ONE OF THEM

Also by Kitty Zeldis

The Dressmakers of Prospect Heights
Not Our Kind

ONE OF THEM

A Novel

KITTY ZELDIS

HARPER
An Imprint of HarperCollins*Publishers*

This is a work of fiction. Names, characters, places, and incidents are products of the author's imagination or are used fictitiously and are not to be construed as real. Any resemblance to actual events, locales, organizations, or persons, living or dead, is entirely coincidental.

HarperCollins books may be purchased for educational, business, or sales promotional use. For information, please email the Special Markets Department at SPsales@harpercollins.com.
harpercollins.com

FIRST EDITION

Ivy art © NadzeyaShanchuk / Shutterstock

Library of Congress Cataloging-in-Publication Data has been applied for.

ISBN 978-0-06-335284-1

25 26 27 28 29 LBC 5 4 3 2 1

For Ken Silver, who was with me every step of the way

PART I

VASSAR

ONE

ANNE

Fall 1946

The cookie platter was nearly empty. Disappointed, Anne Bishop surveyed the gold-rimmed porcelain oval. Gone were the ginger snaps, the snowballs dusted with coconut flakes, the molasses drops, and her favorites, the pecan sandies. All that remained were two chocolate sandwich cookies, their thin layer of filling overly sweet and gritty besides. But what could she expect? It was already 4:45, and the daily tea served in the Rose Parlor, one of Vassar's long-standing traditions, was nearly over. Still, she was hungry, so she poured herself a cup, placed the remaining cookies on her saucer, and made her way across the room. She kept her eyes on the tea because she hated sloshing it into the saucer; it made her feel inept and clumsy. Only when she'd gotten to the other side of the room—just a few tiny drops had spilled over—did she look up.

There they were, the little group she'd fallen in with last year, sitting together as they always did. Graceless and large, Midge Tucker looked too big for the delicate armchair into which she was crammed, while Peggy Sawyer and Tabitha Talbot—sometimes they called her Tabbie—were jammed together at one end of the velvet settee. Carol

Wyland faced Midge on a matching armchair, and Virginia Worthington sat squarely in the middle of the settee, taking up more than her share of the space. When Anne reached them, she saw that even though she joined them for tea almost every day, no one had saved her a spot.

"You can squeeze in here." Tabitha shifted over on the settee, and so did Peggy; Virginia, the acknowledged leader of their set, did not yield an inch. Tall, with a mane of dark-blond hair and a lean, athletic body, strengthened and honed by the kinds of rough team sports that made Anne cringe, she wasn't exactly pretty; her eyes were too close together, and her nose was too long. But she projected certainty and confidence; these qualities gave her power, power that drew all the other girls to her and kept them in line.

"That's all right." Anne set her teacup down and went to retrieve an ottoman she had spotted over by the windows. When she returned, one of her cookies was gone. Virginia looked up at her, expression ever so slightly mocking.

"Hope you don't mind." She patted her lips with a napkin.

"Of course not." There was nothing to be gained by challenging Virginia, especially in front of an audience. Anne sat down and tried to make the lone cookie last. At least the tea was hot, and with the three spoonfuls of sugar she'd added, something of a consolation.

". . . so last night I saw her in the hallway and she was acting so peculiar. Almost like a sleepwalker," Peggy was saying.

"What time was that?" asked Midge.

"Oh, maybe around midnight," Peggy said. "I'm not sure."

"She always seems to be doing something . . . odd," said Peggy. "There's something different about her. Something not quite right."

The subject of this conversation was a girl named Delia Goldhush; she lived on their hall in Main. Delia was not friendly with any of them, and never seemed to register their presence or even their disdain; Anne wondered how she managed to rise, seemingly without effort, above it. She knew that the ill will of these girls would have tormented *her.*

"Well, I saw something even stranger," Virginia said, and everyone looked expectantly in her direction. "Early this morning she was walking along the path, all the way to Main Gate. She walked right through it and off the campus. By herself. At dawn."

"Where do you think she was going?" This was from Tabitha, who'd moved from Raymond; she hadn't lived in Main with the rest of them last year, and so the subject of Delia was relatively new to her.

"I'm sure I don't know," Virginia said. "But wherever it was, I'm guessing she didn't want to be followed." She paused for effect. "Because it was probably a place where she had no business being."

"Do you think she was doing something . . . illicit? Illegal even?" Tabitha sounded mildly titillated by the possibility.

"Could be . . ." mused Peggy. "Maybe she's a thief? Or a spy?" The war was only just behind them; there had been a lot of talk about spies.

The girls fell silent for a moment as they tried to imagine Delia's clandestine mission, but no one had anything concrete to offer.

"Well, even if it's not anything like that, it's still strange," Midge finally said. "She's a strange girl. But they all are."

Anne was well aware of what *they* meant; she'd heard it used the same way many times before.

"What can you expect?" said Midge. "Everyone knows they're a bit devious. And that they keep to themselves."

"Exclusive," added Virginia. "And superior. Like they think they're better than other people."

There was a general murmur of assent. Although no one said the word *Jewish* aloud, Anne knew that that was what they were talking about. Being one of the few Jewish girls at Vassar, Delia was immediately set apart, and her background had been a subject of intense interest and scrutiny since freshman year. This turn in the conversation—and indeed all such conversations—made Anne hugely uncomfortable, and she often tried to steer their talk in another direction.

But today she had not said anything, and now she realized her silence could be interpreted as a form of support for Delia, a dangerous assumption, one that she had to dispel. "Virginia's right," she forced herself to say. "Wherever she was going at that hour of the morning had to be suspicious." She was rewarded with a smile from Virginia, so she continued. "I know I wouldn't do it. None of us would, right?" There was nodding all around.

"I could report her, you know," Virginia said. "I'm sure the dean would want to know about these excursions. How could Miss Goldhush explain them? She might be suspended. Even expelled."

"Expelled . . ." said Midge in a tone that conjured the shame such a fate would bring.

"She'd talk her way out of it. They always do," Carol said. Again, the vigorous nodding.

The more time they spent on this topic, the more quietly agitated Anne felt. She tried to think of something, anything, to change the subject, but her mind was like an empty box—nothing was inside it.

Then Tabitha said, "Would you really do that, Virginia?"

Anne was surprised that Tabitha, the newcomer, had dared to ask. But Virginia was invigorated by the question. "Maybe," she said. "She certainly deserves it."

Deserves what? Anne thought. She hasn't actually done anything. But she dared not say it.

"It's not as if I'd be doing it out of spite or anything," Virginia continued. "I have a responsibility to our classmates." She looked around. "We all do. After all, we know those people can't be trusted, not really. My father found that out the hard way." Virginia's father owned a large paper company and felt he'd been taken advantage of by the owner of another company. That this man was Jewish was a fact Virginia never failed to mention.

"I don't know," Peggy said. "There's nothing to tell really. At least not yet. I mean, she hasn't done anything."

"Yet," said Virginia. "She hasn't done anything yet."

"So let's keep watching," said Tabitha eagerly. "And then report back to each other."

"Good idea," Virginia said, and Tabitha beamed. "I'd like to know more about what she's up to. And I also like knowing I *could* tell on her if I wanted. It gives me a little advantage."

"Even if Delia doesn't know you've got it?" Since Virginia had signaled her approval, Tabitha must have felt she had license to ask.

"*Especially* if she doesn't know it," said Virginia sharply.

Now Tabitha's face turned pink and she looked flustered; the other girls erupted in nervous titters.

In that moment, Anne pitied her. Tabitha hadn't yet learned the rules that governed this group of girls. Now she had. Yes, Virginia had smiled at her, but that didn't make Tabitha an equal. She would know better next time.

Why Anne—or the rest of them—put up with Virginia's subtle and not so subtle bullying was still a mystery. Anne didn't even *like* Virginia. But if she alienated her, she would be ostracized, a truly dismal thought. Freshman year had been a hard, even miserable time. Her father had suffered a fatal heart attack when she had still been in high school and she hadn't fully recovered from the loss. Her mother had died when she was a baby, so she'd never known—or missed—her. And anyway, her father's lavish and abundant love had expanded to fill the gap. He'd been devoted to her, far more so than the fathers of any of the other girls she knew, and though he worked long hours during the week, he went into the office early so that he could be home for dinner almost every night, and he spent most weekends with her too. He read to her, talked to her, listened to her. She had been his adored companion, his princess, his kitten, his bunny, his kumquat—one of his favorite names for her. Now she was no longer any of those things, and never would be again.

Thankfully, the conversation had moved on, and even though it was early in the semester, there was talk of midterms, and beyond that, the Thanksgiving break. Anne would spend the holiday with her aunt, but oh, how she would miss the way she and her father had celebrated. On this one day a year, he joined Hannah in the kitchen and enlisted Anne's help as well. He'd have ordered an enormous turkey, and together they'd have made two kinds of stuffing, several side dishes, and at least three pies: pumpkin, apple, and chocolate cream. Anne's eyes welled with tears when she thought of it.

"Are you all right?" Carol asked.

"Me?" Anne blinked. "I'm fine. Why are you asking?"

"I thought you were about to cry."

Everyone turned to stare at her; Anne felt her face get warm.

"No," she said. "My eyes have been watering lately. Maybe it's allergies."

"You never mentioned you had allergies," Virginia said.

"Allergies can pop up anytime," said Carol. "Out of the blue, I became allergic to cats."

Anne gave her a grateful smile. "I've always had sensitive eyes," she added. "Very sensitive."

Virginia looked at her a moment longer before she turned her attention elsewhere.

Relieved that she was no longer on the spot, Anne made sure to compose herself—just thinking about her father could totally undo her. Before his death she'd been excited by the prospect of Vassar—he'd been proud she'd been accepted—and not at all bothered by the fact that she was the only one of her class at Nightingale-Bamford who would be attending that year. So she had not been prepared for just how unmoored she would feel when she got there. How lonely.

She had been rather desperate when she'd fallen in with this group of girls; they lived on her hall, and she'd been relieved and grateful that they had accepted her. This little clan had propped her up, kept her going—Carol and Peggy, Tabitha and Midge. Midge was a bit whiny, and Tabitha very naive, but Carol had a caring, even nurturing way about her, like a big sister. And Peggy was funny; Anne always had a good time with her. They had become her friends, her bulwark against that lost, untethered feeling she'd battled almost all last year. Now she had a place. She belonged. Only Virginia was the problem. Unfortunately, she was also the leader, and the key to knowing the rest of them. So it was essential that Anne do nothing to upset the delicate social scaffolding she'd managed, just barely, to erect.

They were still nattering on about Delia, and Anne let her gaze stray out the window and toward Main Gate. What grass was left between the dormitory and the gate had started to pale and dry, but the trees, bedecked in brilliant fall foliage, were imposing. Majestic. Many of them had been planted nearly eighty years ago when the college was founded, and they had become part of its history, its present and its future too. Now she was poised to become part of that history, if she could manage to navigate both the academic and social shoals of her life here. She somehow thought that the latter was the more treacherous of the two.

Abruptly, she stood. Unsatisfying as it had been, the lone sandwich cookie was gone and the tea that remained in her cup was now cold. She said goodbye to her friends, grateful to slip away. She said she was going to study—she had a French quiz coming up, and French was not her strongest subject—but when she got outside, she found she'd been craving the air, the light, the space. Even though it was a bit chilly, she walked over to Daffodil Hill. There were no daffodils in bloom now, but the hill overlooked Sunset Lake, a small, placid body of water in which a few goldfish—large, fat, glowing—swam slowly around. Anne didn't see any goldfish today, but she happened upon a gaggle of geese. A couple were gliding along the surface of the lake, but most were on the bank, engaged in what looked like various kinds of fractious social behavior—two were harassing a third, who flapped its wings in agitation, while the others looked on. Did this have to do with food? Territory? Mating? Anne couldn't tell; she knew nothing about geese. But she could see that even these birds had to conform to a particular social hierarchy; it seemed no one was spared. She thought about that even when she had turned and headed back to the dorm.

The next afternoon, Anne was on her way to tea again when she caught sight of Delia Goldhush closing the door to her room, brushing back the tight, springy curls from her face and striding down the hall. Anne immediately looked away, but not before she'd had a chance to register the details of the other girl's outfit: camel skirt, camel cashmere twin set, pearl choker. All this seemed typical attire for a day on campus, spent in class or at the library, but draped over Delia's shoulders was a slightly worn, honey-colored mink coat. And instead of brown, black, or even navy shoes, she wore a pair of dark-red pumps, the color rich yet almost brooding. Though the day was nippy, she wore no stockings of any kind, and her bare legs propelled her quickly down the corridor.

Anne found herself analyzing—and admiring—the seemingly artless way Delia had put herself together, the conventional garments somehow rendered fresh and interesting because of an unexpected addition—the mink—or color—the shoes. She watched until Delia had disappeared down the stairs. It was just after three o'clock; was she headed to the Rose Parlor? Doubtful, as Anne had never seen her at tea. But she was curious, so she too went downstairs and peeked into the room. Just like yesterday, the tea service—plate, not sterling, but still elegant—was laid out on a long table, and all around the room sat girls drinking from delicate gold-rimmed cups and nibbling on cookies. No, Delia was not among them.

Too restless to sit, Anne grabbed the two pecan shortbread squares still on the oval platter and ate them on her way back to her room. There was enough time before dinner for a trip to the library. She slipped into her navy chesterfield coat. Back in August, she had thought it so sophisticated. But now the velvet collar struck her as fussy and precious, like something more suited to a twelve-year-old than to the sort of young woman she so badly wanted to become. The sort of young woman Delia Goldhush already seemed to be.

Anne headed toward Taylor, and upstairs to the Art Library. At this point in the semester, it would be sparsely populated. Quiet. And there, seated at one of the tables, was Delia, the mink heaped in a chair beside her. Delia looked up, and while she didn't exactly smile, something in her expression made Anne feel it would be all right if she sat down at the table too. Delia's gaze returned to the book she had been reading. It was a book Anne had with her as well—Helen Gardner's *Art Through the Ages*, assigned to everyone taking Vassar's introductory art history course. So Delia must be taking Art 105 too. It was midway through the semester, but Anne had never seen her at any of the lectures. Well, they were held in a large auditorium, 150 or so students, and besides, the lights were dimmed to facilitate the showing of the slides.

Anne sat down and casually laid her own copy of Gardner on the table. Delia didn't look up. Opening to the assigned chapter, Anne dutifully studied the images—Gothic cathedrals in their soaring splendor, statues of saints, of Jesus enthroned—but she was finding it hard to concentrate. Maybe she should say something? Nothing clever or witty sprang to mind. For some reason, she wanted Delia to notice her. She herself admired Delia's seeming independence and disregard for what other people thought about her. Anne couldn't imagine ever feeling that way, but she wanted to see, up close, what it was like for someone who did.

Anne looked at her watch. It was now close to five o'clock. She'd been sitting here unproductively for almost an hour; she hadn't even turned a page of her book, but instead read the same two paragraphs over and over. At some point Delia had gotten up and left the library, and though Anne had the urge to follow her, she had remained where she was. Delia might think it was strange, might think that *she* was strange. So she waited another fifteen minutes before gathering her things and leaving; the dining room in her dorm would be open, and she could have an early dinner. Maybe afterward she'd be able to summon the concentration she needed for her schoolwork.

On the way back to Main, she ran into Peggy and her friend Josie, who lived in Lathrop, and stopped to chat. By the time she'd gone back to the dorm and left her coat and books in her room, dinner was already in progress and the dining room was full. Standing in line to receive her meal of meat loaf, carrots, and lumpy mashed potatoes, Anne looked around. Delia was already seated, accompanied only by a book—not Gardner—propped up on the table in front of her. She seemed oblivious to the lively conversations and occasional yelps of laughter that eddied around her. Instead, her attention was focused on whatever it was that she was reading.

Though the room was crowded, the seats directly alongside and across from Delia were, as usual, empty. On impulse, Anne headed for one of them and placed her tray on the table. Delia looked up but said nothing.

"Is it all right if I sit here?"

"Why wouldn't it be?"

How rude. Anne was humiliated by the question, but walking away would be even more humiliating, so she sat down anyway. Delia's gaze settled back on the book whose title, Anne now saw, was in French. Hadn't she heard that Delia's American parents had raised her in Paris? Yes, that was it; Tabitha's father, an ambassador or something, had known the family over there. Anne had never been to

Paris, though she longed to go; the idea that Delia had been brought up there was just another intriguing thing about her.

Looking down at her meal, Anne's sense of discomfort grew. Why had she decided to do this? She was aware of Peggy and Midge sending anxious looks in her direction, not pointing exactly, but clearly taking note. This had been a mistake, and she ought to get up—

"What do you think of Abbott?" Delia asked, closing the book and setting it beside her empty plate.

"Excuse me?"

"Martin Abbott? He gave the lectures on medieval and Gothic art." When Anne didn't immediately respond, Delia went on. "You're in Art History 105, aren't you? I saw you in the library with a copy of the Gardner book."

"That's right," Anne said. "I am." So Delia *had* noticed her there.

"I was wondering if you found Professor Abbott's lectures stimulating. Enlightening, even."

"Well, not exactly *stimulating*—" Anne thought Professor Abbott was exceedingly dull.

"Of course not. He's an intellectual clod," Delia said. "All head and no heart. Listening to him talk about architecture puts me right to sleep. I've seen those churches, I know how they can make you feel—"

"Weightless. Or so I would guess." Anne had never been in France or anywhere else in Europe, but the photographs of Gothic cathedrals, with their vaulted ceilings and attenuated columns—the way the light poured down from above and filled those lofty spaces—had nonetheless stirred her. "Like you've left the ground and are floating way, way up there . . . like you've somehow defied gravity, and become more spirit than body."

"Exactly." Something in Delia's expression changed; she now looked interested in Anne, or at least in what she had to say. Anne, who understood she'd said the right thing, was absurdly pleased. "But you'd never guess that from listening to him," Delia added. "Too bad Katzenellenbogen isn't teaching this semester."

"Katzenellenbogen?" Anne had never heard the name. She thought it sounded ridiculous, like something made up, but wasn't about to say so.

"He's written so much on medieval iconography—*Allegories of the Virtues and Vices in Medieval Art*, *The Central Tympanum at Vézelay*—he's just so smart, so insightful."

"So why isn't he teaching this section?"

"He's on leave this semester. But he should be back in the spring, and if he is, I'm going to take a seminar with him. Germany's loss was our gain."

"What do you mean?"

"He had to leave the country."

Anne waited for Delia to say more, but when nothing else was forthcoming, she said, "You sound like you have very high standards."

"Don't you?"

"I've never taken an art history course before. I wasn't sure what to expect."

"You should expect more. I hope Abbott doesn't ruin it for you."

"You've taken art history courses?"

"Not in any formal way. But my father had a gallery in Montparnasse, and we had a house in Vence too, so artists were always visiting. Picasso, Matisse, Dali, Léger, Chagall—he was friends with everybody."

"You said he *had* a gallery," Anne asked, not wanting to reveal that not all of the names Delia rattled off were familiar to her. And where, exactly, was Vence? "He doesn't have it anymore?"

"The war ended that," she said. Her expression was unexpectedly serious, even grim. "Now we're back here, and he's been trying to reinvent himself. He opened a gallery in Greenwich Village. But it hasn't been the same. Actually, nothing has."

Before Anne could reply, Carol appeared at the table. "There you are," she said. "I was looking for you. Don't you remember what we had planned for tonight?"

"Tonight—oh, right." It was Virginia's birthday, and a few of them had arranged a little surprise for her—a cake, some silly hats, and a bottle of champagne bought from a liquor store in town.

"Aren't you going to help me set up?"

"Of course." Anne hadn't finished the meat loaf, but it was no longer hot and hadn't been all that appetizing even when it was. Carol was making a point of ignoring Delia, and while this made Anne uncomfortable, she knew Delia wasn't invited to the party and couldn't think of a graceful way to include her in the conversation. But Delia had picked up her book again. She barely responded when Anne said goodbye.

"There," Carol said when they were out of earshot. "I thought you needed rescuing."

"So this wasn't about the party?"

"No, though Tabitha bought some balloons, and I suppose you can start blowing them up. I just thought you'd been sitting with her long enough."

Anne said nothing. Carol didn't have to explain that sitting with a Jewish girl was not going to enhance her social standing here; quite the opposite. Anne thought of Delia striding through the streets of Paris, conquering the worn cobblestones in her dark-red shoes. But that was Paris, not Poughkeepsie. Carol was only looking out for her, trying to protect her. What would she—or any of them—have said if they had known that despite her name, Anne Bishop was Jewish too?

TWO

DELIA

Fall 1946

Delia knew that girl Anne was watching her. They all watched her—checking for horns, no doubt. She was used to it by now. Used to it and didn't especially care. But that one, the one with the straight brown hair and alert expression who lived at the end of her hall, seemed different. Not disdainful or critical like the others. Just curious. And unsure of herself. Well, Delia knew herself to be something of an outcast here, so Anne's showing any interest in her wasn't going to win her any friends. Didn't she know that?

Midge, Delia's roommate from freshman year, had been one of the most disdainful ones. When they lived together, she droned on about her horse, Jester. How handsome he was. How fast. How smart.

"It sounds like you want to marry him." Delia had endured at least ten nonstop minutes of this blather.

"Marry him?" Midge was clearly offended. "Is that supposed to be a joke? Because it's not funny."

"Joke? No. I was quite serious," Delia said. "Given what a remarkable creature he is, you might not do any better."

After that, Midge shut up, but her prior mild disdain hardened into active dislike. It had been such a trial living with her, but now Delia had a room to herself—what a relief.

Her father hadn't understood why she even wanted to go to Vassar. "You can go to Barnard," he said. "Stay in New York." He thought Poughkeepsie was a backwater, especially after Paris, and of course he was right. But Delia had her reasons for leaving New York; the chief one among them was him.

Simon Goldhush had come from two prosperous families, diamonds and banking respectively, but he had not wanted to be part of family tradition or go into either of those businesses. Instead he had shocked his parents by going to art school, where, along with studying drawing and painting, he rubbed shoulders with the creative types he met there. He soon realized his true gift was for finding and nurturing talent, coaxing it out like a delicate bud and allowing it the air, space, and light to thrive. He traded New York for Paris in the early 1920s and opened an art gallery. Delia's mother, Sophie Rossner, a sculptor and fellow expat, was one of his early discoveries.

The Paris gallery became something of a sensation, at least among a certain group of people—artists, intellectuals, culture makers, and taste shapers—and Simon and Sophie were at the center of it. They were both tall, and almost always towered above everyone else in the room; Simon's hair was dark, and slicked back with pomade, while Sophie's hair was a brilliant russet, worn long and loose, though that was not at all the style. Simon was easygoing and good at charming the clients, while Sophie was more unpredictable, a woman of great enthusiasms but also prone to voluble outbursts and the occasional tirade. People liked Simon and felt comfortable with him, while they were in awe of Sophie, and even a little bit afraid. But afraid or not, people were drawn to her sculpture. She worked in stone—mostly but not exclusively marble—and often on a small, even intimate scale, though every now and then she'd surprise her admirers with a large-scale, even enormous, piece. The forms were recognizable—figures, animals—but their streamlined simplicity gave them an almost abstract elegance, which made them very modern.

Their apartment in the white-tiled building on the rue Vavin displayed some, though by no means all, of Sophie's work; it was a home, not a gallery, and was full almost every evening. There were long, wine-soaked dinners, themed costume parties at which guests sang, danced, and occasionally removed one or more articles of clothing. There were loud, heated arguments over art or politics, readings of plays, games of charades, and entertainers, such as an amateur magician who filled the room with doves or pulled a dozen brightly colored silk scarves out of his seemingly empty hat.

Delia was mostly a spectator at these gatherings. She didn't mind; what she minded was when her father would try to draw her in, trotting her out as if she were a wind-up toy—*Delia, sing for us, you have such a beautiful voice*, or *Dance for us, chérie, you're a little Pavlova, yes you are*. Delia was neither a gifted singer nor dancer, so why did he keep saying these things? And when he and her mother had been drinking long enough, they stopped paying any attention to her at all. She wasn't given dinner, but went around picking up food left on people's plates; once she consumed a full glass of abandoned wine and got drunk, which they found hilarious, even when she threw up all over the floor. There were nights when no one thought to put Delia to bed, and she would fall asleep on the couch or carpet. Once some late arrival tossed a fur coat over her sleeping form; later Sophie told her that she and Simon had spent twenty frantic minutes searching for her, thinking she had somehow wandered outside on her own. That story became one they repeated often and with great amusement, though it made Delia feel less like her parents' child than like their pet.

The Paris of Delia's childhood was muted and somber, composed of grays that ranged from the palest, coolest tint to the deepest charcoal, and also ocher, mud brown, sable, and oyster white. Against this subdued background—the grisaille of the stately old buildings, the black ribbon of the Seine that wound through the city—were set occasional bursts of color: the red raw-silk cushions her mother had made for their gray divan, the drapes in the front room, forest green shot through with golden threads, the vivid kilims scattered on the dark wooden floors. These colors seemed reflective of Sophie's temperament. She was an often distracted and even inattentive mother, leaving Delia with a nanny or sometimes her father while she went off to her nearby studio, but every now and then she would surprise Delia with a burst of attention and enthusiasm, bright as the red cushions or gold threads in the drapes.

When Delia was seven, her parents forgot about a school holiday. Neither Simon nor the nanny was available, so it looked as if Delia would have to go to the studio with her mother. Sophie was clearly annoyed. "Why can't you take her?" she said to Delia's father. And when he explained why not, she redirected her annoyance toward the nanny. "Why are we paying her?" she grumbled. But in the end, there was no alternative, and she told Delia to hurry up so they could leave.

Delia wished her mother didn't see her as such a bother. Though she didn't say so, she was eager, even excited, to see this place that had an almost magnetic pull on Sophie, one that even seemed to transform her into a different version of herself—her abundant mane of hair coiled into a loose bun, her usual fitted jackets trimmed in fur or velvet, soigné dresses with full skirts, and silk or ruffled blouses replaced with a dark-blue canvas smock and pants. On her feet she wore heavy work boots, filmed with a layer of some chalky substance, instead of the elegant high-heeled pumps she usually favored. She strode so quickly along the street that Delia had trouble keeping up. Sophie didn't notice; she was intent on reaching her studio as soon as she could.

When they got to the building, Delia followed her mother up, up, up four—or was it five?—flights of stairs. At the top, Sophie unlocked the door to let them both inside. "You can go and play," she said. Delia didn't move right away; she was captivated by one of Sophie's large-scale figures, a woman with a fish's tail—she was a mermaid, that was it—who was coiled around a large shell-like object. She was made of some green-and-white stone, and the white veining was made into part of her hair, as if it were illuminated by a light above or behind it. When Delia could finally turn her gaze elsewhere, she saw that the vast space was punctuated by big windows at the front and rear and a skylight above. The wide-plank floorboards were so bleached they were almost white, and the walls were blistered with bubbles of paint. Against one of them stood many slabs or hunks of stone of differing shapes and sizes. Sophie went over to a pegboard on the wall and took down her tools, her attention directed toward another large, unfinished sculpture in the center of the room. At first Delia couldn't quite make out what the thing was supposed to be, but then she saw it was a person—no, two people, entwined in a passionate embrace. The woman's long hair—not unlike Sophie's—streamed down her back, and the man's arms were wound around her, his hands cupping the cheeks of her derriere. This seemed naughty to Delia, but also exciting in some way she couldn't explain.

Sophie circled the figures, absorbed in examining them from different angles. Then she noticed that Delia hadn't moved. "Chérie, I told you to go over there and play," she said, a touch impatient. She waved her arm toward the opposite side of the room. "Vas-y." *Go on.* Delia walked across the room and opened the satchel of things Sophie had packed for her. There was a book, but not the story of Babar that Delia loved and was now able to read on her own. Instead, she found an alphabet book that told her *P* was for *Pomme* and *C* was for *Chat*. Babyish and boring. She set it aside to examine what else was in the satchel. There was a cloth sack of marbles, but marbles needed another person to play. And instead of her beloved Coco, a sleek, plush leopard, Sophie had packed a bisque doll that had been her own as a child, and which she seemed to think Delia ought to love. But Delia found the doll's unsmiling face, with its row of shiny, feral teeth and staring glass eyes, disturbing. Still, this was all she had, so she brought the doll with her to the wall where the stone slabs were clustered.

She began to make her way between the slabs, pretending that they were a forest of petrified trees, trees that she could bring to life again if she uttered the right words. She explained all this to the doll as she ran her fingers over the varying surfaces, some smooth, others rough and pebbly. The syncopated sounds of her mother's efforts—hammering, chiseling, banging—became a form of music; the air grew cloudy with stone dust.

There was a tall piece of stone, almost a column, whose top she could see but the rest of which was hidden behind another piece. It seemed to sparkle, and Delia wanted to see it better, to touch it, even lick it. She set down the doll and tried wriggling first her hand and then her arm behind the stone in front of it, as if pulling it in for a hug. But the stone in front tipped, and then the one behind it did too, pinning Delia against another large slab and hitting the doll that was lying beside her, cracking the bisque head wide open. Delia let out a small, high-pitched yelp. The two stones were heavy, their weight a shocking affront to her small, trapped body. She tried to wriggle free, but she couldn't. Her shoulders hurt. Her back too. And her knees, oh her knees felt like someone was pressing down on them with a spatula, the way their cook pressed down the egg-soaked bread when she was making *pain perdu*.

Sophie dropped whatever tool it was that she was using and rushed over. With some exertion, she shoved one of the stones aside so Delia could scramble out. "Are you all right?"

Delia nodded dumbly.

"You need to be more careful, chérie. You could have been hurt."

Then her mother looked down at the broken doll. "Delia, look what you've done! And she was such a pretty thing." Sophie frowned. "Next time, pay more attention to what you're doing." Sighing loudly, she picked up the pieces and went back to work.

Delia remained where she was. She *had* been hurt—her shoulder and chest still throbbed, and later blurred purple bruises appeared on her skin. But her mother didn't bathe her that night or dress her the next day, so she didn't see them. And when her nanny asked Delia what had happened, Delia didn't want to say.

In the spring of 1939, Simon bought a house of roughly hewn stone that seemed to grow right out of the hills above Vence; he called it Le Piol. This purchase was the result of months of conversation about what was happening in Paris. The city was changing; it felt different, even threatening. Even though the rise of Adolf Hitler and the harrowing events of Kristallnacht took place in Germany, Germany was a country with which France shared a border. It seemed better, *safer*, to leave the city for a while.

But none of this felt very close to Delia. It all seemed like grown-up talk, and not anything that concerned her. She was more interested in getting to know this new environment, enchanted by the house, the landscape, and most of all, the colors—glowing, confection-like—that exploded all around her. There was peach, goldenrod, salmon, robin's-egg blue, lilac, and celery, all contained by the vivid greens of the surrounding trees and capped by the blue dome of the sky. The lively and sometimes raucous meals continued, only now they were eaten outside at the big table of *pierre chaude* that came from Lacoste, which also provided the material for some of Sophie's sculptures; she rented a studio somewhere in town. Delia never went with her, never even asked, but Sophie seemed happier here—less irritable, less distracted. She laughed more, and her manner was easier, less tense. Delia began to relax. She wished that they could stay here forever.

At dinner, large blue-and-white faience platters—Sophie had started collecting them—were filled with roasted eggplant and tomatoes, anchovies, and olives—and that was before the main dish was served. Loaves of bread sat in wicker baskets, and bottles of wine circulated freely. Sometimes discussion of politics and current events crept into the conversations about art and culture that were the mainstay of the evenings, but all that seemed less pressing here, less dire. Guests included Messieurs Picasso and Matisse, though never at the same time—her father said that they were rivals. "Friendly rivals," he'd said. "But rivals all the same." Delia especially liked M. Matisse, who entertained her with sketches of flowers and pretty ladies in hats, and who said Simon must bring her to his studio so he could draw her. Sophie loved that idea and brought down one of her large straw hats for Delia to model. "See how chic she looks," she said to M. Matisse, who regarded Delia appraisingly.

Some days later, Sophie scheduled a time for Delia to visit M. Matisse's studio in Nice, and she drove Delia there. Sophie took the sharp turns in the narrow roads at such speed that Delia was terrified. Papa never drove like that, and he was always chiding Sophie for doing it. But finally they arrived safely. After parking the car, Sophie took Delia into the grand building, a former hotel where Queen Victoria of England had once stayed, and where M. Matisse had bought himself a large flat the year before. They were offered citronade and little sugar cookies, but Sophie declined both and left almost at once, saying she'd be back in an hour or so. Delia was alone with the artist.

During the dinner at Le Piol, M. Matisse had been engaging and chatty, but now he was preoccupied with his work and spoke tersely: *Turn your head*, *Put your hands in your lap*, and the like. One hour stretched to two; M. Matisse got up, paced a bit, and then sat down again. Delia's leg fell asleep, and her back hurt. Also, she had to use the bathroom but was afraid to say so. Why had her mother left her here for so long? Would she ever come back? It was nearly three hours later when Sophie breezed in, face flushed and skin glowing. M. Matisse seemed happy to see her and declared Delia to have been an exemplary model. He gave Sophie—not Delia—one of the pen-and-ink drawings he had done. Sophie was so thrilled that she talked of nothing else on the way back to their house—not a word of explanation or apology about her prolonged absence, not a question about what it had been like to pose for a famous artist. At least she didn't drive so fast.

Sometimes Delia's parents drove to the beach at Antibes or Juan-les-Pins; other days, they went to Nice for the big *marché aux puces* near the port, where Sophie was always on the hunt for things that excited or enchanted her—a woodcut of two lambs in a manger, an oval mirror with an ornate gold frame, a whole box containing nineteenth-century petticoats, slips, chemises and bloomers, all made of white cotton that had grown soft and fine from years of wear and washing. The box sat at her feet in the restaurant where they went for a lunch of fish soup and langoustines, Delia squealing with delight as Sophie pulled out one frothy white garment after another and shook it over the table.

Delia loved being in Vence, maybe even more than she loved Paris. The summer had been one of fresh mornings, hot afternoons, and mild evenings, of riotous flowers in purple, magenta, and blue, and of the rippling warmth of the azure sea. She was older now, and when her father wanted her to perform for the guests—*Read everyone that essay you wrote on Molière, it was brilliant!*—she could smile and shake her head before escaping to the tranquility of her room or the garden behind the house. Maybe next year she would invite her best friend Gabrielle along, so she would have a companion her own age. An ally even.

But that summer in Vence turned out to be not only the first; it was also the last. By the time they returned to Paris in September, Germany had just invaded Poland. They felt the tremors, like aftershocks, all around them. The Poles had capitulated so easily, emboldening Hitler; where would he turn next? The adults were anxious, jittery; the after-dinner conversations chez Goldhush were no longer about art and culture but about the possibility of invasion or, God forbid, full-scale war.

On a sickening June day in 1940, Nazi troops marched into Paris. Almost at once it became a different city, one Delia no longer knew. The beautiful edifices were obscured by bloodred bunting, always emblazoned with a circle on which a black swastika sat, intimidating and hideous. The Palais-Bourbon was converted into the office of the Kommandant von Gross-Paris, and a huge banner was spread across the front of the building. The German words—DEUTSCHLAND SIEGT AN ALLEN FRONTEN—meant nothing at first, but Delia soon learned they proclaimed *Germany is victorious on all fronts!* Instead of the familiar red, white, and blue *tricolore*, swastika-emblazoned flags snapped in the breeze. Rifle-toting soldiers were everywhere, their black leather boots polished to a menacing gleam.

Most Parisians were on edge, waiting for the worst. Delia, to her shock, was no longer welcome at the homes of her gentile friends. Even Gaby, who lived upstairs, was now avoiding her; likewise, many of her parents' friends and patrons stopped coming to the gallery, and the apartment too. The dinners and parties stopped abruptly, and now it was only the three of them, an uneasy triangle in which Delia was largely ignored while Sophie and Simon sat across the oval dining table like a pair of adversaries. Delia didn't like to see her parents like this, glaring at each other, barely civil when they did speak. So she slipped off to her room, but once she was gone, they began to quarrel, their voices escalating as if they had totally forgotten that she could hear them. She turned out the light and put her pillow over her head as she tried to sleep, those angry voices snaking through her dreams.

One morning after a particularly vicious quarrel, Delia came to the table where her parents sat in a fraught silence that was even more frightening than their fighting. Delia looked down at the tartine her mother had prepared, the butter and jam spread in a smooth coating, just the way she liked it. But she had no appetite and went off to school without eating. The atmosphere—her erstwhile friends keeping their distance, the way the teacher would not call on her, even when she waved her hand earnestly—was deeply unsettling. Soon the term would be over, though, and she would be released from this new reality, the one in which she felt she was both invisible and at the same time marked by an indelible stain. The bell rang, signaling the end of the school day; she gathered her things quickly and was one of the first ones out the door. But there was no refuge at home either. "You need to start packing," her father said before she'd even put down her satchel. "Right away."

"Packing? What for? Where are we going?"

"New York," he said. He wasn't looking at her, though; he was looking at Sophie, who, clearly agitated, was moving quickly around the apartment, rifling through drawers, opening cabinet doors, and almost immediately slamming them shut.

"I don't want to go to New York," Delia said. What she didn't say was that she didn't want *any* of this—her parents' brittle, barely concealed anger, the snubs at school, the growing unease in the city. She wanted to go back to the previous summer, the sun-filled days at Le Piol where her parents had seemed happy and the house was always filled with guests, bees buzzing and bobbing lazily through the jasmine-scented air.

"I don't want to go either," said her father. "But we have to."

"Why?" she asked, though she already knew the answer.

"We're not welcome here anymore."

Yet they were luckier than most. They held American passports, and so Simon had been able to secure train tickets to Lisbon; from there they would be among the first group of Americans to set sail for New York since the occupation had begun. They were to leave in two days, days in which the tension in the apartment continued to grow. From the room in which Delia was hastily packing her belongings, she could hear her parents quarreling again, their words clear and biting.

You never—

Why can't you—

Don't lie to me—

I can't look at you anymore—

Liar! You're nothing but a liar—

Then the words had stopped, replaced by the ragged sound of her mother weeping. Delia stood there holding her by now old and very worn plush leopard, Coco. At twelve, she was too old for such a thing, she knew that. But even though her attachment to the toy embarrassed her, she couldn't bear to give it up. She pressed the animal tightly to her chest. How she wanted to comfort her mother, to say something that would stop the tears. Yet she remained where she was, unable to summon whatever it would have taken to walk into the other room. A moment later she heard the rushed, staccato sound of her mother's high heels.

"Where do you think you're going?" her father shouted.

The loud bang of the door was the only reply.

Warily, Delia emerged from her room. Her father was sitting at the table, sipping a glass of wine; the bottle, nearly empty, sat beside it.

"Is she gone?" Delia already knew the answer. This was not the first time her mother had stormed out of the apartment.

Her father avoided looking at her, and instead gazed intently at his glass before he nodded.

"When is she coming back?"

"Soon enough." He poured the remaining wine into his glass and downed it quickly.

Delia was not terribly worried; her father was right about Sophie's return, which usually happened within hours of her departure. There would be tears and apologies, then embracing and kissing; sometimes this was followed by her parents going into their bedroom, the door slamming and bolting shut behind them.

But this time was different. Sophie did not come back at dinner, and she was not back at bedtime either. And even more concerning was the fact that they were supposed to leave the day after the next. Now Delia *was* worried. Would Sophie stay out all night? Her father had changed into his pajamas and robe. "Let's get some sleep," he said. "I'm sure she'll be home in the morning." Delia lay awake for a long time, listening for the sound of the key turning in the lock. It never came.

In the morning, she awoke with a vague sense of dread. As soon as she remembered about Sophie's disappearance, she rushed into her parents' room to see if her mother had returned. She hadn't.

"Should we call the police?" Delia asked. "Maybe she's hurt. Or sick."

"Calling the police would *not* be a good idea," her father said. He looked haggard and pale; was his hand actually shaking as he poured the coffee? "We have to keep packing. The train leaves at noon tomorrow. I'm sure she'll show up soon." When Delia didn't move, he added, "Maybe you want to start gathering some of her things? That would be a big help."

Delia was grateful for the suggestion. Her mother had taken the handbag she always wore—cognac-colored leather with brass trim and clasp—but her valise was here, so Delia began to fill it. First in was Sophie's favorite nightgown—ice-blue satin with lace straps and a matching robe. Then this gauzy dress, splattered with enormous cabbage roses in all shades of pink—Sophie had worn it often last summer at Le Piol. Next was her favorite Hermès scarf, still faintly redolent of her signature perfume, Guerlain's Shalimar; she sometimes dabbed a bit behind Delia's ears and on her wrists, promising to buy her a bottle when she was older. Handling all these familiar objects was reassuring; it made Sophie's return seem expected, even inevitable. She'd be back any time now, of course she would. It was late afternoon; there was still time.

After dealing with the clothes, she turned to the rosewood writing desk Sophie had used. In the bottom drawer, way at the back, Delia found a journal with an olive-green embossed leather cover. She'd never seen it before. Not sure if she ought to open it, she turned it over. There on the back was a tiny sticker from the shop where it had been purchased. Delia knew that shop; it was on the rue Madame in the sixth arrondissement, and it was where her mother had gone to buy pens, ink, and the creamy, deckle-edged notecards she used for correspondence. So most likely it did belong to Sophie.

"Delia?" her father called from the other room.

"I'll be right there." She hastily stuffed the journal into the valise. Something told her that if she did decide to read it, she would want to be alone.

The rest of the day passed with a maddening slowness. Once Delia finished packing for her mother, she had to pack for herself, an awful process that required looking at every single thing she owned and making a decision—quickly—about what she would bring with her and what would have to be left behind. No books—they were too heavy. But maybe she could manage a few—two? Three? And she had to take her favorite dresses, and the glossy black patent leather pumps—her very first pair of heels, albeit low ones. Also the fur-trimmed boots she wore in the winter. Where were they, though? Not in her closet or the hall closet either. Could they be with Sophie's things? As she was on her way to look, she paused in front of one of Sophie's sculptures. It was a double portrait, carved so that the larger of the two faces nestled into the concave shape of the other. Both were female, and looking at the curve of the noses—like Sophie's, like hers—Delia had always thought of them as images of herself and her mother. Never mind about the boots—she had to take this. Unwieldy as it was, she brought it into her room and shoved it deep into the recesses of her valise. Elsewhere in the apartment, Simon was making a similar set of choices. She heard the thump of a valise being dragged, the sound of drawers and cabinets opening and closing, the occasional expletive—*merde!*—uttered as he worked.

Sophie had still not returned by dinnertime, so they sat down to eat without her. During the makeshift meal of cold chicken, wilted greens, and—since no one had remembered to go to the *boulangerie*—stale bread, her father filled her glass with wine, not bothering to dilute it with water. Delia took a sip. Sharp, but she welcomed the bite. There were boxes ringed around the table, penning them in. After a few more sips, Delia felt emboldened enough to say what had been on her mind all through this dreary, excruciating day.

"What if she doesn't come back?"

"She'll come back. She always comes back."

"You mean she always *came* back. Maybe this time is different." She realized this was true, and it scared her that she knew something her father wouldn't let himself know.

"No." Simon set his own wineglass down on the table, hard. A few drops flew up, staining the white napkin with dots of pink.

"But the train is tomorrow. And the ship the next day."

"You think I don't know that?" he said angrily.

"Then we're still going?"

"Of course we are." His tone softened, and he reached for her hand. "We have to go," he added. "We're not safe here."

"Neither is Maman," Delia said.

After dinner, Delia went back into her room, where Sophie's valise now stood next to her own. Unsnapping the locks, she dug through it until she found the journal. Maybe there was something in it that would provide a clue about what her mother was thinking or where she might be. Sophie had a neat, easily legible hand, and she had dated all the entries. Delia flipped through the pages. Here was one written about a show of hers that had almost sold out and received several fine reviews; here was another about a quarrel, one of many, she'd had with Delia's father. Delia kept going; she didn't want to relive those moments. She kept looking for mentions of her own name, and there were a scant few. Not as many as she would have hoped; she was stung by the omission. Yet another name, Serge, began to appear with some frequency. Delia wasn't aware of anyone named Serge in her parents' immediate circle; whoever he was, he had existed somewhere outside it. But as she kept reading, her memory snagged on something. Hadn't there been a day when they had taken a ferry from La Tour Fondu to a little island off Hyères to . . . what was it called? . . . Porquerolles, yes that was it. Porquerolles. There was someone named Serge, she was almost sure of it, in the group that sat laughing and toasting everything—the meal, the wine, the clouds above, and the glittering sea before them—over lunch? And hadn't her mother been eager to go back again? She had said she was visiting her friend Elena; Simon had seemed unhappy about these trips, but he hadn't tried to stop her. Could there have been another reason she'd kept returning?

Delia kept reading, hoping to find an answer. But then she came to a place where the pages, which were perforated, had been neatly removed from the diary. The previous—and last—entry had been written last week. So these missing pages were even more recent. What was in them? Frustrated, she put the diary into Sophie's valise.

A couple of hours later, she heard a soft knocking. For a wild moment she thought it was Sophie, but that was ridiculous; her mother wouldn't need to knock, she had a key. When Delia went to the door, she saw Gaby. They had grown up together and been the best of friends, but when the Germans invaded, Gaby, like all the others, had kept her distance. And yet now here she was.

Delia had been angry when Gabrielle first retreated. She'd expected better of her friend. But she'd missed her too and now was glad to see her, glad she had come. Gaby was still afraid to enter the apartment. But standing on the threshold, she leaned forward to kiss Delia on both cheeks. "Adieu, ma chère amie, adieu," she said. Hearing those words, Delia understood then that she might never come back to Paris, or that if she did, it would not be for a very long time.

After Gaby had gone, Delia went into her room and opened her valise. She dug around until she found what she was looking for—Coco. Delia stared at the animal's face, the thick and now dusty fringe of its lashes, the nose that was slightly dented from having been dropped so many times. The leopard had been given to her when she was what, five? Six? She remembered her excitement in untying the red satin ribbon and opening the box. But now it was time to let her go, and she set Coco on her nightstand. She thought of Gaby's words earlier, and she repeated them now—"Adieu, ma chère amie, adieu." And even though it was late, she took the bedraggled toy downstairs and kissed her a final time before leaving her in a trash can behind the building. It was only then that she wept.

THREE

ANNE

Fall 1946

Since Anne and her father shared a birthday—October 10—he'd always taken special delight in planning the festivities, often held jointly. One year there had been a tea party at the Plaza for some of her friends, followed by an evening performance of *Swan Lake* at the Metropolitan Opera House with some of his. When she turned ten, he arranged for a whole busload of guests to travel upstate for a day of apple picking and horseback riding. Then there was the time he'd rented out a restaurant in Chinatown, and her entire class at school had been invited. No one else's father or mother had come up with such an original idea; for days afterward, everyone had talked about the paper fans and the fortune cookies that were given out just as they were leaving.

But since her father's death, Anne hadn't wanted to celebrate her birthday, and this year, she didn't even tell anyone about it. Instead, she went to her classes just like it was any other day. It was only when she was alone that she took out the photograph album she'd brought to school with her, looking at each image as if it were a portal back to the before time. Here she was at age three, in a frilly party dress and paper crown. Another photo showed her a little older, poised on the ice at the skating rink in Central Park, her hands tucked deep into a small black muff. But she spent the longest time gazing at a picture in which she and her father were together; he was holding her in his arms, and they were looking not at the camera but at each other. Then she closed the album. Her father wouldn't have wanted her to be unhappy, she knew that. Yet she was unhappy, and the dark mood persisted into the next day, and the day after that.

Then she began to see signs posted around campus for a dance at Yale. These "mixers," she knew, were a tradition, a chance for the girls and boys of the two colleges to meet and hopefully get together. She'd heard about several girls who'd met their boyfriends that way, and even one who went on to get engaged. A dance might be fun, and even if not, it would certainly be distracting. And since most of the girls on her hall were going, Anne decided she would join them. Peggy told her that a bus would pick them up early on Friday evening and take them to New Haven; later that same bus would drive them back to Vassar again.

Planning for the dance set off a low-level hum of excitement among the group. Dresses were purchased, compared, accessorized, sometimes exchanged or loaned. Attention was given to shoes and stockings; new shades of lipstick and rouge were tried, considered, and rejected in favor of others. Some of the girls made appointments at the beauty shop on Raymond Avenue, pulling pages from *Mademoiselle*, *Vogue*, *Glamour*, and *Harper's Bazaar* to use as inspiration. A sleek Veronica Lake look or a glamour updo, bangs or a side part. After some serious thought, Anne settled on a black dress whose belt had a rhinestone buckle, and a jade necklace that her father had given her on her sixteenth birthday. She thought the jade was an unusual choice, something that even Delia Goldhush might admire. But why did that matter? She highly doubted Delia would be on that bus to Yale.

On the night of the dance, the girls on Anne's hall came downstairs in a group, the mingled scents of their perfume—Tabu, Evening in Paris, White Shoulders, Chantilly, Arpège—enveloping them in a heady cloud. Anne chose a seat by the window but scarcely noticed the scenery that unfurled before her; she was thinking about the night ahead. Her experience with boys was limited; they hadn't been too important to her before, though she was ready, even eager, for this to change. Her Vassar friends were beginning to couple off; there had even been an engagement in their group—Midge's boyfriend had proposed, though they would wait until graduation for the wedding. It was hard for Anne to imagine; she'd never even been kissed. In high school she'd had a crush on her friend Astrid's older brother Erik, but he scarcely noticed her, and while she'd had a few dates during her senior year, none were of any consequence. But this night would be different. The boys she would meet would be smarter, more interesting, more worldly. Or so she hoped.

Soon enough they had arrived, and were pulling up to the Payne Whitney Gymnasium, where the dance was being held.

"I heard that the boys swim laps stark naked," Virginia said.

"Really?" Tabitha asked. "Is that true? Or just a rumor?"

"It's absolutely true," said Virginia.

"But how can you be so sure?" Peggy asked. "Did you see them with your own eyes?"

"If I did, I wouldn't tell *you*," Virginia shot back.

The girls were still giggling as they got off the bus.

Inside the vast space were groves of papier-mâché trees, dense with silk leaves—gold, orange, and scarlet. On one side of the gym, tables covered in white cloths held drinks, sandwiches, and cookies; on the other side a dais had been set up where a band was playing; several couples were already dancing to "Doctor, Lawyer, Indian Chief."

Virginia was immediately approached by a tall boy in a navy

blazer, and Peggy was surrounded by a small cluster of girls Anne didn't know at all. The music was lively, and the dancers spun and twirled; though she longed to join in, something held her back. Then Midge appeared. "There you are! Duane's been waiting." Midge's boyfriend—no, her fiancé—Cliff Danforth was a junior at Yale, and he had arranged dates for some of the Vassar girls who came with her. Duane Lancet had been chosen for Anne, so she followed Midge across the room to where a ruddy-cheeked young man stood waiting, blond hair slicked back from his forehead.

"Nice to meet you, Anne." He extended his hand. "Would you like to dance?" Duane was stocky and at least two inches shorter than Anne; nothing about him appealed to her. But maybe she was being too judgmental. Midge gave her a little shove in his direction. "Go on!" she whispered. "You didn't come all this way to be a wallflower."

Duane put his arms around Anne, and they started to move across the floor. He was an adept dancer, and to her surprise, Anne felt graceful in his arms. Then the song ended, and the next one, "I Love You for Sentimental Reasons," was considerably slower. Duane took the opportunity to pull her close. Anne could smell the aftershave he wore. But it felt all wrong—she'd only just met him—and she pulled back, putting some distance between them.

"What's the matter?" he said.

"Nothing."

"Then why act so stuck up?"

Was it stuck up not to allow him to press up against her? "I'm thirsty," she said. "Can we get some punch?"

"Sure thing." Duane released her and walked toward one of the tables; the cut-glass punch bowl was surrounded by small cups, and he politely filled one and offered it to her before taking one of his own. The punch was pink and slightly fizzy, and she tried to make it last so she wouldn't have to dance with him again right away. As she watched, he pulled a small flask from his pocket, unscrewed the cap, and poured some of its contents into his cup. Anne was surprised, but the flask disappeared quickly, and when he noticed her gaze, he asked, "Do you want some?"

"No!" Anne was more emphatic than she'd meant to be, but she was sure this wasn't allowed; he might be asked to leave, and she would be blamed along with him.

"What a wet blanket."

What a horrid boy was her silent retort. Wanting to get away from him, Anne said, "I need to use the powder room."

"There isn't one."

"Excuse me?"

"This is a *men's* gym," he said. "Yale's a school for *men*. No powder rooms here."

"Well, I'm sure there must be some accommodation for the ladies," she said icily, and went off to find a chaperone, who in turn escorted her to a private restroom somewhere upstairs. Anne remained there for a long time, and when she eventually returned to the dance floor, Duane was nowhere to be seen. Good riddance. Then she spied Peggy, who came up to her. "Where's your date?" Peggy asked.

"Oh, he stepped outside for a minute." Anne wasn't inclined to tattle on Duane; it would only get back to Midge. "Where's yours?"

"He stepped outside too."

Something about the way she said this made Anne laugh; maybe she thought her date was a dud? Soon they were both giggling, and Anne felt better than she had all evening. Then Peggy said, "Do you know a girl named Miriam Bishop?"

Anne felt the air had suddenly been sucked from her lungs. *She* had been Miriam Bishop all the way through school; she'd only decided to use her middle name, Anne, when she started at Vassar. "Why do you ask?"

"I ran into someone named Elizabeth Hunnewell. She went to Nightingale-Bamford. Isn't that where you went?"

"Yes." Anne was buying time, but she was running out of it. Quickly.

"That's what I thought. So if you went there, you must have known her."

"No, I didn't. Maybe this girl—you said her name was Elizabeth?—is confused."

"She seemed very sure. And she also said that she and Miriam had been very good friends."

Just hearing Elizabeth's name was like a small electric shock, and Anne wanted to end this conversation. And look, there was Duane. She waved to him; could he see how desperate she was? She didn't wait to find out but marched right over, leaving Peggy where she stood. "Let's dance!"

He seemed doubtful, but when Anne practically heaved herself into his arms, his slightly wary expression relaxed, and he grinned and pulled her to him. She didn't find him any more appealing than she had an hour ago, but this time she knew better than to resist. She needed him now; he was her defense against anyone exposing her secret.

As Duane spun her around the room, Anne forced herself to smile, even though she felt the anxiety thrumming inside. Why hadn't it occurred to her that this dance might draw girls from other nearby colleges, and that she might easily run into someone she knew? Anne and Duane danced to three songs in a row, the last one quite fast, and this time, he was the one to say he needed a cup of punch. So they stopped dancing and drank two cups of punch each; to Anne's relief, the flask didn't reappear.

When the band started playing a slow song, she tried to pull Duane back onto the dance floor, but he stayed where he was. "I need some air," he said. "Let's go outside." Anne didn't especially want to do that, but being alone with Duane seemed preferable to having to talk to Peggy or, even worse, be confronted by Elizabeth. She allowed him to steer her away from the music, the press of people, and lead her into the night. She too was overheated from the dancing, and she didn't feel the cold at first. Then the flask glinted as Duane swigged from it. When he'd finished, he thrust it in her direction. "Are you sure you don't want some?"

This time Anne took the flask and brought it to her lips; the alcohol was almost tasteless, but left an unpleasant burning sensation behind; should she risk going back inside for water or punch? Before she could decide, Duane pulled her head down and kissed her, his tongue—fat, slippery, repulsive—an alien thing in her mouth. She jerked away.

"You're a little tease, that's what you are. An ice queen and a tease." Out came the flask again—was there anything even left in there?—and this time, when he'd finished, he shook the thing at her, the last colorless drops splattering the front of her dress, and stalked off. Shivering now, Anne brushed off the drops of alcohol, and then she spat, lavishly, to rid herself of his taste. To think this had been her first kiss—revolting. But chilled as she was, she waited until she was sure Duane was gone before she went back into the gym to find her coat and leave the building.

The bus that had brought them here was waiting not far from where Anne stood. She went over and saw that it was empty; the door yielded to her gentle pressure. She climbed aboard, walked to the very back, and took a seat. Alone in the dark, she tried to calm herself. Duane, that boor, wasn't the real source of her agitation. More pressing—and alarming—was the way her past, which she had forced to the periphery of her life, was now pushing forward again, insistent and demanding.

Peggy was right—she *did* know Elizabeth Hunnewell, though back then she'd been Lizzie, and Anne had been Mimi. *MimiandLizzie, LizzieandMimi*—everyone said their names together. They had been a unit, a pair, best friends in school and out. Mrs. Hunnewell had become a kind of second mother to Anne. She'd been close to all of them, really: Lizzie's father, often comically distracted but always affable, and her two older sisters, glamorous Genevieve and high-spirited Maud. Their black Standard Poodle, Lady, with her long, graceful legs and intelligent expression. Even Opal, the maid, fussed over her when she was there.

Yet despite all the dinners Miriam had eaten at their table and the nights spent in Lizzie's room, there had always been a way in which she felt herself at some remove, not just from the Hunnewells but from the other girls at school too. The source of this feeling was simple but inexorable: it was because she was Jewish. It felt like she'd always known that her friends seemed to pity her, just a little bit, because there was no Christmas tree in her apartment, no joining them for caroling on the cold winter evenings when crystals of glistening snow turned the ordinary gray sidewalks into something almost magical, no frenzy of tearing paper and ribbons from the pile of boxes the next morning. And they pitied her exclusion from the mad race to find the hidden eggs on Easter Sunday. For Anne, there had been no excelsior-filled baskets in which chocolate bunnies and lambs nestled, no proud walk to the church on Park Avenue in a new pastel spring coat and matching hat. Back then, being Christian had seemed like more than a religion; it was the fabric of life itself, rich and glowing, the holidays touchstones for everyone but her. It wasn't as if she and her father didn't have any celebrations. He always lit a menorah and gave her little gifts—chocolate coins, a handkerchief, new hair ribbons—each night of Hanukkah. She liked the ritual, and the game with the dreidel they played, but how could any of this compete with Christmas—the store windows with their fabulous displays, the fragrant wreaths and trees, the way everyone seemed to be swept up in the grand tide of the season? It was the exclusion that grated on her, never glaring but always there.

The summer after seventh grade, Lizzie was getting ready to go off to Camp Oneida in Maine. Excitedly, she showed Mimi the dress outfit the campers wore every Sunday: crisp white shorts, white socks, and white sneakers, topped with a red blazer that had a turtle—the camp mascot—embroidered on the pocket. Miriam envied that blazer, just like she envied everything else Lizzie described—nature walks, arts and crafts, archery, and swimming. "Tell your father you want to come too," Lizzie had said. "My mother knows the director. I'm sure she can find a place for you."

But it turned out the camp was restricted, and so no, Miriam wouldn't be going after all. She wasn't *allowed*. In her humiliation she'd gone to her father; surely he could fix it. "What difference does it make that we're Jewish?" she'd asked.

"It doesn't," he said. "Not in any real sense. In fact, some of these bigoted people forget that Jesus himself was a Jew. The differences they see as crucial aren't truly differences at all. We're from the same tradition. We have the same foundation—we both rejected the pagan world and all its childish, spiteful gods."

Miriam was used to her father answering her this way; he never patronized or talked down to her but acted as if her intellect deserved nothing less than his most serious and thoughtful response. Yet she still didn't understand. "If that's true, why can't I go to camp with Lizzie?"

"I wish I could answer that," he said.

Then something else occurred to her. "Why do we have to be Jewish, anyway? Why do we have to be anything at all?"

"If only it were that simple," her father said. "In the eyes of the world, once a Jew, always a Jew. Besides, a Jew is *what* I am, it's what made me *who* I am."

"But you changed your name. Our name. Wasn't that because you didn't want to be Jewish?"

"No. I didn't want to *appear* to be Jewish, at least with people who didn't know me—it was getting in the way of my getting ahead in my career. But as for *being* Jewish, well, I can't be anything else. And neither can you." The way he said it, with such finality, made Miriam wilt inside. It was as if he were delivering a life sentence. The idea that she was bound by who her parents and their parents had been seemed so unfair.

Lizzie sent her postcards from camp, and when she returned, she presented Miriam with a friendship bracelet she had made for her. Miriam looked at the tightly woven network of beads: orange, white, green, blue, and black. "It's very nice," she said. "Thank you." But she still burned for the blazer, and for the entitled status that would have allowed her to have made her own bracelet, one that she would have given to Lizzie.

Then, in the spring of her senior year at Nightingale, there came another of those snubs, arguably the worst, the culmination of all the others. Elizabeth's mother—she was Elizabeth now, having discarded Lizzie as too babyish—had invited a small group of girls to the Colony Club on Park Avenue for lunch. The Colony was the premier all-women's club in the city, and Mrs. Hunnewell said it would be a nice way to introduce them, in case they wanted to join when they were a bit older. Miriam was familiar with the exterior of the building on Sixty-Second Street—red brick, marble base, marble trim, columns supporting the upper floors—but she had never been inside and so had only heard about the lounges, dining rooms, and bedrooms as well as the two-story ballroom, the basement swimming pool and spa that connected via an express elevator to a gymnasium on the fifth floor, the squash courts, servants' rooms, and kennel, where members could leave their pets.

The girls were abuzz with excitement, and the Colony was all they talked about. That the war in Europe had just ended—all the boys and young men would be coming home! No more ration cards!—only fueled their mood; the entire city felt jubilant. They chattered endlessly about what they would wear, eat, do. They envisioned starched white tablecloths, lace-edged napkins, dainty finger sandwiches, cucumber soup, strawberry shortcake, rosebuds densely packed into small crystal vases. Naturally, they had to dress up—their school uniforms wouldn't do at all.

Elizabeth decided on a black taffeta skirt and pale-pink silk blouse. Astrid's mother promised to lend her a strand of pearls, and a pearl brooch to adorn the deep purple dress she planned to wear; Willa, who was Astrid's best friend, went with her mother to Saks, and came away with a smart checked suit—her first—and peaked cap with a feather on the side. Miriam studied her own wardrobe and decided that nothing she owned was sophisticated enough, but she knew her father would allow her to go shopping—maybe Bonwit Teller?—to buy a dress and a pair of pumps too. And new gloves—she definitely needed new white cotton gloves.

Two days before the much-anticipated event, Miriam went over to Lizzie's apartment to show her the wine-colored dress and jacket she'd found at Saks just the night before; it was so grown-up. She was on her way to Lizzie's room—Opal had let her in—when Lizzie's mother stopped her in the hallway. "Hello, Mrs. Hunnewell," she said. "Do you want to see my new dress? I have it right here." She patted the paper shopping bag on her arm.

"Maybe later." Mrs. Hunnewell seemed—what was it? Uncomfortable. "Can I speak to you for a moment?"

"Of course." Miriam felt a small twinge of apprehension.

"It's about the luncheon at the Colony."

"Oh, I'm so looking forward to it! We all are. That's why I want to show Lizzie the dress. And you too."

"I'm sure it's lovely, dear," Mrs. Hunnewell said. "And I'd love to see you in it. But you see, something's come up. I'm afraid you won't be able to go to the luncheon after all."

"Why not? Has it been canceled?" Miriam asked.

"No, it's not that." Mrs. Hunnewell seemed to be struggling for words. "The luncheon is still on, and the other girls are going. It's just that you won't be joining them."

"I don't understand." Miriam was growing more confused.

"Well, it's because of your father."

"My father? What does he have to do with it?"

"The secretary at the club knew of him, and since the club is restricted . . ."

"Restricted." Miriam repeated the hateful word. It had kept her from going to Camp Oneida, and now it had come back to haunt her.

"I *wish* it weren't so, but those are the rules, and even though I advocated for you, I really did, it seems that they are quite inflexible on this point—" Somewhere in the apartment the phone rang, and Mrs. Hunnewell's relief at the distraction was painfully evident. "Excuse me," she said. "Opal just left, so I'll need to get that."

Miriam opened the door to Lizzie's room without knocking. "Did you know?" she asked without any greeting. "Did she tell you?"

Elizabeth didn't pretend not to understand. "She did. Just a little while ago."

"I thought your mother liked me."

"Oh, she does, she's *very* fond of you. But given your background and all . . ."

"You mean because we're Jews?" There, the word was out, pulsating and hot. Neither of them spoke for a few seconds.

"Mimi, please don't be angry, it's not Mummy's fault." Elizabeth began to twist the end of her ponytail. "She wanted you there. We all did. It was only when she gave them your name that someone connected it with your father, and—"

"And everyone knows that he's a Jew," Miriam said bitterly. "That *we're* Jews." Did they talk about it when she wasn't there? Call them yids, or worse? Her father had changed his name from Jacob Berkowitz to Jay Bishop, but that was when he was just starting out as a young lawyer. And though in the intervening—and highly successful—years, he'd not gone out of his way to advertise his background, he'd made no special effort to hide it either. So people did know that both he—and of course she—were Jewish.

"I'm so sorry, and if you only knew how sorry my mother is—she feels just terrible—"

"Don't go."

"What do you mean?"

"You heard me. Don't go. Not you, not Astrid, not Willa. If they won't let me in, don't go to that stupid, snobby club." But even as she spoke, she knew it was pointless. And the look in Elizabeth's eyes only confirmed it—neither she nor any of the others were about to take such a stand on her behalf. They would say they were sorry a dozen, a hundred times, they would tell her they'd miss her, that it wouldn't be as much fun without her, but they would go. Of course they would. They were all on a single path, headed in a single direction; it was just one that didn't include her.

Anne heard voices outside. Was the mixer over yet? She hoped not. Sliding even farther down in the seat, she waited to see if the voices got closer. They didn't. Whoever was out there wasn't heading to the bus. Her chest, which had tightened from anxiety, relaxed a little; she had a reprieve. She'd replayed that conversation about the Colony many times in her mind, and each time, her sense of indignation flared again. The club, Mrs. Hunnewell, and the girls had wronged her. But there was still another incident, a memory Anne did her best to bury.

It had been a chilly, early spring day. Miriam and Lizzie had spent the entire afternoon in the Hunnewells' living room, assembling an enormous jigsaw puzzle. Music from a radio in another room drifted in; rain tapped delicately on the windowpanes. The bell rang and Lady emitted a single, dignified *woof.* Opal went to the door.

"Oh, that must be Mr. Feinstein." Mrs. Hunnewell came into the room as Opal was taking the man's umbrella and coat.

Miriam looked up from the puzzle. Mr. Feinstein wore a rumpled shirt, and suspenders that were visible because he had on a vest that wouldn't close over his big belly and no jacket. Two bunches of white curly hair sprang from the sides of his bald, pink head, and he carried a canvas bag splattered by dark drops of water.

"Nice to see you again, Mrs. Hunnewell," he said. His accent was familiar to Miriam—it was an accent that her grandparents had, as well as some of her older relatives, like Aunt Riva and Uncle Max. It conjured images of cramped houses with dirt floors, glasses of schnapps, a woman, hair hidden under a scarf, lighting candles, loaves of challah baked to a shellacked shade of brown, cows mooing balefully outside. "I've brought you some new samples—they just came in. Wait until you see them." He reached into the bag and pulled out several rolls of fabric, which he unfurled with great fanfare. "Look at this brocade," he said. "Fit for a queen, for a castle! Touch it! And this chintz—did you ever see such a beautiful pattern?" His voice was booming, and he pronounced the word bee-YOU-tee-ful.

On and on he went; Mrs. Hunnewell nodded and smiled, occasionally extending a hand, its slim wrist encircled by a lovely gold charm bracelet, to indicate the ones she liked best. She was as cordial to Mr. Feinstein as could be, but when he left, she turned to the girls and sighed deeply. "Some people . . ." That was all she said, but Miriam knew *exactly* what she meant, and she was mortified. Was this how Mrs. Hunnewell saw her and her father, who, it had to be admitted, did stand apart from the parents of her friends and classmates? His voice was louder, his gestures more dramatic, his words flowed more quickly. He operated at top volume, and even though she adored him, Miriam had begun to wish he would turn it down, even just a little. So no wonder she didn't want to think about that rainy day; she'd been complicit, wanting to align herself with the Hunnewells and keep as much distance as she could from Mr. Feinstein.

Elizabeth and the others had gone to the luncheon, and to their credit, they tried not to mention it in Miriam's presence. But sometimes a reference slipped out, like the time they served a Waldorf salad in the cafeteria and Willa said, "Oh look, it's just like the Colony!" There had been an awkward silence that lasted until Elizabeth started chattering about something else. And afterward, she seemed to assume that their friendship would continue on as it had before. She was wrong. Miriam couldn't forget, and, it turned out, she couldn't forgive either.

Summer came, and with it an invitation to join the Hunnewells in Darien. Other invitations followed: Greenwich, Newport, Marblehead. She declined every last one. Now that she fully understood the weight of that hateful word, *restricted*, she could imagine the country clubs and beaches where, though her name wouldn't have given her away, the fear of discovery would have hovered around her, never allowing her to fully relax. Her father had rented the same house in Deal Beach, New Jersey, every summer since she was a small child. She would go to the shore with him.

But just a week before they were set to leave, her father died. Miriam had been grateful that her aunt Betty and Mrs. Shifrin, wife of the rabbi at the Temple of Israel Synagogue on East Seventy-Fifth Street, where her father had been a sporadic congregant, organized first the funeral and then the shiva. Those were slow, somber days, the reality of the loss gradually sinking in, like a series of boulders placed on her shoulders and back, each one bigger and heavier than the last. She couldn't believe that he'd never again come striding through the door, calling her name, leaving his ever-battered fedora, coat, briefcase, and newspaper scattered around the apartment for Hannah, the maid, to pick up. No more accounts of his day in court, or questions about hers at school. No more singing—he had a full-bodied baritone—no humming, no expostulating over an article in one of the several newspapers he subscribed to, no heated phone calls with his clients, his partner, Barney Weiss, or his devoted secretary, Miss Fishbein. He had been such a large presence, physically and every other way. How could he just be—gone? And even worse was thinking about how she'd begun, just the littlest bit, to disdain him, and to wish he'd been more polished, more refined. She burned in shame, remembering all that.

Along with this monumental loss was the loss of the only home she'd ever known; Barney sold the apartment and put its contents into storage. She was to spend school holidays with Barney and his family—they had a town house in the East Thirties—and summers and vacations with her aunt upstate. "Everything will be stored away," Barney said, "ready for you if you want it someday." Someday? She didn't want to wait until someday; she wanted everything she knew and loved, every scrap of it, from the dotted Swiss curtains and matching bedspread in her room to the small Oriental rug with its jewel-like colors in the foyer, *now*. The chesterfield sofa, the mahogany sideboard in the dining room, the pair of blue-and-white ginger-jar lamps that sat on the mantel, the enormous Windsor chair that had been her father's favorite and which he would not hear of having reupholstered despite the fact that its faded fabric was practically in tatters. Her aunt fussed and clucked, and told her repeatedly that she should consider the house in Skaneateles as her home. How could she say that? It wasn't her home now, and it would never be.

Still, she miserably succumbed to her aunt's insistence that she spend the rest of the summer upstate. Really, where else could she go?

The sound of voices brought Anne back to the present; the Yale mixer was ending, and the girls were heading back to the bus. Virginia's voice carried through the night, and she thought she could hear Peggy too. She didn't want to talk to either of them, so she slid down in her seat, hoping that would hide her. The darkness was like an animate presence, heavy and enveloping. The girls were filing into the bus now. Soon the driver would appear, shepherding them back to Vassar's campus. She'd never been to Yale before, and after tonight, she didn't think she would ever be back.

FOUR

DELIA

1940

Delia woke up very early the next morning; the sky was still black, and the sparrows that usually twittered on the windowsills were quiet. Lying in bed, she had to face the fact that her mother was not coming back. But her abrupt disappearance might mean that she was in trouble. Was she sick? Had she been hurt? Or arrested? German soldiers were everywhere, and the French police were cooperating with them. Sophie was a Jew; they were all Jews in their family, not that it had ever mattered before. There might have been some circles where they wouldn't have been welcome, but those were not circles they cared about. The arty, bohemian crowd they surrounded themselves with was disparate enough to accommodate them. And though her parents did not hide who they were, they didn't seem particularly tied to their heritage either. Rather they considered themselves citizens of the world, and it was art and the making of art that was their true religion. Delia attended a lycée where the students mingled freely, and every year she celebrated Christmas with Gaby, whose mother served a *bûche de Noël* decorated to look like a yule log, lines scored into the chocolate icing to mimic bark, marzipan mushrooms and leaves surrounding it. Delia had her own wooden sabot in their apartment, set out alongside Gaby's the night before; in the morning, it was filled with little trinkets and bonbons. But now all of a sudden being Jewish was a liability, and because of it, something could have happened to her mother. Something bad.

Her father came into the kitchen and started to prepare the coffee. Now there was no bread, stale or otherwise, but Delia didn't think she could eat anyway. Where was her mother? They had to find her. She waited until Simon was seated at the table—the coffee in his cup was black since there was no milk either.

"Good morning, Papa," she said.

"Bonjour." He lit a cigarette, and a ribbon of smoke coiled and then dispersed somewhere above his head.

"What are we going to do?" She was frustrated by his calm demeanor; why wasn't he frantic with worry?

He looked at her blankly and then said, "Do? We're going to finish packing. And then we're leaving." He glanced up at the clock on the wall. "And we've got to hurry. There isn't much time."

"But what about Maman? Aren't we going to look for her?"

"Where?" he asked.

Delia didn't have an answer to that, so she got up to help him; it was better to do something, anything, than to let the worry completely consume her.

Two hours later, they were done, and Delia looked around the apartment. It seemed to have exploded, its contents disgorged and strewn everywhere—just like their lives. There hadn't been time to pack even half of what they owned; they would have to leave the rest behind. Just as they would have to leave her mother. This stark fact was like a death—if not Sophie's, then the death of Delia's family, imperfect as it was but still hers, still dear, still all she'd ever known. Something inside felt like it was burning, charred. Yet she shed no tears; they had all been dried up by the awful scalding heat inside her.

With just a few small bags, Delia and Simon arrived at the Gare de Lyon to wait for the train. There was a crush of people, all seemingly as anxious as they were, and her eyes scanned the crowd, hoping to see her mother somewhere in it. Simon had Sophie's ticket—Delia had checked—so if she did show up, she'd be able to accompany them. But when it was time to board, there was still no Sophie. Delia felt as if her feet were glued to the platform; she couldn't make herself get on the train.

"Come on," her father said, taking her elbow. His voice was exasperated; so was his expression. Still Delia did not move, though the knot of people behind her were jostling one another in their eagerness to board.

"Do you need any help, mademoiselle?" A harried-looking railway employee appeared in front of her.

"No," Delia said. "I don't."

"Then you'll need to step aside. You're blocking the way."

Delia was about to cede her place when her father grabbed her roughly by the wrist and yanked her up three steps and into the train.

"Papa, stop!" she cried. "You're hurting me!"

"Hurting you?" said Simon. "Leaving you here on this platform would be hurting you. I'm saving you, you silly girl! Can't you see that?"

Delia glared at him and rubbed her wrist. But she had to admit he was right. She couldn't stay here. And she had to accept that Sophie really and truly wasn't coming with them.

Her father was looking at her with some concern. "I'm sorry," he said. "For everything."

"So am I," Delia said, but so softly it didn't seem that he heard.

The trip to Lisbon took eighteen long hours, and the train was noisy and so crowded that some people crammed a few to a seat. Delia and her father weren't seated together; he was two seats in front of her on the aisle, while she was shoehorned in by a window. At first she was grateful that she could look out at the landscape; even the slight distraction from her thinking about her mother was welcome. But then she became aware of the man sitting next to her, who was pressing his thigh against hers; even through the wool coat that she wore, she could feel the pressure. She initially thought it might be accidental on his part, so she shifted whatever fraction of a centimeter that she could away from him. The pressure continued. And the man kept his face averted, so she couldn't even hope to discourage him with an angry stare.

Then he replaced his thigh with his open hand, and then his fingers began to creep under her coat, then her skirt. This could not be accidental. Delia cast panicked looks around her. No one noticed anything, no one could rescue her, not even her father, unless she found a way to alert him. Now the fingers had found their way to the tops of the ribbed stockings that she wore, and were kneading her bare flesh. What could she do? She was frozen by his audacity until she understood: her failure to react was read as acquiescence, a kind of permission. The realization goaded her into action. She dug into the pockets of her coat and found what she'd prayed would be there: a pearl-topped pin from the time she needed to secure her first grown-up hat—navy-blue felt with a black grosgrain ribbon—to her head. Carefully extracting the pin, she kept it concealed as she positioned it right next to the place where the man's thumb joined his hand. Then she pressed, as hard as she could. For a second there was resistance, but then she could feel the pin push deep into his flesh. He jerked his hand away; she was flooded with triumph. He didn't bother her for the rest of the ride.

Once in Lisbon, they boarded SS *Quanza* and embarked on the voyage across the ocean. Delia spent most of the time in her cabin; the idea of socializing with the other passengers was intolerable, though her father seemed to enjoy it. Maybe it was because he was mildly intoxicated much of the time. But on the day they were scheduled to arrive in New York, she made her way up to the deck. The ship was close enough so that she could see the Statue of Liberty on the horizon. She'd only seen it in photographs, but she knew her mother had loved the gigantic sculpture—the size of it, its strong arm thrust boldly into the sky. Sophie should have been here now, when Delia was seeing it for the first time. Delia was once again awash in anger at her mother's impulsive flight from the apartment, which had led to this moment. She turned away from the shoreline.

When they first landed, Delia and Simon stayed with his parents in their sprawling apartment on Riverside Drive. Having met her paternal grandparents only twice, Delia scarcely knew them. They seemed stilted and uncomfortable around their son and granddaughter, as if Sophie's disappearance was too shameful to be discussed. Well, that was all right with Delia; she didn't want to talk about Sophie either, at least not with them. She might have turned to her maternal grandparents, but they had died some years ago, and so she felt quite alone in her sorrow.

She was relieved when her father found them a house on West Eleventh Street, in Greenwich Village, so they could move out of the Riverside Drive apartment. He covered its walls with the paintings that he'd managed to take with them, canvases pried carefully from their stretchers and rolled up tightly in the valises. Seeing the paintings made Delia long even more for her mother's sculpture, those sleek, sinuous forms—everyone had praised Sophie's fluid line—made of marble or granite. Most of that work was in storage now, her father said. But Delia possessed the double portrait, and she was so glad she'd taken it. She loved the way the two faces were distinct yet connected, the spare and even austere form, its alabaster so white and glowing that it seemed lit from within.

"So you took it with you, after all," her father said when he saw the sculpture.

Delia waited for him to say more—to question her, chastise her, *something*. But he just turned away, uttering a small sound—was it a *sob*?—as he did. She placed the sculpture in a prominent spot in her new room, which was on the top floor of the house; her father's room was on the floor below. If he didn't want to see the sculpture, he didn't have to come up here.

Her grief over her mother's absence grew smaller but heavier, more compact. It burrowed deep inside her, a small, hard nugget of pain that she tried to numb by acclimating to her new life in New York. At least she spoke English—her parents had made sure of that—and Greenwich Village was not altogether unlike the Rive Gauche, filled with small shops, cafés, and bars. Their neighbors were actors and artists, poets and writers. Her father talked about opening a gallery; he said this would be a good place for it.

Delia enrolled in the Little Red Schoolhouse on Charlton Street. She excelled there, as she always had, and even made friends, though she told them her mother had died. It was just easier that way; they didn't need to know the truth. She and her father heard news about the war they had left behind, but they weren't shunned as they had been in Paris, and they didn't feel they were in danger.

Then the Japanese attacked Pearl Harbor. The United States joined the war, and now there were food shortages and ration cards to deal with them. People on their block tended victory gardens behind their houses, and joined together to collect scraps, paper, tin, and rubber. Soon enough Delia started seeing blue stars in many of the windows, indicating that someone who lived there had gone to fight. First it was just a few, then more and more appeared.

A tall, lanky boy next door, George Frost, had knocked on their door when they first arrived, offering a coffee cake on a flowered plate.

"My mother told me to bring this."

Delia took it from him; the cake was still warm.

"She wanted to say welcome to the neighborhood." But instead of leaving, he remained where he stood, looking at Delia. He was older than she was—sixteen or seventeen—with fine light-brown hair and crisp features that looked as if they'd been carved with a penknife.

"Thank you so much," she said.

"Let me know if you and your dad need help with anything, especially anything in the backyard."

"Do you keep a garden?"

He nodded enthusiastically. "We've got flowers, and a little vegetable patch too. Also herbs."

"Sounds nice."

"You can see it from your yard," he said. Some of his hair had fallen across his forehead, and to her own surprise, Delia felt an urge to brush it away; she had never thought about touching a boy like that before. "Or you can come over sometime."

"I will," she said. "Thanks again."

After that, she made a point of looking at the Frosts' well-tended garden. Their own garden was overgrown, even wild, but Delia had no patience for cultivating it. Looking at George Frost's garden was horticulture enough for her. Delia also kept track of his comings and goings, so she came to know the small, fluffy dog George walked regularly. With its pointed snout and plume of a tail, it was fairly ridiculous, as was the way it pranced along, as if on perpetual tiptoes. Although the dog yapped incessantly and was known to growl and even nip, George seemed devoted to it, something Delia found endearing. He always smiled when he saw her and sometimes stopped to chat. She had the thought—hope?—that he might ask her on a date. But that was silly; he would think she was too young, wouldn't he? She never had the chance to find out because one day a blue star appeared in the window of his family's house—that meant he'd enlisted or been drafted. She found herself looking at that window regularly; she was hoping the blue star wouldn't be replaced by a gold one, the symbol for a soldier who'd been killed. She also realized she no longer heard the little dog yapping; maybe the family had given it away. Annoying as the dog had been, she found herself hoping that was the case, and not that it had died. By springtime Delia noticed that the entire garden had been abandoned, with plants either withered and dead or else growing out of control.

Every night Delia and her father sat together listening to the radio's news from Europe. Unlike the French, the English would not cooperate with the Nazis, and so London was bombed week after week, month after month. Mussolini allied himself with Hitler, and then Hitler turned around and attacked his allies in Russia. In the midst of all this chaos, where was Sophie? Was she even alive, and if so, did she know her husband and daughter had left Paris without her?

These questions tormented Delia, but there was no one to ask, no way to find out. And so their lives went on. She continued to do well in school; Simon opened a gallery on Cornelia Street that, though moderately successful, never seemed to develop the same cachet as his gallery in Paris. Maybe it was because he was different now—less charming, less engaging.

And he drank too much. Delia began to help out at the openings, pouring the wine and chatting with the people who attended. Her father retreated, grateful, it seemed, to let her assume the dominant role. At first she pitied him, but pity turned to disdain, and then disdain calcified into anger. Why wasn't he more interested in looking for his wife?

The years passed. Delia moved on to Elizabeth Irwin High School and began to think about college. Thoughts of her mother were always there, often lacing her dreams, but they no longer dominated.

Then on a warm spring day, the news broke that the war in Europe was over. Over! The Germans had surrendered unconditionally. Hitler was dead, by his own hand. Paris had been liberated, London was ecstatic. Delia was in school when the city erupted; classes were canceled, and she and all her classmates rode uptown to Times Square to join in the massive parade. People in the packed streets were laughing, singing, even dancing. Strangers pumped each other's hands and kissed. Confetti rained down, and Delia smiled as she brushed it from her hair. She and her friends stopped for ice cream along the way, and the woman behind the counter wouldn't take their money, but insisted on piling their cones with sweet, cold scoops.

But when she got back to the house on Eleventh Street, her elation faded. Simon had slept through the entire day, and when he emerged from his room—disheveled and no doubt drunk—it took him a moment to understand what she was saying. Exasperated, she turned on the radio so he could hear it for himself. Even when he did finally comprehend what had happened, it didn't have much of an impact.

"We can start looking for Maman," she told him. "Maybe we can even go to Paris."

"I don't ever want to see Paris again."

She looked at her father with something bordering on disgust. How could he say that when, for all they knew, Sophie was still there? Well, if he wasn't going to take any action, she would. Without telling him, she began writing to anyone whose address she remembered and who had known her mother—there was Yvette, who had lived nearby on the rue du Faubourg Saint-Jacques, and Marie-Pierre, who lived near Saint-Sulpice. She also found the receipt for all the artwork that had been in the gallery and wrote a letter to the storage company. Weeks later, that letter came back, with the words ADRESSE INCONNUE—address unknown—stamped on the front. Yvette wrote back to say she hadn't heard from her mother since before the war, and Marie-Pierre didn't write back at all.

The elation Delia had felt in May slowly dried up as spring turned into summer; it was especially hot that year, with record high temperatures that kept Delia home and glued to the fans she had set up all around the house. The war in Europe was over, but the fighting continued in Japan until that morning in August when the United States dropped an atomic bomb, first on Hiroshima, and then three days later, on Nagasaki.

The enormity of the devastation seemed to pierce through the cloud of inertia that had enshrouded her father; he pushed the newspaper with its shocking headline in her direction, his face wet with tears. All those people—old women, new mothers, babies, men with canes, in wheelchairs—incinerated instantly. He got up and came to put his arms around her, and even though she was still angry with him, she let him comfort her. He was all she had. This was followed by a few days during which she felt close to him and again brought up the subject of her mother. It had been five years since she'd seen her; so much must have happened in that time. Unless of course Sophie was dead—a thought she tried to keep at bay.

"Don't you care anymore?" she asked her father. "Don't you at least want to know?"

"I did care," he said, clearly measuring his words.

"But you don't anymore?"

"You know who your mother was," he said. "She could wear you out. She wore *me* out."

"Is that it? You're worn out? You're done with her?"

He nodded, reached for the pipe with which he'd lately replaced his habitual cigarettes, and lit it. The tobacco smell was too sweet, almost sickening.

Delia thought about this. Was she finished too? Done with her mother? She didn't think so. She might not have been ready to return to Paris—not yet—but she didn't want to be in New York either and decided to apply to colleges that were elsewhere. She needed to be out of this house, away from her father and her constant disappointment in him. And when the acceptances came in, she decided on Vassar, largely because she liked its campus—serene, gracious, beautiful. She would be able to breathe there.

It was shortly before she was scheduled to leave for Poughkeepsie that the letter arrived from Paris. It was from Marie-Pierre—she'd written back after all. Delia stared at it for a moment before tearing it open. She brought the thin, blue onionskin sheet to where her father sat in the parlor and began to read aloud.

Dear Delia,

How long it's been since I have seen you; you were a child when I last did but I imagine you are all grown now, a lovely young woman just starting out in life. I could tell from your letter—you sounded so mature and poised. Your mother would have loved to see the person I know you have become. But this can never be. I was told by people who were there that your mother was killed. She had been living in Paris and working for the Resistance. Even though Sophie was an American, she felt so allied with the French, and her disgust for the Nazis was so all-consuming, that she felt compelled to join in on this effort. She understood the risks she was taking and was willing to accept them, but she wouldn't have wanted to put you or your father in any danger, she was very clear about that; she was relieved you were out of the country and glad you were safe.

I'm not sure who betrayed them, but it was either late in 1942 or early in 1943. I heard that they, along with some of the other members, were discovered and shot. I know what a shock it will be to read this, and I am sorry to have to be the bearer of such terrible news, but maybe it is better that you know than spend the rest of your life wondering. I hope and pray that you and your father find peace and happiness; your mother would have wanted that too.

By the time Delia had finished reading the letter, her face was slick with tears. Sophie was dead. Shot. How had it come about? When and where? The questions were so loud in her mind that they seemed to be howling. She looked at her father, ready to go to him, to seek comfort in his arms, but his face showed no emotion. "Papa," she began. "Papa, I know you were angry with her, that she hurt you . . . but she was murdered . . . Can't you forgive her now, Papa?"

"If only she hadn't left . . ." He took a few deep, heaving breaths. "I could have kept her safe," he said. "The tickets . . . for the train, for the boat . . ." He looked at his hands as if the tickets were in them. Then he turned away and began to weep.

Delia went over and put her arms around him. But there was no consolation there, not for him, not for her. The war might have ended, but its devastation would live inside them. It had taken her mother and transformed her father. She thought again about Vassar; she couldn't wait to go.

And now, here she was, in the fall of her sophomore year. She still nursed a private, searing grief at her mother's death, but along with it was an enormous sense of liberation. At Vassar, no one knew about Sophie's horrific end. Delia could be just another student, unmarked by the tragedy, at least not externally. The little snubs and slights of her classmates were rendered harmless. The girls on her floor, Midge, the philistine who had been her roommate—all immaterial.

But then there was that one who seemed different from the rest—Anne Bishop. She'd even broken away from that little pack she moved in and joined Delia at dinner one night. Delia told herself she didn't care about making friends, that she was fine on her own. But it wasn't true. She'd been a popular girl back in Paris, and she missed being part of a group, just as she missed Gaby and how close they'd been. There seemed little hope of replicating that here at Vassar; she felt estranged from almost everyone she'd met.

Maybe Anne could be a friend. Once Delia had formed the thought, it took on a concrete shape, a form of its own. She'd pursue the possibility, see where it led, and if it turned out to be a dead end, so what? She'd lost so much already; there was hardly anything left to lose.

FIVE

ANNE

Fall 1946

Anne reached into her mail cubby and pulled out an envelope. The return address was unfamiliar, but that didn't matter; she would have recognized Elizabeth Hunnewell's handwriting anywhere. As she stared down at it, her heart began an unpleasant erratic thudding.

"On your way to breakfast?"

Anne looked up to see Peggy. "Uh, no, I'm not hungry," she said. "I'll just get an early lunch." In fact, she *had* been on her way to the dining room, but now, with the letter held tightly in her hand, she changed her mind.

"All right," Peggy said. "Maybe I'll see you at tea."

"Maybe." As soon as Peggy had turned away, Anne hurried back upstairs to her room, fumbled with the key and slammed the door behind her. Then she tore the letter free from its envelope.

Dear Mimi,

I was at the Yale dance and met someone from your class at Vassar but she didn't seem to know you, yet she knew someone named Anne Bishop. Anne is your middle name, right? Do you have a cousin named Anne? I thought I knew all your cousins but maybe not. Or maybe you're using it now that you're in college? Anyway, none of that matters. What matters is that we no longer seem to be friends.

Even our last spring at Nightingale I could feel that things were different, but I didn't bring it up. I thought that if I didn't talk about it, it would just go away and that the feeling would go away. I guess that was pretty naive of me. It was that thing about the Colony, right? Of course it was. I don't even need to ask because I know how hurt you were. I understand that. I do. Maybe I should have listened to you and not gone either. But it would have disappointed my mother so much, and the other girls too. So whatever I did, someone was going to be hurt. Anyway, I am sorry about what happened, and I hope you can forgive me. I want for us to be friends and to be close again. I miss you, Mimi, I really do.

With love,
Elizabeth

Anne put the letter down. She was transported back to Elizabeth's—Lizzie's—bedroom, with its pair of twin beds and its violet-sprigged wallpaper. All the hours she had spent in that room, eating oatmeal raisin cookies and breaking off bits for Lady, who waited patiently for a treat, poring over comic books and, later, copies of *Calling All Girls* they'd filched from her older sisters, experimenting with lipstick, eyebrow pencil, and rouge, also filched; she could still remember the two of them staring into the mirror above Lizzie's dresser, startled by the vividly colored and wholly unfamiliar faces staring back at them.

Yes, she missed Elizabeth too, and wished she could ease the hurt that was still knotted inside her. Wished that they could, as Elizabeth had said, be close again. It had been easy to avoid her, to avoid all her old friends. Along with three other girls from their class, Elizabeth had gone to Smith. Astrid had gone to Wellesley, and Willa to Mount

Holyoke. There were two scholarship girls, Maureen McAndrews and Nora Cribbs; both of them went to Barnard, where they could live at home and not have to pay for a dorm. Cornelia Travis, the class valedictorian, had gone to Radcliffe. No one else had opted for Vassar, so Anne didn't have to face anyone she knew from Nightingale here. She was glad about that.

And she didn't spend time in the old neighborhood. The apartment on East Eighty-Third Street that she had shared with her father was gone now; she spent summers and holidays with Aunt Betty's family in Skaneateles or with Barney and his family. But even if she'd wanted to see Elizabeth, the facade she had carefully constructed here at Vassar made it impossible. She could just imagine the reaction if her new friends found out that she had deceived them about who she was. Virginia and the rest of them would turn on her, of course they would. She could imagine the chatter, the rumors . . . *Anne Bishop? Oh, she's the girl who tried to hide the fact that she was Jewish. And she thought she'd actually get away with it. Can you believe it? It's just like them, though. Pushy. Deceitful. Dishonest through and through.*

Panic swelled. Anne grabbed her coat and left her room. But she wasn't heading to her nine o'clock philosophy class; she was going to skip it. The truth was, she didn't like the class at all. The readings confused or bored her; everything they talked about seemed so abstract. Not like art history, where you communed directly with a painting or a statue and tried to tease out its meanings. Still, she was a person who never missed a class unless she was sick. Well, today she *did* feel sick, just not physically, but in some bone-deep way. Her past was like an octopus, its strong tentacles extending outward to grab and crush her present. And maybe her future too. The thought propelled her out the door, down the stairs, and away from the dorm.

It was only when she passed through Main Gate and followed Main Street in the direction of the train station that the panic subsided. The day was cold, and at first she walked quickly, trying to generate some warmth. She'd only ever taken this route in a taxi, so this was the first time she'd had the opportunity to absorb the gritty texture of the city, to notice what it was really like. Despite the chill, she found herself slowing down. Navigating the cracked sidewalks and sidestepping the liberally strewn litter, she became aware of how the street rose and dipped; sometimes a bit of the Hudson River was briefly visible, a winding thread that seemed to give her journey both a shape and a direction. The sight of it helped calm the awful, frantic feeling inside, the knowledge that she was an impostor, and she began to look more closely in the windows of the stores that she was passing. Unlike those on Raymond, which catered to students, the shops here had a sad look, evidence of lives far less privileged than her own. But something about them spoke to her, and she stopped to peer at the jumble of things—a dented tricycle, a three-bladed desk fan, ice skates, a basket of what appeared to be socks—behind the grime-smeared window of one of them, April's Attic.

"Anne?"

She turned, and to her surprise, there stood Delia Goldhush. She wore her mink—of course—and a dark-red beret that matched her shoes. "So you're a secret shopper too?" she asked.

"What?"

"This store—" Delia gestured to the grimy window. "Are you a regular?"

"No, no." Anne had no intention of actually going *into* such a place. Looking in from the street was enough.

"Too bad," Delia said. "You don't know what you're missing."

"You mean you shop here?" Anne could not align this idea with her image of Delia's Parisian-inflected elegance. Only poor people bought used clothing, and she knew Delia was far from poor.

"Of course I do," Delia said. "You can't imagine what you might find!" She pushed open the door. "Come on."

Anne followed her into the shop and watched as Delia made her way methodically through jammed racks and overstuffed baskets. It was musty in here; Anne didn't like the smell.

She had no desire to touch or examine any of these castoffs and was rather amazed that Delia did both with such intention and purpose. Also no apparent fear. What if there were vermin in these clothes—lice? Bedbugs? Fleas? Anne shuddered.

Not Delia. "Look at this!" From the tightly packed rack, she had extracted a floor-length black velvet coat with velvet-covered buttons. A glimpse of the lavender lining was visible near the collar. Tentatively, Anne touched the front of the coat—so plushy, so soft. "That's silk velvet," Delia said. "And the lining is silk too. I'm going to try it on."

Anne watched as Delia slipped into the coat and then did a small twirl; the velvet rippled around her ankles. "Perfect," Delia said and, taking off the coat, walked up to the counter, where an older woman sat working a crossword puzzle. "Would you hold this for me? I want to keep shopping."

"Of course." The woman set aside her pencil and began to fold the coat. "Glad you found something today, Miss Delia."

So they knew her here. Anne had to admit the coat was exceptional. It also had to be at least fifty years old, something her grandmother might have worn. And yet it didn't look outmoded at all. In fact it seemed very chic, much more so than something that came from one of the nicer shops on Raymond Avenue, or even one of her beloved New York City department stores.

Meanwhile, Delia had continued her hunt. She held up a black crepe de chine dress with a dropped waist and bodice adorned with jet bugle beads. This too was from a bygone era; Anne remembered seeing a photograph of her mother wearing a similar style.

"Such fine workmanship." Delia touched the constellation of glittering beads. There was no fitting room, but she was not deterred; she slipped the dress right over what she was wearing.

"What if it doesn't fit right when you're not wearing anything under it?"

"That's what seamstresses are for." Delia took off the dress and brought it to the counter, where she placed it beside the coat.

Anne turned to a box of scarves, drawn by their colors. She still didn't think she would want a dress or blouse that had belonged to someone else, but she would consider a scarf—it seemed less intimate somehow. She extracted a silk square from the tangle; a brownish stain—blood?—bordered an edge, and she hastily put it back. Then her eye was caught by a bit of something black, and when she pulled it out, she was rewarded with a lavish pattern of red poppies interspersed with green leaves and slender green stems that wound their way through the blossoms.

"You should get that."

Anne turned to see Delia right behind her.

"I don't know . . ."

"You'll wear it with a black cashmere sweater and skirt. It'll be smashing."

"But it was someone else's. . . . You don't mind wearing clothes that belonged to another woman?"

"Not at all. In fact, I like that they were worn by someone else."

"You do?"

"I like to imagine their lives before they ended up here." She gestured to the racks and bins. "I feel that I'm rescuing them."

"Rescuing clothes?"

"I'm giving them new life."

Anne didn't know what to make of this. Delia was the most unusual—and original—girl she'd ever met. She realized she was still holding the scarf.

"Let me buy it for you," Delia said. "And if you decide you really can't wear it, give it to me."

"Thank you." Anne was astonished. Why was Delia being so nice to her? All the bad things she'd said about her started echoing loudly in her head; Delia didn't hear them, but Anne did, and her complicity made her feel awful. She forced herself to focus on the scarf. Of course Delia would wear it. Wear it and look, as she said, *smashing*. They left the shop, and now Anne was intrigued enough to follow Delia to another, and yet another such place; there were so many. Each time, she was struck by how Delia seemed to move right past the dross to find a treasure: a single crystal candlestick for her dorm room desk, a real leopard collar that she planned to stitch onto a sweater, white net gloves still in their satin-shirred box. And afterward it seemed only natural to go with her into a diner where they sat at the counter and ordered cream of tomato soup and grilled cheese sandwiches.

As they waited for their food to arrive, Delia handed the scarf to Anne. "I hope you wear it."

"I will. Or at least I think I will." Anne found the big, splashy flowers a bit daring, but she yearned, oh how she yearned, to be the sort of girl who could carry off a pattern like that.

"Let me show you how to tie it." Delia reached over to loop the scarf around Anne's neck.

Anne couldn't see herself, but the colors seemed to warm her face. "You really know how to shop in these places."

"My mother shopped in flea markets in Paris and near Vence too. She was so good at finding things. My father said it was because she was an artist."

"An artist?"

"A sculptor. Her name was Sophie Rossner. She used her maiden name professionally."

A mother who lived in Paris. And who was a sculptor. To Anne, this seemed remarkable. "What are her sculptures like? Could I see one? And is she still living in Paris?"

"She was killed during the war."

"Oh, I'm sorry." Anne was mortified she'd asked.

"I wasn't there when it happened, and that made it even worse. One of her friends wrote to tell me about it. Even though I've imagined it hundreds of times, I'll never really know." Delia's eyes shone brightly.

"That must have been terrible." Suddenly it felt like the place had gone silent, and everyone could hear their conversation.

"It was."

Their food came, and Anne was quiet as she picked up her sandwich and began to eat. Then she said, "I never knew my mother, so I've never missed her. She died when I was a baby. But my father died when I was in high school. I still miss him so much." She hadn't spoken of this to anyone at Vassar yet; the loss still existed in a tightly locked place inside her.

"How?" Delia asked.

"Excuse me?"

"How did your father die? Suddenly? Or had he been sick?"

Anne wouldn't have dared to ask such a thing. But she admired Delia for having done so, and she found that she wanted to talk about it. "Heart attack," she said. "Quite sudden."

"And you were close?"

"Very." It was only a single word, and yet Anne's eyes brimmed.

"That must have been nice . . . being close to your father." Delia sounded wistful.

"It was." Anne blinked the tears away. "You and your father . . . aren't close?" She was taking a risk, but she sensed that being friends with Delia would allow for such risks.

"No . . . not exactly. I love him, but it's hard to get his attention."

"What about your mother? You must have been close to her—the trips to the flea markets and all?"

"It was hard to get her attention too."

Anne found this sad; Delia seemed sad as she said it. Then Delia added, "So you know."

"Know what?"

"How when someone you love dies like that, you can't believe it's real—you keep thinking it's a bad dream."

"Yes," Anne said. "I do know." After a moment she asked, "Does that change after a while?"

"No. It doesn't."

Something about Delia's quiet certainty was reassuring, even comforting. She seemed like a girl who was not afraid to face the most difficult truths, and Anne could see how facing them would make them easier to bear.

They started eating again. Anne's sandwich and soup had cooled, but she finished both quickly. She had not realized how hungry she was; it was no wonder, she hadn't eaten anything all day.

Fortified by the meal, Anne was willing—no, ready—to be more actively engaged when they went into the next store, and after pawing through a big basket of lingerie, she showed Delia what she had found: a white cotton nightgown, collar, cuffs, and hem dense with lace.

"Oh, that's been done by hand!" Delia fingered the lace. "My mother loved those old white nightgowns. Bloomers and petticoats too. She had a whole drawerful."

"Do you have any of them?" Anne asked.

"No," said Delia. "Though I wish I did. But we were in such a rush when we had to leave Paris. Things got left behind. Most of my mother's sculpture is still there . . . we couldn't possibly take it with us. We were lucky to get out at all."

So now they were back to the war. Anne thought they had moved past it, but evidently they hadn't. And of course, this too had to do with their both being Jews, even if Delia didn't realize that she and

Anne shared that. Though Anne was aware of what had happened to Jews during the war, she hadn't actually talked to anyone who had lived through it.

"It was frightening," Delia said. "And confusing. Before the occupation my parents had lots of friends, we got along with our neighbors. My father ran a successful gallery, my mother's work was well-known. Well-regarded. People liked them. They liked *us*. And then all of a sudden, they didn't."

Anne wished she could say, *I know just how that must have felt—to be pushed out not because of anything you'd done, but just because of who you are*, but that might lead to a revelation she wasn't ready to make. Instead she said, "Please take this." She handed the nightgown to Delia. "And you have to let me buy it for you." Delia looked as if she might protest, but in the end she accepted the gift.

On the way home, Anne had trouble paying attention to what Delia was saying, not because she wasn't interested but because she kept thinking about what Delia had told her about leaving Paris. Anne had pouted over not being allowed to go to the Colony Club; Delia and her family had faced deportation, imprisonment, or death. Yet Delia did nothing to disguise her Jewish background, and Anne had yet to acknowledge her own.

Luckily, Delia didn't seem to be bothered by Anne's silence. By the time they reached the campus, it was late; tea would be over. They said goodbye, and Delia went upstairs while Anne went straight to the dining room, where she found herself in line behind Peggy.

"Where have you been all day?" Peggy asked. "I didn't see you at tea."

"I didn't go." Anne did not offer any other details, and since the line was moving quickly, she was able to take her plate and busy herself with arranging it on her tray. Then she followed Peggy to a table where their group was already gathered.

"Nice scarf!" Carol said.

"Thank you," Anne said as she sat down.

"Wherever did you find it? You didn't get it in Poughkeepsie, did you?"

"The pattern is unusual." Now Virginia had noticed. "And the colors too—they're really bright. Really bold." She seemed to be trying to decide whether this was a good thing or not. "Carol's right about it not looking like anything you'd find in this dump of a town. Is it from a store in the city? Lord & Taylor?"

"It was a gift." Anne looked down at her baked chicken and rice. When she looked up again, Virginia had lost interest in the scarf and was saying something to Tabitha. Delia had come into the dining room. She sat alone, as usual, but she glanced in Anne's direction and held her gaze for a moment. Did she want Anne to come over and join her? It seemed like the answer was yes, she did. Anne had thought Delia was unaffected by the way she was excluded, but now she wasn't so sure. And she did want to go and sit with her; their conversation earlier that day had been both a balm and a tonic. But Anne was already sitting down with her little group of friends, even if they were starting to grate on her; it would be so awkward to get up at this point. And as for inviting Delia to join them, well, that wouldn't work at all. Anne was just going to have to let the moment pass, even though she could feel the prickle of guilt.

She touched the scarf, a barrier against Virginia's little abrasions. But when the meal was over and she went back up to her room, she saw Elizabeth's letter—incriminating and possibly dangerous—right where she'd left it. No scarf could protect her against *that*. Anne held the letter in her hands one more time before crumpling it into a wad and depositing it in her wastebasket. That letter was not going to come back to haunt her—she refused to let it. And if that meant keeping her distance from Delia, that's what she would have to do.

SIX

DELIA

Fall 1946

Delia slipped into the back of the classroom, slightly out of breath. She'd been hurrying to class and was now overheated in her mink coat; she peeled it off and draped it over the back of her chair.

"Showoff," hissed a voice behind her.

Delia didn't have to turn to recognize Virginia Worthington, the seeming ringleader of that odious bunch of girls, who never passed up an opportunity to insult her. Ignoring the comment on her coat—she was already late and wanted to attract no more attention to herself—Delia settled herself in her seat and opened her notebook.

"Ah, Miss Goldhush, so good of you to join us." Mr. McQuaid raised his head to look at her, but along with the gentle tone of sarcasm, there was a hint of something else. Delia smiled. She loved this course, and today was the first and only time she'd been late; she'd been up until 3:00 a.m. finishing her paper on *Othello* and then slept right through her alarm. It had been worth it, though; she thought it was one of her very best papers, and she hoped Mr. McQuaid would think so too.

His class was her favorite since she'd arrived at Vassar. It wasn't only the intellectual aspects of the material that engaged her; it was Ian McQuaid himself—his melodic Irish brogue, his fair hair and pale-gold lashes, the way his light eyes changed from gray to green and back again. He couldn't have been more than thirty. Delia had learned all she could about him, that he'd come from Dublin and read English at Cambridge. His first name was Ian—a Scottish mother perhaps?—and he was married, with twin daughters, a fact she knew because his wife had posted a notice in the English department office seeking a babysitter. Delia let herself entertain the idea of applying for the job. She'd get to see where he lived, and chat with him outside of class. But she'd also have to meet his wife and his children, and she didn't like the idea. No, she wanted him to herself—a ridiculous idea, but still, there it was. She was smitten, and even though she was clear-eyed enough to understand the hopelessness of her feelings, they nevertheless bubbled up and over whenever she thought of him.

Today they were discussing *Romeo and Juliet*, a play Delia had read in high school and privately disdained: the stupidity of the protagonists' deaths, the colossal *waste* of it. And it was all so melodramatic. Delia had been forced to flee from her home, endured the murder of her mother, and reinvented herself in a new country. Your parents disapproving of your boyfriend? Hardly a reason to kill yourself.

But Mr. McQuaid said that it was his favorite of the tragedies, of all Shakespeare's plays in fact. "Did anyone realize that if lifted out of the play, the first fourteen lines that Romeo and Juliet speak to each other form a sonnet?" he asked the class. Delia had not considered the idea at all, but found herself intrigued. She did admire Shakespeare's sonnets; who knew that he'd tucked one into this play?

"Now, if we examine these lines in terms of their power as dialogue, look what he's able to accomplish here—I'm going to read it aloud to show you, but I need a partner." He looked up, and his eyes met Delia's. "Miss Goldhush, would you please read Juliet's lines?" Thrilled that he had chosen her, Delia didn't trust herself to look at him, so she cast her eyes down and simply nodded.

"Romeo's come to this party in search of another girl, Rosaline," said Mr. McQuaid. "He's in love with her, or so he thinks. But when he sees Juliet, everything changes. He's drawn to her—she has a magnetic pull for him. He *has* to meet her. So he walks right over, takes her hand, and this is what he says: 'If I profane with my unworthiest hand / This holy shrine, the gentle sin is this / My lips, two blushing pilgrims, ready stand / To smooth that rough touch with a tender kiss.'" He looked at Delia, who started reading Juliet's reply: "'Good pilgrim, you do wrong your hand too much / Which mannerly devotion shows in this: / For saints have hands that pilgrims' hands do touch, / And palm to palm is holy palmers' kiss.'"

Mr. McQuaid, warming to his subject, stood up. "Look at what Shakespeare's done in just two lines. He's established character—Romeo is more impulsive, Juliet more controlled and cautious; he's given us a clever bit of wordplay—the way hands touch is likened to the way lips touch—which he'll carry through until the end of the exchange." Delia had never thought of it this way, but she found herself drawn into Mr. McQuaid's enthusiasm, and as she spoke Juliet's lines, the words newly meaningful and resonant, she was drawn in.

"'Have not saints lips, and holy palmers too?'" read Mr. McQuaid.

"'Ay, pilgrim, lips that they must use in pray'r.'" Delia, as Juliet, was once again the voice of caution, of restraint.

"'O then, dear saint, let lips do what hands do / They pray—grant thou, lest faith turn to despair.'"

"'Saints do not move, though grant for prayers' sake.'"

"'Then move not while my prayer's effect I take.'" Mr. McQuaid was looking, even staring, straight at Delia. "And what does he do? He kisses her! All that in fourteen lines, fourteen lines that establish character, that move the play along—he's just met her and now he's kissed her!—and that are interesting and engaging all on their own. And the very next time these two meet, it's on the balcony, where they declare their love and make plans to marry. Shakespeare doesn't waste any time here. He gets right to it."

Delia felt the crackle and spark of excitement that she always felt in this class. How had she not appreciated all this before? It was because of him, he was the one who unlocked this treasure and shared it with all of them, but maybe, just maybe, he was particularly interested in sharing it with her, sensing a responsive spirit. A quiet joy spread through her, an awakening. The way he had looked at her when he described the kiss—Delia felt as if she, and not just Juliet, had been kissed. She was confused, both titillated and embarrassed at the same time; she could feel the heat in her cheeks, and the nervous fluttering of her stomach.

When the class ended, Mr. McQuaid collected all the papers from the students before they left, but Delia stayed behind, pretending to look for her own paper—she knew full well where it was; she'd put it carefully in the front flap of her notebook—to buy a little time. When she finally extracted it, she and Professor McQuaid were alone in the classroom.

"Thank you for reading with me, Miss Goldhush. Shakespeare's words are meant to be read aloud—they're plays after all. Have you ever seen a performance of *Romeo and Juliet*?"

Delia shook her head.

"Well, I hope you will. I have a feeling you'll appreciate it." He smiled and took the paper from her.

I hope he likes it, she thought as she was leaving. I hope he thinks it's the best thing from a student that he's ever read.

The following week, Mr. McQuaid handed back all the papers. Delia ignored the comments in the margins and turned to the last page, where a bold red A+ filled the space. *Incisive, engaging and impressive* were the words beneath it. Delia felt a flush of pride—and of happiness—come over her. But there was no surprise. She'd known all along that the paper was good; it had seemed to write itself, as if the thoughts and words were being spoken to her, and she was transcribing rather than creating them. Typing quickly if erratically, her fingers had flown along the keys of the Corona Comet, articulating how Shakespeare dismantled the idea of evil as a supernatural force, describing it instead as something completely and utterly human. In act 5, scene 2, Othello has just learned how Iago has tricked him into murdering Desdemona. His first horrified thought is that Iago is a devil, only then he says, "I look down towards his feet; but that's a fable." The line refers to hooves, a mark of the devil—yet Othello quickly realizes that no, that's not it at all. Iago isn't a monster, isn't a devil. He's just a man—flawed, consumed by jealousy—who is hell-bent on Othello's undoing, and this truth is far more devastating than anything Othello could have conjured. On her desk sat the crystal candlestick she'd bought on Main Street, and a tall white taper flickered as she worked. She was well aware that the flame was purely an affectation; there was ample light from both a lamp and an overhead fixture. But she liked the atmosphere it conjured; Shakespeare would have written by candlelight.

"So he gave you an A-plus."

Delia turned to see Virginia looking down at the essay, and she quickly put her hand over the grade to hide it. Virginia's hair was held back from her face by a punishingly tight black headband, and her thick brows made her eyes look small and mean. "Well, it's no surprise—the way you spend every class simpering at him. I wonder why he doesn't see right through it."

"And I wonder why you even bother coming to class," said Delia. "You haven't made a single original comment or observation all semester." She was gratified by the sight of Virginia's mouth falling open into a small O of astonishment and savored the feeling even as she put the *Othello* essay away after Virginia had stalked off. She didn't realize the room had emptied out until she saw Mr. McQuaid was standing in front of her.

"Miss Goldhush, may I have a word with you?"

"Of course." It didn't matter what it was about; she wanted to hear anything he had to say.

"Our babysitter called to say she can't make it tonight—she has strep throat. So if there's any way, any chance at all, you could step in, I'd be very grateful."

Babysit for his children? That was what she most decidedly did not want to do.

"It's our anniversary, and Maggie's been looking forward to this evening. We have tickets to a concert."

Now this put the request in a different light. *He* needed something from *her*. How could she say no? But even as she was jotting down his address on a page in her notebook, she had the distinct sense she was doing something wrong.

Several hours later she arrived at the house. It was rather ordinary looking, brown-shingled and three stories; the paint was peeling on the front door and the window trim. But the lawn was neatly raked, and several pumpkins and ears of multicolored corn had been arranged on the steps, giving it a welcoming air.

Mrs. McQuaid opened the door. "Thank you for coming on such short notice," she said. She was a delicate, pretty brunette with pale skin. "Ian's been singing your praises for weeks, so I'm glad we're getting a chance to meet. You're his favorite student, you know." Mr. McQuaid—Ian!—had been telling his wife about her? What else had he said? Delia wished she could have heard every word, every syllable.

Mrs. McQuaid brought her inside, introduced her to the twins, Violet and Dorothy, angelic-looking babies with wide blue eyes and hair in a deep, glowing shade of red—their father's hair must have been that color when he was young. Mrs. McQuaid gave her a list of instructions, as well as the phone numbers of the pediatrician and pharmacist.

"They'll be fine," Delia assured her. "You go and have a good time. And happy anniversary."

By 7:30, the twins were sleeping peacefully. Delia went downstairs, where she sat on the sofa and unpacked her textbooks, legal pads, and pens. But she was too restless to study, and too restless to do anything really, other than prowl around this house, looking for . . . well, exactly what was she looking for? The sofa on which she sat was covered in a faded floral fabric; across from it were a pair of lumpy armchairs, and behind them, a playpen. Anchoring the whole sorry group was a marble-topped coffee table, a handsome piece of furniture that only made the others look that much more woebegone. The kitchen was somewhat cheerier—red-and-white gingham curtains and matching seat cushions, a cloth covering the round table in a bright pattern of apples, pears, and cherries, two high chairs in the corner. There was a radio on the windowsill that she switched on and then off again.

What she really wanted to see were the rooms above, where the more private parts of Professor McQuaid's life unfolded. She went up on the pretext of checking on the babies; a quick peek in their room revealed that they were both still asleep, Violet's tiny hands splayed like starfish, Dorothy curled up on her side. Stepping into the hallway, Delia peered into the other open doors. One led to the bathroom, another to what appeared to be a study, and a third to the bedroom that Mr. McQuaid shared with his wife.

Hesitating in front of the bedroom, she pivoted and instead went into the study. It was a small but inviting room, books lined up on the shelves and piled on the floor too, with a graceful Queen Anne desk on which sat a typewriter and yet another pile of books. Several tarnished silver vessels held pens and pencils; upon closer inspection,

Delia saw that they were engraved trophies—for rugby, for rowing, for tennis, and even for golf. So he was an athlete as well as a scholar. In one corner was a leather armchair worn to a glorious brown patina, and next to it was a standing lamp. Delia sat down in the chair and tried to imagine the life that he led here, the things he read and wrote about.

She turned to look at the small painting hanging near the chair. It was of a tiger, and the image was accompanied by lines of what appeared to be verse. Closer inspection revealed it to be William Blake's poem "The Tyger," rendered in an elegant black script. She looked again at the image, painted in gouache, and quite expertly at that. The feline lurked against a dense backdrop of deep greens and blues, his body, orange-gold with black stripes, glowing against the dark tones. The paint was thickly applied, the brushstrokes swirling yet controlled, a metaphor for the animal's power and grace, latent for the moment but ready to lunge forth at any second. Delia knew that Blake had illustrated his own verse with watercolor images, but she'd seen them reproduced, and they did not resemble this gouache. Then she saw the letters IMM in the right corner. The artist must have been Ian Michael—she'd found a reference to his middle name—McQuaid.

She had a crush on him. A crush and nothing more. Mr. McQuaid was more than a decade older than she was, married, with a family. She might be his favorite student, but she was still a student. Unfinished. Unformed. Abruptly she stood and, though she knew it was a transgression, walked into the bedroom. There was a tall bureau on one side of the room and a lower, wider one on the other. A closet door, no, two. A rocking chair and a pair of nightstands, also marble-topped, like the table in the living room. And dominating the room: an ornate and highly polished brass bed topped with a white coverlet. This is where he slept, dreamed, and presumably made love to his wife. To Maggie. The thought of this made Delia burn with jealousy. She stretched out on top of the coverlet. What she was doing was wrong, but she remained where she was. She didn't imagine herself in this bed with him, but she did, with some shame, imagine the two of them entwined. Her experience was limited—she'd dated a bit in high school but had been put off by the inept fumbling of boys her age. Mr. McQuaid was a grown man. He would know what to do, how to guide her. Though Delia felt she was more worldly than many of the girls here at Vassar, she knew that some of her sophistication was only an act. With Professor McQuaid, she would be able to stop pretending and leave her girlhood behind.

Delia got up, smoothed the coverlet, and went downstairs, where she washed the little bowls and spoons she'd used to give the twins their dinner, wiped down the high chairs, and scoured the sink. Then she parked herself on the sofa, opened her biology textbook, and forced herself to sit still and keep reading. When the McQuaids arrived home, they found her in a pool of lamplight, the legal pad covered in her notes.

"Were they good? Did Violet fuss much when you put her to bed? I should have told you she could be fussy," said Mrs. McQuaid. She started unbuttoning her coat, and Mr. McQuaid was immediately beside her, helping to take it off and then hanging it in the coat closet. Delia's coat was in that same closet, and when he brought it to her, he helped her into it. How gallant he was. Mrs. McQuaid was rummaging in her purse. "Ian, do you have money for Delia? Somehow, I've left myself with only coins." She smiled at Delia warmly. "We can't thank you enough."

"Yes, I have it right here." He took out his wallet, handing Delia several bills; she realized she hadn't even discussed what he would pay her. "I think that should take care of it." He'd given her five dollars, which seemed quite generous. Delia didn't want to take so much, but she put the money away and thanked him.

"You're welcome. Now, let's get you safely home."

"I can walk," Delia said, but only because she felt it was the right thing to say. Inside, she was jubilant—she'd get to be alone with him, even if only for a little while.

"Nonsense," said Professor McQuaid.

"Ian's right, Delia. It's too late for you to be wandering about on your own."

"I'll be back in a flash," Mr. McQuaid said to his wife as he ushered Delia out the door and into the car.

"How was the concert?" She was trying to cover her excitement—and awkwardness—with small talk.

"Superb," he said. "It meant the world to Maggie. She adores the twins—we both do—but taking care of two babies all the time is a lot, even for the most adoring of mothers."

"I'm sure it is."

"You didn't have any trouble tonight, did you?"

"None at all." This wasn't true. Dinner was messy—most of the creamed spinach and pureed chicken ended up on the floor—and changing the diapers was even messier. Also Violet *had* resisted going to sleep, which meant Delia had to walk her back and forth, back and forth, before she settled her down for the night.

"Thank you so much, Delia. You saved the day. Or rather the evening."

Delia. He'd called her Delia, and not Miss Goldhush, for the first time. Did that mean something? They were almost at Main Gate; she'd be getting out in a moment, saying goodbye to him before she'd had a chance to offer something, anything, clever or witty, something he would remember. Her heart was beating very hard when she turned her head to look at his profile. She had the mad thought that he would kiss her. She *wanted* him to kiss her. But he did nothing of the kind and kept his eyes on the dark road ahead.

When they had passed through Main Gate, he slowed the car and pulled up to her dorm.

She stepped out into the chilly night and watched as he drove away.

Then she went upstairs and got into bed. What if he had kissed her? Then what? She lay awake for a long time, embellishing and embroidering such a scenario.

By the time the Shakespeare class met again, Delia had gotten herself under control. Mr. McQuaid—*not* Ian—was not going to kiss her, *ever.* She needed to put a stop to these fantasies. But when the class had ended and the students were filing out, he once again asked her to stay. She was aware that Virginia Worthington had heard this as well, and could feel the other girl's animosity, rising like steam around her.

When everyone had left, and Delia and the professor were alone, he said, "Mrs. McQuaid and I were wondering if you'd like a regular job watching the girls. Our babysitter's had some family emergency, and she's had to go back to Albany."

Delia stared down at the clutch of books in her arms. She knew she should say no.

"My wife is very much hoping you'll say yes," he said. And then, after a few seconds, "So am I."

Delia looked at him then; there was indeed something hopeful—bashful even—in his expression, and she found herself saying yes, she'd love to watch the babies. From then on, at least once and sometimes twice a week, she walked over to the McQuaids' house on Church Street. The McQuaids would then go out—to a faculty party, a movie, dinner in Rhinebeck or Garrison—while Delia minded the twins. She soon got to know them better and could discern their differences—Dot was the more outgoing, boisterous baby, while Vi was more reserved. Delia found herself falling in love with both of them, just as she was falling in love with their father. Because it *was* love, this feeling she had for him.

Then there was an unusually mild night for the beginning of November. Delia sat in the passenger seat of Mr. McQuaid's car and rolled down the window so she could see the wisp of the moon up above. It wasn't that she cared so much about the moon, but the exquisite tension of these drives back to the dorm—he continued to insist on driving her, and she'd stopped protesting—had been wound and tightened to such a degree that she felt she couldn't stand it. She needed something, anything, as a distraction.

"It's a lovely evening," he said. "It's almost balmy."

He had stopped the car right before passing through Main Gate. Why? Could it be that he was feeling what she was feeling? Delia turned to look at him but said nothing. The space between them—mere inches, a foot at most—felt electrified. To her own shock, she leaned across the seat and pressed her lips to his. He was clearly taken aback. But his hesitation was no match for her desire. Inhaling something redolent of pine—his bath soap? His shampoo?—she traced the unfamiliar contours of his lips with her tongue and then, all at once, he was responding to her kiss, returning it with greater ardor than she could ever have imagined. When they moved apart, Delia was breathing heavily. She waited for him to say something, but he didn't, so she just mumbled a hasty good night and jumped out of the car. She ran up the stairs and threw herself onto her bed, grateful that she had no roommate and could replay what had just happened in the privacy of her own quivering soul.

The next time she babysat for the twins, she could barely contain her excitement or her unease—what would happen when he drove her home? Would he bring up the last time they'd been together? Would he scold her, tell her she'd done a terrible thing and that it could never be repeated? Initiate the contact? Maybe he wouldn't even offer her the lift home at all. Or maybe he would say nothing, pretending it hadn't happened. To Delia, that would be the worst of all.

But no. When he and Mrs. McQuaid got home, he jingled the car keys merrily in one hand and said, as casually as could be, "Come on, Miss Goldhush. Time to get you back to campus." Delia said good night to Mrs. McQuaid and followed him out into the dark. They were both quiet on the drive. Then he took a slight detour and, instead of driving through Main Gate, turned a corner and parked on a side street, away from the streetlight. There he took her in his arms and kissed her passionately, kissed her until she felt giddy. Then it was over, and she once again got out of the car without any mention of what had just taken place. She ran up the stairs to her room and bolted the door behind her. He was a married man! A married man with a beautiful wife and two darling babies. And he was her professor. But this was what she'd been wanting, yearning for, practically since the first day she'd walked into his class. How astonishing, how *wonderful* that he wanted it too.

When the next time came, she couldn't wait to be alone with him in the car, and for the next few weeks, this became their pattern. They rarely spoke, or if they did, it was about something inconsequential, not about what they were doing to and with each other. That was fine. She didn't need to talk to him then. She had spent hours listening to him talk in class; she was well aware of—and admired—the clarity of his thinking, of his eloquence. What happened between them when he drove her back to campus was a different form of communication, one that needed no words. They always began by kissing, but soon things progressed to more intimate caresses. He slipped his hands first inside her sweater, then her brassiere, and finally her underpants, stroking her with such sureness, such delicacy, that she was surprised by the shuddering wave of pleasure that washed over her. She was still shuddering when he guided her hand inside his trousers and showed her what to do. She grew greedy for his touch, demanding of it; the more it happened, the more she craved it. Delia felt herself split in two—there was the wordless girl in the parked car and then there was the composed, self-possessed girl in her classes.

She began to find reasons to walk past Avery, where the English department was located, in the hope that she might run into him. She didn't know what she'd say if she did, but that didn't matter. And early one evening, when the sky had already darkened, she walked past the building and saw just a single light in a window on the second floor. Ian's office was on the second floor; she'd been there to see him for meetings a couple of times early in the semester. She was pretty sure the light was coming from his office. And if that was true, it would mean he was inside, and most likely alone.

The building was unlocked, and she was able to slip inside and up the stairs. On the second floor the hallway was dark, but at the far end she saw the light, the same light she'd seen from below, and she began to walk—slowly, quietly—toward it. All the doors she passed were closed. All but one. When she reached it, she stopped, her heart galloping. He looked up. "Delia." The word was a caress. He had never called her that in this building; it was always Miss Goldhush. Now what? She had no reason to be here, no reason other than that she wanted to see him, and to have him see her.

"Won't you come in?" he asked, as if they were mere acquaintances, as if he hadn't touched her everywhere. When she didn't move, he crossed the room, pulled her inside, and closed the door. Locked it. The click startled her for a second, and then he was kissing her, pulling at her clothes, only this time they weren't in a car, but in his office, where a sofa covered in some scratchy fabric of an indeterminate color beckoned. Above it was a window whose shade was halfway down. He stopped for a moment to pull it down completely. Then he led her to the sofa, still kissing, still loosening her clothes and his. When they had undressed, Delia found that she was trembling; as much as she wanted this to happen, she was frightened. And she knew it would hurt. Her trembling intensified.

"I've never known a girl like you." He brushed the hair from her face. "A girl who kissed me first. A girl who came here looking for me . . . for this." He gestured to their naked bodies. "You're a marvel, Delia," he breathed into her ear.

Was she? He seemed to think so. Her fear was subsiding, and

desire took its place. She tilted her face up and kissed him, and then he lay back against the sofa. "Here," he said. "Let me show you how." Gently he guided her so that she was straddling him. Then he pulled her down so that her body lowered gently onto his. Slowly he began thrusting his hips as his hands stayed at her waist, anchoring her. She felt something sharp and tearing, but though it hurt, the pain was muted by the soft pressure of his lips on her nipples, his fingers touching her, arousing her, the tension building and building until it exploded like a shower of petals raining down. He kept thrusting in a rhythmic, rocking motion; his body arched slightly, and he cried out.

Delia was quiet. She had never felt so close to anyone, and she leaned over to kiss him. They remained like that for a moment until her legs began to ache and she gingerly pulled herself off of him. Inside her thigh was a small smear of blood; she put her fingers to it with a kind of wonder but also fear. This was more than kissing and caressing; she'd just crossed a line, and she understood that, having done it, she'd never be able to cross back.

She started gathering her clothes in kind of a trance. Here was her brassiere; over there her slip; her skirt had found its way to the floor. He'd gotten up and was getting dressed. When he'd finished, she moved closer, so she was standing before him, waiting for something—a sign that what had just happened between them was not debased and ugly but beautiful and even sacred. She'd come here because she couldn't help herself. That had to make it all right. It *had* to. Now if only he would reassure her—

"Darling" was all he said, but it was everything she needed to hear. He took her in his arms and held her for several minutes. Finally, he moved out of the embrace. "Will you be all right getting back to your dorm?" he asked.

"I'll be perfectly fine," she said.

"Let me at least walk you downstairs," he said. They went quietly and stood in the doorway for a moment, shivering. Was it because she was cold, even in her mink, or because of the exhilaration of what had just happened upstairs? Before she left, Ian pressed the back of his hand to her cheek, a small but infinitely tender gesture. She smiled all the way back to her room. And for the rest of the night, and most of the next day, she felt euphoric. She was still aware of the transgression against his wife and family. But that wasn't her concern; if he felt the need to stray, she told herself, it meant something was amiss in that marriage, and she wasn't responsible for that.

The next time she babysat, Delia could barely stand the hours she had to wait until the McQuaids returned. The time passed slowly, even painfully, but finally—finally!—they were at the door, unlocking it, coming into the room. Mrs. McQuaid chatted with her while Ian fetched her coat and scarf from the closet.

"Good night, Delia," she said. "We'll see you again next week. But the evening may need to change. Is that all right?"

"Yes, that's fine. What night did you need me to come instead?"

"Well, that's just it—I'm not entirely sure." Mrs. McQuaid launched into a long—and tedious—explanation while Delia composed her expression into one of attentive interest. All the while she was thinking about what would happen when she and Ian were alone again. Finally Mrs. McQuaid finished, and Delia was able to leave.

She walked quickly to the car, and as soon as she and Ian were both inside, she pulled him close and started kissing him, a small frenzy of pent-up longing.

At first he seemed surprised but quickly responded with an intensity that matched hers. "You saucy girl." He started nipping at her throat, running his fingers through her hair. But all at once he stopped.

"What's wrong?"

He didn't answer but turned away, looking past her, through the car's side window. She followed his gaze. There was Mrs. McQuaid, clutching the ivory cashmere scarf Delia had, in her haste, left behind.

The combination of shock, hurt, and outrage on her face was too painful to look at; Delia had to avert her eyes. And she had to get away from here, but how? Squeeze past Ian in the driver's seat? Or exit the car on her side where his wife was standing? Mrs. McQuaid yanked open the door, ending the need for a choice.

"Get out," she hissed. "Now."

"Maggie, please, I—" Ian started to say.

"Not in front of *her*." Mrs. McQuaid spoke to her husband, but she was staring at Delia. "I told you to go! What are you waiting for?"

Delia climbed out of the car, grabbed the scarf, and fled. Somewhere on the way she must have dropped it, because when she got to the dorm, it was nowhere to be found. She wasn't about to go back and look for it. Instead she kicked off her shoes, let her coat slide to the floor, and slipped into bed, where she kept replaying the last thirty minutes in her mind. It was only after the third or fourth time that she realized Ian had not said one single word to her; it was as if she hadn't even been there. Why was she surprised? His wife came first, she now realized, and even if she hadn't discovered them, she would always come first. Delia could now see that she had thrown herself into a relationship both furtive and complicated. This had mattered less during their heated, wordless encounters, encounters that seemed to exist in their own realm, without consequence or repercussion. But she'd slept with him; she'd surrendered her virginity to him. She thought of the blood on her thigh, and the solitary walk and night that followed. Where had she thought this would lead? Now she knew: straight to the reckless kiss in the car, and the pain that contorted Mrs. McQuaid's face into a mask of rage and grief. Even then Delia knew it was an image she would never be able to forget.

SEVEN

ANNE

Winter 1947

Even though Anne arrived at Kenyon Hall just after seven a.m., there was already someone in the pool. It was mid-January, and second semester had just started. Who else would be swimming now? It was silly to be disappointed, though; there were plenty of empty lanes available. But she enjoyed having the pool all to herself. She watched for a moment before getting in. Whoever this was, she was an excellent swimmer—graceful as a seal, arms and legs slicing through the water smoothly with only a minimum of splashing. Anne turned away. Why was she standing here? Better get in the pool before someone else showed up.

The water was cold, but that was all right—she liked the initial shock. It made her feel alert and alive. And once she was immersed, she took no notice of the other swimmer, concentrating only on doing laps. Anne was a competent though hardly exceptional swimmer; it didn't matter. The steady rhythm of her arms and legs and the light filtering down softly from the high windows gave her a sense of release and liberation that was hard to find anywhere else.

After she'd been swimming for about twenty minutes, she stopped at the shallow end, where she could stand for a break. That's when she noticed that the other swimmer had gotten out of the pool. The girl in the college-issued gray maillot and white bathing cap stretched out on the tile was Delia Goldhush. She recognized Anne just as Anne recognized her.

"Seems we keep a similar schedule," Delia said. "First Main Street, now Kenyon."

"I like to swim before it gets crowded," Anne said.

"Same with me."

Delia swung her legs around and slipped back into the pool. "I was just resting for a minute. But I wasn't finished yet. I like to do forty laps before breakfast." She adjusted the cap on her head before taking off.

Forty laps! Anne rarely did more than twenty-five. She resumed her laps as well, but now she was keenly aware of Delia's presence, plowing through the water as if she'd been born to it. Her crawl seemed effortless, and she interspersed it with a powerful breaststroke and a more languorous backstroke. She was still swimming when Anne got out of the pool and headed for the shower.

Standing under the hot, pulsating spray, Anne wondered why she hadn't seen Delia here before, especially given that they both liked morning swims. She had dried off and gotten dressed when Delia appeared in the locker room; though she was patting herself with one of the tiny white towels the gym provided, rivulets of water streamed down her back and legs.

"Swimming makes me so hungry! Do you want to go out and get pancakes? I can be really quick in the shower."

"Pancakes sound good." Anne's first class today was not until eleven, so she had the time. And pancakes also meant that they would be going off campus to eat, so no one would see her with Delia. She was a little ashamed of herself—she really liked Delia. Admired her. But having breakfast with Delia on campus? Not a good idea.

The day was cold but bright; here and there, crests of a recent snowfall glinted in the sun. They walked quickly away from the campus and toward the diner that many of the students liked to frequent. Anne did have the thought that someone from school could see them here, but on a Tuesday morning it was unlikely; most of the girls came here on the weekends. Her breath came in little white puffs, and her hands, even in their mittens, felt icy. She was glad when they reached the diner and sat down in the generously sized booth with its red leatherette covering.

"Good morning, ladies," trilled an older waitress with the kind of marcelled bob that had been popular twenty years ago. Without asking, she placed two mugs of black coffee on the table, along with a metal creamer and a bowl of sugar cubes.

"Menu's up there." She gestured to a chalkboard over the counter. "I'll be back in a jiff."

Anne added cream and sugar to her coffee; she was glad it gave her something to do. Delia, normally talkative and opinionated, had said nothing on the walk to the diner. Maybe she'd decided she didn't really want to be here with Anne. But she was the one who'd suggested it.

The waitress—the maroon embroidered script above the pocket of her pink uniform read "Bunny"—returned. "What'll it be?"

"Pancakes." Delia had finally spoken up. "For both of us."

Bunny nodded and left to place the order.

"I've never seen you at the pool before." Anne knew it was a lame remark, but the silence was a bit unnerving, and she wanted to fill it.

"I guess we missed each other." Delia took a sip of coffee to which she'd added neither sugar nor milk. "I'm usually there a few mornings a week, but this is the first time I've gone since the break. I'm glad I did—I really needed it."

"The exercise lifts you up, doesn't it?"

"Body and soul." Delia put the mug down. It looked as if she might cry.

Anne didn't know what to say to that. Then the pancakes arrived and

Bunny bustled about, setting them up with maple syrup—heated!—and pats of butter on little white plates. Anne concentrated on eating; she had quite an appetite and the pancakes were delicious. Then she looked over to see that Delia had taken only a couple of bites before putting down her fork.

"I thought you were hungry," Anne said.

"I thought I was too. But apparently not." She pushed the plate away.

"Are you all right?" Anne asked, although it was obvious that something was wrong.

"I'm fine."

"Is it something that's happened at school?" Maybe Anne had been wrong about Delia's thick skin; maybe she was bothered by the routine exclusion, and the barbs. Maybe she didn't like being such an outsider. "One of your classes? A test or a paper?"

"Nothing like that. It's something else . . . more personal. A romance that's gone wrong. Ended, actually. We broke up."

"Oh," said Anne. It was hard to imagine that anyone would have broken up with Delia, though. "Did he tell you why?"

"It wasn't exactly his decision."

"It was you? Did you decide you didn't like him anymore?" Anne had stopped eating now; she was entirely focused on the conversation, and the new side of Delia it exposed.

"I *loved* him."

Anne was quiet. She had never been in love, so she didn't know what it would feel like to navigate such a loss. But Delia was confiding in her, and she yearned to understand. And to be of help, or if not help, then comfort. "So then why did you break up with him?"

"He was married. And his wife found out. She *saw* us."

Married. Anne wouldn't have guessed. There were of course girls who did such things, but she'd never known such a girl, and she wouldn't have thought that Delia was one of them. What could she even say to this? But she was spared saying anything. Delia had started to cry, at first just a few tears that she brushed aside with her fingers and then a whole onslaught that caused her to bury her face in her hands.

Anne was as shocked by this as she had been by Delia's initial revelation. Only now she knew just what to do. She got up from her seat and slid in next to Delia. Then she put her arm around her and let her weep.

Bunny appeared, a look of concern on her face. "Everything all right here, ladies?" she asked.

"Everything's fine," Anne said. "I'm taking care of it," an assertion of guardianship that made her feel more adult, more her own person, than she ever had before.

Bunny nodded and left.

"If you want to tell me about it, I want to hear."

Delia raised her tear-wet face. "I knew it was wrong from the start, but I couldn't stop myself. I didn't want to hurt anyone, though. But I did. I hurt his wife—I'll never forget the look on her face. I hurt him. And I hurt myself. It was the worst thing I've ever done, and now I have to live with that."

Anne took Delia by the shoulders and turned her so that they were facing each other. "No," she said firmly. "You shouldn't think that. Even if you did a bad thing, a terrible thing, you're more than that—much more. The worst thing you did doesn't define you."

"It doesn't?" Delia sniffed.

"No. It does not." Anne didn't know where this certainty came from, but she had utter faith in her own words.

Delia seemed calmer after that. Still sitting next to Anne, she reached for her plate and began to eat.

Once again, Bunny was standing in front of the booth. "Those pancakes must be stone cold," she said. "I'll get you a fresh batch."

She looked over at Anne's half-eaten food. "And for you too. On the house." She smiled sympathetically as she took the plates away and was back quickly with new ones.

"Thank you so much." Though Delia's tears had stopped, her voice still quavered. Anne put a hand on her arm. "Let's eat before these get cold too."

They walked back to campus in silence. Before they parted–Anne was going to get her books and head over to her class—Delia took Anne's hands in her own. "Thank you. I'd been repeating the same awful things in my head over and over, I couldn't even consider that they might not be true. It was good to get another perspective."

"I'm glad if I helped."

"You did." Delia leaned forward and pressed her cheek to each of Anne's, that charming French gesture Anne had seen in movies but of which she'd never been on the receiving end. And if that weren't surprising enough, Delia didn't move away after the cheek-press; she enveloped Anne in a brief but powerful hug. "More than you know," she said.

Anne returned the hug. She was facing away from Delia, so Delia couldn't see her wide smile. For the first time, she felt like she might be worthy of a friendship with Delia.

Later that afternoon, when Anne headed to the Rose Parlor for tea, she found that Virginia and the others were not seated in their usual spot, but standing by the wide double doorway.

"You're late," Virginia said.

Had they agreed to meet at an exact time? Anne didn't think so, but she apologized anyway.

"Well, you're here now. Get your tea and some cookies if you want. You can take them to my room. That's where we're all going."

"To your room? Why?"

"There's something we need to talk about. Something highly confidential. I'll explain when we get there." Virginia turned to the rest of them. "Come on." They followed her out of the parlor. Anne watched them go and then hurried to catch up; she decided to skip the tea.

All the girls filed in. Peggy, Carol, and Tabitha found places to sit on the bed while Midge sat on the wooden desk chair. There were no more seats, so Anne took a spot on the floor. Virginia presided over them from an armchair upholstered in pink-and-green satin stripes. "I've got news," she said. "Big news." Then, for maximum effect, she waited.

"Well, what is it?" Midge said. "Aren't you going to tell us?"

"Of course I'm going to tell you," said Virginia, delaying her revelation still longer. She had a genius for orchestrating social interaction, thought Anne, not for the first time. "That's why I asked all of you to come. It's about Delia Goldhush."

Delia. The name started an awful clanging in Anne's head, reminiscent of the way she'd felt when her own real name, Miriam Bishop, had recently reemerged at the Yale mixer. But she was not surprised; some part of her sensed that Delia would be at the center of whatever Virginia had to tell them.

"Why are you dragging this out?" Carol said. "Just tell us already!"

"I'm *dragging this out* because it's really good. Or really bad, depending on your point of view." Virginia looked around at all of them, her gaze skipping from one face to the next, clearly brimming with anticipation. "Delia is having an affair with Mr. McQuaid!"

"You're kidding!" said Midge.

"She wouldn't," Carol said. "Would she?"

"How do you know?" Tabitha asked.

"I believe it," Peggy said. "I really do."

Only Anne was quiet. Although she hoped for Delia's sake this wasn't true, the pieces fit. Delia had told her, just hours ago, that she'd had an affair with a married man. As she listened to all the chatter, she felt dread slowly rising inside her, like foul, oily sludge.

"How can you be so sure?" Carol asked. "Delia didn't tell you, did she?"

So Carol had doubts too.

"As if she would!" Virginia was obviously annoyed. "But it's not like I needed her to tell me. I found out on my own."

"How?" Carol wasn't letting this go so easily.

"I got suspicious watching her in the Shakespeare seminar. Week after week, she would be giving him these little looks. Mooning over him, really. She'd stay late to talk to him. And he gave her paper an A-plus."

"I'm still not getting how all this adds up to an affair," said Carol. "I mean, I know you don't like her—none of us do—and that she acts superior and haughty in the way all of them do. But an affair with a professor? I don't know . . ."

"Carol's right," said Peggy. "And as for that grade, well, no one ever said she wasn't smart. She studies all the time."

"I saw them kissing in his car." Virginia had clearly been saving this prize, this jewel, and was now quiet so they could absorb the impact.

"You didn't!" Tabitha said.

"Oh yes, I did. I knew she was up to something. After all that business in class, I started following her because I'd overheard her talking about going over to his house—she's been babysitting his little girls. But somehow I didn't believe that was the only reason. So one night I drove past the house. I saw them come out together, and Delia got into his car. I stayed behind them—they didn't see me." Virginia was exceedingly proud of the shiny green Ford convertible her parents had given her for her eighteenth birthday—none of the other girls in their set had a car. Cars owned by students weren't allowed on campus, so she had to park elsewhere, at a nearby garage. "He didn't go right back to campus. Oh no. He took a little detour, and it was quite a while—maybe twenty minutes—before he drove her to the dorm. That's happened at least two more times." She leaned back and gripped the arms of the chair as if it were a throne. "And who knows—it may have even happened more than that."

"What do you think they were doing?" asked Tabitha.

"Please, Tabitha, do you have to ask?" Virginia inquired in a withering tone.

"That's really . . . shocking," said Peggy. "I wouldn't have thought she'd have the nerve."

"There's more." Virginia sat up straighter now. "I saw them one night at the door of Avery."

"Kissing? Really?" Tabitha's need to know was so strong that she risked Virginia's disdain.

"No. But it was late, and the building was empty—no lights on anywhere but one room; it must have been his office. So she had been in there with him. Alone."

Everyone was quiet, absorbing the implications of what Virginia had told them.

"I wonder if they had been drinking," Midge said. "I know *she* drinks."

"How do you know that?" asked Carol. "It's not like you spend any time with her."

"She was my roommate last year, remember? She kept a case of wine in our room and had a glass every night. Then she'd be up for hours, conjugating her Latin verbs—out loud—and she read those French poems out loud too."

"Plenty of girls drink," Carol said.

"Not wine, and not in their rooms, all by themselves."

"Did she get drunk?" asked Carol.

"Well, no . . . She just had one glass, never any more."

"It's because she grew up in Paris," said Peggy.

"You're getting sidetracked," Virginia said. "None of that is important. What matters is that she is clearly violating every code of conduct that we're supposed to obey."

"Virginia's right," Anne found herself saying, and hating herself as she did. "Okay, let's say Delia and Mr. McQuaid are having an affair. What are we supposed to do about it?" Because that was really the point, wasn't it? Virginia wasn't going to be content just dropping this bomb and then expecting them to sit still; she would want to *do* something.

"Do? Why, report her to the dean of course."

"She'll be expelled." Anne knew that attempting to put the brakes on anything Virginia wanted was risky. But she had to try, however feebly, to protect her new friend.

"Don't you think she deserves to be expelled?" The challenge to Anne in Virginia's tone was unmistakable.

Anne was quiet. It was scary to go up against Virginia. And she had yet to sort out her feelings about Delia's behavior—carrying on an affair, if that was what she was doing, with a married man was wrong, even reprehensible. But what had she herself just told her? *You're not defined by the worst thing you've done*. And did this "worst thing" deserve expulsion? "What do you suppose will happen to Mr. McQuaid?" Anne asked.

"What do you mean?" Virginia seemed not to have thought about this.

"Anne has a point," said Peggy. "Does Mr. McQuaid just get to carry on as if he had no part in any of this?"

"It's her fault. She seduced *him*." Virginia sounded so certain. Smug. "You know what she's like. What they're all like. Devious. Cunning. They almost can't help it."

These words made Anne feel sick. But she'd already gone as far out on a limb as she dared to go. She couldn't face having Virginia and all the others turn on her now. If she defended Delia any more, she'd be tarred with that very same brush.

"I'm going to write a letter to the dean," Virginia said. "I'll tell her what I saw, and she can decide what to do."

"I think we all know what she'll do," said Anne quietly. But her tone didn't reveal how panicked she felt as she glanced around at the other girls. Maybe someone, even one of them, would balk at the idea of getting Delia expelled. They might not like her, but getting someone expelled was a serious thing to have on your conscience.

"Well, the punishment fits the crime. She's not the sort of girl who belongs here. None of them do, really. Maybe the administration will think twice about letting them in next time." Virginia reached for the pad and pen that sat on the desk and began writing. No one spoke, and when she finished, she read it out loud.

Dear Dean Schoales:

It has come to our attention that Delia Goldhush has been carrying on an affair with Mr. McQuaid in the English Department. I've seen the two of them alone in his car, and they have been alone in his office too, at night when no one else was in the building.

I'm also aware of the favoritism he has shown her in class and of her obvious attachment to him. Some of the other girls on my hall have taken note of her behavior, and we all think she should be punished for her transgression. It's for her own good. She needs to find out that there are consequences to her actions and it's better she finds this out sooner rather than later. As it is, her presence here casts a shadow on Vassar's fine reputation, a reputation we are all honor bound to uphold.

"I'm going to sign it first, and then the rest of you can too. Put your dorm and room number next to your name," Virginia said.

"You want all of us to sign it?" Anne asked. "Why?" This was even worse than she had imagined.

"There's strength in numbers."

The letter was circulating now—Midge, Peggy, Carol, and Tabitha each signed and then passed it on. Now it was Anne's turn. Hours ago, Delia had confided in her. She'd wept in Anne's arms and hugged her when they parted. And now Anne was going to betray her trust, and poison a friendship that was only just starting to blossom. "I don't know if I can," she said.

"Why on earth not?" Virginia sounded incredulous.

"It just seems like too much. I mean, we can avoid her. Ignore her—we kind of do that anyway. But do we really need to get her kicked out of school?"

"If you don't sign, it's like saying you condone what she did. What kind of a girl does that make you?"

"Of course I don't condone an affair with a married man." Anne felt her face growing red and most likely blotchy, which was what happened when she was upset.

"Then you have to sign." Virginia pushed the pen in her direction.

Anne saw the other girls watching. This had become something more than whether or not she signed the letter. This was Virginia exercising her power. If Anne resisted, she'd have to face the repercussions, the cold shoulders, the very real possibility of being lumped with Delia, her reputation ruined. Still she hesitated.

"Anne, I don't have all day."

Anne took the pen and gripped it tightly as she wrote her name at the bottom of the page; it seemed much larger than all the others. She handed the pad to Virginia so she wouldn't have to see it.

"There, that's done." Virginia tore the sheet of paper from the pad.

There was murmuring from the girls as they got up and moved toward the door. Anne was the first to leave. She didn't want to be alone with Virginia for a single second.

But though she could flee from Virginia, she couldn't flee from herself and the lacerating knowledge of how she'd betrayed Delia. She never imagined she'd find herself in this position. Deciding to keep her Jewishness to herself, she'd thought she'd found a shield against a hostile world. And for a time, it seemed to have worked. She did feel a part of things; she was grateful and relieved to be spared the worry about her background, the fear that it was going to trip her up, or keep her from—from what? Just living a happy life, she thought. A life that she made for herself, not based on other people's biases. She hadn't thought about the other side of it, though. Pretending not to be Jewish meant that the Gentiles with whom she mixed felt entirely unfettered; they said even *worse* things about Jews in her presence because they assumed she shared their noxious beliefs and opinions, that she was one of them.

Guilt stalked her for the rest of the day, and all night too; she was unable to sleep. As the sky lightened to gray and then pale blue, she got up, dressed, and left her room. She couldn't imagine how she would be able to concentrate in her classes that day. But somehow she muddled through, and late that afternoon, as she left her French class, she caught sight of a notice pinned to the bulletin board just outside the department office.

APPLICATIONS FOR STUDY ABROAD
NOW BEING ACCEPTED

Do you want to improve your foreign language skills, gain proficiency and fluency, expand your horizons and see the world? Then apply for the Junior Year Study Abroad programs being held in these four European cities:

Paris ***Madrid*** ***Rome*** ***Lisbon***

Application forms are available in the Study Abroad Office, Main Building, Room 202.

Paris. What if she applied to go? It would be an escape, a way to get herself out of this horrible predicament. And she'd been longing to visit the city, to see for herself its fabled streets and landmarks, improve her admittedly execrable French. Tired though she was, Anne sped out of the building and across the campus to Main. "May I please get an application form?" she panted as she stood in front of the desk.

"Can it wait until the morning?" said the white-haired woman—the name plate on her desk read Miss Vane—with the hankie pinned to the front of her dress. She was straightening a pile of papers. "We're about to close up."

"It really can't." She must have sounded so desperate that Miss Vane took pity on her and reached down into a drawer.

"Here you are," Miss Vane said. "Oh, look—" She turned and pointed to the calendar that was tacked up behind her. "The deadline is tomorrow. I guess you really shouldn't wait."

"Thank you," said Anne. "Thank you so much." She took the form to her room and filled it out immediately. She had the money to do this—her father had left her well provided for—and in her mind, there was no better way to spend it. She thought Barney Weiss, her father's partner and the executor of his estate, would agree.

That night she skipped dinner and ate only the banana and the orange she'd taken from a previous meal in the dining room. She was able to fall into a deep, if troubled sleep. In her dreams, she was forced to take long, complicated French examinations that were well beyond her capability; the other students seemed to know, and jeered at her. The room emptied, she was the only one left, but the more she struggled to answer the questions, new ones kept appearing; the test would just go on and on.

The next morning Anne was back at room 202 even before the office opened; she brought the application to Miss Vane as soon as it did. And when, a couple of days later, she received notice that she had been accepted into the program and would spend her junior year in Paris, she was flooded with relief. This opportunity represented a new chance, and she was going to take it. But it didn't stop her from feeling terrible about the way she'd betrayed Delia, and she knew it wouldn't. What it would do was put some distance—thousands of miles and an entire ocean—between her and the worst thing *she'd* ever done. She'd told Delia she wasn't defined by a single, reprehensible act. Was that true for her as well?

EIGHT

DELIA

1947

The house on West Eleventh Street throbbed with music, but not the music Delia's father typically played. Instead of the dulcet strains of Mozart, Bach, or Vivaldi, this was some kind of jazz: low, sultry, hot. How strange.

"Papa?" She set down her suitcase and followed the sound downstairs to the kitchen, where a party was in full swing, radio blaring. Her father was at the center of the group, regaling his guests with one of his elaborate, meandering stories; he'd always been a skilled raconteur. Catching sight of her, he called out, "Delia my dove! To what do we owe this lovely surprise?"

"I told you I was coming down for the weekend," said Delia. "We talked about it on the telephone." Could he be losing his memory? God, she hoped not.

"And so we did!" said Simon. "But I've been so busy. It must have flown right out of my head." He reached out for a quick hug, and Delia inhaled vetiver, a scent he'd worn in Paris but not since. She shook hands with several well-dressed men and women, not recognizing any of them. Since arriving in New York, Simon had not been in the habit of hosting parties or gatherings at the house the way he and Sophie had in France. But here he was in his dark blazer and his paisley ascot, a full glass held aloft and commanding all the attention.

"Everyone, this is my brilliant and beautiful daughter."

Delia stood there mutely. There he was, doing it again, praising her in such an exaggerated way that it had the opposite effect—instead of bolstering her confidence, it made her feel unseen, as if she were some girl he'd invented, and not the one she really was.

"If you'll excuse me," she said. "I'm a little tired, so I think I'll go upstairs."

"Don't you want a glass of wine? Or some lamb stew? I have to say Helga's outdone herself." Helga, the cook and housekeeper, had set out a chafing dish, surrounded by bowls, spoons, and napkins, on the damask-covered table. A crusty baguette, sawed open and partially sliced, sat beside it.

"No, thank you." Delia was in fact hungry, and the stew was tempting, but she didn't want to stand around and have to make conversation with all these strangers, so she retreated to her room.

The next day the house was filled with guests again, this time for a lunch served in the dining room. Helga had made some sort of baked egg dish and filled a basket with popovers, hot from the oven; Simon, dressed in a silk smoking jacket and black velvet slippers with golden bees embroidered on their fronts, was passing them around. What had happened to him since she'd last been home? He seemed to have emerged from his years-long cocoon, now as resplendent as a butterfly. This resembled the father she recognized from Paris, from Vence—her mother's sophisticated and gregarious husband. How did it happen?

Delia paid more careful attention to the guests gathered around the table and realized that the voluptuous woman sitting next to him—brassy blond hair that looked as if she doused it in peroxide, bright-red lipstick—had been there the night before. Her father seemed to like her very much. And when he kissed her fully on the mouth, smearing the red lipstick, some of which ended up on his chin, she understood: this was the reason for the change. Her name was Harriet Curtis, and she stayed after the other guests had gone home, so Delia was able to learn that she was now Simon's assistant at the gallery; he must have dismissed Gordon Braithwaite, who had held the position before. So her father had a new woman in his life. Delia turned that over in her mind. Well, Sophie was gone; he was free.

It didn't take long for Delia to track how Harriet was different from her mother. She was nice looking, though her style was a bit obvious, even vulgar, which was wholly unlike Sophie. She was not an artist, and by her own admission had no talent in that area. She was also completely acquiescent to Simon; she agreed with him about everything, whereas Sophie had constantly challenged him about matters large and small. Today Simon was holding forth about Jackson Pollock's drip paintings, which Sophie had thought laughable. She'd called Pollock a fraud. But today Sophie was absent from the conversation, and when Simon declared that Pollock's *Lavender Mist* "heralds a new chapter in the history of art," Harriet's head bobbed furiously in agreement.

Then Simon began talking about a new show he was planning; it seemed Harriet was going to play a key role in putting it together. "It's going to cover a lot of ground—women artists from the last twenty years—and we've already started talking to some of them."

We? Now it was *we*? In the past her father had sought Delia's help in organizing his openings. She could also see the way he looked at Harriet. It was as if the light had been switched back on.

"It's going to be an exceptional show," he was saying. "We've got works by Mary Cassatt, Lee Krasner, and some lesser-known names. Harriet's been superb in tracking them down. I was even thinking we could include that double portrait of your mother's, the one you brought from Paris."

"You mean it would be for sale?"

"Well, yes. That's the point of a show, isn't it? I run a gallery, not a museum."

"No," said Delia. "Absolutely not. I'll never sell it. How could you even suggest such a thing?"

"Oh, so now selling her work is suddenly verboten?"

"That sculpture is not for sale" was all Delia said, but annoyance crackled inside her. Her father had gotten his energy back, yet he'd said nothing about resuming the search for Sophie's missing work. Well, he might have pushed it aside, but Delia had not. She began to think about returning to Paris, maybe even over the summer. The more she thought about it, the more urgent it seemed. She could visit Marie-Pierre and find out more details.

For the next two days the house was noisy, perpetually filled with strangers and loud music. Delia found half-finished glasses of wine and plates of food on the bookshelves or on the stairs, overflowing ashtrays, hand towels wadded into balls; poor Helga was having a hard time keeping up. She had even come upon a couple passionately kissing in her bedroom; they broke away from each other and scurried out without looking at her.

Delia watched them go, but instead of remaining in her room, she went downstairs and through the kitchen to the yard. Everything was frozen or dead, but at least it was quiet out here. Then she heard a rustling nearby and glanced over at the yard next door. A tall figure bundled in a dark coat and knit cap was busy doing something—it was George Frost, the gardener with the little dog. So he'd come back from the war—no gold star on the window, thank God.

"Hello!" she called.

He straightened up and looked around.

"Over here." Delia went over to the wooden fence—rather decrepit, it should really be replaced—so that she wouldn't have to shout.

"Delia Goldhush," he said, recognizing her. "It's been a long time. How are you?"

"I'm pretty well," she said. "How about you?"

"I'm keeping busy." He too approached the fence.

That was when she saw that the empty sleeve of his dark coat was pinned to his shoulder. He must have lost his arm in the war. He used the other one to poke at a pile—it looked like leaves and such—with a pitchfork. "I've started composting." He must have seen her confused expression.

"Composting?" She had only a vague idea of what that was.

"I put in leaves and other garden material—twigs, stems, dead flowers, and also food scraps—into a pile and cover them. Nature does the rest." When he saw that she didn't understand, he added, "Everything in the pile decomposes, and eventually turns to rich, black soil." If he saw her distaste, he showed no sign of it. "Not that much happens in the winter, but I like to check on it anyway."

"Food scraps and leaves," she repeated, but the only thing she could really focus on was his arm. How had it happened? Had he adjusted to its loss?

"I can give you some if you like."

"Some what?"

"Compost. By the spring I'll have plenty." He smiled. "You can't believe what it does for the garden. People call it black gold."

Delia understood he was trying to be nice. Neighborly. But wouldn't that mixture be crawling with worms and such? She knew that was a good thing, but the thought was nonetheless revolting. Noisy and smoky as the house was, she said a hurried thank-you and went back inside.

When Sunday night came, Delia was more than ready to leave. Vassar would be a relief, an oasis. Fortunately, Harriet was not there when she said goodbye to her father. He was seated in his study on the parlor floor, a room dense with books, paintings, wall hangings, and an elaborately carved wooden screen from Morocco. He looked up from the magazine he'd been leafing through. "I wanted you to know that I *have* been trying to find the rest of your mother's sculpture," he said.

"Why, so you can sell everything?"

"No, of course not." They glared at each other for a moment before he said, "Delia, your mother wanted to sell her work. It made her feel seen in the world as an artist. Valued. Important. You remember how happy she was when she made a sale, don't you?"

Delia did remember, but she didn't want to give him this.

"In any case, I couldn't track down any of the sculpture."

"You've never gone back to Paris, Papa. You could have gone back when the war ended."

"I don't think I can." He suddenly looked deflated as he said this; his shoulders slumped, and he leaned back in the chair as if he needed its support.

"I can," Delia said. "And I want to."

"All right." He waited for a moment. "I won't try to stop you. But you should be . . . careful. You may think you're going in search of the sculpture . . . but sculpture isn't the only thing you might find."

"I don't know what you're talking about."

Simon shook his head. "Never mind. But Paris won't be the same anymore. You'll see."

Delia went over to give him a peck on the cheek, and he absently patted her head, mussing her hair in the process.

On the ride back to Poughkeepsie, she went over the conversation in her mind, and then she resolved to stop thinking about it. Certainly there were enough other things to compete for her attention, like Ian McQuaid. Since that terrible day when Mrs. McQuaid had discovered them kissing in the car, there had been no word from him, not a thing. It was as if she'd ceased to exist.

She slogged through the days, and on a couple of occasions walked past Avery, not sure if she was relieved or disappointed when she didn't catch sight of Ian. The single time she did see him—the winter light turning his hair gold, the brief but powerful sensation of not being able to breathe—his eyes met hers, and then he turned abruptly away. Delia felt as if she'd been slapped.

But even so she couldn't stop the hummingbird of hope that continued to flutter around her. Every time she checked her mail, she imagined that he would write to her and say—what? That he was sorry, that he missed her, that he was going to leave his wife for her? On one of these days, she did find an envelope with a Vassar College logo on it—was it from him? But no, her name had been typed on the front; he wouldn't have done that.

Opening the envelope, she found a brief note from Miss Schoales, the sophomore dean, asking her to come in the following morning at 9:00. Whatever for? The note gave no clue. Delia tried to think of any reason the dean would be summoning her. Could it have anything to do with Ian? That thought throbbed quietly but persistently for the rest of the day and interfered with her sleep.

The next morning Delia sat in an unyielding Windsor chair outside the dean's office, which was on the second floor of Main building, past the Rose Parlor and down a long hall. "She'll be right with you," the secretary said. Did Delia detect a strange look—pity? contempt?—on the secretary's face? She didn't have to wonder for long. Within minutes she was called in by the dean and seated across from her. This chair had a padded seat and back, but it was no more comfortable than the other had been.

"Good morning, Miss Goldhush," said the dean. She was a thin woman with exceedingly good posture; her fading ash-brown hair was coiled into a tight bun from which not a single strand had been permitted to escape. "I've had a chance to review your grades and learned that you are an excellent student—one of the very best, if not the best in your class." Delia said nothing; she could sense a very damning *but* about to be uttered.

As if on cue, Dean Schoales said, "But it has come to my attention there are some issues of character that override academic excellence." She paused, knitting her long, bony fingers together. Did she expect Delia to say something here? When it was clear that Delia was not going to speak, the dean continued, this time prefacing her words with a deep and what seemed heartfelt sigh. "Really it boils down to one single issue—that of character. And it concerns Professor McQuaid."

Hearing his name in this context was a heavy lead weight dropped in Delia's lap; her whole body seemed to clench. This was followed by panic, voluminous and engulfing. How did the dean know about them? Delia thought they had been careful. And yet, looking into the dean's pale and not unsympathetic eyes, Delia realized that apparently they had not been careful enough. "I've learned that you and Mr. McQuaid have been engaging in some . . . behavior that is very unbecoming both to him and to you."

Delia still had not said a word. She couldn't; any words she might have wanted to say had frozen in her mouth. Yet even through her panic she began to see that her silence was in its own way powerful; it was obvious that the dean was expecting—hoping?—that she would break down crying, deny, explain, beg. Delia did none of those things, though her reaction was not by design but instinct. Her transgression had been exposed, and she wanted nothing more than to cover it, cover herself. Dean Schoales would have to spell it all out, every ugly and sorry syllable. "It was more than unbecoming, actually." It was evident that the dean was nervous. "It was unacceptable, at least at this institution." She paused, but Delia remained mute.

"I have a letter here"—the dean reached into a folder and took out a lined sheet of paper—"written by one of your classmates, and signed by several others. I don't think their names matter, but I bring it up to underscore the idea that this was not an isolated complaint. And that my office made sure to verify the accusations before I called you in."

Just then the phone on the dean's desk rang, and though she looked distinctly annoyed, she answered it. "No," she said. "I can't. I told you I was in a meeting and not to be disturbed." The hand that held the letter turned slightly, and Delia's eye went straight to the bottom, where the signatures were. Most of them did not surprise her, but there was one that did—very much. "I'll deal with this later," said the dean. She put the receiver down and looked at Delia with what seemed like exasperation. "Aren't you going to say anything?"

Delia couldn't say anything. Though she was aware that she seemed calm, inside she was a volcano, an earthquake, a storm at sea. After a couple of excruciating minutes, she replied, "You seem to know everything already. There's nothing more to add."

"I should think you would want to apologize for tarnishing your good reputation and the reputation of this institution." When Delia didn't offer this apology, the dean went on. "All right, then. You aren't required to say anything, but you do understand there will be a consequence. You'll be receiving a formal letter from the president's office, and your parents will be getting a letter as well. You should have your things packed and be ready to leave by the end of the week."

Delia stood up. "May I go now?"

The dean looked surprised, and Delia had that small satisfaction to take away with her. She'd already grown skilled at ignoring her classmates, assuming a blank, impervious look as if her face had been wiped clean of expression; she hadn't expected that this would work with the dean, who was far more powerful than a bunch of college girls.

But once she was outside the office, she was shaking so hard that she had to stop and place her hands against a wall, just to steady herself. After taking a few deep breaths, she left Main and headed outside. She had no particular destination in mind; she just had to get out of there. It was still winter—gray sky, sharp wind, and a fine, cold rain that stung her forehead, cheeks, and lips.

Where was she going anyway? She turned and went back inside. She shook off the water from her hair and then brushed the droplets from her coat. Two girls in the dorm lobby walked by without looking and Lottie, the girl who lived next door, walked up to her. "Delia, do you have a hot water bottle I can borrow?" Delia said yes, and they went upstairs together. So no one knew—yet. But once the secret was out, her life here would become intolerable.

She gave Lottie the hot water bottle and then retreated to her own room. Once alone, she said the words *I've been expelled* several times out loud. The dean had not actually used the word, and Delia needed to say it, to hear it, for herself. Being expelled meant she'd never have to see Ian again. That was a relief. Also a torment. And what about him? Would his wife leave him or put him out?

She hung her coat in the closet. She had the urge to get undressed and climb into bed, pull the covers up, and not stir. She'd skip lunch, skip all the meals in the dining room, and just go off campus to eat; she thought of Bunny and how she'd brought Delia a fresh, hot stack of pancakes. But no. Something defiant in her wanted to fight back, to not make it too easy to dismiss her, to pretend she'd never been here. She wasn't going to let herself be erased.

And then it hit her. Her time at Vassar wouldn't be so easily erased either. Now that she was about to leave, everything she loved about her life here was suddenly so clear, so vivid. There was a kind of mental stimulation, an energy that she'd never encountered in France. She found it not only in Ian's class but in others too. There had been Miss Havelock, who brought the imperial splendor of ancient Rome to stunning immediacy. Also Miss Digby, who'd unlocked the wit and humor of Chaucer's storytelling. And then there was Mr. Gregg, always in the same grease-spotted khaki pants and threadbare tweed jacket, who despite both a stutter and a lisp was an excellent lecturer, so chatty and affable that it seemed he was on a first-name basis with Leo Tolstoy, Fyodor Dostoyevsky, and Nikolay Gogol. She would miss all that, just as she would miss the feeling of walking into the sacred silence of the library, with its lofty ceiling and finely grained wood paneling, the four Japanese maples in the quad that turned a brilliant scarlet in the fall, and the lilac bushes that grew so lush and tall, arching overhead, to form a fragrant bower in the spring.

That night Delia dressed for dinner in a suit she'd bought when she was last in New York. It was made of navy gabardine, piped in white, and its narrow, fitted jacket topped a full, flowing skirt. It was too formal, too dressy, for an ordinary dinner, but that was the point: the suit was imposing, like armor. By the time she'd reached the dining room, the news must have already traveled through the dorm; she was aware of the way the other girls looked at her, how they gave her a wide berth in line. She stood there silent, almost motionless, a wax figure in a blue wool suit.

When it was her turn, she accepted the food ladled onto her plate, though she had no appetite and knew she wouldn't eat it. Then, finding an empty place, she put her tray down on the table. She sat alone, but that was nothing new; she almost always sat alone. Looking surreptitiously around the room—she didn't want to catch anyone's eye—she saw Virginia. Though she was now dressed in a pleated skirt, white blouse, and sweater vest, in Delia's mind she was traipsing back from the hockey field, her legs coated in mud, her uniform sweaty and dirty.

Of course Virginia's had been the first name on that list; that was the reason she wore such a gloating, satisfied expression now. The other names were attached to the other girls who sat around her, girls who had made no secret of their feelings. Well, so what? She held them in contempt; they were a bunch of sheep, bleating in unison.

Tonight they seemed animated by a sizzling, barely concealed excitement, looking her way and nudging one another.

There was only one whose expression set her apart, and that was Anne. Unlike the others, she looked miserable. Then Delia had a thought that was like a hot branding iron applied to her skin. What if *Anne* had been the one who'd gone to Virginia, who'd betrayed her? She remembered that morning at the diner, Anne's arm around her shoulders as she'd wept. Had all that been just an act? Before, she would have said no. Anne had seemed so genuine. And her words had brought unexpected solace: *You're not the worst thing you've done.*

Seeing Anne's name on the letter was scalding in a way Delia wouldn't have believed possible. She looked down at her plate and began to cut up her bland baked fish—she would not miss the food here, that was certain. She raised a small forkful to her lips. Swallowing was an effort all its own; the food remained in her mouth, an unpleasant lump that she couldn't make go down. She wished she could spit it out, but she wouldn't do that—not with everyone watching. No, she had to continue the pretense, save face, save *her* face, in this, the most humiliating moment of her entire life.

Finally she was able to swallow and then she forced herself to repeat the process again and again, until her plate was nearly clean. Only then did she dare to look up, ignoring the girls who were watching her so carefully, until her gaze found Anne's. Although there were no words between them, Delia's look was beseeching. *Why did you go along with the rest of them? How could you have signed that letter? Did you mean what you said at the diner?* She kept looking, waiting for something in Anne's expression to communicate some kind of response. But Anne turned to Midge, who was sitting next to her.

That was enough. While her former roommate whispered something to Anne, Delia stood up and took her tray to the conveyor belt near the kitchen. Then she walked slowly—she refused to look as if she were fleeing—out of the dining room. Whatever she had thought set Anne apart from those others must have been an illusion. She'd been deceived. Anne was just like the rest of them. That her betrayal had burned a hot little hole in Delia's heart was something she would have to get over. In the meantime, she had plenty to do. She went upstairs to begin packing.

PART II

PARIS

NINE

DELIA

1947

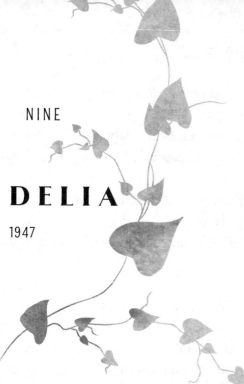

Delia left the campus at the end of the week. She packed up all her belongings and arranged for them to go into storage at a warehouse near the Hudson River, not far from where they lived on Eleventh Street. That way she could show up with a small overnight bag, so it would look like she was just home for the weekend, and put off telling her father what had happened, at least for a while. But when she arrived home, Helga told her that Simon and Harriet had gone to Long Island for a few days, which gave her a reprieve. Also a chance to intercept the letter, on Vassar stationery, that the dean had sent: *Dear Mr. Goldhush, I regret to inform you that it has been decided not to allow your daughter, Delia, to continue her education at Vassar. Although she is an uncommonly bright girl, it has come to my attention that . . .*

Delia didn't need to read any more. Neither did her father. And when he did return a couple of days later, he was glad to see her and didn't bother to ask why she was there, preoccupied by his own plans and with Harriet, who by this time had moved into the house. Still, Delia knew he would notice that she was staying longer than a weekend. Before he had a chance to ask, she told him that she'd applied to—and been accepted by—Barnard as a transfer student. "Poughkeepsie is so dull," she said. "I needed to be in a city again."

"Brava!" said her father. "I always thought Barnard was a better choice for a girl like you. Is there any paperwork for me to sign? A check I need to send?"

"I've taken care of all that," she said. "And if it's all right, I'd like to live here. Dorm life isn't exactly for me."

"Of course you can live here!" He smiled and gave her hand a little squeeze.

So it had been as easy as that. Well, her father always had been this way—loving but fundamentally inattentive. And with Harriet in the house, there was even more to distract him. His girlfriend's various belongings—gloves, bedroom slippers, a paper fan, packets of hairpins, reading glasses, lipstick-smeared hankies and napkins—joined the general clutter, which Delia found upsetting; Harriet had supplanted Sophie so easily. But when it came to the gallery, Harriet was extremely organized and kept things running smoothly. She cultivated relationships with a number of critics, which would help in getting reviews of the shows when they opened. And more importantly, Harriet and Simon never seemed to quarrel; Delia had to admit that she didn't miss the combative atmosphere of her childhood. Also, Harriet made an effort to include Delia; she would invite her to go shopping or to dinner if Simon was otherwise engaged. If Delia declined—and she usually did—Harriet would bring her some small treat: a package of lavender-scented sachets for her drawers, a pair of embroidered slippers, a pin in the shape of a poodle. But Delia had to wonder how long she could keep this fiction going. At some point her father would expect her to graduate from Barnard, and then what would she do? She had no answer for that, at least not then.

As spring approached, she frequently saw George Frost out in his garden. Soon his coat was replaced by a jacket, and then a nubby oatmeal-colored sweater. The pinned sleeve made it seem as if someone were touching him on the shoulder, a comforting, even tender, gesture. He seemed very engrossed in his activities back there, and managed to do a lot—dig, rake, carry—with his single remaining arm. But while she admired his spirit, she kept out of the yard and did her best to avoid him; his self-sufficiency seemed like a reproach.

Instead, she found herself leaving the neighborhood entirely, and several mornings a week, took the train uptown and got off at 116th Street, where the Barnard campus was located. At first she just wandered around, looking at the imposing iron gates, the various patterns of the bricks lining the ground, and the large and not particularly interesting buildings; the architecture at Vassar was certainly superior. She watched the students walking around in groups of twos and threes—chattering, laughing, sharing a cigarette in the chilly air—and realized that she missed the friendship and camaraderie of other girls. She was lonely. But when a girl actually approached her, Delia hurried away. Not that she wouldn't have welcomed the conversation, but she was worried her outsider status would be exposed, and she'd be banned from campus.

Sometimes she went inside; she looked like she could be a student, and no one questioned her presence when she sat in the library reading or poring over back issues of the *New Yorker* and *National Geographic*. When that began to wear thin, she found she could slip into some of the larger lecture classes where her presence would not be noticed. There was an anthropology class that met three times a week, and she found that interesting enough. Better was a music appreciation class where she could sit and listen to recordings of symphonies and chamber quartets.

Best of all was the astronomy class, where, as for the art history lectures at Vassar, the lights were dimmed and the professor showed slides of star-filled skies, renderings of the solar system, and the pocked surface of the moon on a large, flat screen at the front of the auditorium. Listening to these lectures was absorbing in and of itself; it also gave her enough conversational fodder to participate in dinner-table talk, though in truth her father never really listened to what she said, despite his habit of heaping both lavish and inaccurate praise on her. When she mentioned the music class, he turned to Harriet and declared that Delia had an "exceptional voice." Exceptional? Hardly, and besides, when had he even heard her sing? She remembered his prodding in Vence, in front of their guests. But she just smiled. Her father's blurry and vague form of love made it possible to avoid his scrutiny and any probing questions it might lead to.

In April, Simon told Delia that he and Harriet were taking a trip to Santa Fe. "We're going to meet with Georgia O'Keeffe!" he said. "I think she's going to let us have a painting for the show. Maybe even two."

"That sounds exciting." Delia was familiar with O'Keeffe's work—the animal skulls, the giant flowers. "How long will you be gone?" It would be nice to have the house to herself.

"A week. Maybe two. I love that part of the country. Spring in the desert . . ." He seemed to be picturing it in his mind. Then he looked at Delia and said, "Come with us. You'll get to meet her. A once-in-a-lifetime opportunity."

"I have classes." This was, of course, a lie, but he didn't know that.

"Skip them. Or at least some of them. She's a great American artist. What class is more important than that?"

"I'll think about it," Delia said. But she knew she wouldn't go; she would just be a third wheel. By the next day, Simon seemed to have forgotten that he'd brought it up. Amid hugs, kisses, and Harriet's promises of souvenirs—*We'll bring you a turquoise cuff, no, a squash blossom necklace, like the ones O'Keeffe wears*—her father and his girlfriend finally climbed into the bulbous yellow cab that would take them to Idlewild.

Once they were gone, Delia could feel the house relax and expand around her, as if it too were catching its breath. Without Harriet and her penchant for creating a mess, Helga embarked on a cleaning frenzy, tossing, scrubbing, and polishing as she went. When she was done, the windows shone brightly, the floors were washed and waxed, the beds crisply made with fresh sheets, and the pillows plumped and standing proudly on the sofa and the chairs.

"Take a few days off," Delia told Helga.

"No, Miss Delia. It's not right."

"It is if I tell you it is."

"But you'll be alone . . ."

Exactly, Delia wanted to say. But instead she said, "I'll be fine. You've been working so hard, and you deserve a rest."

Helga finally agreed, but before she left, she prepared several dishes for Delia to heat up—chicken paprikash, her notable stew, and baked cinnamon buns, chocolate chip cookies, and a nut cake with a filling of raspberry jam. There was no way Delia would eat it all, but she appreciated the effort.

Since for the time being she could drop the pretense of being enrolled at Barnard, she could stay in the neighborhood and also in the house. It was the latter that interested her. She had the feeling that Simon wasn't being entirely truthful about the missing sculpture. Maybe there was something he wasn't telling her, information he wasn't sharing. He was still angry at Sophie. Perhaps he didn't want to extend himself to look for her work. But Delia did, and this was her chance.

On the first morning after Helga left, she went straight to the desk in his study. After twenty or so minutes of fruitless searching, she turned instead to the pair of gray-green metal file cabinets that stood side by side. These were more organized than the desk, on which papers, letters, and the like had been heaped rather haphazardly; the files, in contrast, were alphabetically arranged, and it was a very easy matter to find the sheets listing all the sculptures that had been stored in the Paris warehouse. But Delia had seen these before; there was nothing new here.

Frustrated, she turned her gaze elsewhere. There was an armchair with a tufted ottoman; next to it was a standing lamp whose shade dripped fringe. The floor was covered in rugs, some of them overlapping, and the windows were lined with long velvet drapes. There was the Moroccan screen, an intricately carved thing with four folding panels. Behind it was an armoire, which her father used for storage, since the room had no closets. She decided to look there. Inside were some boxes that contained large envelopes, and she began to go through them methodically. A couple of them contained clippings from newspapers and magazines; another contained receipts dated from one, two, three years ago. Delia grew impatient. Maybe her father had been telling the truth—other than the inventory sheet from the warehouse, there was no more information available about the sculpture.

On the top shelf of the armoire were still more boxes; one of them was labeled *Correspondence*. She eased it off the shelf and sneezed; the box was dusty. Sitting down on the floor, she began to go through the papers in the box. Most were letters having to do with the gallery, and they all seemed to be recent; nothing from Europe. But then she noticed a thin blue envelope stuck between two larger sheets of paper. She pulled it out.

The shock of what she saw caused a sharp intake of breath and a small fit of coughing. It was an unopened letter from her mother, addressed to her, and sent to her grandparents' address on Riverside Drive. She clawed apart the envelope and extracted a single sheet of onionskin paper. Her eyes scanned the page; certain sections jumped out:

. . . the police came to Serge's apartment, and they were intent on taking him down to the station for questioning. They insisted I go along as well. I was frantic. I knew you would be leaving soon, that we were all

scheduled to leave, but when I told them this, they ignored me. We were held for three days, and when I was finally released, I went straight to the apartment. You were gone, of course; I knew you would be. I wanted you gone—it meant you would be safe, an ocean away from the war.

But I was sick, knowing that you would think I had abandoned you like that. Yes, your father and I fought. We always fought. That was nothing new; you'd witnessed plenty of our fights. And I do have a temper, I admit. Still, I wouldn't have disappeared like that of my own volition, and I hope you will believe me, and believe how sorry I am. It must have been terrible to leave without me, wondering where I was and why I hadn't come back.

Delia felt dizzy. She had to put the letter down. So there was an explanation for what had happened, and for her mother's disappearance—but Simon had kept it from her. How could he do that? And that name, Serge. She vaguely recognized it from the diary pages she'd read. Who was he, and what was Sophie's relationship to him?

She resumed her search and found two more letters from Sophie. Like the first, they were addressed to her and unopened. In one of them, she read:

Please tell your father I'm sorry. I would tell him myself, but I know he won't hear it from me. He's simply blotted me out—I know him so well. My temper burns hot but then cools down. His is slower to build, and slower to fade. He can keep it going for days, weeks and even months. I couldn't take it any longer. That's why I've gone to live with Serge. I'll be back in touch and tell you more when I can. When all this is over and we can breathe again.

Delia had to read those last sentences several times. Live with Serge? The idea whipped through her like a gale-force wind. Setting the letters down, Delia looked desperately around the room, searching for something that would anchor her again. There was nothing.

Still shaken, she was about to return the box to its shelf when she noticed lined sheets of paper peeking out from the pile and instantly recognized Sophie's writing. When Delia extracted them from the pile, she saw that they had perforated edges—the missing diary pages. The diary was still in her possession, hidden in her closet; she had not looked at it in years. She remembered how badly she'd wanted to know what was in those missing pages. Now she would get her wish.

I've decided to leave. There, the words are out now. Real. Not just in my mind, but here on a page in this book. They declare an intention. A challenge that I have to meet. I know that leaving will break Simon's heart, and I wish I didn't have to do that. But not leaving will break mine, and in the end, I have to save myself. I never expected to feel this way about another man, I didn't plan it, or go looking for it. But it happened, and I can't undo it. I worry about Delia, but she's a strong girl, stronger than me, stronger than Simon. She'll get through this. And because of her, Simon will get through it as well. It will be better for her to stay with him. Better for all of us. We'll still be able to see each other, of course I want that. But if I want to live with Serge, I can't have her too, it will never work. She'll hate him and he'll resent her and, ultimately, me. None of us will be happy. At least this way, two of us will. And Delia, she'll be able to understand it one day. Not right away. But in the future. The war has made everything more complicated; it's blown apart all of our plans, so we've been revising them, even making them up as we go along. For now, the goal is to head south, and then to Spain. We'll be safe there. I haven't told Simon yet; I haven't been able to. But I will, and very soon.

Sophie had filled in all the blanks. But how had Simon come to have these pages? And why had he kept Sophie's plans from Delia?

Painful as it would have been, knowing would have been better. Delia put the box back where she'd found it, keeping the letters and diary pages. She would read them all again, but not here. She had to get out of this room; it reeked with her father's deceit. And there was something else too: the memory of Mrs. McQuaid's face, standing outside the car where Delia and Ian had been kissing. The hurt she must have felt was like the hurt Delia was feeling now, imagining her mother in love with someone else, ready to leave her family for him. Maybe Delia deserved this pain. After all, she'd caused it in someone else.

Downstairs, Delia ignored the overgrown tangle at the back of her own house; it seemed to mirror her family's chaos. Instead, she looked over the fence to the orderly beds and neatly swept paths of the Frosts' garden. Things were growing already. The sight made her feel calmer, and she took several deep and steadying breaths. She still had so many questions, and what she'd just read only added to the list. Her father wouldn't be able to answer them; she knew that. No, the answers were somewhere else: Paris. Yes, that was it. It was April now; her father would be home by the beginning of May. Classes at Barnard ended in May, so she could tell Simon the semester was over and that she was planning a trip. Ever since she was expelled, she'd been treading water, trying to figure out what to do next. Now she knew. The very next day, she went uptown to West Thirty-Eighth Street, where the office of the French line was located. She was the first one through the door, and by ten o'clock she had booked her passage.

Exactly two months later, on June 15, Delia arrived in Paris for the first time since she'd fled seven years before. The city looked grayer and drabber than she remembered. More worn down. And it felt both familiar and strange at the same time. Sitting in the taxi that took her to the hotel she'd booked, she recognized the names of so many streets from the past, but she herself was so different. The girl she'd been when this was her home was gone.

The cab stopped in front of the hotel, and the cabbie helped her take her bags into the lobby. There were only two, one large and one small. She didn't know how long she would be staying, and if she needed anything else, it would be easier just to buy it.

Hotel Delambre was in Montparnasse, not far from where she'd grown up on the rue Vavin, and she spent the first couple of days traversing the streets she'd known so well. The past was all around her, shimmering in the distance, or close by, breathing softly at her neck. Familiar Métro stations, landmarks that she'd visited or passed a hundred times, even the sound of French being spoken everywhere, summoned her memories. They hovered alongside her wherever she went; there was no avoiding them.

Not everything was familiar though; there were differences. Shops she remembered were now gone, sometimes replaced by others or else just boarded up and empty, a reminder that the people who'd once occupied them were now gone too. She wondered what had happened to them, if they'd managed to survive the war.

But she was intent on finding out more about what had happened to her mother; she had to know. And then there was the sculpture, which was another aspect of her mother's personality and life, not the often distracted or mercurial mother Sophie had actually been. Not the mother who had abandoned Delia or the mother who'd betrayed Simon. No, she wanted to find the mother who'd created that nesting pair of faces, the mother who felt so close to her daughter that she'd shaped a form containing them both.

Late on the second day of her walking, Delia went in search of Marie-Pierre's apartment on the rue Saint-Sulpice. It took her a few minutes to find the six-story limestone building with the sheared-off corner. There were terraces in that spot, and she remembered standing at the iron railing, looking down at the city while her mother and

Marie-Pierre talked, talked, talked inside. Now the building seemed dirtier than Delia remembered, and one of those iron railings—the one below Marie-Pierre's apartment—was broken. Delia found her name still on the bell; so she hadn't moved. But when she rang, there was no answer, and she soon left. She tried again the next day, but this time, when there was no response, she decided to wait at a café on the corner. After a while she saw a woman she thought she recognized at the door to the building; she was carrying a string bag in one hand and using the other to rummage for her key. Delia jumped up, leaving her unfinished café au lait on the table along with a few coins.

"Marie-Pierre!" she called out.

Startled, Marie-Pierre dropped the bag, and Delia dove to pick it up and hand it to her.

"C'est toi, Sophie? Is that really you?" Marie-Pierre spoke in French, which Delia felt quite comfortable with, after the few days she had been in Paris.

"Non. C'est Delia. Sophie's daughter."

"Mon dieu!" Marie-Pierre stared for a moment. "You look so much like your mother for a moment that I thought it was she, even though I know that's not possible. *Ce n'est pas possible.* Come upstairs, let's talk."

Once inside, Marie-Pierre brought her to a room that appeared to be a parlor and also a workspace; there was a tilted table at one end, and next to it stood a small cart that held jars of ink, pens, and brushes. On the walls, ink-drawn fashion illustrations had been tacked up by their corners—a woman with a flouncy dress and parasol, another in a hooded cape, and many others. Delia remembered now that Marie-Pierre had been an artist and illustrator; she and Sophie had moved in the same circles.

"I'm shocked to see you," said Marie-Pierre. "When did you get here?" She had produced a bottle of wine and poured a glass for each of them.

"Just a couple of days ago." Delia took a sip. "Can you tell me about the last time you saw my mother?"

"That fall of 1940, the one right after the occupation began. She was horrified that the French were cooperating with the Germans. Sophie was very attached to France. She always said that coming to Paris felt like coming home."

Delia remembered that too.

"She was already talking about the Resistance. Serge was an early member, and she wanted to join as well." Then she stopped talking, studying Delia's face for—what, exactly? "You knew about Serge?"

"Yes. I know about Serge." Delia didn't say how she knew, and Marie-Pierre didn't ask.

"Toute façon, I heard that they got involved early on, and that they, well, your mother really, became essential to the movement." Marie-Pierre had finished her wine and poured herself another glass; she tipped the bottle in Delia's direction, but Delia shook her head. "Once she became immersed in that work, I didn't see her. None of her friends from outside the group did. Later I heard that someone within the group was working for the other side. She and Serge were both found out, and—well, you know the rest."

Delia left Marie-Pierre's apartment in a daze. Not knowing how her mother had died was a quiet torment, but there was no way for her to find out. What she *could* find out was what had happened to the sculpture. She set out for Mercier & Girard, the moving and storage company on the boulevard Raspail. The area was one where many artists lived, and she tried to remember if she'd been here before. That little bar on the corner with the green-and-white awning—had she sat at one of those outdoor tables while her parents shared a bottle of wine? Or maybe she and Sophie had stepped into the little boutique that sold knitted and crocheted garments? There was a black sweater in the window with lavish crochet work at the neck and lapels; it had tiny red buttons and was certainly something Sophie would have liked. Several more shops were empty or boarded up, reminding Delia once again that the wounds of the war hadn't healed yet.

Finally she reached the big brick building of the warehouse, but saw nothing that would help her take the next steps. She stared at the sign, which now hung from a single corner. Several of its letters were missing. She tried ringing the bell; it emitted a weak, faraway sound. No reply, so she walked around the perimeter of the building. Occasionally she jumped up to try to see inside, but the windows were high, and dirty besides. As she stood there catching her breath, she spied a wooden crate and brought it over to the window. Now she could climb up to look inside. But a prolonged view of the interior was as disappointing as those glimpses had been. The big space was empty.

"They're long gone," said a voice behind her.

Delia turned to see an old man with a fat little dog on a leash. "Do you know where?"

He shrugged. "No."

"Maybe you know when?"

"I can't say exactly. But it was a few years ago already. While the Boches were still here." He spat on the ground, and the little dog looked alarmed. "Stuff scattered all over the street. What a mess."

"Stuff?" Delia got down from the crate. "What sort of stuff?" Had it included Sophie's sculpture?

"Eh, I wouldn't know." He tugged on the leash and walked away, the dog waddling beside him.

In addition to the invoice, Delia had a list of three storage companies that the telephone directory listed in or near Montparnasse; she spent the rest of the day calling or visiting all of them. It was a futile effort. None of the places had any records of her mother's sculpture, and two of them had not even heard of her.

The day had grown hot, and Delia was now sweaty, tired, and discouraged. She found herself walking along the boulevard de Montparnasse, where she had walked so many times. She slowed when she came to La Coupole and stood for a moment in front of the entrance to the celebrated and vast brasserie. The red awning with its sans serif lettering was the same. And the two women walking in—one in a tight black skirt, fishnet stockings, and frilly white sleeveless blouse, the other in a halter dress with a pattern of sunflowers all over it—looked like the kind of customers she remembered. There had been so many dinners here, either alone with her parents or with their lively entourage; they always ordered the onion soup, a tower of fresh seafood, and a platter of oysters. Delia had loved the oysters and devoured them greedily when they were set before her; the waiters had been tickled by how she, such a little girl, could eat so many and with such apparent delight.

The maître d' saw her standing there. "Voulez-vous entrer, mademoiselle?" No, she did not want to come inside. She shook her head vigorously and hurried along the boulevard until she came to the Café de la Rotonde, another place they had frequented. This time she walked by quickly without stopping. Nor did she stop at Le Dôme, but why would she? That was the place where the English speakers gathered, and her parents never went there; they held it in disdain. She kept walking, almost without volition headed not to the Métro station but toward the rue Vavin.

Here too were the empty stores emblematic of this new postwar Paris. The seamstress Sophie had used was gone, and so was the cobbler. But these were not just boarded-over shops; Delia had known the owners, the seamstress with her head of very tight red ringlets and her pumps with bows in the front, the cobbler who always managed to produce, from somewhere amid the heaps of shoes and boots piled on the counter, a single foil-wrapped caramel, which he presented to Delia with a flourish. But then she saw that some shops still remained:

her mother's favorite patisserie, the butcher, the newsstand where her father bought his packs of Gauloises and the daily edition of *Le Figaro*.

Soon enough she came to number 26. It looked the same as it had when she had lived in the neighborhood: seven impressive stories, crisp white tiles, contrasting blue details, and a stepped structure that had been designed to let more air and light into the apartments. Delia's family had lived on the third floor; who was living in what had been their apartment now? Gabrielle had been on the fifth floor, and the two girls were always running up and down the stairs to visit each other. Delia looked up to the windows she knew had been Gabrielle's. Could she still be here, or if not, was her family?

Just then someone left the building, and Delia slipped through the open door and took the elevator up to the fifth floor. Rapping sharply on the door, she waited. The sound of footsteps grew louder, and when the door was opened, there stood Gaby—taller and with shorter hair, parted on the side, but Delia recognized her instantly.

"May I help—" She stopped and threw up her hands. "Delia! Is that you? I can't believe it. Come in, come in!" They hugged, and Gaby stepped aside. Delia recognized the marble-topped chest in the entryway, the gilt mirror above it, the round Chinese rug on the floor. "It's been so long. I didn't think I'd ever see you again."

Delia sat in the small kitchen she remembered so well. The same copper pots hanging above the stove, the same checkered dishcloth on a hook near the sink. Gaby was slicing a baguette and setting out cheese and ham when a little boy burst into the room and flung himself at her knees.

"Félix! So you're awake, are you? That was quite a nap that you had." She scooped him into her arms; he put his head on her shoulder and his thumb in his mouth.

"Is he—" Surprised, Delia looked from the boy's face to Gaby's and back again.

Gaby nodded. "He's mine. I was just going to tell you."

"Are you . . . married?"

"I was. Do you remember Christophe Fornier?"

"From school?" Delia recalled a tall, awkward boy who hardly ever said a word. He had been a year or two ahead of them, not one of their friends or companions.

"Yes. Well, after I graduated, I would see him around the neighborhood, and we started spending time together. . . . He was really very sweet once you got to know him."

"I never would have guessed that you two—I mean, we barely even noticed him." She didn't add that when they had, it was to make fun of him.

"Neither would I. But he was different outside of school. And of course, we were both older by then. We fell in love and got married. That was in 1944. November. We found a little place of our own, just a few blocks from here. Despite everything, we were happy. In the spring, he was drafted. The war was almost over by then, and so we thought he'd be home very soon. But he didn't come home at all."

"Oh Gaby!" Delia took her hand and pressed it hard. "I'm so sorry."

"I miss him terribly. Still, he left me a gift—a miracle, really." Gaby kissed the top of Félix's head. "This little one saved me. I don't know what I would have done without him. Félix, do you want to say hello to my old friend Delia?" Félix sucked harder on his thumb and didn't answer. "I moved back here after he was born. Papa had died by then and Maman was alone. So it seemed like the best thing to do."

"Where is your mother?" Delia asked. "I'd love to see her."

"She died last year," said Gaby. "She was never the same after she lost my father." There was a silence, and then Gaby asked, "And what about you?" She sat down at the table, repositioning Félix in her lap. "You went to New York, yes? Is it as exciting as people say? And how are your parents?"

To her own surprise, Delia started to cry—to wail, really, with great, heaving sobs. She almost never cried. But Gaby had known her when she was young and innocent; she was still young, but her innocence had turned to ash.

"Delia! What's wrong?!"

Delia told her the story, every single, shameful bit: her mother's disappearance, her affair with Ian, getting expelled from Vassar, the letters she'd found from her mother, and her current search for the lost sculpture.

Gaby listened quietly before she said, "You've lost so much."

"So have you."

Somehow this mutual acknowledgment—and recognition—was more comforting than Delia would have expected, and once she'd calmed down and the tears stopped, she felt more hopeful than she had in a long while.

TEN

ANNE

1947

In late August Anne sailed to Europe on a large ocean liner that had seen better days. An outdated brochure showed photographs of its first-class dining room, lounge, grill room, swimming pool, theater, and winter garden. But the ship had been used as part of the war effort, and the present reality did not live up to the travel agent's promises. Yes, there were still spectacular entryways, grand rooms, and long, wide staircases, but everything, from the stained carpets to the frayed draperies, had a battered, beaten-down air. Anne's room was spacious and well-appointed, but the drawers of both bureaus were missing knobs, the dressing table surface was scratched, and every time she sat in either of the faded velvet armchairs, the cushions exhaled small clouds of dust.

None of this really mattered, though; she was consumed by seasickness and spent much of the trip either vomiting or trying hard not to. It was better when she was on deck, where the wide expanse of sky above and the dark, glittering ocean below calmed her stomach. On a couple of occasions she parked herself in a wooden deck chair and, covered by several blankets, slept there all night long. Finally, after seven interminable days, the ship docked in Le Havre, where she boarded the train that would take her to Paris.

Paris! The very word was magical. Her nausea mercifully gone, Anne now felt invigorated, as if she'd just woken up from a fevered sleep. She sat by the train's window, riveted by even the most commonplace of sights—a tangle of bushes, a wooden fence, a willow tree, a flock of small, dark birds whose name she did not know. These were *French* bushes, a *French* fence, *French* birds, and so were special in ways that were not quite apparent to her but would be soon enough.

The dormitory where the foreign students were housed was on the Left Bank, and as she tried to get her bearings during those first few days, Anne saw street names she recognized—rue du Bac and rue Madame were just two of them. Delia had mentioned those streets, and others too. Delia: she seemed to be everywhere in Paris, hovering at the periphery of Anne's awareness. Anne could easily imagine that Delia had played in the Tuileries and the Jardin du Luxembourg and licked a *glace au chocolat* while strolling along the rue de Rivoli. Delia had stood in front of the paintings at the Jeu de Paume, had looked down from the Eiffel Tower, walked briskly across the Pont de Neuf. Delia's imaginary presence was a small torment, and one Anne had not expected. The vast distance between them did nothing to erase the knowledge that she had behaved shamefully. But there was nothing she could do about it now. Her name had been on the letter the dean received, and as they had all expected, Delia had been asked to leave Vassar. Virginia had gleefully reported this to the rest of them. Anne told herself that she had to put this out of her mind. If not, Paris would be ruined for her.

The city seemed a little shabbier than she had imagined, and dirtier too; the war had taken its toll. It had a slightly ravaged beauty that shone through, perhaps because, and not despite of, the suffering it had endured. There were still the wide, spacious avenues, the enduring majesty of the old buildings. Unlike London, Paris had surrendered to the Nazis and thus had not been bombed—the gardens, the plazas and squares, remained untouched. And she felt an excitement, even a giddiness, in the air. People seemed so happy to be engaging in the ordinary life of the city. Young women hurried along the cobblestone streets and down the steps leading to the Métro. Were they off to work? To meet friends, or perhaps boyfriends? A couple sat ignoring their *steak frites* in a bistro, instead holding hands and leaning over to whisper to each other. Two silver-haired ladies, one in a dark dress and the other in a bright-red one, were sitting close together at a marble-topped round table and chatting amiably. A solemn-eyed baby in a starched bonnet surveyed the world from her vantage point in a shiny black pram; three little girls in navy pinafores, jackets, and berets skipped down the street, one of them holding a yellow balloon, buoyant and bright against the gray of the sky.

Bakeries and patisseries propped open their doors, enticing potential customers with the smells of butter, vanilla, cinnamon, and caramel; charcuteries displayed their cured meats and their pâtés, *fromageries* sold cheeses she'd never tasted—never even heard of—in an impressive array of geometric shapes: wheels, wedges, blocky rectangles or squares. She passed shop windows filled with chic hats trimmed in flowers, ribbons, or both, with handbags and shoes of the softest, most supple leather. Here was a store that sold only handkerchiefs, the merest scraps of printed or embroidered cotton and silk, lavish lace trimming their borders; another sold perfume, silk stockings galore—no more rationing!—satin slips, brassieres and tap pants, umbrellas, gloriously patterned scarves, and jewelry. And then there were the Parisian clothes—dresses, suits, coats, and sweaters in fabrics and styles that surpassed anything Anne had ever seen or tried on before. She'd seen a photograph in *Harper's Bazaar* in which a model, viewed from behind, was caught as she walked across the place de la Concorde, her full, flared skirt opening out around her like petals stirred by a breeze. Delia had worn a suit in that style the last time Anne had seen her, in the dining room at Vassar. Although they hadn't spoken that night, Delia's expression seemed to say that she knew Anne had betrayed her.

While Anne was falling in love with Paris as so many Americans had before her, Paris also engendered in her a kind of melancholy she hadn't expected, something that had nothing to do with Delia. Try as she might, she felt she would never measure up to the glamour and sophistication with which the women here seemed to have been born. She'd hoped that if she came here, some of it might rub off on her. Her French was improving, but her accent was still poor—there were sounds, like the *r*'s that came from deep in the throat, that she simply couldn't master. And keeping up in her classes—all taught in French—was more of a struggle than she'd imagined. She'd met very few actual natives; the French students were intimidating or else seemed tightly bonded to each other, with little interest in outsiders like Anne. The dorm where she lived was filled with American students like herself. At least she was able to make some friends among them, chiefly her new roommate, Nancy Gilchrist. Nancy's French was even worse than Anne's, but to Anne's surprise, it didn't seem to bother her at all. She spoke gamely and without any apparent embarrassment to waiters, shopkeepers, museum guards, and anyone else who crossed her path. There was something refreshing about Nancy's ease with herself; this, along with her affable nature and her ready smile—punctuated with a single dimple on one side—was a balm to Anne's own insecurities, and she was able to relax in her new friend's company. Nancy came from Portsmouth, New Hampshire, and didn't know any of the girls Anne had known in New York—another reason Anne could let down her guard a bit. So when Anne decided she wanted to explore the vast *marché aux puces* that she remembered Delia talking about, she invited Nancy to go with her.

After consulting her guidebook, she led the way to the Métro, which they rode to the Porte de Clignancourt station. When they emerged, they found themselves at the Puces de Saint-Ouen, which the guidebook listed as "the oldest and largest antique market in Paris." According to the book, it was best to walk along the rue des Rosiers, so that was what they did, stopping at the Marché Malassis, where a menagerie's worth of porcelain animals—lions, monkeys, bears, rabbits, dogs, and more—were lined up as if waiting to board the ark. On the next table was an elaborate three-story dollhouse filled with exquisitely crafted miniature furnishings, and then they came to the Marché Dauphine, crammed with brocade sofas, gleaming dining tables, and row upon row of chairs, and farther on, the Marché Biron—chandeliers dripping crystals, an imposing pair of alabaster lamps. They passed stalls selling long-stemmed wineglasses, goblets, pitchers, and vases; sterling flatware and platters; stacks of gold-rimmed plates, delicate teacups and saucers. Anne, who had grown up in a realm of plenty, was still dazzled, even overwhelmed, by the sheer volume. Finally they came to Marché Vernaison. "We're here," Anne said.

"Where?" Nancy looked around at the tables piled high with clothing, and the hangers from which were suspended everything from ball gowns to nineteenth-century bathing costumes.

"Exactly where we want to be." Anne remembered what Delia had told her about shopping here with her mother. "Come on." Nancy didn't move for a moment, so Anne took her arm. How unusual that she, for once, was the leader. She made her way methodically through the mounds of clothing—a billowing cape, silk blouses in shreds, cashmere sweaters sporting holes small and large, embellished with beads or sequins, dresses in styles popular ten, twenty, forty years ago. Nancy was happy to follow in her wake, even though she clearly thought that some of what caught Anne's eye was peculiar at best.

"You'd wear that?" she asked as Anne held up a paisley silk robe.

"Why not?" Anne thought the colors—garnet, shot through with bits of orange, black, and lapis—were beautiful.

"Well, for one thing it's a man's robe."

"So what?" Anne slipped the robe on over her dress and jacket, just as Delia had done on that day when they shopped together.

"You know, it looks good on you." Nancy was nodding her head approvingly. "It really does." She picked up another silk robe, this one a deep burgundy enlivened by a pattern of small white dots. "Who'd have thought a man's robe would look so good on a girl?" She slipped on the robe; the dark color flattered her complexion. "Let's get both of them. We can wear them together in the dorm. The other girls will be very impressed!" They bought the robes, as well as pairs of tight-fitting gloves, shiny black satin for Anne and brown suede for Nancy. They also tried on over a dozen hats each, and Nancy chose one of black felt with a jaunty red bow while Anne came away with one made of pale pink straw, embellished by an even paler pink ribbon held in place by a cluster of blue silk hydrangeas. "Are you sure you want that one?" Nancy asked. "You won't wear it for months."

"It's worth the wait," Anne said. By this time the light was fading and the wind had picked up. They stopped at a patisserie where they bought a box of éclairs and devoured all of them, sticky and delicious, on the Métro ride back to the dorm. It was the best day Anne had spent in Paris since arriving.

It poured for almost a solid week after their excursion, one soggy, rain-soaked day following another. It was late September, a month Anne had always associated with bright, crisp days, but here in Paris the weather was gloomy and depressing, engendering a wave of homesickness she hadn't expected to feel. But after five days, the skies finally cleared. Or at least it was no longer raining, and when Nancy suggested a day trip to Chartres, Anne was more than ready to join her. They took an early train from the Gare Montparnasse, eating the buttered tartines they had bought at the station along the way. Anne thought back to the photographs of the cathedral she'd seen in Art 105–106, the light streaming down from above, illuminating—and transforming—whatever it touched.

There was a ten-minute walk from the train station. Chartres Cathedral, with its two mismatched towers, was the tallest structure she could see. Soon the carved facade came into view. Up close, the stone was gray, like the sky, and sooty. Would it be too gray to appreciate the brilliance of the cathedral's windows? Maybe they should have waited for a better day. But once they entered, Anne's concern dissolved. The drabness of the day could not dull the blazing effect inside. The architecture of the cathedral, with its daring combination of ribbed vaults and flying buttresses, coupled with the windows made Anne feel she'd stepped into a glowing glass palace. Cobalt and red, a lighter, celestial blue, emerald green, and a rich egg-yolk yellow—the intricate patterns seemed animate, as if the panels might begin to shift and move, like the pieces in a kaleidoscope.

They walked around the interior in silence, stopping when Nancy wanted to place a coin in a small box and light a candle. "For my grandmother," she explained. Anne lit no candles, offered no prayers. She was put off by much of the sculpture; the tall, gaunt figures seemed so mournful, even grim. But the combination of glass, light, color, and pattern was a miraculous contrast. The experience was nothing she could have anticipated.

And then Anne understood. The tortured, tragic figures rendered in stone were just the support for this—the light, which was the real exaltation, the reason the cathedral had been built. The light was forgiving, healing, and glorious. To her surprise, she found that being a Jewish girl in this splendid Christian place did not make her uncomfortable. What mattered was the feeling she had when she walked through those doors. Here was a place for everyone, not just those who adhered to a particular set of beliefs. That was what the light seemed to say, the light so enveloping and palpable that Anne felt it like a warm cloak around her.

The two girls were both quiet on the walk back to the station, and Nancy dozed for most of the ride home, giving Anne time to be alone with her thoughts. Even if the visit to the cathedral hadn't been a religious experience for her, it was nevertheless spiritual in some inchoate way, and she was touched by it. Changed, somehow. Delia might have understood. Delia. Just thinking of her made Anne feel small, even despicable.

As they pulled into the Gare Montparnasse, Nancy woke up and was her usual chatty, cheerful self all the way back to the dorm. Anne was glad; it was a welcome distraction from her own troubled thoughts. When they arrived at their dormitory, a young man wearing a thick cable-knit sweater and a bright red scarf called Nancy's name. She whirled around, and then flung herself into his arms. Anne stood back, watching. He was dark-haired, and dark-eyed too. Also handsome—the nose, the jaw. He seemed a bit older than Nancy; was he her boyfriend? If so, she'd never mentioned it.

Finally Nancy released him and started peppering him with questions. In English. "What are you doing here? Why didn't you tell me? I thought you weren't coming for another week at least."

"You didn't get my letter?"

"Letter? What letter?"

"I wrote to say that my plans had changed and I'd be here today. I was disappointed when I didn't find you. No one seemed to know when you'd be back."

"We went to Chartres today, and it was"—she turned to Anne—"how would you describe it? Are there even words? But where are my manners?" She turned back to the man. "You startled them right out of me." She squeezed his shoulder affectionately. "Drew, meet Anne."

"Pleased to meet you." Drew extended his hand, and when he smiled, Anne saw just a single dimple, on the right side of his face. Like Nancy's. What was it about that dimple that was so, well, adorable?

"Andrew's my brother," Nancy said. "He's a photographer, well, a photojournalist with the *New York Herald Tribune*, and he's just arrived. He's going to be here for the next few months. Isn't that grand?"

"Pleased to meet you, too." Anne now noticed the camera he had slung on his shoulder. It was compact and easy to overlook; he kept a hand on it protectively.

"Have you had dinner yet?" Nancy asked.

"No, and I'm starved! Let me take you to my favorite place—my treat."

"You have a favorite place already?" Anne was confused; hadn't Nancy said he'd just gotten there?

"Oh, I've been to Paris before. Several times, actually," said Drew. "So I know my way around a bit."

Drew led them confidently to Le Petit Saint Benôit, a bistro on the street of the same name in Saint-Germain-des-Prés. There were people at every single one of the tightly packed tables in the long, narrow room, and they had to wait a few minutes to get one. Anne watched as waiters hurried by, carrying three plates on each arm and setting them down before the diners; they also poured wine, whisked away dirty dishes, and adroitly managed to avoid colliding with one another.

When the three of them sat down, Drew ordered for all of them; to Anne, his accent sounded flawless. Their waiter—gruff, frowning, and with the bushiest eyebrows Anne had ever seen—wrote down the order not on a pad but right on a corner of the white paper covering the table. "He'll tear that off and total it up at the end of the meal," Drew explained. He wasn't that much older than she was—twenty-six to her twenty—but he seemed so much more sophisticated and at ease in the world.

The food arrived quickly, and everything—the roast chicken, the beef bourguignon, the apple clafouti—was uncommonly good. Was the food that good, or was it Drew? He'd been to the Soviet Union to photograph Stalin, to Dresden to photograph the ruins of the bombed-out city, to India to photograph Gandhi. "While I was there, I got sidetracked and took pictures of an elephant giving birth. You should have seen it. All the other elephants were gathered around her, like they were cheering her on. It was such an amazing thing to watch, but I thought I would get in trouble—it wasn't what I was sent to do. But my editor went crazy for the pictures and ran them as a sidebar. I was lucky he saw it that way."

"Did you always know you wanted to be a photographer?" Anne was loving all his stories; he was so widely traveled.

"I didn't even know that it was a profession, at least not the way I'm doing it. No, I went to art school in Boston. I wanted to be a painter."

"He was really good!" said Nancy. "We have his paintings and his drawings hanging all over our house."

"So what happened?" Anne asked.

"I was too restless. I just wanted to be out—outside. Looking. Seeing. One day I passed this pawnshop that was near the art school, and I saw a camera in the window but didn't go in. It was there the next time I passed, and the time after that, almost like it was waiting for me."

"Is this it?" She gestured to the camera she'd noticed when they met earlier; it was a combination of brushed metal and something black and pebbly. There were tiny numbers etched around the lens and the word *Leica*, in script, at the top.

"This?" He touched it lightly but lovingly. "No. It was a Canon. Not as sleek but still a good camera. I finally went into the shop to have a look at it, and because it was cheap, I bought it. I thought I'd just fool around, have some fun. But it turned out to be the thing I wanted to do most."

Anne drank in every word. She also drank the wine he poured without asking, and she was soon feeling tipsy. "Your French is really good," she said. "And mine is really terrible. I cringe every time I hear myself."

"It's just a matter of practice."

Anne shook her head. "No, it's more than that. You have the ear. I don't, and I never will."

Drew seemed to consider that. "You may be right. We all have our qualities, don't you think? Some special talent or trait that sets us apart?" He looked straight at her. "What's yours, Anne?"

"I haven't found it yet. It's waiting for me to unlock it." The wine had erased any shyness she might have felt, and she held Drew's gaze.

"I'd like to be around when you do."

That was certainly bold, Anne thought. He continued to gaze at her with a look both curious and interested. She liked the way he seemed to be assessing her, trying to figure her out. It made her feel as if he saw something special in her. But what? She yearned to know, and even more, to see herself as he saw her—whatever that turned out to be.

ELEVEN

DELIA

1947

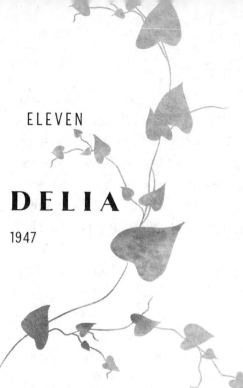

Delia stayed for dinner at Gaby's, and because they had stayed up so late talking, Gaby invited her to spend the night. She offered Delia her room, but Delia said she'd be fine on the sofa. Sometime before dawn, she heard Félix calling *Maman, Maman*, in a sleepy, plaintive voice; a moment later, she heard Gaby shuffling in to comfort him. Delia and Gaby were the same age, but Gaby's life had moved on; she was someone's mother, and that gave her a direction and purpose Delia lacked. Maybe it was because of her own mother's death, or the missing sculpture? The losses were in Delia's way, impeding her path forward. All the more reason to find out what had become of Sophie's work so that she too could get on with her life.

The next morning, Delia planned to go back to her hotel to change her clothes.

"Why stay in a hotel when you can stay with me?" Gaby asked.

"Are you sure? I don't want to put you out."

"I'm sure," said Gaby. "You can get your things and come back tonight."

Delia was grateful; staying here would ease her sense of dislocation and sadness. Over the next few days, she canvassed other storage companies elsewhere in the city but these efforts were, like the first one, in vain. Then she expanded her search to suburbs like Saint-Denis and Asnières. Reaching the storage companies by telephone was inefficient and haphazard: someone put the phone down to check something and never returned, or she was abruptly cut off in the middle of a call. So she decided to try an in-person visit; perhaps she would have more luck that way.

It drizzled on and off the day she went to Saint-Denis. She picked her way through the wet streets and occasional puddle until she found the moving company, which seemed like it was kilometers away from the train station. Delia had high hopes for this place; the woman she'd spoken with said they had acquired some lots from Mercier & Girard when the Parisian company had gone out of business.

But when she finally did reach the warehouse, she was turned away. No, she could not come in and look around. It was against all rules and protocols. She left the office, discouraged. Maybe there was a way she could sneak in, but would that help? The storage units would be locked, she knew that. Still she waited for a while, out of sight, until she saw the snippy woman from the front office leave the building. Then she tried the back door, and another on the side. It was useless. Both doors, like the front, were locked. There was nothing to be done but head to the station and catch the train back to Paris.

The futility of the search had begun to grind her down, so she decided to take a little break. Gaby had a part-time job in a bookshop, and Delia offered to watch Félix, taking the little boy to places she had loved when she was young, like the zoo in Vincennes, the Jardin des Tuileries, and the carousel near the train station in Montparnasse, where Félix rode on a sky-blue horse, or the one at Sacré-Coeur, where they spun around in a giant teacup. Being with the boy made her think of the time she'd spent watching Vi and Dot, Ian's little girls; she imagined they might have started to walk and talk by now. Would they remember her? Did she even want them to? No, it was their father she wanted to remember her. *Stop it*, she scolded herself. *Stop it right now*. But though she could eject Ian from her waking thoughts, the nights were a different matter entirely; he was a regular presence in her dreams. In some of them, he was excoriating her, telling her what a terrible girl she was in front of a crowd of people—at Vassar? Somewhere else? In others, she would be calling out to him and he'd ignore her completely, striding by, or even shoving her aside. But the most painful ones were those in which they were kissing as he unbuttoned her blouse and reached under her skirt.

One Sunday afternoon she and Félix were slowly making their way back to the rue Vavin when Delia noticed a small piece of sculpture in a gallery window. Although it first appeared be an abstract form, she saw that it was actually the body of a woman—a pregnant woman. It was made of a gleaming, brownish-red stone that Delia wanted to touch. Had the gallery been open, she would have gone inside for a closer look; as it was, she could only stand in front of the window until Félix tugged on her hand. "Allons-y," he whined. "Je dois faire pee pee."

"Of course. We're going right now." She turned away from the window.

The next day Delia left the apartment early, intent on returning to the gallery. She couldn't stop thinking about that sculpture, its cunning shape, its lustrous surface. It was drizzling again, but in her haste to leave she'd forgotten to take an umbrella. Well, so what? She wasn't going back to get one. Her long, swift strides brought her there quickly, and the rain was tapering off. She went inside.

There was the statue, just where it had been the day before. Up close, she could see that the stone, which was highly polished, had subtle variations in color, darker in some places and paler, with an almost milky vein running through it, in others. It was a lovely thing, compact and unadorned yet utterly complete. She had been so taken with it that she hadn't even looked to see the name of the artist, but she was curious and now looked down at the label.

Sophie Rossner
Mother
Carnelian, 1946

Blood rushed to Delia's head, and she heard a whoosh, a roaring in her ears. No wonder she had been so drawn to it. But the date—how was that possible? It was a mistake. Marie-Pierre said she thought Sophie had been shot in 1942 or 1943.

"Isn't it a beautiful little piece?"

Delia turned to see a woman in a chic black dress and rhinestone pin.

"So simple, yet so sophisticated," added the woman.

"Where did you get this?" The roaring in Delia's ears had grown louder.

"Excuse me?" The woman looked slightly affronted.

"This piece of sculpture—where did it come from? How did you manage to get hold of it?" Delia was aware of how agitated she sounded.

"I'd have to look up the provenance," said the woman. "But I can assure you it's here legitimately. We have impeccable records and take great care to authenticate all of our pieces—"

"It's the date. The date is wrong."

"I highly doubt that, though as I said, I can check." Her tone was frosty.

"It doesn't matter what your records say. It can't be right."

"And why is that?"

"Because Sophie Rossner was killed during the war."

The woman looked at Delia as if she were deranged. "I think you have been misinformed, mademoiselle. Sophie Rossner is most certainly not dead."

"How would you know?"

"Because I've seen her. Recently."

"You have? Where?" The roaring in Delia's ears stopped all at once, replaced by an eerie, terrible quiet.

"Why, right here, mademoiselle. Right where you're standing. She's been to the gallery."

"She's been here? When?"

"I don't remember the exact date, but not all that long ago—late last year, I think. It was in the winter."

"Do you have an address for her? Or a telephone number?"

"She doesn't live in Paris."

"Then where does she live?"

"I'm not at liberty to give out that information to just anyone."

"I'm not just anyone," Delia said. "I'm her daughter."

"You?" The woman seemed skeptical. "I didn't know she had a daughter."

"Yes. Me."

"Mademoiselle, I don't wish to be rude, but you seem . . . troubled. I think it would be best if you were to leave now."

"I'm sorry, I didn't mean to—"

"Please." The woman gave her a stern look. "I'd like you to leave immediately. And if you don't, I'll need to get someone to help me escort you out."

"I can prove that I'm Sophie Rossner's daughter. I'll bring you my passport!"

"Your passport?"

"Yes, my passport." As the woman considered the idea, Delia's mind began exploding with questions. How could this be possible? Had Marie-Pierre been mistaken? Then there were the letters—they were from a few years ago. Could there have been others that Delia never received? Or since Delia hadn't written back, could Sophie have stopped trying?

"Well, that might be all right . . ."

"I'll go get it." Now she had two reasons to hurry back to Gaby's apartment—the passport *and* the letters. She had brought them with her and wanted to read them yet again. Maybe there was something she'd overlooked, something she hadn't fully understood.

So chaotic were her thoughts that she barely registered the two people, a young man and woman, who had just come into the gallery, and she bumped right into them. *Oh, I beg your pardon*, she was about to say, but the words never left her mouth. Standing in front of her was Anne Bishop, the girl who'd betrayed her.

TWELVE

ANNE

1947

It was eight o'clock on a Sunday morning, and Anne had already been up for almost two hours, hours during which she'd finished all the assignments due for this week's classes, brushed her hair until it shone like a gleaming cap, and changed her outfit three times, finally settling on a plaid skirt and matching vest worn over a silk blouse with a pussycat bow at the neck. The bow just peeked out from the collar of her coat, and Anne thought the effect was very pretty. She quietly gathered her hat, gloves, and handbag; Nancy was still sleeping, and Anne hoped she could slip out of the room before she woke. But just as her hand turned the doorknob, Nancy sat up in bed. "Where are you going?"

"For a walk." She had wanted to avoid a direct question like this.

"So early?" Nancy's hair was sticking up on one side and squashed flat on the other; she patted it tentatively.

"It seems like a nice day."

"Does it?" Nancy turned her gaze to the window. The sky outside was gray and filled with clouds.

"Well, I was just feeling restless, and—"

"You're meeting my brother, aren't you?"

"Why do you ask that?"

"Because you've met him at least once a week for the last month. Or is it month and a half?"

Anne didn't know what to say. That she had a crush on Nancy's older brother was obvious, but until now, she hadn't thought Nancy minded. And as if Nancy had read her thoughts, she tossed a cushion in Anne's direction and laughed. "I know you're crazy for him," she said. "And it looks like he's pretty sweet on you. You haven't told each other yet?"

Anne felt her face getting hot; she retrieved the cushion, which had landed in a corner. Was Drew really "sweet on her"? "He has the day off, so we're going to the Louvre," she said. "You could come with us."

"Mmm, not now." Nancy settled back down into the bedclothes. "I'm still sleepy. But let's meet later. How about three o'clock at Les Deux Magots?"

Anne left the dorm and walked the few blocks to Drew's hotel. As she walked, she kept looking up at the clouds, dark and threatening. Too bad she'd been so eager to rush to leave that she hadn't thought to take an umbrella. Just then it really did start to rain, lightly at first and then more heavily. She quickened her pace.

Rounding the corner, she saw she needn't have worried; there stood Drew with a wide smile and an even wider black umbrella in one hand, with ample room under it for two. His Leica was on a strap and slung over his shoulder, and in his other hand he held a small bunch of flowers in a waxed cone.

"Good morning!" he called out, and when she'd gotten close enough, he handed the flowers to her.

"Thank you." She looked down at the small bunch of violets, their velvety purple blossoms, their tiny yellow centers, each one as bright as a spark. He'd bought her flowers! Surely that meant he was indeed sweet on her. But she could read nothing different in his eyes; he could have been a doting older brother or a favorite cousin offering this gift. She couldn't tell. "They're beautiful. Maybe we should put them in water and leave them in your apartment. We could get them later."

"I have a better idea." He extracted the violets from the paper and fastened them to the lapel of her coat with a pin he'd pulled from his pocket. "There—that's perfect."

Anne thought *he* was perfect. Sheltered by the wide black silk dome, they set off for the Louvre. Since it was so early, they stopped for café crème and croissants and then waited by the entrance of the museum until it opened. Anne had been here several times before, and had seen many of the most famous works of art—the Nike of Samothrace, the *Mona Lisa*, *The Wedding at Cana*—and so was happy to follow Drew into rooms where lesser-known works were hanging.

She stood in front of a painting by Piero di Cosimo that showed the Virgin Mary and the infant Jesus. Drew walked over to join her. "Do you like it?"

"I do," said Anne. "She seems thoughtful. Sad. And she's not looking at the baby, not even holding him very tightly. It's almost like she's not sure that he's hers."

"I see what you mean."

Anne felt encouraged, so the art history student in her continued. "Maybe she's thinking about the future. *His* future—nailed to a cross, the crown of thorns still on his head, the awful men who give him vinegar when he asks for water and who play dice for his clothes."

"That could be." Drew was looking at her intently.

"And then there's the dove." Anne pointed to the white bird in the bottom right corner of the painting.

"What about it?"

"Well, it's a symbol of the Annunciation—I know that—but I also think the artist just really liked painting it. Look at how deftly he's done the tail."

"You're right. When I was painting, I never could get the texture of feathers. It always eluded me somehow, though God knows I tried."

"Maybe the camera is better for that."

"Not better. Just different. Paintbrush, camera—they're both tools."

He moved away to look at another painting across the room. Anne remained where she was, not quite ready to move on. She loved Renaissance painting. Almost all the imagery was religious, but it was nothing like the religious imagery that came just before. In the medieval period Jesus was a judge, either standing or sitting on a throne, intent on sending people to heaven or hell. Even when he was supposed to be a child, he didn't look remotely like one. He was that same stern, imposing figure, only smaller. Anne thought of the figures she'd seen at Chartres; compared to this pensive mother and plump naked baby, they were abstractions, austere and impenetrable, not real people with whom she could empathize and whose emotions she could understand.

"You're still here." Drew had wandered back over to where she stood.

"Still here." She wasn't done looking, wasn't done seeing. What she was thinking—but not saying—was that despite being Jewish, she found all this religious imagery, this *Christian* imagery, so resonant. Jews took the injunction about graven images very seriously; their visual tradition didn't include any human figures. But looking at all these painted characters, the whole arc of life from birth to death, made Anne think this rule was a limitation, even a loss. Besides, Mary and Jesus, along with Joseph and all the characters in that story, were Jews, a fact that had somehow been obscured over time.

When they emerged from the museum, they found that the rain had stopped and the sun was making a valiant effort to shine. Since they still had time before they met Nancy, they decided to stroll across the Pont Neuf to the Left Bank. Below, the Seine was dark, the inky blue almost black, but above, a faint rainbow arced over the tops of the buildings; Anne wanted to read it as a sign, though of what she wasn't sure. Something good, though.

They came to the window of an art gallery, and Anne noticed a small piece of sculpture, its reddish-brown stone polished and shining. "Can we stop?" she asked.

"Of course."

They went inside so Anne could get a closer look. At first it looked like an abstract form, but wait, wasn't that a face, and the curve of a body—oof! Someone had slammed right into her, and her hands flew to her shoulder, throbbing from the impact. She looked up to see who had been in such a hurry and was astonished to see that the someone was Delia Goldhush.

For a moment no one spoke. Then Drew asked Anne, "Are you all right?"

"I'm fine," said both Anne and Delia, almost at the same time.

"Then what—"

But for once, Anne ignored Drew and gave all her attention to Delia. "What a surprise to see you here."

"It's hardly a happy one," Delia said coldly.

"I know, and I just wanted to say . . ." But Anne *didn't* know what she wanted to say. She fell silent.

"To say what? I saw your name on that letter. I know you were part of it."

Anne couldn't utter a word, or believe that this confrontation, which she had both longed for and dreaded, was happening here, in a Parisian art gallery. Delia was still talking. ". . . getting me expelled. I might have expected it from them. But not from you. I thought we were becoming friends."

"We were!"

"Excuse me? That's your idea of friendship?"

Just then a woman in a severe black dress and glittering pin stepped in. "Ladies, what's going on here?" She looked at Delia. "Mademoiselle, I can see that you are overwrought, but I can't have you speaking this way to people who come into my gallery. I'm going to ask you again to leave."

But Delia ignored both the woman and Anne, and spoke directly to Drew. "Don't waste your time with her. She'll betray you just like she betrayed me—wait and see." And with that, she turned and marched out into the street.

Anne was aware of Drew's confusion. How could she explain this to him? Her gaze darted around the gallery, as if she could find an answer there. Then she saw the sculpture, the very thing that had drawn her eye in the first place and made her want to stop in, and she walked right up to it.

"Sophie Rossner," she said.

"What?" Drew looked puzzled.

"Sophie Rossner, that's what the label says."

"I don't understand," said Drew. "Who is Sophie Rossner, and what does she have to do with any of this?"

"The girl who just stormed out of here? That was Delia Goldhush. I knew her at school. And Sophie Rossner was her mother. She was a sculptor, and she was killed during the war."

"Did you really get her expelled?"

Anne didn't answer. All she could focus on was the extraordinary coincidence of running into Delia here, and asking herself if this piece of sculpture had something to do with it. Delia had talked about the pieces that had been left behind and gone missing. Was this one of them?

"Anne, I still don't—"

Drew didn't finish because the woman in black had joined them and began talking right over him. "I overheard your conversation, and I can assure you that Sophie Rossner is not dead, mademoiselle. She's alive and well and, the last I heard, living in Palestine. She moved there after the war—to one of those collective farms, whatever they call them. Somewhere in the south," she said. "In the desert."

"I see," said Anne. "Thank you for letting me know." She took Drew's arm and led him out of the gallery, remaining quiet as they walked toward the café where they were to meet Nancy.

"Do you want to tell me about what just happened?" Drew asked.

"It's not important," Anne lied. Upset as she felt about Delia, she was elated by the fact that Drew had taken her hand and given it a gentle squeeze. They remained hand in hand for the rest of the walk, a glowing, vital connection that made her momentarily forget Delia, forget everything but this.

Nancy was waiting for them at Deux Magots. Drew dropped Anne's hand as he sat down. Had Nancy noticed? If so, she said nothing, and the conversation moved in other directions. But later, when Anne was alone, she allowed herself to think about the encounter at the gallery. To her surprise, she found herself wanting not to flee from Delia but to seek her out. To apologize. Something had changed. Was it being here in Paris—the city where Delia had been born and raised, the city that was just beginning to open itself up and let her in—that made her want to assume responsibility for what she'd done? And as she thought about what form that apology would take, something like a plan began coalescing in her mind. The more she considered it, the more viable it seemed. It just might work, she thought. It might be a way to begin repairing her friendship with Delia.

The next day Anne returned alone to the gallery. In her navy leather handbag was a note in a sealed envelope. She had a strong feeling that Delia would come back here too. The sculpture—that was what would draw her; she wouldn't be able to stay away.

Today the gallery's owner wore a bloodred dress with white polka dots, a white collar, and big white buttons down the back. "Ah, mademoiselle, I'm so glad you came back, and that the unpleasantness yesterday didn't deter you."

Anne assured her it hadn't, and she let the woman show her around, complimenting the various works of art. And then she did something very bold, something she had told no one she was going to do: she bought the piece of sculpture made by Sophie Rossner. It was expensive, which meant that she'd have to scrimp a bit, at least for the next couple of months.

The woman in the red dress clucked and purred as she packed the sculpture securely; clearly she was very pleased by the sale. "You must take a taxi going home," she said, and Anne agreed, a taxi would be just the thing. And after the francs had changed hands and the tissue-swathed sculpture had been slipped into a burlap bag and was ready for transport, Anne pulled the envelope from her handbag and gave it to the woman. "I have a favor to ask," she said. "Two favors, actually. That girl? The one who made all the fuss? I have a strong feeling she'll be back, and if she is, would you be kind enough to give her this?"

"Mais oui," said the woman. *But of course*. Smiling, she pressed the envelope to her dress, where it stood out starkly, even brighter than the white collar.

"I'd also like an address for Sophie Rossner. You said she was living in Palestine."

The smile faded, just a bit. "Well, yes, but that's not the sort of information we usually share with the public. If you wanted to be in touch with her through me, I might be able to arrange that—"

"Oh, but I would never try to buy work from her without going through you," Anne said quickly, "if that's what you're worried about. I respect your eye too much for that. It's just that I'd love to ask her questions about her background, her work. Now that I've bought this piece, I'm interested in buying others. You do handle her work, don't you? You might be getting new pieces, and you could let me know when you do."

"In that case . . ." The woman apparently deemed this reason enough to grant Anne's request, and she went into a back room and returned a few minutes later with a slip of paper that she handed to Anne.

After taking a taxi back to the dorm, Anne unwrapped the sculpture and studied it closely. The piece was about fifteen inches high, and its reddish-brown stone had a glossy sheen, as if it had been shellacked. Now she could see that it was a pregnant woman, lush and bursting with life. The woman's face was devoid of features, so Anne couldn't read her expression, but her carved arms cradled her belly in what seemed like a protective and loving way. She wrapped it back up and returned it to its bag. All she had to do was wait.

THIRTEEN

DELIA

1947

Delia sped back to the apartment on the rue Vavin, where Gaby was putting away the groceries she'd just bought. Gaby paused, a bunch of carrots in one hand, when Delia came clattering in. "What's wrong?" she said.

Throwing herself onto the sofa, Delia told her about the gallery where she had seen her mother's sculpture, and the gallery owner's startling news about Sophie being alive. "Do you think it could be true?"

Gaby put down the vegetables and joined Delia on the sofa. "Of course you *want* it to be true . . . but I don't know."

"Marie-Pierre said she thought my mother and . . . Serge had been caught and killed. But she didn't have any actual proof. And since I hadn't received any more letters from my mother . . ."

"Letters could easily have gotten lost, especially if she was writing during the war. Did the woman at the gallery say anything else?"

"Only that she'd seen my mother at the gallery sometime late last year. And that she'd had letters from her. I wanted to get an address, but the woman didn't believe me when I said I was Sophie Rossner's daughter. I told her I'd bring her my passport. But I just realized that won't convince her—the name on it is Goldhush. I wasn't thinking of that when I made the offer." Delia put her head in her hands. "She thinks I'm a troublemaker. Or crazy. If I go back there, I'm only going to make things worse."

"I can go." Gaby looked at the clock on the wall. "But not today. What about tomorrow afternoon?"

"Oh, Gaby!" Delia leaned closer to hug her friend. "That would be such a help. She said she could produce the provenance, but we never got that far. I want to know how she acquired it. Also when. And if there's any way to get an address for my mother, that would be the best of all."

The next day, Gaby was off from work. She took Félix to a playmate on the floor below, so when she left, Delia was alone in the apartment. She was too unsettled to do anything but sit by the window, waiting and watching for Gaby's return.

When she spied her friend crossing the street toward the building, she ran to the door and flung it open. "Well?" she asked. "What did you find out? Did you see the sculpture?"

"No, I didn't." Gaby unbuttoned her jacket and took it off.

"Why not? It was right in the window."

"Actually, it was sold."

"Sold!" Delia was crushed. "Really? It was just there yesterday. Who could have bought it?" It seemed so unfair to have stumbled upon the sculpture at all, only to let it slip through her fingers. Why hadn't *she* thought of buying it? She felt tears of frustration welling in her eyes.

"But she gave me something to give to you." Gaby handed her a sealed envelope.

Delia tore it open immediately, scanning the few lines it contained:

I bought the sculpture that was in the gallery. I would like to give it to you. I also have some information about where your mother is now. I'm usually home by 5:00 p.m. The dorm is on the rue Gay-Lussac, near the Sorbonne, and my room number is 401. If you meet me there, I can tell you what I know.

Yours,

Anne

In her haste to get her coat and bag, Delia knocked the table, sending the large ceramic bowl at its center skittering to the floor. It cracked neatly as a melon.

"What's the matter?" Gaby said.

Delia thrust the letter into Gaby's hand. "It's almost five o'clock. I have to see her, talk to her. Now." She gestured to the mess on the floor. "Oh, so sorry about all this! Can I clean it later?"

"Go," said Gaby. "I'll take care of it. Just get your things and go."

Delia grabbed her coat and took the Métro to Anne's dorm. Racing up the stairs, she passed other students, talking, laughing, some arm in arm. Their world felt so distant from hers that it pained her. But this was no time to brood about that. She rapped on the door, and Anne opened it.

Now that she had a chance to observe Anne more closely, Delia thought she looked older. No, not older. More sophisticated, somehow. Paris had a way of doing that; even American girls were not immune. Delia sized up the gray flannel dress enlivened by the silk scarf at her neck—she'd obviously learned a thing or two about scarves since that day they'd gone shopping in Poughkeepsie—and the several thin silver bangles on her wrist. All in all, it was a definite improvement. Then she looked into Anne's eyes and saw . . . what? Not fear. Not even shame. No. It was an acknowledgment of some kind.

"I'm glad you came," Anne said.

"You said you had the sculpture. Where is it?" She sent an anxious glance around the room. It didn't look to be there.

"My roommate will be back any time now. Let's go somewhere else to talk."

They went to a café around the corner, where they ordered coffees that neither one of them drank.

"What's this all about?" Delia asked. "The only reason I came is because of the sculpture. But I didn't see it anywhere upstairs. Do you really have it? Or is this some kind of trick?"

"No trick," said Anne. "I owe you an apology. About what happened at Vassar. And about what I did."

Delia snorted; she couldn't help herself. "You can apologize all you want. But you don't expect me to believe it, do you?"

"There was a reason I signed that letter." Hard as it was, Anne kept talking. "A terrible reason, but a reason all the same. I felt awful about it. I still feel awful about it."

"Then why did you do it?"

"Because I didn't want anyone to know."

"Know what?"

"Know that I'm Jewish."

"Jewish?" Delia was stunned. "You?"

"Yes," Anne said. "Jewish. Me."

"I had no idea. . . . You never said . . . and your name."

"My father changed his name before I was even born. He was having trouble launching his career, and he thought a name like Bishop would make it easier. As it happened, he was right."

"But you knew you were Jewish? You were raised Jewish?"

"I was. But the other girls at school—my friends—weren't. I was the only Jewish girl in my class. They liked me, they accepted me—to a point. There were always these little snubs, little exclusions. It was as if they couldn't help it. They couldn't even *see* what they were doing as hurtful in any way. It was just how they were brought up, part of who they were." Anne seemed to be feeling the hurt washing over her again. "I couldn't understand it at first—I felt like one of them. I *was* one of them. Only I kept finding out that I wasn't. It made me angry. Furious, really."

"So you lied."

"Not exactly . . ."

"Yes, you did. You lied, and you kept lying."

"I didn't plan it!" Anne burst out. "It was after my father died, and I was so unhappy. I missed him so much."

"I don't see what that has to do with hiding the fact that you're Jewish."

"I know, it doesn't seem to make sense, but to me it did. I wanted to escape all that unhappiness. Escape from myself and be someone else."

"Someone not Jewish."

"Well, yes. I'd already been accepted to Vassar, and I wanted my life there to be different. *I* wanted to be different. So I started using my middle name—my first name's Miriam—and though I never told anyone I was Christian, I just let them think I was if they chose to. I thought it would be easier."

"Was it?"

"Yes. No. I mean, at first it was. No more worrying about those little remarks, about that *attitude*. And feeling like I belonged. But I had to listen to the worst things about Jews, much worse than what they would have said to my face. And then Virginia was set on telling the dean about—"

"About my affair with Mr. McQuaid?"

Anne paused and then said hesitantly, "Yes, that. Though at first I didn't know who it was. You never said. Virginia knew, though. She . . . followed you. And you had told me that you'd broken up with a married man. So I put two and two together. But I wasn't the one who told her, I swear it."

"Why should I believe that?"

"Because it's true, and now I'm telling you the truth. When she said she was going to go to the dean, I tried to discourage her, I really did. But I was afraid to try too hard, afraid she would figure it out and turn on me. I was a coward. I'm so sorry."

"Maybe it wouldn't have mattered if we didn't know each other. If I hadn't confided in you that day. If I hadn't thought you were my friend."

"I wanted to be," Anne said. "I wanted that very much."

"Not that much, it seems." Delia paused. "Anyway, you did what you did, and you have to live with it, just like I do. Despite those snotty girls, I loved being at Vassar. You took that away from me, and I can never have it back."

"I know," said Anne. "But there is something I can give you—the sculpture."

"So you keep saying. Where is it? And you said you had something to tell me about my mother. What is it?"

"The sculpture is upstairs. I'll get it for you." Now Anne was the one who paused. "Your mother—she's in Palestine."

"What?" Maybe Delia had misheard. Palestine? Sophie? That made no sense.

"The woman in the gallery said she left Paris and went there to live. On one of those collective farms. There's a name for them, right?"

"Kibbutzim." This was even more unlikely—weren't those farming communities? Sophie might have loved fresh flowers, fruit, and vegetables, but the idea that she would actually have anything to do with growing them, with growing anything, seemed ridiculous.

"I have an address." Anne handed Delia a slip of paper. "And I can get the sculpture."

Anne walked out of the café, and after a moment, Delia followed. The sky had darkened, and the air was cold; she pulled her coat more tightly around herself. She had never wanted to see or speak to Anne again. But the sculpture. She wanted that. And she wanted to hear more about her mother in Palestine—she wanted to hear anything that Anne could tell her.

Delia waited in the street until Anne returned with a burlap bag. She handed it to Delia. As soon as it was in her arms, Delia felt the weight of the thing, its solidity. "Thank you." She knew she was being ungracious, but she couldn't offer anything more.

"I'm glad—glad you want it. And glad you're willing to accept it from me." She paused. "And I hope that we can see each other again while you're here."

Delia didn't answer.

"You know where I live," Anne said. "But where are you staying?"

"In Montparnasse. On the rue Vavin."

"Do you mind giving me the address? Just in case I find out something else about your mother—I'll need a way to reach you."

Delia hesitated before answering. She was starting to have a better understanding of Anne's behavior now. If she and her own family had stayed in France, they would have hidden their Jewishness too. They would have had to lie—it would have been a matter of life and death. Anne, of course, hadn't had to face anything like that in New York. But Delia wasn't insensitive to how it felt to be an outsider, to be scorned or avoided not because of something you'd chosen, but simply because of who you were. She herself had felt some of that at Vassar, even if it hadn't bothered her all that much. She *could* understand Anne's need for acceptance, even if the length to which she'd gone—joining those other girls in hounding her out of Vassar—was reprehensible. Would she have done that? She had to admit, if only to herself, that she wasn't entirely sure that she wouldn't.

The sculpture was too heavy for her to carry all the way back to Gaby's, so she found a taxi. When she got it up the stairs, she set the bag down on the table, but she didn't open it right away. She was too preoccupied with what she'd just learned about Sophie. It was only later, when she'd brought the sculpture into Gaby's room, that she loosened the string and peeled back the layers of tissue. The form was as simple and strong as Delia had remembered, the color as rich and as radiant. She thought of her father then; should she tell him what she'd just found out, or wait until she had something more substantial to share? But a decision didn't have to be made immediately. Just having this object in her possession was enough for now. She ran her fingers over the cold, unyielding surface, and when she removed her fingers and replaced them with her cheek, she didn't even flinch.

FOURTEEN

ANNE

1947

Even though she was here in Paris and not in Poughkeepsie, now that she'd done it—actually told someone from her Vassar life that she was Jewish—Anne felt unexpectedly elated. Ever since she boarded that train to Poughkeepsie more than two years ago, she'd kept this part of herself hidden. Sharing the truth was such a relief. Even Delia's reaction—cold, judgmental—didn't dim that. Not a bit.

The disclosure had a ripple effect. She became more confident in her classes, raising her hand, answering in French that wasn't so terrible after all and soon became passable—even decent. One of her professors, Monsieur Leblanc, took note. "Très bien, Mademoiselle Bishop. Maintenant vous parlez couramment le français." Anne thought that "fluently" was a generous assessment of how she spoke French, but she was definitely more comfortable. Paris was beginning to feel more accepting, even welcoming, to her. She felt like she belonged. She and Nancy became regulars at Le Petit Saint Benôit; the gruff waiters seemed a little less gruff, and one of them even smiled in recognition when she came in, albeit the smallest smile imaginable. The woman at the bakery put an extra *pain aux raisins* in her bag for no discernible reason. Her term paper—written in French!—on the depiction of Jesus Christ in three paintings she'd seen at the Louvre received a top grade. One day she took the Métro back to the *marché aux puces*, alone, and tried on a secondhand fur coat of sheared beaver, the dense brown plush of it so dark that it read as black. She looked at her reflection in the cheval mirror that the fur dealer had standing at the back of his stall and almost didn't recognize herself. She felt like a different girl now, the change visible in her face and even her bearing: the coat was a talisman, a portal ushering her into a new phase of her life. She bought it without a second's hesitation, counting out the franc notes into the dealer's eager, outstretched hands.

Best of all, she and Drew had fallen into an easy routine. On Sunday afternoons they often strolled around the city together, and Anne soon realized that these walks gave her a chance to see the world through Drew's eyes. He always carried the Leica and frequently stopped to take photographs. At first she didn't understand what caught his eye—a boarded-up store window, a group of people sitting on a bench, torn newspapers and bits of trash in the gutter. But soon she began to see what he saw: the boarded-up store had a melancholy, wistful feel, the grain of the wood in the boards an intricate, engaging pattern of its own. There were little interactions and even dramas between the people on the bench, one person talking, another listening or instead looking away. Someone clutched a glove, someone had been caught fiddling with a button or leaning over to tie a shoe. And the detritus in the gutter formed an unexpected kind of urban collage—an apple core next to a torn headline from *Le Figaro*, a lone tarnished key, a broken baby's rattle. Random bits and pieces of the city that somehow made poetic sense when they were all contained by the frame of the photograph.

Sometimes he took photographs of Anne, but never a formal portrait; he liked to take candid pictures of her looking at a painting in a gallery or museum, or raising a cup to her lips for a sip of coffee. Now she could literally see herself through his eyes, a vision both illuminating and flattering.

During the week they were often too busy to get together, but sometimes they found the time to meet at a café midway between the *Herald*'s Paris office and Anne's dorm. Drew ordered beer or a glass of wine, and soon Anne began to do the same. She found the taste of beer offensive, but Drew guided her on the subject of wines, and soon she developed a taste for some of them, like burgundy and cabernet, as well for the sweeter, lighter whites and aperitifs like Lillet. Anne remembered how Delia had shocked some of the other girls at school by drinking a nightly glass of wine. But now she understood this daily ritual as civilized and even ceremonial, with Drew always touching his glass to hers before he drank. She let the unfamiliar flavors fill her mouth, trying to sort them out and identify them; the experience was nothing like that time she'd joined that horrid Duane in swigging from his flask at the Yale dance.

On a gray and cold afternoon in early December, Anne arrived at the café first. She was wearing the fur coat for the first time, and when Drew saw it, he made her spin around a couple of times before she sat down. "Where in the world did you get *that?*" he asked. "You look just like a Parisian girl." Anne beamed; she could think of no better compliment.

"I bought it at the flea market. Do you like it?"

"Flea market! You really *have* become a Parisian girl." He helped her out of it, first touching the dense fur and then her shoulder before he hung the coat on a hook behind the table. As always, even the slightest, most casual physical contact between them felt like a small electric shock to Anne, one whose effect lingered for several seconds.

The wine had arrived, and Anne waited for Drew to touch his glass to hers. When he didn't, she realized that he looked disturbed, even anxious. Was something wrong? The feeling seemed to flow straight from him to her, and she absorbed it as if she were a piece of gauze.

"There's something I need to tell you," he began. Was he going to say that he didn't want to keep on seeing her, that she was really too young and inexperienced to be a good companion? Or even worse—that he'd met another girl he liked better, and wanted to spend what free time he had with her?

". . . and I'm going to be leaving Paris the week after next," he said.

"What? Leaving?" With her mind spinning all sorts of scenarios—none of them good—she had missed the first part of what he'd said. "Where are you going?"

"Palestine. The UN just voted to partition the state, and I've been assigned to cover the region."

"I don't understand." Palestine? Drew was at the paper's Paris bureau; Palestine might as well have been on Mars, although, amazingly, it was also where Delia's mother was living. How strange that a place she'd never even thought about should now crop up twice in a matter of days.

"It's not a war zone yet, but it's probably going to become one. They want me to photograph what's happening there—not any actual combat, but what life looks like on the street and in the public spaces."

"I'm not sure I understand."

In between sips of wine, Drew told her about this part of the Middle East. There had been a lot of tension in the area, especially in the last thirty or so years. Jews and Arabs both claimed it as their own. "The Jews are Zionists. To them, Palestine is their ancient homeland, and that's where they want to establish a Jewish national state," he explained. "But the native Palestinians—Arabs—see Palestine as *their* homeland. It's where they've been living for centuries. They want to limit Jewish immigration and set up a secular Palestinian state." He leaned close, both hands lightly touching the Leica that sat on the table between them. "The British got there around 1917," he said. "And they've been trying to appease both sides. It hasn't worked. And after the war, Jews flooded into Palestine—illegally. The more radical Jewish groups thought they'd been betrayed by the British and started using guerrilla tactics, as if the Arabs had no right to be there. But the Arabs felt justified in protecting land they saw as theirs. The whole thing was getting too much for the Brits, so they threw up their hands and turned it over to the UN."

Anne was quiet during this history lesson. "How long will you be gone?" she asked finally, since that was what mattered most to her.

"I can't say. And I can't say I'm not a little scared. But I'll be the youngest photographer there. It's a big opportunity for me."

"It sounds dangerous."

"It could be. Okay, most likely it will be. But that's part of the job—going where there's trouble. Conflict. Change. And maybe this will be a change for the better."

"You really think that?"

"It's hard to say." Drew said that Zionists had been going to Palestine since the nineteenth century, and there had been talk of establishing a Jewish state for years. But it was what happened during the war that made the whole thing seem more urgent. It became clear that nationhood was what counted. "Jews found out that in order to survive, they needed a homeland. And they claim Palestine is theirs."

"I understand." And she did. Her father had talked about how Jews in Germany, Austria, and France had all thought of themselves as German, Austrian, and French—they had lived and worked in those places for generations, and fought in past wars. Overnight they became outcasts. Reviled. Shunned. Delia had talked about what had happened to her family a few years ago in Paris. They had been lucky; because they were Americans, they could escape. The Jews of Europe didn't have an easy way out. When they tried to flee, no one wanted them. Anne remembered what happened to the MS *St. Louis* because her father had been glued to the radio while the drama played out. The ship was carrying over nine hundred Jewish refugees and was refused landing in Florida. Jacob Bishop had put his face in his hands and wept when that was announced. Anne had never seen him break down like that before; it was a terrible thing to witness. "Daddy, why are you crying?" she'd said.

"Why?" He looked up and dug for his handkerchief. "I'll tell you why. I'm crying for those terrified passengers, gazing at the lights along the coastline. I'm crying for what it was like when they were turned away—their bitterness, their disappointment. And I'm crying about what I think will happen to them when they're sent back."

Anne began to sense that this conversation with Drew was heading somewhere unfamiliar and even frightening, somewhere she might not want to go. Or did she? Her heart started to beat more quickly. It was possible she did want to go there. Yes, all at once she realized that she did.

"I guess I'm looking at this with a certain bias."

"What do you mean?"

"What I mean is that I'm Jewish." There, she'd said it. The words had weight, like dense stones dropped in a pond.

"Excuse me?"

"I'm Jewish. Jewish parents, Jewish girl."

"Really? I would never have guessed—not with the last name Bishop. It just hadn't occurred to me."

"That was my father's decision. The law firms where he wanted to work wouldn't hire him, so he changed his name to get a foot in the door."

Drew seemed to be studying her now, evaluating her through a new lens. "You don't exactly look Jewish."

"What does that mean? That I don't have dark skin, or curly hair?" Anne bristled, instantly wounded. "Or maybe you mean my nose—that it's not particularly big, or worse, *hooked* . . ." To her own dismay, she felt tears rising up and threatening to spill.

"Anne, I'm sorry." Drew looked stricken. "That came out all wrong. I didn't mean to be rude. I would never want to hurt you." He put his fingertips under her eyes where the tears were pooling. "Your being Jewish doesn't change how I see you . . . or how I feel about you." He took his hands away. "But I'm a little surprised that you hid it from me. It makes me wonder what else you're hiding. Don't you trust me?" They sat in silence for a little while until he said, "Maybe we should go now."

"We haven't had dinner."

"That's all right. I don't have much appetite anyway." He signaled to the waiter and paid for their wine before escorting her out of the restaurant.

Anne was miserable on the walk back to the dorm; she had mistimed her revelation, and now she'd gone and ruined everything. He thought she was a liar, not trustworthy, not someone he wanted to spend time with anymore. Or he was anti-Semitic, like those vile girls at Vassar. And he was leaving soon, so there might not be time to patch things up before he left. He would forget about her, forget that he'd ever liked her at all. That thought made her feel terrible—shredded inside—and she had to fix it. Or at least try.

"I'm sorry. I should have told you sooner that I was Jewish." They were almost at the dorm, but she stopped walking and turned to face him.

"Why didn't you?"

"I don't know." But she did. "Maybe I thought that it might put you off, and I wanted to wait."

"Wait for what?"

"Wait for you to like me better, so that when it did come out, it wouldn't matter."

"I *do* like you. A lot. I even thought . . ." He hesitated, and in that taut silence between them, Anne felt the hope floating up inside her.

"Thought what?" she asked softly.

"Thought that I might be falling in love with you."

In love with her! Was she really hearing this? And when he pulled her into his arms to kiss her, she knew that she was in love with him. The kiss was gentle, a question, not a demand, and it lasted for a long time, long enough for Anne to luxuriate in the sensation of their two mouths pressed together. The kiss completely wiped out that abomination at Yale, and everything surrounding it. The kiss seemed like a promise, and even a pledge.

Finally he stepped back and smiled. Did he see the stars in her eyes? Hear the whoosh of her heart? But all he said was "You know what? I'm suddenly hungry. Starved, actually. Do you want to get something to eat?"

She laughed; this struck her as funny. Then he started laughing too, and they went hand in hand, still laughing, to a nearby café.

Later that evening she told Nancy about the kiss. "Finally!" said Nancy. "He's been talking about you for weeks. I told him that he really needed to make a move soon, or some Parisian boy would sweep you off your feet."

"There's something else," Anne said. "Something I told your brother that I should probably tell you too."

"You look worried," said Nancy. "Is it something bad?"

"I hope you won't think so. It's that I'm Jewish."

"You are? When we went to Chartres, you seemed so affected by being there. I thought Jewish people didn't go to church. Or if they did, it didn't mean anything to them."

"Who told you that?" Anne was relieved that Nancy didn't seem angry or judgmental. But it was frustrating to have to explain or defend her response to one of the most beautiful cathedrals in all of France, if not the world. And one that Jewish art historians had written about with such sensitivity and insight.

"Well, no one told me," Nancy said. "I just assumed." She too looked at Anne as if she were seeing her with fresh eyes. "I don't know many Jewish people."

"So," Anne asked. "Now that you know one, what do you think?"

"I think she's the same girl I knew and liked before she told me that. Should I think anything else?"

Later, when Anne got undressed and into bed, she realized she was a bit agitated, and not at all sleepy. "Nancy?" she said quietly. "Are you up?"

"Uh-huh." Nancy shifted in her bed so that she was facing Anne. "Something on your mind?"

"It's Drew. He's leaving, you know. He's going to Palestine."

"Yes, he told me. But Paris is his home base. They'll want him to come back soon. I'm sure of it. You'll see."

"I suppose." Anne was not convinced.

"And you can write to each other. It will be very romantic."

Anne remembered a line in a John Donne poem she'd read in her British poetry class: *letters mingle souls*. But she didn't believe it would be enough, at least not when things were so new between them. She was quiet again, and closed her eyes as she relived the evening—the revelation of her secret, Drew's response, and the kiss, the kiss, the kiss. And then—Palestine, and his imminent departure. She was awake until dawn.

It was only after she'd reluctantly responded to the insistent sound of the alarm clock a scant two hours later and was walking to her morning class that she saw a possibility that hadn't occurred to her during those fitful, fretful hours. Drew had said that he was leaving in a couple of weeks. In a couple of weeks her winter break would start; classes wouldn't resume until the third week in January. She and Nancy had talked about taking a trip together, maybe Spain, maybe Italy, but then Nancy had been invited on a ski trip to Switzerland. "You could come too," she told Anne. "I'm going with Rosalie

Barnes. Her parents rent a chalet, and there's plenty of room." Rosalie was another exchange student; maybe she went to Radcliffe, or was it Mount Holyoke? But it didn't matter, because Anne didn't ski and had no interest in learning.

What she was interested in, now, was Palestine. Drew said it was a Jewish homeland, an impassioned, zealous response to the wholesale destruction of Europe's Jews during the war. What would such a place look like, *feel* like? She wanted to know. Then she thought of Delia. Of course. Delia's *mother* was in Palestine. Delia had a *reason* to go to Palestine. So did Drew. And now she did too. Perhaps she and Delia could go to Palestine *together*. As soon as the thought came to her, she understood how necessary this trip would be. How important, how right. Now she just had to figure out how to make it happen.

FIFTEEN

ANNE

1947

For the next week, all Anne could think about was going to Palestine. She scoured the newspapers for any mention of the region, consulted maps in an atlas so she could situate it in her mind. Despite her preoccupation, she didn't entirely understand her own reasons. Was it part of her effort to apologize to Delia, to rekindle the friendship that had sparked at Vassar? Given how Delia had acted when they last met, it didn't seem likely that she would ever want to be Anne's friend again, but still . . . She also had to admit the possibility that she was being guided more by self-interest. A single girl following her boyfriend to another country might raise eyebrows in a way two girls traveling together would not.

Whatever it was, the idea of accompanying Delia to Palestine took hold, buzzing in her head, her soul even, until it felt imperative that she make this trip. It would be more than a trip. It would be a pilgrimage to her own disavowed heritage. Yet still she told no one about it. Until she had a concrete plan of action, it would be better to keep quiet. Drew had gotten very busy at work and could not meet until Saturday evening. Good. She had a little time to figure it out.

Sitting at the desk in her dorm room, she penned draft after draft of notes to Delia, but every one of them seemed wrong. Soon she'd created a small mountain of crumpled pages that filled the metal wastebasket. Saturday arrived, cold and clear. She got up very early, slipped on the fur coat, and went to the Montparnasse building where Delia was staying. She had no clue as to when or if Delia would emerge, but she was almost out of time and needed to do something. And after an hour or so during which she stamped her feet and balled and opened her gloved hands in the pockets of the coat, Delia did step out of the apartment building.

"What are you doing here?" She seemed startled, and not altogether pleased to see Anne.

"I have something to ask you. Something important. Can we talk?"

"I'm going to the market." Delia indicated the wicker basket on her arm; inside was coiled one of those string bags all the Parisian women used. "You can come along if you like." As she began to walk quickly away, Anne hurried to keep pace.

"What did you want to ask me?" Delia said.

"Palestine."

Delia stopped abruptly. "What about it?" She looked very glamorous to be embarking on such a mundane task, what with her mink coat and the royal-blue-and-brown-patterned silk scarf over her hair and tied under her chin.

"I'm thinking of going. And I thought you might want to go with me."

"You want to go to Palestine? Whatever for?" Delia started walking again.

"I'm not sure. I want to see it, experience it. From what it sounds like to me, it's a different way to be Jewish."

"I hadn't thought of that." Delia seemed to be considering the idea.

"Your mother is living there." Delia nodded, so Anne continued. "You've been on her trail—first her sculpture, and now her. It seems logical that Palestine would be the next place you would want to go."

They had reached the open-air market, dozens of tightly crammed stalls under a corrugated metal roof, the contents of some pushing out into the street. A vendor selling live chickens was vainly trying to call out prices but couldn't be heard because the birds made so much noise; a woman carried a baguette almost as long as she was tall; an old man inched along, weighed down by string bags filled with apples, onions, and celery.

The conversation paused as Delia wound her way through the cramped space, touching, examining, sniffing, considering. Into the basket went a handful of potatoes, a head of cabbage, a bunch of beets to which black dirt still clung, and a round, fragrant loaf that Anne knew was called *pain d'épice*. She also bought two wedges of cheese, one deep yellow, the other pale and buttery, and a log of goat cheese dusted with ash.

Finally she turned back to Anne. "So, when are you thinking of doing this?"

"In a couple of weeks."

"A couple of weeks. That's quite soon."

"Someone I know is going there. I wanted to be there with him."

"The man you were with when we ran into each other at the gallery? Is that who you mean?"

Anne felt her face grow warm and was sure she was flushing. She hadn't wanted to reveal the part about Drew yet, but here it was. "Yes," she said. "Him."

"And why does he want to go?"

"He's a photographer. He works for the *Herald Tribune*, and they're sending him."

"He's your boyfriend?"

"He is." The kiss had solidified it, and Anne couldn't keep the smile from spreading across her face.

Delia looked away to examine bunches of flowers in tall metal buckets. After a moment she extracted a dripping bunch of white mums interspersed with red berries and set it atop the vegetables in her basket. When she'd paid the flower vendor, she turned back to Anne. "You must be in love with him."

"I am," Anne said, realizing it was true. She *was* in love with Drew, and he'd said he might be falling in love with her too.

Delia said nothing to that, and when she started walking back to the rue Vavin, Anne did not follow but called out, "You'll think about it?" There was no answer at first, so Anne tried again, her voice louder this time. "You'll let me know?"

That seemed to do it; Delia paused and turned around. "I'll let you know," she said before she resumed walking. Anne watched until she reached the corner and disappeared from view.

That night, she and Drew met at Le Petit Saint Benôit, which she now thought of as their place. He embraced her when she came close, and she clung to him for a moment, the wool of his scarf soft against her face. Over dinner, she brought up his impending trip and said, "Remember that girl we met in the gallery?"

"The one who bumped into you? And was so rude?"

"She had her reasons," Anne said.

"So you've told me."

"She came to Paris because she was looking for her mother."

He nodded. "Did she ever find her?"

"No, because it turns out her mother is in Palestine. That's what the gallery owner said."

Drew leaned back in his chair. "Well, that's a coincidence. And it's significant because . . . ?"

"Delia may want to go to Palestine. To look for her."

"And you want to go too?"

"Well, yes." Anne took a deep breath. "I do."

"Anne." He leaned in now and took her hands in his. "I'd love to be there with you, to be anywhere with you. But I'm going to be really busy. And like you said, it's not exactly safe."

"I know you'll be busy. And I know it could be dangerous. But this is something I want to do for Delia. That I need to do for Delia."

"Because you helped to get her expelled?"

"Yes." She felt shame flooding her. "I was a coward then. I don't want to be a coward anymore."

"I admire your wanting to make amends, I really do. But isn't there some other way?"

"Not one that would mean as much. And it wouldn't just be for her—it would be for me too." Their dinner came, and he let go of her hands. "I hadn't ever thought about Palestine before you told me you were going. I didn't even know where it was. But now I can't stop thinking about it. I want to see it for myself. Can you understand that?"

He put down his fork and put a hand to her cheek. "I can. I do."

"So then . . . ?"

"Well, you're a very determined girl," he said. "I don't think I could stop you even if I tried."

After dinner, he walked her back to the dorm. All along the way, she wondered if he would kiss her again, and what she would do if he didn't. She needn't have worried; when they got to the entrance, he took her in his arms like she was meant to be there, and this second kiss was as wonderful as the first. She floated up the stairs and to her room, opening the door and shutting it quickly behind her. The room was empty; Nancy had said she would be out that night. That was all right, because Anne wanted to savor the last few minutes—the whole evening with Drew, really—all by herself for a while. She hung up her coat and slid her feet out of her pumps before walking over to the mirror above her bureau. Her hair was mussed by the wind; unlike Delia, she hadn't worn a scarf to cover it. Anne picked up a comb, and the gentle, repetitive movement calmed the nervous, fizzy excitement she'd been feeling. It was only then that she noticed it—a cream-colored envelope with her name written across the front that had been slid under the door. She put down the comb and picked up the envelope. The single folded sheet inside said only this:

When do we leave?

PART III

PALESTINE

SIXTEEN

DELIA

1947

Delia stood looking out the large plate glass window at the Orly airport. There was the plane that would take her to Tel Aviv. It was a dull brushed silver and had four small propellers, two under each wing. She'd never been in an airplane before, never even been this close to one. It looked magnificent, this sleek machine that could rise up into the sky and soar through it. Would they go through clouds? Rain? She looked impatiently at the large clock on the wall; still another twenty to thirty minutes before they boarded.

When they were finally aloft, Delia peered out the tiny oval of the window and watched the buildings, trees, and roads drop away and then disappear from view. The sound of the propellers was like the beating of a thousand birds' wings. Anne sat next to her, face pressed against the seat, eyes closed. How was she able to sleep? Delia was feeling more charitably disposed toward her, which was surprising. Every time Delia thought she knew Anne, she found out something new about her, another facet of her nature.

The plane stopped in Turkey to refuel, filling the cabin with a biting noxious odor. Anne opened her eyes and looked around briefly before closing them again. Delia leaned forward, eager for the plane to ascend once more. When the refueling was completed, the plane took off smoothly into the air. Glorious. Delia looked out the window at the voluminous banks of clouds and remembered the game she'd played as a little girl, trying to decipher the shapes they made—this one a whale, that one a pig, still another a leaping rabbit. The effort distracted and even lulled her; without realizing it, she too fell asleep, waking when the plane hit the ground.

Passengers started unbuckling their seat belts, gathering their belongings, and pressing into the aisle. Everyone was eager to disembark. Delia and Anne joined them but had to wait; it took another twenty minutes for them to actually leave the plane and find their way into the crowded terminal.

Drew was there waiting for them, and Delia stood quietly apart as he and Anne moved into an embrace. Then they all found their way to the baggage claim area. Once their valises had been retrieved, Drew led them outside and hailed a taxi that drove along a broad, bustling street lined with trees and modern-looking buildings, most of which had terraces. The buses were double-deckers, like in London. They passed a fountain, then a minaret, and turned onto a roundabout. Delia spied a sign, in English and what had to be Hebrew, that read "Allenby Road." Soon they stopped in front of the hotel where Anne had gotten them two rooms. Though she was exhausted, Delia agreed to have dinner in the hotel dining room, which, with its minimal decoration, cheap, heavy china, and bent and dinged cutlery, was serviceable and nothing more.

"I thought I'd go with you tomorrow," Anne said after they had ordered.

"To the kibbutz?"

Anne nodded. "I'd like to see it. And you probably shouldn't go alone."

"She's right," Drew said. "You should have someone with you.

I've gone ahead and hired a guide for Anne so he can help you get to the bus station. You're going to Be'er Sheva, right?"

"Yes, Be'er Sheva."

"And what about after that?"

"I don't know. Maybe a taxi?"

"There won't be a taxi."

"Well, then I'll figure out something else." Delia wanted the conversation to be over.

"What if the guide goes with you? I've paid him for the day, so he'd be willing."

"All right." Delia wanted to appease him. "Thank you for the offer." She excused herself before dessert.

Her room was bare-bones—a narrow metal-framed bed, sheets that were clean but of a coarse cotton and covered by a worn blanket, a small bureau, a single chair—but she didn't care. Not even bothering to undress, she stretched herself out on the bed nearest the door and fell into a deep, almost drugged sleep. She woke before it was light. Good. She had no intention of letting Anne accompany her; she had gotten herself a map and a little Hebrew phrasebook she'd been studying on the plane. She could find her way to the bus station on her own. And once she got to Be'er Sheva, she'd figure out a way to get to the kibbutz.

Breakfast wasn't being served yet, though she was able to order coffee in a small white cup; it was so thick and gluey as to be almost undrinkable, and she abandoned it after a couple of sips. She stepped out into the day. The sky was a clear, almost impossible blue, so bright and cloudless that it hurt her eyes. She would need to buy sunglasses; somehow, she hadn't even thought to pack them. She passed block after block of crisp white buildings—Delia recognized them as International Style, from photographs she'd seen—that glittered like sugar cubes. Even though it was December, the sun was so warm that she unbuttoned her mink; she really didn't need it here.

On her way to the station, she passed an open-air market that was louder and more chaotic than the French markets of her childhood. The voices were strident, even yelling, and there was an uneasy kinetic energy to the place. Two men argued loudly over something—price? Quality?—and a woman wearing a kerchief, a long skirt, and an apron squatted in the middle of the bustling place, leaving a large wet patch in the dirt.

Along with the bread, cheese, olives, and figs for sale, Delia saw brightly painted and glazed ceramic dishes, battered pots and vessels of copper or bronze, and live animals—chickens, geese, a calf, a trio of goats with coarse, bristly fur, black eyes, and delicate little hooves on which they seemed to perch rather than stand. Most of the vendors seemed old, or at least as if their lives here had prematurely aged them—worn and creased skin, gray or white stubble, hands calloused, skin like leather. Judging from the caftans they wore, many looked to be Arabs. But there was one woman, quite young, really no older than Delia, standing in front of a grouping of woven rugs, many of which were unfurled and almost glowing in daylight. Above the rugs, on a length of twine secured to a pair of metal posts, hung a few caftans, mostly black, a few white, all covered in the most meticulously embroidered designs—stylized leaves, flowers, a pattern of vines that ran across the entire front and up over the shoulders. Delia slowed to look.

"You like?" said the girl. Beneath the dark headdress that covered her hair, her face was an elegant oval, with dark brows, small, very dark eyes, and smooth skin that seemed to be without pores.

"I do." Delia touched the careful stitching of a black caftan whose embroidery was mostly gold, with a few touches of brilliant red—long sinuous lines, delicate arcs, and multifoliate shapes like exploding stars.

"I give you good price." The girl named a sum that Delia, even with her limited grasp of the local currency and its relative value, thought was very low. That red, somehow even more arresting and vivid than the gold, made Delia think of those red pillows in their Paris apartment. Paris. That was a time when her family, though standing on a fault line, had been more or less intact. A time before her mother had shattered it. Sophie would have loved the caftan. But did Delia really care what Sophie would have loved?

Then she looked up and saw the eager expression on the girl's face, the hope in her eyes. She was clearly expecting Delia to buy the caftan, and Delia couldn't disappoint her. She reached for her money and started counting out the shekels. The girl smiled broadly and began to fold the garment, but Delia shook her head. "No," she said. "You keep it. Keep the money too." The girl looked puzzled, but finally she seemed to understand and tucked the bills into a pocket buried deep in the folds of her dress.

Before she walked away, Delia stopped and waved. The girl waved back. "Todah rabah," she called after her. *Thank you.* Delia knew that much from the phrase book.

The bus station was as crowded and chaotic as the open-air market had been; Delia had to fight her way in, and then make her way to the line where she could purchase a ticket. When she told the man behind the counter she wanted to go to Be'er Sheva, he waved both hands at her: *Hurry.* She ran outside to a pale-green bus that was about to pull away, but when she knocked on the door, the driver let her on.

"Be'er Sheva?" she asked, and he nodded, as if saying anything were too great an expenditure of energy. There were no seats, though, and Delia had to hold on tightly as the bus swerved and lurched. Soon they were out of the city, and the green foliage—it must have rained the night before, because the leaves glittered with droplets—gave way to a landscape that was drier and more barren than any she'd ever seen. This must be the Negev—vast, parched, and mostly empty except for two boys trudging along the side of the road with a donkey.

She followed their progress briefly until the bus outpaced the pair, leaving them behind in a plume of dust.

In Be'er Sheva, Delia climbed down from the bus and looked around. The station was smaller, and on a chalkboard she saw departure times for buses heading north—Chadera, Haifa, Jerusalem, or back to Tel Aviv. But there seemed to be nothing going south, and when she told a ticket agent where she was headed, he shook his head. "No bus." Like the girl in the market, his English was thickly accented but still comprehensible.

Delia looked at the scrap of paper she'd carried with her since Paris, and she told him what was on it.

"Chatserim." He grunted. "There's a wagon."

"Wagon? When?"

He shrugged. "You wait. I tell you."

Delia sat down on a hard, uncomfortable metal bench. She was hungry. Several people around her were eating sunflower seeds encrusted with salt, so she went outside, bought a bag from the man selling them from a small cart, and went back inside to eat them. Soon there was a pile of shells in her hand. Everyone else was just spitting them out onto the floor, but Delia couldn't bring herself to do that; it seemed so crude. Ten minutes passed, then twenty, then thirty. Would this wagon really come? What would she do if it didn't—take the bus back to Tel Aviv? But just then the man behind the ticket counter called out loudly and in English, "Girlie! Wagon!" Delia got up and grabbed her bag and hurried over.

The wagon was a crude thing. In front of it stood a horse, an exhausted-looking creature too apathetic to shake off the flies that had settled around its ears and eyes. It took Delia a few tries to climb up and position herself on the splintery seat. Since the day had grown even warmer, she took off her coat and folded it under her as a cushion. She was the only passenger and had to carve out a space for her feet and legs; the floor of the wagon was filled with burlap bags of what might have been flour or sugar, a large tin of what she thought was oil, flimsy cardboard boxes whose contents were unknown. The man yanked on the reins, and they began to move.

The ride was bumpy and slow; occasionally the driver muttered something—was he talking to himself? To her? The horse? If it was the latter, the horse ignored him. The sun was beating down, and Delia rolled up the sleeves of her blouse. She wished she could have taken off her stockings too.

The landscape around her looked so alien, the earth parched and cracked, the sky bleached of the vivid blue she'd seen in Tel Aviv. She sat quietly, and soon glimpsed a low building of some kind, an unadorned ocher rectangle covered by a roof that gave off a dull metallic gleam. She stared at the building as it grew larger and more solid, and as they approached, she could see that around it were smaller structures with peaked roofs—no, they weren't structures at all, they were . . . tents. Yes, that was it. The building was surrounded by tents. Was it possible that Sophie lived in a tent? Sophie, with her Guerlain perfume, her net gloves, the leopard-print swing coat she'd worn with that jaunty maroon beret covered in beads? Delia still couldn't picture it.

The driver stopped abruptly in front of a low, roughly fashioned fence. The horse shook himself, lifted his long face up toward the sky, and let out a mournful neigh. Two armed guards sat at either side of a gate; there was also a pair of dogs that looked like German shepherds. One was sleeping, head resting on his crossed paws. But the other sat straight up, ears pricked, gaze alert. When he saw the wagon, he emitted a low, throaty growl that sounded like a warning.

The driver called out something, and one of the guards called out something in return. Then the driver hopped down and extended a hand to Delia, who took it gratefully. She watched while he lugged first the bags, and then the tin, inside the rectangular building, and when he came back out again, she handed him some of the boxes and took a few herself. His face cracked into a smile—the first since she'd laid eyes on him—and he gestured for her to follow him into the building, which appeared to be a dining room. Inside, sheets of oilcloth covered low wooden tables flanked by benches, and bare bulbs suspended from the ceiling gave off a low, staticky buzz. Delia waited while the items from the wagon were taken away and a few of the people seated at the tables got up and came over to the driver. One gave him a hearty slap on the back; they all seemed glad to see him. Since their conversation was in Hebrew, she didn't understand any of it. Instead she looked anxiously around the room. Was Sophie here?

Then the lone woman in this small group noticed her. She said something that Delia presumed was in Hebrew, and when Delia didn't respond, she said, "Hello. I'm Esther, but here they call me Hadas. Can I help you in any way?" She wore baggy canvas pants, a stretched-out sweater that might have once been black, and heavy lace-up work boots; her accent was British.

"I'm looking for Sophie Rossner. I was told that she's living here now." Even saying her name caused Delia's heart to jump.

Hadas studied her carefully. "You look so much like her. Are you related?"

"I'm her daughter."

"Her daughter? She's never mentioned you."

Never mentioned she had a daughter. How could Sophie have just erased her from her life? Now Delia felt lightheaded, even dizzy, as if she might faint. Looking at her watch, she saw that it was almost one o'clock. No wonder she felt this way; apart from those sunflower seeds, she'd eaten nothing all day.

"Are you all right?" Hadas reached out a hand to steady her. "Here, why don't you sit down? Can I bring you a glass of water? Lunch is going to be served in a little while. Do you want to join us?"

"Just the water," said Delia gratefully. "Thank you." The room smelled overwhelmingly of cabbage, which, despite her hunger, Delia found revolting. She sat down at one of the long tables, keenly aware that people were looking at her. She looked away, and when the glass of water appeared in front of her, she drank it down quickly. There. That helped.

"Did you want me to go get her? She usually doesn't get here until a little later, but I can try to find her now if you want."

"Can't I come with you?"

"Of course."

There were baskets of rolls already on the tables, and when Hadas saw Delia eyeing them, she said, "Please help yourself." So Delia took a roll and munched on it as she followed Hadas across the room. She was eager to escape the stench of the cabbage. But still, she looked up and noticed the muslin curtains that hung over the windows, pulled closed against the sun. They had been embroidered, the coarse fabric a backdrop for brightly colored flowers and leaves. How odd to find these panels in such a bare, unadorned place. Then she realized that some of the panels had not been embroidered but painted instead, with bold, even raucous forms. They seemed familiar, and she realized they had been done by Sophie—she was sure of it. And were those tiny initials in the corners Sophie's? She didn't paint or draw often, but on occasion she had done both. Delia stared at the flowers. They had been made by Sophie's hand, she was certain.

"Aren't you coming?" Hadas said.

"Yes, of course." Delia fell into step beside her, finishing the last of the roll as she walked. Though she'd been ravenous, it sat like a sodden mass in her stomach, and now she was sorry she'd eaten it.

They went outside, passing tent after tent as they walked.

"Is this where people live?" she asked.

"Most people, though not the kids. A *beit yeladim*—a children's house—was built for them."

Delia couldn't fathom how Hadas could tell the difference between the tents, which all looked the same, but she seemed to know exactly where she was going.

Hadas stopped in front of one of them. "Here it is." Since there was no door on which to knock, she called out, "Sophie, there's someone here to see you."

"Come on in," called a voice—Sophie's voice, which Delia had not heard in years and had not thought she would ever hear again. For a second she was frozen at the entry, unable to take the next step.

Hadas looked perplexed. "I thought you wanted to see her."

Delia hesitated for just a split second longer. Then she put her hand through the opening, pushed back the flap, and went inside.

SEVENTEEN

DELIA

1947

There she was. Her mother. Sophie. Seated at a small metal table, she looked up when the tent flaps parted. "Delia?" Then she was darting across the tiny space and flinging her arms around Delia, who stumbled backward and did not, could not, reciprocate right away. Pressed against her, Sophie felt delicate, even breakable. She smelled unfamiliar, of something bracing, almost medicinal. Peppermint? Wintergreen?

"I can't believe it," Sophie said into Delia's hair and then released her. "Let me look at you." Delia submitted to the gaze. Sophie was thinner, much thinner, and her once-abundant hair was short, cropped in the back, with little wispy bangs. It was a shock. Sophie's long, wavy hair had always been so essential to her look, her very being. She'd worn it loose, worn it up in a variety of ways, adorned it with silk flowers or scarves, tortoiseshell combs, jeweled barrettes. And now it was essentially gone, and what was left was streaked with gray. But her face was still the face Delia remembered: the angled cheekbones, the elegantly curved nose, the thin lips. Her eyes were the same steely blue, the gaze penetrating, even unnerving. Her clothes, like those of everyone else here, were nothing more than utilitarian, yet she managed to make the white cotton blouse and pleated pants—so faded that the black had become a smudged gray—look elegant. And she still looked beautiful, albeit in some haunted, ravaged way.

Sophie was crying now, and Delia realized that she was too. "Come," Sophie said, leading Delia to the hard-backed chair where she'd been seated. "Sit down." Sophie perched on the cot, her arms wrapped around herself as if to contain all that she was feeling. "You're all grown up." She took in Delia's two-piece silk dress. Then she looked down. "But your shoes!" Delia was wearing black suede pumps. "No one wears shoes like that here. Let me lend you another pair."

"Shoes?" Delia couldn't believe it. "After leaving us, and all those years of silence, and—"

"That's not fair, I wrote to you, I tried—"

"What? Three times in, what, eight years? I'd hardly call that trying. And now you want to talk about *shoes*? What's *wrong* with you?" Abruptly Delia stood, knocking over the chair. "You haven't changed a bit. You'll never change."

"Darling, I'm sorry, I just—" Sophie had gotten up too and was moving toward her, but Delia took a step back, and then another. And then she was outside the tent and walking away as quickly as she could.

"Delia!" Sophie called out. "Delia, please come back!"

Her mother's voice trailed behind her, but Delia didn't turn around. She had no idea where she was going or what to do next. She saw the glances she attracted—she clearly didn't belong here—but no one said anything, they just went about their business. She wove her way through the tents, back past the dining room, and then past another crude structure—a barn, it seemed; several skinny cows stood outside.

She kept walking, faster and faster, fueled by her anger. Now she was actually hot, and also thirsty.

God, what a wretched, unforgiving place this was; she still couldn't understand why Sophie had chosen to be here. And then all at once she did: her mother wanted to be punished. What a thought. Delia had to stop to consider it. She'd wanted to excoriate Sophie, to hurt her the way she'd been hurt. But Sophie had already assumed that burden. She was here seeking penance.

Delia turned and started back toward the tent that was Sophie's. Even if she wasn't ready to forgive her mother, she would listen to what she had to say. Lost in her thoughts, she didn't notice the hole in the dry earth; her foot slid into it, and as she tried to pull it out, the heel of her shoe snapped right off, leaving a jagged edge. Looking down, she stared at the now useless piece before scooping it up. Then she hobbled, as best she could, to her mother's tent.

Sophie was once again seated at the table when Delia walked in for the second time that day. She took in the ruined shoe, along with the shredded stocking on Delia's foot, but said only, "You came back."

"I did." Yet Delia was still angry. "You didn't follow me. Or try to find me."

"What would have been the point? Either you want to talk to me, or you don't."

"Do you blame me for being angry? Not trusting you? You're the one who left us."

"I know. But I wrote to you. Several times. You didn't answer."

"I didn't get the letters. I didn't even see them until a couple of months ago. Papa never gave them to me."

"Then how—"

"I found them in his office. They weren't opened."

"Then you probably don't know that I wrote to him too, telling him that I wanted to be in touch with you. He wrote back and said you didn't want to see me. That you'd adjusted to life in New York and that communicating with me would only upset you."

"And you believed him? How convenient for you. How easy."

"Delia, he threatened me with legal action—a restraining order. I thought it would be best to let things cool down for a while and then try again. And . . ."

"And what?"

"And I was going through a very difficult time."

"And I wasn't? When you left, you didn't think of the consequences, of what might happen. Of how we would feel. We thought you were dead."

"Dead?" Sophie looked surprised. "Why did you think I was dead?"

"Marie-Pierre said so. She said you and . . . Serge had been working for the Resistance and been caught." It was hard for Delia to say his name; it felt foul in her mouth. "And that you'd been . . . shot."

Sophie shook her head. "No, that wasn't true. But it easily could have been."

"I don't understand."

Sophie released her daughter's arms, leaned forward, and took Delia's hands in her own. A gentle squeeze, and then she let go. "It was never my plan to just vanish from your life. Yes, I was going to leave your father, but not then, and not like that. And once I was settled, I would have written to tell you where I was." Delia looked unconvinced as Sophie went on to recount things she already knew and had been over a hundred times: the quarrel, her angry flight from the apartment. But then Sophie started filling in the blanks, telling Delia things she hadn't known. After storming out that day, Sophie had gone to Serge's apartment, thinking she would come home later that night, or early the next morning. "But the police were already at Serge's, yanking out drawers, pulling things down from shelves, from the closets. Serge looked terrified—of course. He thought he'd been found out." Sophie said that they took him in for questioning, and they took her too. The police kept them for two days, and in the end, let them both go. By then, Delia and her father had sailed.

"There were no more boats. You and Simon were on the last one."

"I thought you'd abandoned us. That you'd abandoned me."

"Of course you did," Sophie said. "Simon . . ." She didn't finish the sentence. "Serge was already deeply involved with the Resistance, and since I was with him, I became involved too. I thought that the work we were doing would help end the war sooner. Then I could find my way back to you." After their release, Sophie explained, they didn't return to his apartment. Instead, they went to a workshop on the rue Richard Le Noir, near the Bastille. It had belonged to the grandfather of one of the women in the group. "This grandfather, he'd been in the furniture business—repairing, recaning, something like that. But he'd left Paris, and the place was empty, and it seemed safe, or at least safe enough. There was one member of our group, Guillaume. No one really liked him. But for Serge, it was more than that—he suspected that Guillaume was working as a double agent and feeding information to Vichy officials. There was a day early in 1942 when Serge was able to confirm this hunch. He had the proof. We knew we had to act, but we also didn't want to let Guillaume know we were onto him. Serge went out for a while. Guillaume and I were alone in the building. We were supposed to be working on the wording for some new leaflets—they had to say enough to make the message clear, but not enough to implicate or endanger anyone. I was so nervous. Did Guillaume know that I knew? What would he do if he did? Serge had been gone a long time—too long." Sophie's voice dropped, but rather than ask her to speak louder, Delia leaned in closer.

"I heard something outside the door," said Sophie. "Footsteps on the stairs, shouting. Then the door was kicked in, and there they were—four German soldiers in uniform, screaming, their guns trained right at us. Their words were only noise to me, nightmarish noise. I couldn't understand anything they were saying. But I did understand that they were going to shoot me. That I was going to be murdered."

Sophie stopped, pressing her palms together. "I heard gunfire. I thought it was in the room, but no, it was coming from outside. Two of the soldiers began running, stumbling over the broken door. One of them tripped, and a third helped him up. He barked something to the remaining soldier. This time I could understand—*Erschießen sie jetzt*. Shoot them now. My parents spoke Yiddish. Some of the words were the same. And in the next second, the remaining soldier raised his gun and shot Guillaume, three times, in the chest. The sound was so close, so loud, that I thought my eardrums would burst and my heart would burst right along with them.

"Guillaume collapsed on the floor, his eyes wide with disbelief. The soldiers hadn't known he was working for their side too. His blood was everywhere—his shirt, the floor, the wall behind him. I looked at my hands, my arms—splattered with blood. I was in shock. Seconds ago, Guillaume had been alive. Guillaume, with his silly little goatee, that high, slightly nasal voice, and these surprisingly delicate hands. He was someone I'd known, not well, and what I knew of him, it's true, I hadn't liked. And he was betraying us. Yet to see his life end in such a violent and abrupt way was truly the most horrifying thing I'd ever witnessed."

Delia was still, trying to absorb this.

"I became aware of another sound nearby, a strangled, choking sound," Sophie went on. "It took me a few seconds to realize that it was coming from the German soldier—had he been shot too? But no. He wasn't hurt, at least not physically. Yet he was rocking and sobbing as if his heart was breaking. He'd set his gun down beside him. Maybe I could have grabbed it. I don't know. But it didn't occur to me then. I was just staring at this boy. And he was a boy—I could see that now, no more than eighteen. He was babbling. I could make out *Werden sie mich töten, werden sie mich töten.* They'll kill me. Of course. The three who'd run off—they would most certainly kill him if they saw that he'd broken down, that he was too overwrought to shoot me.

"I put my hand on his shoulder. It was a gesture of comfort, the way I would have comforted a child. Because that's what he was—a child dressed up as a soldier, handed a gun, and pushed into the line of fire. He flung himself at me. I was frozen for a second, and then, well . . . then I put my arms around him and let him cry. Over his head, I could see out the window. The street was empty. Silent. The three soldiers had disappeared, gone off to shoot, maim, kill someone else. The boy and I were still there. Still alive. I began to speak to him, in Yiddish of all things, and he calmed down. The sobbing slowed. Then he lifted his head, and Delia, if you can believe it, he kissed me. Kissed me! Some instinct that I didn't understand told me to obey him. I let him keep kissing me and kissed him back while he started pulling at my clothes. I led him away from that thing that had been Guillaume and was now just a bloodied corpse.

"He pulled me down to the rug and climbed on top of me. I was numb, though I was aware of the rhythm of his movement, what it meant, how it would end. It was all over very quickly, and when it was, he yanked me to my feet and told me to get out, to run quickly—'*Mach schnell*.' So I did. I ran and ran until I couldn't run anymore, and when I was some distance from the warehouse, I found my way to one of the safe houses I knew elsewhere in the arrondissement."

It took Delia a moment to absorb this. "You were raped," she said finally.

"Yes," Sophie said. "And being raped saved my life."

If Delia had wanted her mother to have been punished, she had surely gotten her wish. She realized Sophie had started talking again.

". . . Serge and I left Paris and made our way down to Marseille. At first I didn't tell him about what had happened. But I had to because . . . because I couldn't bear for him to touch me, and I had to explain why. He didn't press me, he understood. I missed a period, and another. The absence barely registered. That my body was off kilter didn't seem strange. Then I started feeling sick. I ignored it, and when I couldn't do that anymore, I ascribed it to something, anything else, unwilling to face the truth. Until finally I did. I was pregnant. Serge wanted me to have an abortion. I told him it was already too late. I had felt the baby kicking inside me, flipping like a fish. An abortion would have been dangerous. That was something Serge *didn't* understand. To him there was only one clear path, and I wasn't taking it. But Delia, I couldn't. As strange and surreal as my life had become, I didn't want it to end on some table, gouged and bleeding. I still hoped to find you again. So Serge went to Spain. I stayed in Marseille, where I had the baby. And what a beautiful baby he was—such eyes, so big and so blue. That German soldier, he'd had blue eyes. And the golden hair—the baby had ringlets—that came from the German boy too."

"Your baby," Delia said. "Where is he? What's his name? Isn't he my . . . brother?"

"Yes, he's your brother. His name is Asher, and he lives here, that is, in the baby house. Maybe, that is I hope . . . you might want to meet him." When Delia said nothing, Sophie went on.

"I know it's a shock. It was a shock for me too—I thought that part of my life was finished. I felt like I should have despised Asher, but I couldn't. No, I loved him, just as I had loved you. But with you, I'd been selfish and distracted. I hadn't been a good mother. I started remembering things from the past, and they were a torment to me. I even began to think there was some crazy logic in what had happened. That I'd been given a second chance—to be better."

Delia had no reply. She remained quiet as Sophie continued her saga. When the war ended, Sophie said, she went back to Paris. She even tried to work again. But her ambition had deserted her. The only thing she was able to complete were a few small pieces. "Remember how I'd done them in the past? Little table-size ones?"

"Like that double portrait. I have it—I took it with me when we left."

"You did?" Something like a smile passed over Sophie's face. "You always liked it."

"I thought it was a portrait of us." Delia felt a bit shy; she'd never said this to her mother before.

"Really? I hadn't thought about it like that, but it makes me very happy to think that you did. In any case, I started working on that scale again, and it felt right to me. These pieces felt alive to me. Like infants or children. I could pick them up and hold them in my hands. I sold a few of them at a gallery that was not far from the rue Vavin; I may have even been in it before the war. The dealer knew and liked my work and she sold all of them—all except one. It was a figure of a pregnant woman and made of carnelian, a stone I'd never worked with before. Only after I'd finished it did I realize it was me—that I'd created a self-portrait. Was the child that stone figure carried you? I wasn't sure. The dealer loved the piece and was eager to offer it for sale. At first I said no. I let her take all the other pieces, but not that one. I wanted to keep it for myself."

This was the statue Delia had, the one that led her here, to this place, to her mother. But she didn't want to tell Sophie about that yet.

"After the war ended, Paris seemed worn down, wounded, even though it had seen almost no fighting until the Liberation," Sophie said. "I went back to Marseille, but it wasn't any better there. I needed to be somewhere else, somewhere not in France, not in Europe. That's when I started to hear about Palestine, to hear talk about a Jewish homeland. You know we were never particularly involved in Jewish life, your father and I. Not that we were ashamed or hid it. It just wasn't at the forefront."

"I know," said Delia. "But we were comfortable that way, weren't we?"

"Until we weren't. That's when I realized being Jewish wasn't a choice for me to make. It was a choice the world was going to make whether I liked it or not. I decided to take a trip. I sailed from Marseille to Haifa. I spent some time there and then made my way here, to the Negev. I had some friends who told me about it—the kibbutz, how people lived there. I didn't like it at first—it was so empty. Harsh. But something began to happen. My feelings changed. I found that the desert wasn't empty at all. It was filled with wind and clouds, with sunsets that unfolded like revelations, with nights that glittered with stars. I got to know the people on the kibbutz, the ones who welcomed us, my little boy and me. I settled in and went to work, in the dairy, and then in the laundry. But what I liked best was working outside, making things grow. Would you have ever imagined it? In Vence, we hired gardeners to do everything; I never so much as picked up a tool. I was disconnected from the place and hadn't even known it. Here, I found the connection that had been missing. And it was here that I saw there was something wrong with my beautiful boy, something that couldn't be fixed or healed."

"What do you mean? Is he ill or . . . deformed?"

"Not ill. And not deformed either. He was a beautiful baby, and he's now a beautiful little boy. But if you meet him, you'll understand. He doesn't look at you when you're talking. He can't seem to focus or connect. And he barely speaks. Just a few words now and then. Mostly he points. Grunts sometimes. And cries, oh how he cries. You were nothing like that," Sophie said. "You had great composure and self-control, even when you were very young."

"Have you taken him to a doctor? There must be a diagnosis, a name for what he has."

"I've taken him to so many doctors—in Paris, and even in Vienna, to someone who studied with Freud. Most didn't know what it was. But one doctor suggested it might be something called autism."

"I've never heard of that," said Delia.

"Neither had I." She raked her hands through her hair. "In any case, there doesn't seem to be any treatment. The way Asher is now is the way he'll always be, only when he's older, he'll be that much stronger, and these fits of his will be harder to manage. But if I stay here, I'll have help."

"The people have agreed to that?"

"Yes." Sophie looked straight at her. "They have. And thank God for that, because I couldn't do it myself. He'll never be truly normal, but here there will always be a place for him. The community will support both of us."

"Really? For the rest of your life?"

"Yes. They do that for all the members. I'm a member now. So is Asher. As long as he's here, I'll be here too. Unless I had the money to support him, there really isn't anywhere else for him to go."

"Do you have any money?" Delia's father's family was rich, but Sophie's was not.

"A little. I had a bank account in Paris, and I took what was in it when I left. And when I sell work, there's money from that."

"And what about Paris? New York?" Delia asked. "And all your friends? Your life as an artist? You cared so much about it back then. Sometimes it seemed you cared more about them than about me."

"I deserve that." Sophie looked hurt. "And maybe someday I'll want to make art again. But for now I need to be a better mother than I was—to Asher, and to you too, if you'll let me." She paused. "You must be in college. You were always so intellectually curious."

"I was at Vassar. Until I was expelled."

"Expelled? You? You always got such high marks in all your subjects."

"I wasn't expelled because of my grades. I was expelled because I had an affair with my English professor. Someone—a horrid girl—found out, and she told the dean."

Sophie studied Delia's face. "Your professor? He must have been older than you. Shame on him. Seducing a young girl, a student . . . that's reprehensible."

"He didn't seduce me. I . . . seduced him." Delia had admitted that to no one. Once the words were out, she discovered that it was a relief to have said them.

"Be that as it may," Sophie said, "he should have known better."

"Just like you should have known better . . . is that what you mean?"

Sophie was quiet. "Maybe," she said at last. "But whatever you think of me, whatever I did, your father was an adult, an equal, and he had a part in what happened. A professor and a student? Not the same thing." When Delia didn't reply, Sophie added, "In any case, that must have been terrible for you. What did your father say?"

"He doesn't know."

"How can he not know?"

"I told him I was transferring to Barnard, and he believed me. You know Papa. He can be very . . . distracted."

"Distracted!" Sophie said. "That's a very forgiving way to look at it."

But Delia wasn't thinking about her father. "Distracted and a bit selfish. Just like you, Maman. You left because you were in love with Serge. But you didn't stay with him. What a waste. You destroyed our family for no good reason."

"Delia, there's always a reason. Your father and I, we weren't happy. You knew that, didn't you? And as for Serge, I did love him. And I would have stayed with him. But who could have imagined that I'd end up with another child? Another child that he just couldn't accept. I can't blame him for that."

"So you gave Papa up for Serge, and Serge for Asher."

"I suppose you could put it that way."

They were both quiet for a moment. Outside, Delia heard voices.

What time was it, anyway? She'd lost all track. And she was hungry; her stomach was growling. But she wasn't quite ready to leave yet. There was still more she had to ask. "That little carnelian figure. The pregnant woman. You left it with the gallery in Paris?" Delia knew the answer, but she wanted to hear it from Sophie.

"Yes, I did. I went back to Paris one last time; it wasn't all that long ago. I went because I had to be sure that I was really and truly done with it, that Palestine was the place. My place. I brought the carnelian sculpture with me. I was ready to let her go, to let that old part of myself go. The dealer was delighted to get it. And she recently wrote to tell me she had sold it."

"I know. Because I have it now."

"You bought it?"

"No. But she sold it to a girl I know from Vassar, who made a gift of it to me."

"I'm so pleased," said Sophie. This time there was no mistaking the smile on her face. "You went to Paris without Simon?"

"Your sculpture was why I went to Paris. I wanted to find out what happened to it. Papa put all of it in a warehouse, but when he tried to get it back, the warehouse had gone out of business. And then when I left school, I had time, and nothing to do really. Once I was in Paris, I found out that you were alive and where you were living."

"I never expected to be in such a place. And yet here I am."

"Here you are," echoed Delia. "You and . . . Asher." Her brother.

"Would you like to meet him?" Sophie asked.

"Yes. I would." She'd come all this way, hadn't she? She had to finish what she'd started.

"All right. If you're sure. I have the afternoon off, and we could go over there now." She looked again at Delia's remaining black pump, now covered with fine, pale dust. "But you're not going to be able to walk with only one shoe," she said with a laugh. She reached under the cot and pulled out another pair of the ubiquitous work boots she had on. It was only then that Delia made the connection: these boots reminded her of those Sophie had worn when she worked in her Paris studio. Yes, she'd changed. But not entirely. Delia had found a thread that bound her to her old life, and to her own surprise, that mattered.

EIGHTEEN

DELIA

1947

Delia left her coat folded on the cot and followed Sophie out of the tent. Together they walked to the children's house a short distance away. Inside the low, stucco-covered building were about twenty-five small children mostly grouped in twos and threes. Many of them sat at small tables; some were coloring with crayons, others playing with wooden blocks. Two little boys rolled a ball back and forth on the floor; a girl leaned over a rag doll in a cardboard shoe box, arranging a scrap of cloth over her like a blanket. And in a corner, by himself, was a boy with blond ringlets and very bright blue eyes—Delia could see them even from where she stood.

Sophie's gaze followed Delia's. "That's him," Sophie said. Delia could hear the anguish in the words. She watched the boy as he arranged some small wooden animals in a row. He was careful about where and how he placed them; he seemed to want them to be equally distant from one another, adjusting the creatures—a cow, a pig, a rooster—again and again, in an apparent effort to get it right. When he was done, he lifted his hand and knocked them all down. The girl looked up briefly; seconds later, she was back to tending to her doll.

Asher picked up the wooden cow and placed it in front of him. Then the pig, the rooster, and some others. And just like before, after he'd carefully and painstakingly arranged them, he knocked them all down again. This time, the girl picked up her doll and box and went somewhere else.

"Does he do that all day?" Delia asked.

"That, or something like it." She continued to watch him. "Come. I'll introduce you." Delia followed her across the room and waited while Sophie spoke to him. Asher ignored her and continued to arrange his animals in the same meticulous order. When he'd set the last of them in place, he finally looked up. His beautiful blue eyes held no expression. Delia tried a small, tentative smile. He did not smile back. His steady blue gaze was disconcerting. She reached out her hand, and for a moment, it seemed like he would take it. But suddenly he grabbed the pig and threw it directly at her face. "Asher!" Sophie seized his wrists before he could throw anything else. The other children looked startled, and the young woman who'd been overseeing the group herded them away.

The pig had hit Delia's forehead, and when she touched her fingers to the spot, they came away sticky with blood. Sophie had her hands on Asher's shoulders and was talking to him, urgently, passionately, in Hebrew, which Delia could not understand. But what she could understand was how deeply engaged with this boy her mother was; how connected. She couldn't remember Sophie ever speaking to her like that; she'd never raised her voice and rarely been angry, only annoyed or impatient. Mostly she was distracted, her attention always wandering, in search of something or someone else. Could Delia actually be jealous of Asher, jealous of how much Sophie seemed to care about him?

Finally, Sophie released Asher, and the young woman, who'd been watching all this time, stepped in. Sophie spoke to her and then turned to Delia. "Are you all right? Can we get you a bandage?"

"I'm fine. The bleeding's stopped." Delia had pressed her handkerchief to the wound; it was nothing more than superficial.

"Still, it couldn't hurt to wash it off and cover it."

"It's okay," Delia said. "Really." She wanted to get out of there, away from this strange child who happened to be her brother.

"If you're sure . . ."

"I am."

Sophie glanced at her watch. "You must be hungry. We didn't have lunch. But it's almost time for dinner. Let's go get something to eat."

"I *am* hungry." Delia hoped dinner would not involve the cabbage she'd smelled earlier.

They left the children's house and stepped outside. Delia took a deep breath, and then another. Sophie had tried to prepare her for meeting Asher. Still, the boy's small act of violence had shaken her. It was not herself that she was concerned about—she'd leave this place soon, and she never had to return. But Sophie couldn't do that; she was bound to this child for years to come. Forever. Again, Delia felt that spiky twist of jealousy. Sophie had been quite able to leave *her*.

The dining hall came into view; people were already heading in. Just outside the doors, Delia saw someone waving at her, calling her, actually—who could it be? Was that *Anne*? It was. Why was she here? But before Delia could call back, a great crashing sound seemed to rise up from behind her, and she was thrown into the air. A small shriek escaped her lips, and for a few awful seconds, she could feel her arms and legs flailing. Then she landed, hard, in the dirt. She was aware of grit in her eyes, dust in her mouth, before the impact knocked the consciousness right out of her.

When Delia came to, she had no idea where she was or what had happened. Then she saw Sophie, her face constricted with worry. "You're awake!" Sophie said. "Finally!"

"Where am I?"

"The hospital in Be'er Sheva. Someone threw a grenade in the window of the dining room. Several grenades, actually. There was an explosion, and you were hurt."

Delia attempted to stitch the recent events together in her mind: the noise, the building collapsing, the screaming. And fire, there must have been fire, because she remembered the acrid smell of smoke. Her head hurt. So did her shoulder. And her, what—foot? Ankle? The entire lower part of her leg radiated pain. "What about Asher?"

"He's fine. All the children are fine. Frightened, of course. But none of them was hurt."

"Was anyone else hurt?"

Sophie's eyes filled with tears. "A few people," she said. "And two were killed."

"What?" Delia didn't even ask who, because apart from being led to Sophie's tent by Hadas, she hadn't talked to anyone else there. But still, it was terrible to think people had been killed. She closed her eyes again.

"Do you want anything?" Sophie asked. "You never got any dinner."

"I'm not hungry now." Delia would no longer describe her head as hurting; she needed a stronger word to convey the sensation of it being held in a vise and squeezed, squeezed, squeezed. There was a burning sensation in both her foot and her ankle; the pain had expanded and made it impossible to locate the source. "What I want is for it to stop," she said.

"You want what to stop?" Sophie looked confused.

"Everything!" Delia burst out. "Please, make it all stop!"

NINETEEN

ANNE

1947

Early on the morning after they'd arrived, Anne waited for Delia in the hotel dining room. When she didn't show up, she went to her room and knocked on the door. No answer. So she went back downstairs to the front desk, where she learned that Delia had gone off on her own very early.

"How do you like that? She left without me," Anne told Drew when she sat back down again.

"But why? She agreed to let you go with her. And the guide would have made things easier."

"Delia's not interested in things being easy."

"Well, you can go to Be'er Sheva anyway. Jim Doyle is taking the bus there in about an hour so you can ride with him." Jim Doyle was a reporter with the *Herald Tribune*.

"I still wish I could go to Jerusalem with you," said Anne.

"I know. But it's not a good time. There'll be lines everywhere, armed forces patrolling the streets. You wouldn't be able to see any of the sights, and you'd barely be able to get around the city because you'd have to show your papers everywhere you tried to go."

So Anne reluctantly agreed, and a little while later she watched as the olive-green jeep pulled away from the curb and started off down the street, sputtering as it went. Drew was in that jeep, along with three other reporters. They all wore helmets. Maybe it *was* better to spend the day in Be'er Sheva and meet Drew later on. On the bus with Jim, she took the window seat. The landscape outside turned from green to brown, and soon they were in the desert. She thought of Delia, who must have come this way earlier today. Maybe her decision to go solo had less to do with Anne and more to do with her need to do this momentous thing on her own. What would that be like—thinking your mother was dead and then finding out that no, she was alive?

The bus pulled into the depot before noon, and Ahmed was waiting in front of it. She knew who he was because he held up a sign with her name.

"Pleased to meet you," he said, extending his hand. His English was excellent, and he was dressed in a pressed white shirt, open at the neck, dark slacks, and black loafers. His very dark, silver-streaked hair was worn somewhat long and combed back from his face. "Be'er Sheva is nothing like your cities in America, but it's our home, and we love it here."

"I'm sure you do." Anne felt there was something just the slightest bit challenging in his comment, but he said nothing more, so she simply followed him past low houses, mostly stone but some made of stucco and painted creamy pastel colors: pink, pale blue, a turquoise that was several shades lighter than the sky. There were almost no cars on the road; instead there were wagons pulled by horses and donkeys. And camels. Anne had never seen so many.

She stopped in front of a camel that had been tied to a rusted metal post. The animal's hump was covered in dense light-brown fur, and its feet were large, flat, and dusty. But it was the face that interested her: the mournful dark eyes, the set of the mouth, which appeared to be smiling, as if it knew an important secret that it would never reveal.

When they started walking again, they came to what appeared to be the main avenue. Rows of evenly spaced date palms lined each side, and the ground beneath the trees was littered with ripe, sticky fruit. Ahmed knelt to pick up a date, which he wiped clean with a white handkerchief drawn from his pocket before offering it to Anne. At first she hesitated—it had been on the ground, after all—but refusing felt churlish, so she took the date and carefully bit into the dark, wrinkled flesh. It tasted sweet but also somehow tangy and even smoky—a complex, lingering flavor. "Delicious," she said. Ahmed smiled.

After that, there wasn't much to see. Anne wondered how they would fill the next few hours. It wasn't even lunchtime yet, and Drew wouldn't be here until this evening. She was hungry, though, and so was glad when Ahmed led her to a small café and ordered a meal for the two of them—something he called falafel. It came served with round, flat bread. Anne tore it open, and steam rushed out, burning the inside of her hand.

"I'm sorry," Ahmed said, dipping the same handkerchief he'd used before into his glass of water; the glass itself was smudged and dirty, but Anne allowed him to press the wet cloth to her palm, where a blister was already beginning to form. The crisp golden balls of ground chickpeas, along with the bread, were like nothing she'd ever had before. For dessert, there were dates, this time stuffed with a mixture of finely chopped nuts, and dark, fragrantly spiced tea.

But after the meal ended, there were still several hours before dinner. Then Anne had an idea about how to fill them. "Could you take me to the kibbutz near here?" she asked.

"Chatserim?" Ahmed looked puzzled. When Anne nodded, he added, "I suppose so. But why?"

"The friend I'm traveling with is visiting. I'd like to see it too." This was true; Anne had not even heard of kibbutzim before Delia had told her about them, and now that she was so close, she was curious. And she wanted to make sure Delia had gotten there and was all right.

"It's not very far," Ahmed said. "I suppose I can get you back to Be'er Sheva by dinnertime."

They made the trip in a wagon that Ahmed owned; it was pulled by a small black horse. As the animal clopped along, Ahmed talked to him, often offering encouragement and praise. Anne knew very little about horses, but it seemed to her that this one was well cared for, and clearly loved. Soon they had left the city behind and were surrounded by the vast expanse of the desert. Anne rooted through her handbag for the small guidebook that Drew had given her and began to read.

> The uninitiated traveler comes to the Negev and sees only a void, a barren, forsaken place. But this is the land where Abraham came face to face with God, and where ancient tribes forged a new relationship with Him. The sons and daughters of the Negev hold the history and majesty of this place within themselves. The Bedouin have been here for centuries. The Ottoman and the Turks came later, along with the Jews. The Negev is big enough for all of them, and it is these privileged souls who know the secrets of the hidden canyons, the brilliance of the piercingly blue sky, and the harsh beauty of the ragged promontories that jut out over the land.

She looked up again. Those canyons were pretty well hidden, and she had yet to see any promontories, ragged or otherwise, jutting out. But she knew about "the privileged souls" who each felt they had a claim to the land. "Has your family lived here a long time?" she asked.

"At least three generations." He seemed surprised by the question. "Maybe four." He was quiet for a few minutes before adding, "It wasn't always like this."

"Like what?" she asked, though she knew.

"The fighting. The endless fighting. The British came because it gave them the opening they needed to conquer Syria and the rest of Palestine. After that, there were riots, and most of the Jews left—most, but not all. And now they're back again. Grabbing the land. Trying to force us out."

Now Anne felt defensive. She wondered if he assumed she was a Jew. She was silent for the rest of the trip. When they arrived at the kibbutz, Ahmed helped her down. It was a primitive, makeshift sort of place, and she saw two young men with rifles sitting on either side of the entrance. The men looked at them quickly, sizing them up, and one of them said something in what Anne now knew was Hebrew. Ahmed answered and then turned to Anne. "There's someone who speaks English well, and I'm going to find her for you. Her name is Hadas. You can wait here." He went off and reappeared a few minutes later with a woman at his side. She wore work clothes like everyone else that Anne saw. Ahmed climbed back into the wagon. "Meet me here at five thirty." He gave a signal to the horse, and they were off, the sound of hooves reverberating in the air.

"Hello," Hadas said to Anne. "What can I do for you?"

"I'm looking for Sophie Rossner and my friend Delia. Do you know where they are?"

Hadas nodded. "Delia came earlier today, and I helped her find Sophie. I'm guessing they're together now, though I'm not sure where. We can go look for them."

As they walked, Hadas pointed to a rectangular, one-story building. "That's the *beit yeladim*—the children's house."

"Children's house?" asked Anne.

"We raise children communally," Hadas said. "It's more efficient, and we think it benefits the children too."

Really? Anne heard at least one baby crying as they passed, and possibly even two. That didn't sound beneficial to her. They kept walking until Hadas stopped in front of one of the tents. "Sophie lives here." Hadas called her name, and when there was no answer, she peered into the opening. "They're not there," she said. "Let's go to the dining hall. They'll be setting up for dinner soon, and I'm sure Sophie and her daughter will be there."

Anne followed Hadas, who pointed to a bench just outside the building. "You can wait here."

Anne sat down and set her small valise by her feet; Drew had said they would be spending the night in Be'er Sheva, so she'd brought a change of clothes. People passed back and forth, all of them in well-worn clothes—heavy pants or sometimes shorts, faded canvas jackets or sweaters that had stretched-out hems and necklines and were punctured by holes. But their attitudes, at least as far as she could tell, were cheerful and optimistic. They were smiling; they stopped to talk to each other, to clasp hands, to hug. The kibbutz may have lacked material comforts, but it seemed rich in communal feeling.

A couple with a little girl walked by. The man and the woman each held one of her hands, and on the count of three, pulled her up so that for a few seconds she was suspended in the air, head thrown back and laughing. After they had passed, Anne caught sight of a young woman in very different clothes—a blue-green silk dress, or was it a skirt and blouse?—and knew instantly who it was.

"Delia!" Anne waved her arm. "Delia, over here!" She saw Delia look in her direction, and Anne jumped up, about to go over to her. But before she took a step, she felt the ground shake under her, and in the next second there was an explosion that shocked her ears. More sounds followed—things smashing, screams. Smoke filled the air, causing Anne's lungs to tighten and her eyes to water. She began to cough, her lungs rebelling against the rapidly forming gray clouds. Whirling around, Anne saw that it was the dining hall—there was a huge hole in one wall, and the roof was on fire. And then, before her horrified eyes, the building collapsed, bringing the roof—and the fire—with it. More screams, and someone was shouting—shouting at *her.* She didn't understand the words, but she understood their meaning. Someone was telling her to run, run for her life. So that's what she did.

TWENTY

ANNE

1947

Galvanized by panic, Anne ran from the scene as fast and as far as she could. She reached the place where the kibbutz ended and the desert began and then stopped, panting from the exertion. The wind had picked up, turning the air cool; it felt good on her hot, sweaty skin. It was quieter here, but in her head the screaming still echoed. Had anyone been hurt? Had *Delia* been hurt? Now the wind was making her cold, and she began to shake. Somewhere in her valise she had both a scarf and a hat, but the valise wasn't there; she'd left it behind, and there was no way she was going back for it.

She stood there, still shaking, unable to form a coherent idea of where to go next or what to do. And then she saw it: the wagon, the glossy black horse. Ahmed! He'd come for her, just as he'd promised. As he approached, she could see the worry on his face.

"What's happened?" He came nimbly down from the cart and stared. "Are you all right?"

"I don't know," she croaked.

"You're dirty." He again offered his handkerchief.

Anne touched her palms to her cheeks; they felt gritty. Then she looked down at herself. Ash and dirt covered the front of her dress, and no doubt the back as well.

"Come on, let's get out of here. You can tell me what happened on the way."

"We can't leave yet." Although she had bolted from the explosion, now that she was safe—or safe enough—she could think of Delia.

"Why not?"

"There was an explosion and my friend is still back there. Maybe she's hurt."

"If she is, there's nothing you can do about it."

"Still. I have to know."

"I'm leaving now and you should too. If you go back, I'm not going to wait."

Anne thought about this as she attempted to clean her face with the handkerchief. She was desperate to know what had happened to Delia but if she went back now, she'd be stuck here all night or even longer. And Ahmed was right—even if Delia had been hurt, what could she do about it?

Extending her arm, she let him help her up to the wagon and as they drove away from the kibbutz, she told him more about the blast that had destroyed the dining hall.

"Grenades. They tossed them through the windows."

"How do you know?"

He didn't answer, and then she understood—he knew because this had happened before. And would happen again.

"Why would anyone bomb a dining hall?" She was almost talking to herself. "Or any place on a kibbutz? It's not a military target. It's just the place these people call home."

"It was a place my people called home too," he said.

Anne was quiet for the rest of the ride. She could still feel the explosion reverberating through her, again and again. Her breathing hadn't slowed. Neither had her pounding heart. Reflexively, she began to pat herself all over, to see if she'd been hurt. Everything felt intact. But what about Delia? Was she all right?

"How can I find out what happened back there?" she asked Ahmed.

"What do you mean? You know what happened."

"I know what happened to the building. But not to the people who were in it or near it. Was anyone hurt?"

Ahmed grunted. "Maybe. That was the plan."

"Whose plan?" Her voice scaled up.

"Whoever did it." Unlike Anne's, his voice was cool and controlled. "Those grenades didn't launch themselves."

Drew was waiting for them when they arrived in Be'er Sheva. "Anne, are you okay? You're a mess!" He hurried over to the wagon.

"I'm okay." It wasn't true, but she couldn't say more just then.

"There was an explosion on the kibbutz," added Ahmed. "She says she wasn't hurt."

"An explosion! Where?"

"I'll tell you everything later," Anne said. "Right now, I just want to clean myself up."

Drew paid Ahmed for the day and thanked him for bringing Anne back unharmed. "I thought the kibbutz would be a safer place."

"Right now," Ahmed said, "no place is safe."

That evening Drew took Anne's hands across the table in the hotel's restaurant. "Do you want to talk about what happened?"

"There was an explosion, and . . . I was terrified. I just . . . ran."

"That was a good instinct," he said. "The best instinct."

"Delia didn't."

"Didn't what?"

"Didn't escape. I saw her in front of the dining hall. It was a moment before the explosion. I called her name. She heard me, I know she did, because she turned to look, and then—"

"And then what?" His voice was gentle.

"And then I was running. Gone. I didn't stay to see if she was all right."

"Of course you didn't. You had to get away."

"But what happened to her? I've got to know."

"Tomorrow I can make some calls and—"

"Not tomorrow. Tonight."

"You mean now?"

"Yes. Please, *please*, you have to do it now."

"All right." He stood up. "You wait here."

While he was gone, the waiter set down their meals, but Anne didn't touch her food.

Finally he came back.

"Well?" she said. "Did you find out anything?"

"I did." He waited for a moment.

"You have to tell me!" she said. "Whatever it is, no matter how terrible."

"Two people were killed," he said finally.

"Was one of them—"

"Not your friend. But she was hurt—a concussion, a broken ankle, a dislocated shoulder."

"Still alive? Not dead?"

"Not dead."

"And where is she?"

"In the hospital. In Be'er Sheva."

"Be'er Sheva. That means I can see her, doesn't it?"

"I suppose so. But not tonight. You're not going anywhere tonight except up to bed."

They went upstairs early and said good night in front of the door to Anne's room. Earlier Drew had gone out to buy Anne some clothes—her valise was back at the kibbutz, and what she had been wearing was ruined—and while he hadn't found a nightgown, he had come up with a pair of cream-colored men's pajamas. They were enormous, but the cotton was soft and smooth, and she rubbed her fingers against it for several seconds before putting the pajamas on and getting into bed. Despite her exhaustion, she couldn't sleep. Two people had been killed. Blown up. Was it wrong to be grateful that Delia wasn't one of them? Eventually, Anne drifted off, but her dreams were filled with the wail of sirens, which turned into the sound of some animal howling. She woke in a sweaty panic and groped for the lamp's switch. Even with the light on, the room felt strange and distorted. She had to get up, get moving, remind herself that she was alive.

The hallway was dim. Still, she knew where Drew's door was. She stood in front of it for a few seconds before she knocked, softly at first, and then louder. It took a moment before the door opened. Drew looked sleepy, and his hair was sticking out on one side; somehow it was endearing. And he was wearing only pajama bottoms; this was the first time she'd seen his handsome bare chest.

"Anne, what is it?"

Suddenly it engulfed her, a great wave of relief, and she began to sob, giving in to the tears she realized she'd been holding back for hours. He pulled her into his arms and pushed the door closed behind her. The room was dark, but the white sheets and coverlet were visible and the bed seemed to glow. He brought her over to it, and she slowly sat down. The tears didn't stop.

"It's all right," he soothed. "You're all right. You can stay here if you want."

Yes, she did want that, and she allowed herself to sink down onto the mattress. He slipped in beside her, not touching. Her tears subsided, and she took a few deep breaths. Now she was aware of the space between them, every inch of it. She'd never been in bed with a man—that was what you did when you were married, not before. She and Drew had kissed, and kissed passionately. Twice he'd slipped his hand under her blouse, and once inside her bra. She'd felt his excitement then, pressing that hard part of himself against her; she'd been excited by that too, excited that she could arouse him. But things had not gone any further.

Anne knew she should go back to her own room—immediately. Nice girls didn't behave this way. Yet she also knew that she would do nothing of the kind, nothing to break this invisible but powerful current that connected them. Tentatively, she reached over to touch his naked back. He didn't react. But his skin—it was so smooth. Warm. She wanted to keep touching it; touching it calmed her. For several minutes, they didn't speak, but she knew he was awake, alert and wholly aware of her hand caressing him. Who was this girl? How had she become so bold?

Finally he turned around to face her. "Anne?" Her eyes had adjusted to the dark by now, and she could see the question on his face.

"Yes," she said softly, as he moved closer and then closer still. "Oh yes, please yes."

Anne woke feeling exhilarated, even giddy. What a wonderful end to an awful day. She sat up and stretched. Drew wasn't there, but on the pillow where he'd laid his head was a note. *I didn't want to wake you; you were sleeping so soundly. Come meet me in the dining room when you get up. I love you.*

And she loved him. She pulled back the covers. There on the sheet was a smear of blood. A slow flush of shame enveloped her. What they'd done in the dark was one thing; acknowledging it in the clear light of day was another. Girls were ostracized for such behavior. Delia had been expelled for it. Anne thought, for the first time in a long while, of Virginia and the others at Vassar—their judgment, their condemnation. If they knew what she'd done . . . but why was she thinking of them? They didn't matter, not a bit. All that mattered was that Drew loved her.

She dressed quickly and took the note with her when she went downstairs—it was her proof and her protection. There he was, smiling, and when she sat down, he reached across the table and took her hand. She smiled back but couldn't find the words that seemed appropriate.

"Good morning." His voice was tender, a caress all by itself. "I hope you slept well."

"I did." That wasn't much but at least she'd managed to reply.

The waiter appeared and took their order; when Drew asked what she wanted to eat, she said, "Whatever would be quickest. We should get out of here as soon as we can." Suddenly it seemed imperative to get out of these ill-fitting clothes—the coarse cotton dress he'd found was too small, the jacket even more oversize than the pajamas. To get away from the violence of the day before, those images returning, diluting the happiness she'd felt earlier. She hadn't found out if he'd heard anything more—had there been any retaliation? But at least she knew that Delia was alive. Drew said she was in the hospital in Be'er Sheva, and Anne would see her soon.

Once again, Drew climbed into the jeep while Anne watched. He was headed to Chatserim to photograph what had happened there, but she didn't want to see it again—the memory would stay with her for a long time. He'd be back that night, and then the next day she'd go to Tel Aviv to catch her plane to Paris. Delia was supposed to be going with her, but obviously, that wasn't going to happen.

Anne got the directions to the hospital from someone at the hotel; it wasn't too far, and he'd been kind enough to draw her a little map on a scrap of paper. Soon she came to a pastry shop and stopped. Wouldn't it be nice to bring a box of pastries to Delia? Silver bells jangled when she walked through the door. Ahead of her was a man in a glowingly white shirt making his selections; it took her a moment to realize that it was Ahmed, her guide from the day before. She said nothing, but when he turned away from the counter holding a string-tied box, he recognized her.

"So it's you again. You're all right?" he asked. "No harm done?"

"I'm fine," she said. "Thank you again for getting me away from there so quickly."

"It must have been frightening for you."

Anne was about to say yes, it was, but then he added, "You Americans are so soft. Nothing bad has happened to you in a long time. But bad things have been happening to us longer than you've been alive."

"Bad things can happen to anyone." She surprised herself by answering back.

"They happen to some people more than others." The bells jingled again as he left the bakery. The sound, so pleasant just a moment ago, no longer was.

To distract herself, Anne looked into the glass case, which held an assortment of sweets—thin layers of pastry shaped into nests or balls or sliced into diamond shapes, crushed nuts oozing from their centers, glistening with syrup that pooled at the bottom of the tray. She bought several before heading back out into the street. Stopping at a wide avenue, she waited to cross. A horse drawn wagon paused almost directly in front of her, the horse's black, unblinking eye seeming to regard her calmly. She wasn't calm, though. Far from it. She was exceedingly agitated, a strange mixture of ashamed, defiant, thrilled, and frightened. The explosion the day before. What she had done with Drew. She didn't think it was wrong, exactly, but it would take some adjusting to; she hadn't thought she was the kind of girl who would go to bed with a boy—or a man—before she was married.

She wished she could talk to someone about this. No, not someone, she wanted to talk to Delia. *Delia*—Delia had done the same thing, more than once, and with a man who was married besides. Anne remembered how shocked she'd been. Now the shock had faded, and she longed to talk to Delia about how you could still be a good girl even if you'd broken the rules, rules that you'd never thought to question before. Well, she was on her way to visit Delia now, although she knew there wouldn't be an opportunity for such an intimate conversation.

She walked past a few small stores, and several storefronts that were empty. Grocery, pharmacy, another bakery, cobbler—nothing really captured or held her interest until she saw, in the second-floor window of a building across the street, several mannequins that displayed lingerie. She was tempted to go up and have a look, but not now. First she had to get to the hospital. If there was time after that, she would do it then.

And look, here she was in front of a three-story building covered in a grainy pale-peach coating that looked as if it had been spackled on. She went inside. Delia's room was on the third floor, no elevator, so she climbed the stairs, bakery box in hand. There, in room 306, was Delia, looking small and shrunken amid the white pillows, sheets, and blanket. Her wrist was bandaged, her eyes were closed, and she was breathing lightly through her mouth.

"Shalom?"

Anne turned to see the woman sitting upright on a chair by Delia's bed. She hadn't noticed her when she came in.

"Hello," Anne said. "I'm a friend of Delia's. From school. I was visiting the kibbutz yesterday, and I was there when the dining room was bombed."

"It's been totally destroyed," the woman said. "But I'm sorry, I should have introduced myself. I'm Sophie Rossner, Delia's mother. And you are . . . ?"

"Anne Bishop." So this was the French-speaking sculptress mother Delia had talked about. Anne tried not to stare at her.

"You said you know Delia from school. From Vassar?"

Anne nodded, not really trusting herself to say anything. Did Delia's mother know she had been expelled? Or that Anne was instrumental in it? But then Delia's eyes opened, and Anne was spared having to say anything.

"You have a visitor," Sophie said.

"Anne?" Delia's brow furrowed in concentration. "What are you doing here? I thought I saw you at the kibbutz yesterday—or did I imagine that?"

"I was there. I was looking for you."

Delia's eyes fluttered shut as she nodded. "I know . . . I was supposed to meet you . . . and the guide . . ." she said. "But I didn't, I went by myself . . ." She trailed off, and soon it was apparent that she was asleep again.

"She has a concussion," said Sophie. "So she's been drifting in and out. The doctor says that's normal." She patted a metal chair beside her. "Why don't you sit down? And you can put your package down too."

"Oh, this is for Delia." Anne handed the box to Sophie. "Maybe you'd like one?"

"Not now," said Sophie. "But thank you."

Sitting next to Sophie, Anne couldn't very well scrutinize her the way she would have liked to, so she focused on Delia, who, though still sleeping, had started muttering. The words were mostly indistinct, but Anne caught a few—*no, stop, why did you, no, no, no.* She sounded fretful. Anxious.

A nurse appeared at the doorway and said something to Sophie in Hebrew. Sophie stood up. "Visiting hours are over," she said. "We have to go. But you can come back this evening if you want."

"All right. Maybe I will." Anne wasn't sure if she would. "You'll take the pastries, though? Delia might like one."

"I think she would." Sophie smiled, and Anne could see that, yes, she had been very beautiful and was even beautiful now. "It was nice of you to bring them."

Once she'd left the hospital, Anne made her way back to the building where she'd seen the lingerie shop. Her visit to Delia had not been entirely satisfying, but at least she'd tried. And she'd seen for herself that Delia, though wounded, was essentially all right—she'd recover. That in itself was an enormous relief. Climbing a narrow, poorly lit flight of stairs, she arrived at a landing with a single door. It was partially open, so she gave it a small push. Once inside, Anne's eyes scanned the room. There were the mannequins she'd seen from across the street. The windows she'd seen were, from this vantage point, revealed to be smeared and dusty; there were clear arcs left where someone had tried to wipe them. She walked toward them, passing a few metal racks from which hung various undergarments, but mostly the merchandise was heaped on glass counters, loosely folded, spilling out of fragile cardboard boxes, frothing from tightly packed drawers. "Hello?" called Anne. "Anyone here?"

"Hello!" a voice called out from somewhere in the back of the shop. "Can I help you?"

Anne detected an accent—German? She looked around until she saw who'd spoken—a small woman who wore a crocheted shawl and dangling pearl earrings. Her gray hair was done in braids pinned on the top of her head, and her thin legs, encased in dark, ribbed stockings, poked out from the hem of her jersey dress.

"Do you mind if I look around?"

"Of course," said the woman. "Take your time."

Despite the haphazard presentation, Anne could see that the slips, chemises, and negligees were exquisitely made—the silks, the satins, even the cotton, of the highest quality—and many were trimmed with lace, embroidery, or both. Much of the stock was quite old and looked like it was from twenty or thirty years earlier. How unlikely to discover such finery here!

Anne picked up a sheer white nightgown and held it against herself. "Come." The woman gestured for Anne to follow and led her to an oval mirror that hung on a rather grimy wall. The nightgown looked as if it would be flattering—that square-cut neckline, the lace strips that made the straps.

"It suits you," said the woman. "And wait, I have something else." She rummaged through one of the boxes and pulled out what Anne could see was a matching robe—also white, with the same lace, but with two white satin birds embroidered on either lapel; the birds held banners in their beaks, and on the banners were rows of tiny white satin hearts bordered by white opalescent beads. "You have to try it on. Make sure it fits," said the woman. Anne looked around. There was no dressing room, but there was also no one else in the shop. She was still wearing the uncomfortable—and unflattering—dress Drew had bought, and she gladly took it off; after this, she was going to buy something, anything, else to wear. She slipped the nightgown over her head.

It was perfect—the simplicity of the neckline and straps was both elegant and luxurious, and when she added the robe, which the woman had handed her, it became an ensemble, just right for a wedding night. Wedding night! Was she really thinking about that?

". . . it's a bit long, but I could have someone hem it for you. Could you come back the day after tomorrow?"

Anne shook her head. "I'll be gone by then," she said. "But I could get it done in Paris—that's where I'm off to."

"Paris." The woman sighed. "A beautiful city."

"It is," Anne said. "Do you know it well?"

"I used to go to Paris on buying trips," the woman said. "But that was before the war. Before everything changed."

Anne saw the way her face instantly changed, the friendly, attentive expression clouded. She gestured to the piles around her. "Are these things you bought on some of those trips?"

"Some of them, yes. But there was more, much more. I had to leave in a hurry, so I took whatever I could carry," the woman said. "I couldn't take everything . . . When I think about what got left behind, I feel sick." She reached into a velvet pouch that hung from around her neck, pulled out a cigarette, and lit it. Then she took a deep drag. "And even sicker to think that my very best things ended up on the back of some Nazi pig's wife. Or mistress." She tilted her chin up, so that the exhaled smoke rose in a stream above her head.

"Are you from Germany?" Anne asked tentatively.

"Vienna. Do you know Vienna? That was a beautiful city too. Quite beautiful. And cultivated. Refined. I had a shop on the Kärntner Strasse. It was in our family for three generations. But when Hitler got into power, it was all over for us." She took another drag. "You see, we were Jews."

"So am I," said Anne.

"But you're from America." Anne nodded. "You were safe over there. Protected. You don't know what we know . . . what we saw, what *I* saw." The woman's hands clenched, creating two small, tight fists.

"It must have been . . . horrible."

"You can't imagine." She gave Anne a hard, penetrating look. "Anyway, that life is over. I escaped with what I could, and I was lucky to get out. I wanted to go to London, even to New York, but those places, those *governments*, said no. But Palestine welcomed me with open arms." She stubbed out her cigarette in a cut glass ashtray. "Why am I going on about all that? You're here to buy a nightgown, aren't you? A nightgown and perhaps a robe." She began to fold the garments. When they were wrapped in yellowing tissue paper and the bundle tied with a bow, she handed it to Anne.

"Thank you." Anne couldn't stop the images in her head: herself in the white nightgown, Drew sliding the straps down from one shoulder and then the other. She pulled out her wallet and paid, but before she could leave, the woman laid a hand on her arm.

"Wait," she said and scurried off again, this time returning with a faded blue shoe box. She ran her hand over the top of it to wipe away the dust before giving it to Anne. Inside was a pair of cream-colored embroidered slippers trimmed with white fur. They looked as if they might fit, and when Anne tried them on, she found that yes, they did. She peered down at her feet, encased in the soft, luxurious materials. These slippers had been part of another life, and now they were going to be part of hers.

"I love them." Anne took out her wallet again, but the woman waved it away.

"A gift," she said. "From one Jew to another." She looked at Anne almost tenderly and extended her hand. "I'm Giselle. Giselle Krauss."

"And I'm Anne Bishop."

Giselle raised her eyebrows. "Bishop?" Then her mouth formed a rueful smile. "Never mind. I understand. Maybe America wasn't Austria. But that didn't mean it was easy to be a Jew there. Maybe it's not so easy to be a Jew anywhere."

Anne knew that her own minor difficulties paled before Giselle Krauss's experience and the experience of so many others; the two didn't exist in the same universe. "No," she said. "It isn't."

On her way back to the hotel, Anne thought about this. Yesterday had been the most alarming, most frightening day of her life. But it was also clarifying in some way. Galvanizing. She'd experienced, firsthand, just how precarious it was to be a Jew. Not that she didn't know that, but she'd known it only in the abstract, from events that had happened long ago or far away. And what she'd known had been on a minor scale—the sting of prejudice, of snide and hurtful comments. But that explosion and her panicked dash gave her an entirely different perspective. Before, being Jewish had been an impediment; now she saw how it could be a matter of life and death.

When she got to her room. Anne put the package away and went downstairs to wait for Drew in the dining room. It wasn't long before he came in and sat down. He looked tired and, as she looked closer, disheveled, even dirty. "Do you want to go up and shower before dinner?" she asked.

"That's just what I want to do. I'll be quick, and then we can eat and I'll tell you about my day. Did you find your friend?"

"I did," said Anne. "She's all right. She was hurt, but not that badly."

At dinner, Drew told Anne about being at the kibbutz, what he'd heard and seen.

"Did they find out who did it? And why?" Though she essentially knew.

Ahmed had made it clear.

"No. But it wasn't a very well thought out attack," he said. "They think it was done by a few teenagers from one of the towns nearby."

"Teenagers? Really?"

"A couple of weeks ago, a few Arab boys and boys from the kibbutz got into a fight, and two of the Arab boys ended up in the hospital. One of them died. So the attack was their way of retaliating."

"But that won't settle it. The people from the kibbutz will want to get revenge." She thought of a line her father was fond of repeating. *An eye for an eye leaves everyone blind.*

"Nothing is going to get settled for a long time." Drew continued eating. "Tell me about your day. What did you do while I was gone?"

When they'd finished eating, they went up to their separate rooms, which was probably the right thing; they both needed to think about how far, all of a sudden, their relationship had come. There was no discussion of their sleeping together again, which of course was the right thing. Sleeping together before you were married was just wrong, wasn't it?

Then why was Anne so disappointed? She knew they should wait; they *would* wait. The one night they hadn't, well, that was an exception. She pulled back the covers, thinking of the white nightgown and robe tucked under the bed. Too soon for her to wear them. Just as she was drifting off, she heard a light knocking outside, in the hallway. She got up and crossed the room.

"Who's there?" Though of course she knew. Knew and was so happy.

"It's me."

Anne opened the door. Drew was wearing the clean clothes he'd put on earlier, after he'd showered, but now his striped shirt was partially unbuttoned. That seemed like a sign to her. An invitation. She didn't say a word but took his hand and drew him over the threshold, so that their bodies were almost touching. Then she closed the door and shot the bolt home.

The next day it was that much harder to say goodbye, especially since Drew was going to be staying in Palestine for another week, and then he was off to other countries in the region—Syria, Egypt, Lebanon.

"I'm going to miss you." Anne felt tears forming in her eyes, but she wasn't going to cry, she just wasn't going to.

"I'm going to miss you too," he said. "That's why I bought you this." He produced a silver ring with an oval stone in a saturated shade of green and slid it onto her finger.

"It's lovely." The tears were still threatening, but their source had shifted. A ring. Who could miss the symbolism of that?

"It's called an Eilat stone," he said. "I hope you'll think of me when you wear it."

Anne's answer was to move closer and press her lips to his. She'd never initiated a kiss before; that was the man's prerogative, she'd been taught. But Drew's passionate response let her know that he didn't mind.

TWENTY-ONE

ANNE

1948

Much as she missed Drew, Anne was relieved to be back in Paris. The city was still cold. Still gray. But what had seemed dirty and slightly seedy when she'd first arrived now, after Palestine, seemed unbelievably luxurious. Her classes resumed, and she threw herself into them—French poetry from the fifteenth through the nineteenth century, French classical drama, Greco-Roman art.

And Drew wrote to her, the thin blue onionskin envelopes filling her mail cubby, sometimes two on the same day. She answered the letters immediately and brought them, along with the letters she wrote to Delia, to the *bureau de poste* near the dormitory.

"He must be crazy about you," Nancy said.

"It's mutual," Anne said. "We're crazy about each other."

"So it's serious?"

Anne looked down, not sure how much to reveal. But her happiness must have been painted on her face, because Nancy said, "Anne Bishop, are you engaged to my brother?"

"No." Anne felt a little deflated by the admission. "But he did give me this." She showed Nancy the silver ring.

"Oh, I'd say that's a major sign," said Nancy. "A major sign." She sighed. "I'm happy for you both. And my mother—she's going to be happy too. She's going to *adore* you—just wait until you two meet!" And then Anne learned she wouldn't have to wait long to meet Mrs. Gilchrist, who had planned a trip to Paris in time for Easter.

Spring began to make its first fitful overtures. One day the temperature climbed and the sun shone brightly, but the next day was gray again, with a wind that whipped around Anne's face, making her eyes tear and nose run. Yet even when it was chilly, she could see the tender green buds on the shrubs, and the early flowers—crocuses, snowdrops—starting to peek out.

Most days, Anne still needed her fur coat, though sometimes she left it open, or even wriggled her arms out of the sleeves and wore it on her shoulders. That was how Delia had worn her coat when Anne first noticed her. It seemed such a long time ago. She'd written to Delia, but had not heard back. Maybe she ought to write again.

But she didn't. She had reached out to Delia so many times, apologized, tried to help her, and yet she always felt rebuffed. Maybe it was time to accept that this friendship, unlike the spring flowers, would never blossom. It looked as if Anne had squandered her chance with this interesting, intriguing person, and she wasn't going to get another.

So she threw herself into her schoolwork and spent time with the new friends she'd made in Paris. Some, like Rosalie, were from the United States, but there were others who came from different places—England, Scotland, Hong Kong, and even Australia. Anne felt like her view of the world—and of herself—was being pried wide open. Still, she somehow missed Delia—her sense of independence, her courage. Anne still had the address of the kibbutz; she would write to her mother and see if she was still there.

One night she walked to Le Petit Saint Benôit for an early dinner with Drew. Ever since his return to Paris he'd been so busy; there hadn't been much opportunity to get together. The restaurant was nearly empty when she walked in. She spotted him right away, sitting at a table near the window. He got up from the table and kissed her on both cheeks, adopting the French custom she liked so much. When they were seated, the waiter brought a carafe of wine and two glasses before whisking off to another table.

"How was your day?" she asked.

"Hectic. And things are only going to get worse." He poured the wine and took a long drink before she'd even raised her glass to her lips. "In fact, I just found out my trip's been moved up. I'm leaving tomorrow."

"Tomorrow?" The word felt like a punch.

He nodded. "I don't have a choice."

"Where are you going?"

"Back to Palestine. Things are really heating up again."

"More fighting?"

"More fighting."

Anne didn't reply, and she was glad when Drew changed the subject.

"I was hoping I would be here when my mother arrived," he said. "But that's not going to be possible, so Nancy will introduce you. She's looking forward to meeting you."

"What have you told her about me?"

"That you're uncommonly pretty, extremely smart, and—"

"But not that I'm Jewish."

"It didn't exactly come up, no."

"Drew—" Anne reached across the table to put a hand on his arm. "It's not going to come up unless you *tell* her. Your mother is not going to ask about my religion, is she?"

"Well, no. She'll just assume that you're Christian." He finished the wine in his glass and poured himself another. "That you go to church. Regular observance is pretty important to her."

"But not to you." She knew this because he'd told her so. Back in February, on Ash Wednesday, Nancy's forehead was smudged with ash but his had not been. Also, he was having sex outside of marriage and using rubbers when he did, both things the church frowned upon. Still, she couldn't help feeling apprehensive about how Mrs. Gilchrist would take the news that she wasn't Christian at all.

"No, you know that. We've been through it already." Did she detect a touch of . . . asperity? Annoyance? Then his tone grew gentler. "I just wanted her to meet you first, to see how wonderful you are, before I brought it up. Is there anything wrong with that?"

"I suppose not." She had a sip of wine and then another.

"You're getting all upset for nothing. But there's no reason for it." He leaned across the table and took her hand. "Everything will work out. You'll see. I just need to be careful with my mother. Ever since my dad left, it's the role I've had to step into, like it or not."

Anne knew about how Drew's father had deserted them when he was ten and Nancy was four and how he'd become the man of the family, and felt the need to act strong for his mother and sister. She also knew how he'd not seen his father again until he was eighteen; they had run into each other on the street, and he had found out that his father had made another life for himself—new wife, new kids. He never told Nancy or his mother about that meeting; he bore the burden of that secret all alone. And when he later learned that his father had died and left them nothing, he was glad he'd not brought it up. It would only have hurt them all over again. He'd been a good son, a good brother. A good person. Anne felt the tension of the last few minutes ebbing away. He was right. This divide between them—call it culture, call it religion—didn't have to be a major issue for them.

The next day, Anne was with him as he moved briskly around his hotel room, stuffing clothes into his valise.

"I'll miss you." Her eyes strayed to the bed, where they'd made love several times now. She and Drew were lovers, a word that thrilled yet frightened her. It meant she had crossed into new territory; there were no signposts, no familiar landmarks to guide her.

"I'll miss you too." Drew was standing in front of her now, stroking her hair, her face. His hand moved to the buttons on her blouse and undid the top one. "Anne . . ." he said softly as he kissed her neck. She shuddered in pleasurable anticipation. Would they go to bed now, in the middle of the day? They'd only been together at night before, and somehow this seemed even more illicit and compromising. Then he stopped. "I wish we could. But there isn't time," he said. Within the hour, he was gone.

Evelyn Gilchrist arrived several days later, and the next evening Anne and Nancy met her for dinner at La Coupole. She was a diminutive, subdued wren of a woman—dark gray coat, gray hat with a bit of a veil at the front, dark brown suit. The only bright thing about her was the gold crucifix that sat snugly above the suit's top button. It was small, but it shone brightly, and Anne found her eyes drawn to it, making it hard for her to focus on their conversation. But Mrs. Gilchrist was tired from her trip and needed to end the evening early.

"I'm sorry we didn't get to talk more. Might we have lunch tomorrow?" They were out on the street again, standing in a pool of lamplight.

"Yes, I'm free," said Anne. She had only one class in the morning, and it would be over before noon. "How about you?" She looked at Nancy.

"Oh, I wish I could! But I've got classes all day."

"That's all right, dear," Mrs. Gilchrist said. "It will give Anne and me a chance to get to know each other. Anne, let's meet at the hotel.

I'm staying where Andrew is—he got me a room on his floor. And Nancy, I'll see you for dinner instead." She hugged her daughter but shook Anne's hand—no embrace for her.

The next day Anne arrived a few minutes early and stood waiting for Mrs. Gilchrist in the lobby. When she appeared, Anne noticed that she wore the same dark coat—the cross presumably tucked inside—and hat. When Mrs. Gilchrist unbuttoned her coat at the restaurant, Anne saw she was right. Once again the cross, tiny as it was, commanded her attention. She kept looking at it and then away; she hoped Mrs. Gilchrist didn't notice.

"So how are you liking your classes here in Paris?" Mrs. Gilchrist asked when they were seated.

"I'm really enjoying them." Willing herself to look down, Anne took a bite of the asparagus on her plate; the vinaigrette with which it had been drizzled formed a pool around the stalks.

"And Drew says you're majoring in art history?"

"I am. But after the time I've spent here, I've decided I'm going to do a double major—art history and French."

"That's a wonderful idea." Having finished her asparagus, Mrs. Gilchrist patted her mouth delicately with her napkin. "Learning a language—any language—is so enriching."

Emboldened by this bit of praise, Anne said, "Drew's French is so impressive. And he told me he's studied Spanish and Italian too."

"It's helped him enormously in his work." Mrs. Gilchrist smiled. "In fact, he told me he plans to start learning Russian. He thinks that there's a developing situation between the United States and the Soviet Union, and he wants to be prepared."

"I took a Russian literature class at Vassar," Anne said. "I'd love to be able to read those books in the original."

"I don't imagine he'll be tackling *War and Peace*." Mrs. Gilchrist smiled. "But even having some proficiency would give him an advantage."

They had moved on to their main courses—mussels *marinière* for Anne, coq au vin for Mrs. Gilchrist—and Anne was feeling a bit more relaxed. Mrs. Gilchrist seemed friendly, even if they hadn't engaged in anything more than small talk. And when she told Anne to call her Evelyn, Anne felt some test had been passed.

"That was excellent." Evelyn laid her knife and fork neatly across her empty plate. "A quintessential French meal. How about your mussels—were they good?"

"Oh yes," said Anne. "Very." She sopped up the last of the juice with a bit of bread.

"I was surprised when you ordered them," Evelyn continued. "I've been cooking them for years, but that's because we live near the ocean—everyone thinks New Hampshire is landlocked, but we actually have eighteen miles of coastline."

"I learned to like them here," Anne said. "Drew encouraged me to give them a try."

"And to think he ate only the blandest foods growing up, most of them white—he wouldn't go *near* mussels back then, and if I served them at dinner, he refused to try even a single bite."

"His palate has expanded," said Anne.

"Yes, I can see that." Evelyn's gaze was cool and appraising. "Along with his worldview."

Flustered, Anne tried to redirect her focus. "Should we order dessert?"

"That would be lovely, but I've given up dessert for Lent," Mrs. Gilchrist said. "So no sweets for me." She readjusted her hat and looked around for the waiter. "Just because I'm not having any dessert doesn't mean that you shouldn't. Let me get a menu."

"That's all right, I really don't need to have—"

"Please order something." Evelyn put her hand on Anne's wrist. "I'd really like you to."

"All right, then," said Anne. Maybe she'd been apprehensive for nothing. So far it seemed that way. She looked at the menu and chose the crème brûlée, which had become one of her favorites. When the waiter placed it in front of her, she used her spoon to crack the brittle sugar coating, revealing the creamy confection underneath.

"That looks very tasty," said Evelyn. "As soon as Lent is over, I'm going to try it." She took a sip of the coffee she'd ordered. "And speaking of Lent being over, I meant to ask what you're doing on Easter Sunday. Nancy and I are going to church and then out for lunch. I'd love it if you would join us."

"Lunch sounds lovely." Anne tried to speak slowly, even though she wanted to blurt it all out, get it over with. "But I won't be going to church on Easter Sunday." When she saw Evelyn's confusion, she added, "I'm Jewish. I think Drew intended to tell you, but now that it's come up, I see no reason to hide it." She realized she didn't need Drew to say this for her. She could say it herself.

"I'm not entirely surprised." Evelyn was studying her. "I asked Drew if you were Catholic. He said no, but he was vague—and now I see it was intentional—about what your background actually was. So I had my suspicions . . ."

"Well, now you know your suspicions were justified," Anne said.

"I understand." Evelyn set down her coffee cup and pressed her palms on the table. "And I respect that, I really do. Of course, if you two become more seriously involved, there will be things to work out. Children, for instance. I've always assumed—*expected*—that Drew's children will be raised as Catholics." Evelyn looked down at her cup, not at Anne, as she spoke, and the gold cross seemed brighter now. Brighter and, to Anne, somehow accusatory. "But we don't have to go there yet, do we?" Her words said one thing, but her tone—brittle, artificial—said another. It was clear that she thought that they ought to settle this now.

Anne spooned down the rest of her crème brûlée quickly, unable to savor it. She just wanted the conversation—and the lunch—to be over. When the check had been paid and she'd thanked Drew's mother, they left the restaurant. It had started to rain, quite hard, and neither she nor Evelyn had an umbrella. She would be soaked by the time she got back to the dorm. When Evelyn said, "I have an umbrella you can borrow," it seemed like a good idea to go back to the hotel with her to get it.

They hurried through the slick streets, and when they reached the lobby, Anne shook the drops from her hair and her coat. She was intending to wait downstairs, but Evelyn said, "If you come upstairs, I can give you a towel to dry off."

"Thank you—that's very thoughtful." Anne read this as a good sign, and she followed Evelyn into the elevator and then down the hall to her room. It was right next door to Drew's. Why did this make her uneasy? She tried to shake off the feeling. Just then, there was a knock on the door.

"Come in," Evelyn said.

"Pour vous, madame." A maid in a pale blue uniform handed her a neatly folded pile of clothes.

"What is this?" Evelyn asked.

"Votre linge," said the maid. "Your laundry."

"But I didn't send anything to be laundered."

"You didn't?" The maid looked confused. "Monsieur Gilchrist asked that I take care of his laundry, and when I found these things in his room, I thought they were yours."

Evelyn began looking through the pile. With growing mortification, Anne realized that all these garments—the blouses, the peach satin slip—were hers. She'd left them in Drew's room.

"I don't understand." Now Evelyn was holding up the most incriminating things of all—two pairs of lace-edged tap pants, one sky blue and the other gray satin.

"Je suis desolée," said the maid. "I'm sorry. My mistake . . ."

But Evelyn wasn't paying attention. No, she was looking right at Anne, and her stony expression made it clear that she understood exactly whose underwear she was holding, and why it had been found in her son's room. Understood all too well.

TWENTY-TWO

DELIA

1948

Today it was her ankle that woke her, a dull, persistent pain that seemed to emanate from deep in the bone and wrenched her out of sleep. Some days it was her shoulder that throbbed hideously, and on other days her wrist. Sometimes it was everything at once, dull, pounding waves of pain that broke over and over again.

Fully awake now, Delia could feel how dry her mouth was, her lips. She reached awkwardly for the metal pitcher on the nightstand, but when she tried to pour from it, she missed the glass, and water dripped down onto the floor.

This was not the first time she'd done this. She didn't even call out; she knew no one would come, at least not right away. It wasn't an emergency, after all. She'd been marooned here in the *kupat cholim*—the clinic—of the kibbutz for two weeks. Right after the blast, she was taken to the hospital in Be'er Sheva, a trip she barely remembered. But after they put casts on her ankle and on her wrist—both broken—they'd sent her back here to the kibbutz, her plans to leave the country postponed until she'd healed. She couldn't put any weight on the ankle, and the thought of navigating a plane flight with crutches seemed more challenging than it was worth. Besides, she had no compelling reason to be in Paris, or New York for that matter, so she might as well stay here.

The rotating trio of women who took care of her—one named Bila, another Vered, and a third whose name she kept forgetting—were competent, if brisk. Well, she understood that they were stretched thin. The explosion that had landed her here had unnerved and upset the entire community. The dining hall had been destroyed, and plans for rebuilding were already underway; Delia heard the hammering and banging outside the room. She did wonder about the wisdom of this plan; it was clear to her that the question was not whether another attack would happen but when. Just days after the attack here, there had been news of another, this one at Kibbutz Revivim, which was about three kilometers away. That one had been deadly too—it was the baby house that had been bombed, and three children were killed.

The tension that incited the first attack hadn't been eased, or even addressed. But the kibbutzniks were stubborn, and they weren't going to surrender their claim to this land. Didn't they understand that the people they had chased away had an attachment as fierce and as deep as theirs? Not that she said this to anyone, because no one would have wanted to hear it. Mostly she spent the days by herself, first sleeping a lot, and then, after a few days, looking through the window at the desert that stretched out beyond the perimeter of the kibbutz.

Apart from Anne, who came right after the explosion and whose visit was nothing more than a blurry memory, Delia's only other visitor was Sophie, who showed up every morning before she went to work, and every evening when she'd finished. Sometimes she would bring bread, which had been baked that day, and a small crock of butter; she knew how vile Delia found the spread that was used more widely here.

"Where did you get this?" Delia asked.

"Someone brought it to me from Tel Aviv," Sophie said.

Delia was surprised by her appetite, given that she was just lying here most of the time. In the evenings Sophie brought wildflowers that she gathered just outside the confines of the kibbutz—small yellow ones that looked like dandelions, clusters of tall, deep red ones, and irises, which quickly became Delia's favorites.

When the doctor came to check on her, he decided that Delia should start getting up and moving around on crutches. It was Sophie who helped her navigate first around her room, then the hall of the *kupat cholim*, and finally outside. Delia welcomed the chance to move around, hobbled as she was. Walking with the crutches was tiring, so she took frequent rests. Her mother was with her through all of it.

"I think you're getting stronger," she said after the first week, when Delia had walked as far as the children's house.

"Then why don't I feel that way?" Delia was exhausted by the trip.

"Sometimes you can't see the progress when you're in it. But that doesn't mean it's not happening." Sophie pointed to a wooden bench just outside the *beit yeladim*. "You can rest here. I'll go inside and see Asher, and then I'll walk you back to the clinic."

Delia said nothing. She hadn't wanted to see Asher since that day he'd flung the wooden animal at her head, and she didn't want to see him now. She understood that there was something wrong with him, and he couldn't be blamed for his behavior. Still, she found it upsetting to be in his presence. And she resented how Sophie seemed so patient with him. Where had all that patience been when she was a little girl?

Sophie was in the *beit yeladim* for quite a while. When she finally emerged, her expression was tight, her face drawn. Delia heard screaming from inside; without asking, she knew it was coming from Asher.

"Everything all right in there?" she asked.

"Nothing is all right." Sophie's tone was clipped. Hard. "And it never will be."

Delia waited, but Sophie said nothing more. Instead, she helped Delia up, and together they walked back to the clinic.

The next day Sophie brought Delia a thin blue envelope. Who would be writing to her here? She looked at the postmark. Paris. Anne. She was back in Paris now. "Could you open it for me?" Delia asked her mother, and when she had scanned its contents, she set it aside.

"A friend from Paris? Gaby?" asked Sophie.

"No, not Gaby." Delia hadn't given Gaby her address because she hadn't thought she would be in Palestine very long. But now that she was stuck on the kibbutz, she realized she should write to her. "A friend from college, actually."

"The girl who was here the day after the explosion?"

"Anne Bishop."

"It was good of her to come. And she brought pastries. Is she a close friend?"

Delia was about to say no, but stopped to consider it first. Anne was trying to be her friend; was there a special term or status for that? Friend-in-training? Delia remembered eating one of those pastries the next day; it was cloyingly sweet, and she hadn't been able to finish it.

Sophie didn't come the next day. She had told Delia she wouldn't be able to get there in the morning but would be there in the evening. Delia looked around the little room. On the nightstand were a few newspapers and a tattered magazine, but all in Hebrew, which she could not read. Nothing on the walls, though there were curtains at the windows; they were embroidered, like the ones in the dining hall. Someone had spent hours doing that, creating something lovely even here.

Delia swung her legs around and reached for her crutches. Sophie had been right—she was getting stronger, and getting stronger made her feel restless. She didn't want to stay inside any longer; she wanted to be outside, feeling the warmth of the sun on her face and arms, letting the breeze ruffle her hair. She'd become more nimble with the crutches and made her way to the front desk. Vered was sitting behind it.

"You go out?" she asked in her thickly accented English.

"Yes. I'm going to take a walk."

"Sophie go with you?"

"No. She didn't come today."

"She come later." Vered seemed certain of that.

"Maybe. But I don't want to wait."

Vered looked like she was about to say something else, but then someone called to her from down the hall. It sounded urgent, and she got up. "You be careful," she said.

Delia was well aware that she needed to be careful. But she didn't plan on leaving the confines of the kibbutz. Since she'd already proved she could walk to the *beit yeladim* and back, that's where she would go. Outside, the day was mild, though the breeze was stronger than she'd anticipated; it blew sand into her mouth and whipped her hair around her face. Maybe a *chamsin* was on the way; Sophie had told her about that fierce desert wind and the destruction it could cause. When she reached the children's house, she paused in front of the gray metal doors. No sound came from behind them, and she wondered if the children were even in there—maybe they'd gone outside for a walk? But when she peeked inside, she saw that they were seated at a low table with sheets of foolscap in front of them; scattered around were the large, fat crayons that they used to draw.

She went in and stood by the door. When one of the *metapellot*—caretakers—looked up at Delia she was able to string together a simple sentence in Hebrew: "Anee bat shel Sophie." *I'm Sophie's daughter.* The woman smiled and gestured for her to come in.

Delia saw that most of the children worked with some attention and even gravity, though a few were scribbling, loops and lines of color that covered the page. And then there was Asher. He sat still in front of his sheet of paper, not drawing, not doing anything. But with a sudden, deft movement he plucked a crayon out of the hand of the girl sitting next to him. Her mouth twisted into a frown as she tried to get it back, but he'd already gotten up and began to move around the table, snatching crayons as he went. One girl started to cry, and two boys followed him, intent on retrieving their purloined crayons.

Then one of the caretakers—a tall, hefty woman Delia remembered from the time she'd been here before—planted herself in Asher's path and began talking to him. He didn't react, didn't even look at her, but Delia could see that his grip on the crayons hadn't loosened; he still held the bunch of them tightly. Another of the caretakers, this one with red hair done in pigtails, came over and took Asher by the shoulders while the first woman pried the crayons loose; when he finally surrendered them, he threw them all over the floor. He remained impassive throughout this exchange, and then allowed himself to be led to a corner while the crayons were gathered up and redistributed. The girl who'd been crying sniffed loudly before settling down to work.

Delia watched all this from her place near the door. All was calm now. The children were coloring again. Asher was silent and immobile in the corner. There was no expression on his face, and he stared straight ahead. Why did this suddenly fill her with such sorrow? She made her way over to him. It was too awkward to sit down with the crutches, but she stood close and said "Shalom." There was no reaction, and she really couldn't come up with anything else to say in Hebrew, so she switched to French. Maybe Sophie spoke French to him sometimes; it was possible. If he understood her, he gave no sign. Then some words from long ago came into her head; they were from a song her nanny sung to her as a child, and she began to sing them now.

Veux tu monter dans mon batteau?
Ton batteau, c'est pas beau.
Veux tu monter dans mon batteau? C'est pas bien beau, mais il va sur l'eau.

Do you want to ride in my boat?
Your boat's not pretty.
Do you want to ride in my boat? It's not very pretty but it sails on the water.

Silly, but she had liked it, and still remembered it after all these years. And there were other verses too, something about bringing flowers . . . but she couldn't think of them, and so she just sang the one verse she knew a second time, and then again. Asher didn't react to her first two renditions of the song, but just as she'd finished the third, she felt a pressure in her palm, and when she looked down, there was Asher's small hand, tightly grasping her own. His face was still a blank, and he didn't look at her. Still, he kept his hand pressed to hers.

The caretaker with the red hair walked over. "Sophie's girl, right?" she asked, and Delia nodded. "So you've met your brother."

"Half brother," Delia said, but really, did that make any difference? They were both Sophie's children.

"It's good you came," said the woman. "He could use a friend."

A friend? Now she was a friend to this strange, feral boy? But she allowed her hand to remain in his. "What will happen to him?" Delia asked. "What kind of life will he have?"

"Who can say?" the woman replied. "But whatever happens, he'll always have a place here."

That's what Sophie had said too. The other caretaker was now collecting the children's drawings and the crayons. Delia felt a rumbling in her stomach. Time for lunch. Carefully, she extricated her hand from Asher's. He didn't resist, but when she stood up, he surprised her by pressing his face to the front of her skirt. She placed her hand on his buttery curls for a moment. So silky, so soft. Then she left.

That evening, Sophie returned. "I heard you went to the *beit yeladim* today." She'd seated herself in one of the room's two hard-backed chairs. Delia was in the other one, leafing through a magazine, but she closed it. "Asher took all the crayons so they had him sit in the corner," she said.

"I know," Sophie said. "And I know that you sang to him. Why?"

"It just felt like the right thing," Delia said.

"It was kinder and more generous than I have a right to expect from you," said Sophie.

"I didn't do it for you," said Delia. "I did it for him."

Sophie smiled; she was still so beautiful when she smiled. "But you must know that by being kind to him, you're being kind to me." She didn't say anything more, and neither did Sophie, who after a time got up and kissed Delia's forehead before leaving the room. "See you tomorrow," she said.

After a few weeks, Delia was well enough to leave the kibbutz. But she didn't. She wasn't entirely sure why; it wasn't as if she had a compelling reason to stay, any particular ideological attachment to the place and the life it offered. But her own life was at a standstill—no college, no job, no boyfriend—though after Ian McQuaid, the word *boyfriend* seemed ridiculous and sophomoric—and she had nowhere else to be.

She was given a job; everyone who lived there was required to work. First in the field, planting peppers, but the required digging sparked some residual pain in her shoulder, so she was moved to the nascent chicken coop, a hastily built tin-and-wire-mesh structure that housed forty or so plump white hens and a handful of roosters. Several times a day, she was tasked with collecting their eggs.

At first she enjoyed it. With their white feathered bodies, red combs, and small golden beaks, the chickens were appealing, even adorable, as if they had stepped out of an illustrated children's book, clucking and fluffing. And there was time between the egg collections during which she could do what she liked; often this meant going to the children's house to see Asher. He still didn't speak to her, but now she caught him looking at her from time to time, and once, when she got up to leave, he took her hand and tugged it, indicating he wanted her to sit back down.

She asked if she could take him for a walk and was told yes, as long as she never let him out of her sight. So as spring came to the desert, warming the air and enlivening the drab tans and browns of the landscape with brilliant dots of color, she took Asher on walks around the kibbutz. He stayed beside her, hanging on to her sweater or, when she shed that, her shirt. Once he stuck a finger in her belt loop, but that didn't work at all, and he tripped and fell. She worried he'd been hurt, but no, he laughed, a high-pitched, squeaking little sound. Laughed! She'd never even seen him smile before.

On these walks they visited the dairy, where he patted the coarse dark hides of the cows, touched their knobby little horns. They were given tin cups of fresh milk, still warm, the taste unfamiliar and as rich as if an egg or butter had been added. Or they might go to the laundry. Asher wanted to plunge his arms into a barrel of sudsy water where clothes were soaking, and when he pulled his arms out, blow the bubbles into the wind. She saw him laugh again when a bubble landed on his nose; when she reached over to brush it away, he kissed the tips of her fingers. Their last stop was always the kitchen. Sophie would come out to say hello, wiping her hands on her apron. The expression on her face when she saw Delia with Asher was one Delia couldn't identify at first. Then she understood what it was: happiness. Sophie was made happy by the sight of her two children together. Then Delia brought Asher back to the children's house and returned to the coop for the next collection.

But soon she began to distrust and then dislike the chickens. The hens pecked, drawing blood. The roosters attacked from behind; once she was knocked down into the dirt, and the bird attempted to mount her. After that, Delia didn't want to work in the chicken coop. The fluttering, frenzied birds now repelled her; she didn't want to be in their presence. Surely there was another job she could have? She asked about working in the children's house, but was told that only permanent or long-term residents could be considered for that job; her stay here was going to be too short. Then Sophie had the idea of making Delia responsible for Asher, and for Asher alone.

"She's his sister, so it's not like she'll be abandoning him when she goes," Sophie argued. Did Sophie think Delia was going to come back again? Yet the idea of pairing the two met with little resistance and even enthusiasm. Asher was a difficult child. He flouted rules, resisted joining in, was often hostile or combative. Maybe time spent with Delia could soften his edges, lower the volume of his fits, his rages. Delia had to ask herself whether she was equal to this. To her surprise, she thought she was.

TWENTY-THREE

ANNE

1948

"You said *what* to my mother?" Drew's voice was controlled, but he was clearly upset.

"Only that I was Jewish, and I didn't want to go to church with her on Easter Sunday." She felt defensive; this was a tone of voice Anne had never heard Drew use before, and certainly not with her.

Easter had come and gone, and she hadn't seen or spoken to Evelyn since that last uncomfortable encounter. Anne had also done her best to avoid Nancy. She needed to see Drew first, to tell him her side of the story. He had gotten back late last night; she was already asleep, so this was the first time they were seeing each other since his return. She had counted on his understanding. But no, here they were early the next morning, in the Jardins du Luxembourg, passing through that long alley of perfectly aligned trees. Though he wasn't actually raising his voice, she could tell he wanted to.

"I thought we were going to wait to tell her," he said.

"No, *you* wanted to wait."

"But you agreed with me. Or you said you did."

"I know. At the time it seemed all right. But it was different when we were actually together. I could see how she reacted to the idea that her son was going out with a Jewess."

"Anne, she would never use that word."

"Well, she thought it." She glared at him.

He glared back. "The issue of my dating a Jewish girl isn't her only problem."

"What do you mean?"

"Anne, she knows you've been in my room, that we've slept together. In her mind, that damns you more than being Jewish."

"How reassuring. Being Jewish is only slightly less damning than being a slut."

"Don't say that."

"Why not? It's what she thinks, isn't it? And maybe you agree with her."

"That's not true, and you know it." He tried to take her hand, the hand on which she was wearing the silver ring he'd given her.

"Then why don't you tell that to your mother?" She pulled away.

"It's not so simple."

"Why not? To me it seems like the simplest thing in the world. Tell her you love me. Respect me. And that whatever we did or didn't do in your room isn't any of her business. You're a grown man. Why are you so worried about what she thinks?"

"You don't understand."

"No. I don't."

For the next few minutes, they walked in an uncomfortable silence. Then Drew stopped and put the Leica to his face. Usually she loved to watch him do this, loved to try to see what he saw. Not today. In fact, she was irritated. Did he have to take a picture now? She waited impatiently as he aimed the camera, pressed the shutter, then tilted the camera slightly, pressing it again. Click, click, click. Finally, he stopped, and they could continue walking.

When they reached the wide, placid expanse of the Grand Bassin, Anne saw a model boat sailing serenely across the octagonal pond. A young boy in short pants stood watching its progress; next to him was a man whose hand rested lightly on his shoulder. Father and son? Anne thought of her own father, whose death had left her feeling so abandoned. Her father hadn't meant to abandon her. But Drew? His father had known exactly what he was doing, and how it would hurt Drew and Nancy. And thinking of that, Anne felt herself soften—toward Drew, and even toward his mother. She imagined the shock Evelyn must have felt when she'd been deserted, the fear when she tried to imagine how she would raise her children on her own.

Anne hated this rift—surprising and painful—she'd felt with Drew. But she also saw that she could bridge it; she just needed to find the words. She turned to him, ready to back down, to say something conciliatory. Drew was talking, though. She'd missed the first part of what he'd said and only heard, ". . . maybe we put things on hold for a while. Let her get used to the idea of our being together before we move ahead."

"On hold?" Anne repeated. "What does that mean?"

"We can tell her we've decided not to rush into anything. And I have another idea."

"What is it?"

"I think I can find a priest who would be willing to give you instruction, so you could go to confession."

"Confession?" Anne bristled all over again. "Why would I do that?"

"Belief in the sacrament of confession runs deep for most Catholics. Well, for my mother anyway. If you confessed your sin—"

"Sin! What *sin?*"

"Sleeping with me, of course." He looked at her as if it were obvious.

"And what about you? Two people were involved in this so-called sin."

"Oh, I'd go to confession too. We'd be absolved and could start fresh."

"Absolved? Start fresh? Drew, I'm Jewish, remember?"

"I know that." He sounded impatient. "It's just awkward, that's all. If you hadn't left your underwear in my room—"

"I was sleeping in your room. Dressing and undressing there."

"If I told her that we both went to confession and received absolution, it would go a long way."

"Not for me. I'd only be doing it to please her."

"Is that so terrible? She is my mother, after all," he said, and then, his attention snagged by something he saw, he turned and raised the camera. Again.

"Do you have to be taking pictures now?" Anne said. Here they were, having their first fight, and he was taking pictures?

He spun around. "Yes, actually I do. I'm always going to take pictures," he said. "It's who I am. If you don't like it, then maybe you're saying you don't like me." He took a picture, then another. And still another. Anne fumed but said nothing. Finally he took the camera from his face and added, "I don't even understand why you're making such a big deal of this. You told me about that day at Chartres, how much you loved being inside the cathedral. It sounded like you had a kind of religious experience."

"Maybe I did. But it wasn't an explicitly *Christian* experience, at least not for me. And now that I've been to Palestine, I'm seeing things differently." This was true. She couldn't pinpoint the difference, but it was there.

They were still standing by the water's edge, only the boat was no longer gliding along the surface of the water; the boy was gently shaking the drops from its sides. He and the man walked off, the boy carrying the boat in his arms as carefully as if it had been alive.

"You're not going to give an inch, are you?" He looked at her as if she'd become someone else, someone he didn't recognize. "My mother feels insulted."

"She feels insulted? What about me?" Anne said.

"If you'd only try to see it from her point of view—"

"What about my point of view? I'm not a Catholic, and I'm not going to follow a Catholic blueprint just to please her." Just then he turned away to snap another picture. Anne couldn't control herself a minute longer. "Would you just stop that already? Just stop!"

He looked at her with obvious anger. "Really? You're telling me not to take a photograph? When we ran into Delia at the gallery, she told me not to trust you. Maybe she was right."

The comment was an affront, surprising and wounding. But she wouldn't let him see how it had affected her. "Well, if you don't trust me, maybe I shouldn't be wearing this." She pulled at the ring on her finger; for a second it seemed to be stuck, but then she yanked it off and tossed it in his direction.

He looked stunned before scrambling to pick it up.

"That's right. Take it back. Take it back and give it to someone else. Someone your mother will like." But this was a bluff; she wanted him to say *No, that's not what I want at all* and give her back the ring. He didn't, so she turned and walked away quickly, hoping that he'd call after her. But he didn't do that either. Nor did she hear anything from him for the rest of the day, or the next day either. But on the following morning, she found an envelope with her name on it in the wooden mail cubby downstairs. She recognized the handwriting instantly and tore it open.

Dear Anne,

I'm sorry we fought, and sorry for the things I said. But now that I've calmed down, I'm thinking maybe it's for the best. Anger can be clarifying. It showed us differences that we can't seem to reconcile. We said I love you to each other. But love doesn't conquer all. It can't even get us over this hurdle; how about all the others that are bound to crop up? I'll be leaving Paris soon, and I think we shouldn't have any contact for a while. I've told Nancy what's happened, and she's going to move out of your room; there's a single that opened up on another floor. So maybe that's for the best too. I hope you can finish out the semester and take in all that Paris has to offer.

Yours,

Drew

Anne read this several times. Why had she thought she loved him? If he could write this, he wasn't capable of love. And he didn't think they should have any contact for a while? Well, she didn't want any contact either, and not just "for a while." How about no contact ever again? That would suit her just fine. Now she was sorry she'd thrown that ring on the ground; she should have thrown it right in his face.

Spring finally settled in Paris, and its sparkling blue glory enraged her. How dare the leaves unfurl with such a tender green color, the flowers bloom with such profusion, the sun shine with such warmth? But underneath the anger was pain. She should have been sharing these days with Drew; instead she was alone, plagued by a persistent gnawing sensation in her stomach, as if she'd swallowed ground glass. The feeling dulled her appetite, so she barely ate anything, skipping meals in the dorm's communal dining room and instead stepping into nearby cafés for coffee that kept her going all day. At night she allowed herself a single glass of wine. Remembering how Delia had shocked some of the girls at Vassar by doing the same thing, she felt she'd finally achieved some kind of honorary status as a French girl, if only in her own eyes.

Most of her time was spent either in the library or in her room, studying; no one else had moved in, and so she had no one to talk to, no one to distract her. She read, she wrote, she memorized; her efforts earned her the highest grades in all her classes, and her professors praised her fine work. But one of them, Madame Molyneux, added, "Vous devenez très maigre, Mademoiselle Bishop. Tout va bien?" *You've grown very thin, Miss Bishop. Is everything all right?* Anne assured her that yes, everything was fine, but later, back in her dorm room, she took a good look at herself in the mirror. She *had* grown quite thin; her blouse seemed to engulf her, and her skirt hung on her hip bones. Her face was positively gaunt. She dug through a drawer to find a belt; that seemed to help, and later that day she ordered a crème brûlée along with her coffee, but the thick custard seemed to clot in her throat and she couldn't bring herself to swallow it. Making sure she was unobserved, she spat the vile mouthful into her napkin.

But though she couldn't eat, she discovered she could smoke. It started when someone left half a pack of Gitanes and a book of matches on a café table where she sat with one of the day's many cups of coffee. She'd never considered smoking before, though of course she'd seen other girls take up the habit, and so many of her favorite screen actresses—Bette Davis, Lauren Bacall, Joan Crawford—made smoking seem glamorous and alluring.

She fished out a cigarette, lit it, and tried to inhale. Immediately she began to cough, but that didn't stop her. She waited for the coughing to subside and then tried again; this time, she coughed less. And she liked the feeling of the burning smoke in her throat and her lungs—the scalding sensation made her feel she was being cleansed. Purified. Over the next few hours, she finished all the cigarettes in the pack, and in the morning she bought a pack of her own.

She trudged through the next weeks. The semester would be ending soon, and she'd need to think about what, exactly, she planned to do. She was ready to leave Paris, but there was nowhere else in Europe she wanted to be, so she thought she might as well make the arrangements to sail back to the States. The upcoming summer loomed long and empty; maybe she would go to and spend time with her aunt in Skaneateles. Then again, maybe not. Nothing seemed to call to her; everything felt flat and dull. At least she could throw herself into studying—her final exams were coming up. She took comfort in the small immediate pleasures of caffeine and tobacco—the first hot rush of smoke in her mouth, the way the bitter, dark brew—she had taken to drinking it black—made her heart bang in her chest and set up a steady, lilting rhythm in her head.

One day Anne saw Nancy in the hallway and tried to duck into her room. Nancy wasn't having it. "Anne!" she called out, and when Anne didn't answer, she called out again, even louder. Anne's door had been locked, and by the time she opened it, Nancy was standing there in front of her.

"I've been looking for you," she said. "I knocked on your door a bunch of times. It was like you'd disappeared."

"I've been here," said Anne. "I've just been studying."

"You've also been avoiding me."

"I haven't—" she started, but then thought, why lie about this? "You're right. I have."

"Because of Drew."

"Yes. Because of Drew."

"He won't tell me what happened. Or at least he won't give me the details, and neither will my mother. She says you 'weren't compatible.' But that's not what I saw—I thought you two were made for each other."

"Evidently not."

"Anne, aren't you going to invite me in? Talk to me? I thought we were friends."

Telling Nancy would mean telling her about sleeping with Drew, and Anne didn't feel she could confide in Nancy, not the way she could have confided in Delia. Delia. Now, why was she thinking of her again? There had been no contact between them; Delia had not answered her letters. Yet Delia was the one person she wished she could talk to. "We were friends," she finally said. "But things are different now."

"They don't have to be. You have a choice, you know."

"I'm sorry, Nancy, I just can't—" She was opening the door, stepping inside her room.

"Are you sure you're all right? You look very thin."

"I'm fine." She'd stepped into her room and now wanted to close the door, even if it meant closing it in Nancy's face. "I'm sorry, but I don't want to talk anymore." Anne closed the door while Nancy was still standing there. She waited for a moment, and when she didn't hear anything, she went to her desk and pulled out a pack of cigarettes. She'd taken to smoking Sobranies. Imported from London, they had a smoother, richer taste than the Gitanes, and they seemed classy to her. She really needed one now, right now, so she quickly lit up and inhaled. There it was, that feeling she craved—something tightened in her chest, but dilated in her mind, as if the bright, glowing tip—so vivid against the black paper—created some vital neural spark. Not wanting to risk seeing Nancy again, she remained in her room for the rest of the day.

But in the morning she had a class, and so had to venture out again. She opened the door a crack, just to make sure there was no one in the corridor, and when she saw there wasn't, she scurried out, down the stairs, and into the street. It was a perfectly glorious day, the kind of day that every dream or story about Paris conjured—azure sky, fat, fleecy clouds, a light breeze that set the new green leaves quivering. And for what seemed like the first time in weeks, she was hungry. Ravenous. She looked at her watch—8:30 a.m. Breakfast was still being served in the dining room: bread, jam, butter, slices of cheese and ham. The thought was intoxicating. She could go back right now, go back and pile her plate with food. But in the dining room, she might run into Nancy. So she continued on her way and instead stopped at a bakery where she bought two croissants and two *pains aux raisins*. She ate both of the croissants before she even got to class, shards of golden-brown pastry showering her jacket. She brushed them away before she slipped into her seat, pulling out and uncapping her pen. She could barely concentrate on the lecture, though—it was about the sixteenth-century poet Pierre de Ronsard—and she took no notes. Instead, she kept the bag with the *pains aux raisins* under her desk, breaking off small pieces that she surreptitiously slipped into her mouth.

Finally, the class was over. To her amazement, she was hungry again—it was as if she hadn't eaten anything at all an hour ago. She had another class in fifteen minutes, but she had to eat, immediately, and so she left the building and headed straight into the first brasserie she came to, where she ordered onion soup with a layer of molten cheese coating its bubbling surface, a croque madame, with its golden moon of an egg quivering on top, and, as if that weren't enough, *pommes frites* that came hot, crisp, and dotted with salt, overflowing the wire basket in which they were served.

"Vous avez grand faim, mademoiselle." The waiter smiled as he placed the food in front of her. *You're very hungry*. Anne knew he was teasing, but she felt found out in some way, and she wouldn't look at him. She devoured the soup, the bread, the egg, the *pommes frites*. Had she ever eaten anything so delicious in her entire life? Her fingers were coated with oil, and though she knew it was rude, she couldn't help putting them in her mouth to get every last bit. All of a sudden, her stomach lurched. The rumbling in her stomach grew more intense, and she got up from the table. Stumbling a bit, she hurried to the WC, which was not very clean, but at least it was empty. Once she'd latched the door behind her, she threw up in great, extravagant bursts. As she heaved, someone started knocking and then banging on the door. She ignored it and, when the heaving was at last over, washed her face and rinsed her mouth with handfuls of water guzzled right from the faucet.

She looked at herself in the small mirror above the sink. She was pale except for a blotchy patch of pink on either cheek. Beads of sweat dotted her hairline. What was wrong with her? Food poisoning? The flu? It was only then that she remembered it had been quite a while since her last period. One month, or maybe two? Or even longer than that? Her periods had always been irregular; she didn't even worry about it anymore. But maybe, just *maybe*, there was a connection between the missed periods and what had been happening to her these last days: first her lack of appetite, then her voracious appetite, and finally her body's sudden and violent need to purge itself.

She unlocked the door of the WC and walked past the irate man who had been waiting. Could she be pregnant? With Drew's child? Yes, they had used rubbers, but she knew rubbers weren't foolproof. Back out in the street, the day was even more beautiful than before, almost gaudy in its splendor. If it was true that she was pregnant, what would she *do*? She looked up at the celestial blue dome of the sky and realized she hadn't a clue.

TWENTY-FOUR

DELIA

1948

Delia started visiting Asher in the children's house every day. They had already built a fragile rapport, and now when she showed up in the morning, he was always waiting for her. Not smiling—he didn't do that—but alert and seemingly eager for her company. Having all those hours with him was at first challenging; she had no program to follow, though no one seemed to think that she should. Even Sophie was willing to let her take the lead.

"He likes you," she said. "I can tell."

"I like him." Delia realized it was true. She *had* come to like this odd and not-at-all endearing child. And not even because he was her half brother. No, it had more to do with his inalienable sense of identity: rigid though he was, he was very much himself, not willing or even able to tailor his reactions to the expectations of other people. And Delia found this admirable, even exhilarating. She thought of her time at Vassar: the cold shoulder she'd been given, the scarcely veiled contempt of the other girls. Had that bothered her? Not all that much. She had taken a strange kind of pride in their ostracism. They thought it would wound her? They had been wrong. They hadn't mattered to her. Well, except for Anne, who did not fit neatly into any category Delia could devise. Anne had written to her a couple of times and even gone into her hotel room and packed up her clothes, which she'd mailed back to her dorm in Paris. Though she didn't want to admit it, even to herself, Delia missed Anne. Maybe she ought to write back to her. But there was always something that seemed to get in the way; for now, she was focusing her attention on Asher.

As the weather grew warmer, she planned their walks early in the day or late, to avoid the heat of the sun. In addition to all the places she'd been taking him, she started venturing just outside the kibbutz, into that great, unbroken expanse of land and sky. There was so much to explore. Asher could sit for an hour or more, watching the patterned lizards—red, orange, yellow—that darted between rocks or into small crevices, or a tortoise, slow-moving enough for him to snatch up. Delia stopped him; she knew the creature could bite. Asher looked surprised by her intervention, but he did not fight her. Instead, he crouched down so he could follow the tortoise's progress over the dips and rises in the hard-baked earth.

Midday, she brought him back to the children's house to wash up and have lunch. He would be seated at a table with the other children, which made him restless, but when Delia joined the group, he calmed down and ate his food without throwing it on the floor—or at anyone seated across from him. After lunch, the children all went down for naps, and Asher did too. He wanted Delia to sing to him. "Bateau," he would say, clearly remembering the first time she'd sung him a song. Delia complied, and sometimes he sang a few words of it with her. In the evenings she would go to the dining hall for dinner, but later she and Sophie would walk over to say good night.

"It seems like you're fitting in well here," Sophie said as they left the dining hall. It was a cool, clear night; once the sun set, it took all its warmth with it. Delia was wearing a kibbutz-issued scratchy sweater and a knitted cap too. "You've found your place."

"As long as it's not with the chickens." Delia smiled. "I prefer spending time with Asher."

"I know," said Sophie. "It shows. And you've done him so much good. The change has been . . . remarkable."

"You think so?" Delia didn't share her mother's opinion. Asher still barely spoke and didn't engage with the other children. He still lived mostly within himself. Not much of a difference there. "Maybe he's a little less angry."

"Yes. And don't discount that. Even a little less angry is a big improvement. And you're the first person, aside from me, with whom he's been able to make a connection. That's remarkable as well. I'm grateful to you, sweetheart. And proud."

Delia let this wash over her. She'd felt jealous of Asher when she'd first met him. But now she felt something else—empathy. And a sense of kinship. yes. That was it.

". . . and so I've been meaning to ask, what do you plan to do next?"

"Next? As in tomorrow?" Delia hadn't been listening.

"No, I mean with your life. It seems like Vassar is over for you. Will you go back to Paris? Or New York?"

"Maybe." If she went to New York, she could enroll at Barnard; she'd been accepted before and would most likely be accepted again. She wouldn't even mention what had happened at Vassar. Or she could go to work in the gallery. She would find artists. Nurture them. Bring their work to a wider audience. Is that what she wanted?

"What if you stayed here?"

"On the kibbutz?"

"Yes. Or in Tel Aviv. Tel Aviv is a good city for a young person. You could open an art gallery there."

"I don't know . . ." But hadn't she just been thinking about a gallery? "Is there even a market for art in Tel Aviv?"

"Maybe not now. But there will be. Trust me."

They walked into the children's house. The room where they slept was darkened, with just one small light burning in a corner. All the children were tucked in, some asleep, some whispering to a parent who'd come to say good night or read a story. Asher alone was standing in the center of the room. Watching. Waiting. When he saw Sophie, he moved toward her and let her embrace him, kiss his hair. As she led him toward his cot, he reached for the sleeve of Delia's sweater and tugged her along, creating, however imperfect, the only family unit he'd ever known.

After that night, Delia thought about staying in Palestine—what it would mean, what she might do. She'd picked up a little Hebrew during her time here; she'd have to become fluent, but she believed she could. But the kibbutz—no, this wasn't the life for her. Tel Aviv, though . . . She thought of those Bauhaus inspired buildings—clearly someone knew about modernism and was intent on bringing it here. April turned to May, and days grew warm and then hot.

Delia started taking Asher farther outside the kibbutz. Most of those early spring wildflowers had withered by now, but in addition to the lizards—so many, scurrying so swiftly—and tortoises there were other creatures, like the ostrich they saw moving swiftly across the landscape, and the sleek feline, the color of the sand around him, that flitted by at dusk. Was it real, or had she imagined it? She looked at Asher, who didn't seem to notice. But he did notice the herd of deerlike creatures with funny little beards and the most remarkable horns that curved, improbably, backward. When he saw them, he put his hands on either side of his head, fingers extended. Delia realized he was improvising horns of his own. The animals took note, and the nostrils of the one closest to them twitched a few times. Then they all began to step back, small steps that put more and more distance between them. Asher kept his hands by his head, watching until they were too far away to see anymore.

Later Delia learned from Sophie that they were wild goats; they roamed the desert. "But you shouldn't be walking out there," Sophie scolded. "It's not safe."

"What about the grenades, the dining hall?" Delia said. "It's not safe here either."

"You're right," Sophie said. "It's not. But it's even more dangerous now."

"Is it? It seems calm enough."

"That's because you haven't been listening to the news. There's an English radio station that comes out of Jerusalem. Hadas listens to it at night. I'm sure you could listen with her."

Delia began to do that after she and Sophie had visited Asher. Often the program was filled with crackling and static, but she could still get a sense of the rising tensions, the conflict that was brewing. And then, at midnight on May 18, David Ben-Gurion proclaimed the state of Israel. A few people had been up late listening, and by morning, everyone on the kibbutz knew. There was crying, hugging, laughing. Some women formed a circle and danced a *hora* while a man shook a tambourine and sang, loudly and off key. Someone brought a radio into the dining hall, and people rushed in to listen.

Sophie translated for Delia. *Ben-Gurion will be the first premier. The British withdrew yesterday. Fighting has already broken out between Arabs and Jews. An invasion from Egypt is expected. The United States recognized the new state.* Cheers erupted when that was announced.

Delia turned away. The news that made everyone around her happy terrified her. She told Sophie she was going to find Asher and would see her later, in the evening, as was their habit. The mood in the children's house was no less joyful; the children had been organized into a group and were clapping and chanting "Eretz Israel, eretz Israel." *Land of Israel, land of Israel.*

As usual, Asher stood apart, a blank look in his eyes. But something flickered when he saw Delia. She took his hand—he let her do this now—and they began their walk. She made sure they stayed inside the perimeter of the kibbutz, even when he urged her to go past the gate. He raised his hands to his head to remind her of the goats; he wanted to see them again. Not today.

By the next day, she began seeing, in the distance, lines of people moving through the desert. Even from where she stood, she could tell they were encumbered: by satchels, by bags, and by boxes. They were holding the hands of small children or carrying those children, they were leading donkeys and cows, pushing wheelbarrows, pulling carts. Some might have been Jews who had been expelled from the Arab countries where they had lived. Others were Arabs, pushed out of their homes by the imperative of the new state. Delia knew that the lines of this conflict had been starkly drawn: Jew against Arab, Arab against Jew. But where most people saw enemies pitted against each other, she saw a strange and sad kind of affinity: people who'd been displaced and were just trying to find a way to survive.

That brought her back to the occupation and the escape from Paris—the frantic packing, the worry over Sophie's disappearance, the crowded port filled with people as anxious and frightened as they were, the endless wait to board the ship. Europe had been at war then. And the newly minted state of Israel? Now it was at war too: the radio reported on the Egyptian air attack, and the ground invasion of forces from Transjordan, Syria, Lebanon, and Iraq. Things were only going to get worse, and Delia didn't want to be a part of it.

That night she sat across from her mother in the makeshift tent that had been erected until the new dining hall was completed. It was open on all sides, and the air was cool and pleasant. Even if the days were hot, the temperature in the desert always dropped at night. When Delia told Sophie that she would be making plans to go, Sophie stopped eating, her forkful of fried cauliflower suspended in midair.

"I understand," she said finally. "And I'm not surprised. I knew you'd want to leave eventually. This life"—she gestured to the other tables, the people sitting around them—"it's not for everyone. But still I'd hoped . . ."

"Hoped for what?"

"Hoped that you would stay a little longer. There's so much lost time to make up for. So many ways I want to repair what damage I did." She put her fork down.

Delia was about to say that the hurt Sophie had inflicted could never be undone, but she realized that wasn't entirely true. Her mother had changed; she had been there while Delia recuperated, she listened when Delia spoke. And her devotion to Asher was something Delia would not have expected. Sophie was still looking at her; there was something expectant, hopeful, in her expression that Delia didn't think she'd seen before.

"I'm sorry, Maman," said Delia. "But I can't be here anymore. I have to go."

"Asher will miss you," Sophie said. "And I will too."

"I know." Delia reached for her mother's hand across the table.

"Will we see you again?"

"I don't know." This had been such a long, drawn-out journey, a pilgrimage really, and she couldn't imagine making it again. "Would you ever consider coming to Paris? Or New York?"

"Maybe," Sophie said. "Traveling with Asher won't be easy."

Living with Asher won't be easy, Delia thought but didn't say. She hadn't expected this conversation to be so hard. And yet she wasn't about to change her mind. Whether it was by air or by sea didn't matter: she was going to leave this place as soon as she could.

PART IV

VASSAR AGAIN

TWENTY-FIVE

ANNE

1948

Anne stood in the narrow aisle of the airplane, waiting to use the restroom. There were three people ahead of her, two men and a woman the stewardess had to shimmy past every time she needed to go back and forth. Anne shifted her weight from one leg to the other, both as a distraction and as a way to relieve the cramps in her legs that had plagued her during the long flight.

The interior of the plane was filled with a cloudy gray haze—it seemed everyone had either just finished a cigarette or was just lighting one up. Not Anne. Her infatuation with smoking had ended as suddenly as it started, and now the taste or even the thought of it sickened her. She vainly waved at the air in front of her face, but it was no use. The smoke had nowhere to go.

Finally it was her turn. She stepped inside the tiny cubicle, snapped the lock shut, pulled up her skirt, and sat down. That's when she saw it: the bright red splotch of blood that stained her gray satin tap pants, the very same pants that Mrs. Gilchrist—forget about ever calling her Evelyn again—had regarded with such chilling disdain.

Anne stared for a few seconds. Then she did what she was there to do and, after creating a makeshift pad with some toilet tissue and the handkerchief that was tucked in her skirt pocket, scrubbed her hands in the doll-size sink and returned to her seat. The flight was not even halfway over; she had hours to think about what she'd just seen and what it meant. Luckily, she had a window seat and could turn her face from the cabin, toward the dark, framed oval of the sky. That way, no one could see the tears as they began to trickle down her face. Because as relieved as she was—and of course she was relieved—Anne was also sorry *not* to be pregnant, sorry to have lost this last connection to Drew.

Once she was back in the States, Anne split her summer between her aunt's house in Skaneateles and Barney Weiss's brownstone, but was aware that she was marking time until boarding the train to Poughkeepsie in August to begin her senior—and final—year at Vassar. The week before she left, the city had been in the ferocious grip of a heat wave: hot, sticky days had turned into hot, sticky nights. But in Poughkeepsie the mornings already held a hint of the coming season; she needed a sweater or a light jacket when she left the dorm. She'd chosen not to live in Main this year, even though it was tradition at Vassar for seniors to live there, no matter where they'd lived before. This was a last-minute decision, and she was pleased she'd snagged a room on the top floor of Cushing. Even though the dorm was only twenty-odd years old, it had the look of a Tudor manor house from the sixteenth century, and she liked the feeling that she'd stepped back in time.

There was a good reason for this departure from tradition. Though Anne knew she'd have to face Virginia and the rest of the group sooner or later, she didn't want to see them at meals or run into them in the hallways. Better to keep some distance. And for the first few days, her plan worked. She didn't run into any of them on campus, and luxuriated in her sense of relief. But as the days turned into a week, she once more started feeling jumpy. When and where would she encounter Virginia again? That was when she decided that she'd rather be in control of the story, which was why, after her last class on a Thursday in September, she headed over to Main Building at a little after four. Tea was being served in the Rose Parlor, just as it had been served for decades. Anne felt sure that they would all be there, that little set, most likely in their familiar spot by the windows. Virginia would be at the center, with Midge, Polly, Tabitha, and Carol grouped around her. How would they react when they saw her? And even more important, how would she respond?

The parlor was nearly full when she walked in; she heard the sounds of chatter, of laughter, of teaspoons touching the rims of delicate cups. And yes, there they all were. She stood looking at them for a few seconds. Virginia had a new hairstyle, a chin-length bob, with bangs. Tabbie seemed to have come out of her shell and was more animated than Anne remembered—she was telling a story, and everyone was listening to her, even Virginia. Polly leaned over to Midge and whispered in her ear; Midge looked annoyed by what she'd said. Then Carol spied her and called out from across the room, "Anne! Anne Bishop, you're back! Come right over here and say hello!"

Anne felt her face stiffen into an artificial smile. She went to pour herself a cup of tea before walking over to join them. Carol got up to give her a hug; so did Tabbie, and Midge moved over on the settee so she could sit down. Virginia was looking at her appraisingly, as if trying to determine what, if anything, had changed.

"Tell us about Paris!" said Polly.

"Par-lay voo français?" Midge asked. Her accent was terrible, even worse than Anne's had been.

"Oui, je parle très bien maintenant," Anne replied.

"Ooh la la!" Tabbie said. "You sound just like a Parisian girl."

"And you even dress like one." These were Virginia's first words to her, and though they were technically complimentary, she somehow managed to inject them with a hint of derision. Trust Virginia for that. Her hairstyle might have changed, but her essential nature hadn't.

Anne sipped her tea, answered their questions, and caught up on the latest news. Carol had gone to Nova Scotia for the summer. Midge was planning a June wedding at, of all places, the Colony Club. Two other girls from their hall freshman year had dropped out to get married, one to a boy from West Point and the other to a Yalie. One of them was already pregnant. And Polly wasn't going to graduate with them, after all; she'd decided to do a five-year combined BA/MA in chemistry, and would be staying on another year. "Everyone in my family is a doctor," she explained. "I don't want to be a doctor, though—I can't stand blood! So being a chemist is a better choice. Maybe I'll teach."

Then Virginia said to Anne, "So were you in Paris the whole time? Or did you go anywhere else? London?"

"I was in London over the summer," said Polly. "You can't believe how awful it still looks. All those bombed buildings, rubble *everywhere*. It will take years to clear all that up."

"I didn't go to London." Anne felt a pounding in her chest, but she ignored it; she knew what she was going to do, what she *had* to do. "But over the Christmas break, I did some traveling."

"Where?" Tabbie asked. "Rome? Florence? I'm going to Florence in the spring—a semester abroad. You'll have to give me tips for being in Europe."

"Of course," said Anne. "But I wasn't in Italy on my break. I went to Palestine. Though now it's called Israel."

No one said anything for a minute. Then Virginia asked, "Isn't that just a big desert? A wasteland? Why on earth would anyone go *there*?"

"Oh, it's more than that. So much history, so much culture. Jerusalem is a fascinating, ancient city." Not that she'd actually been to Jerusalem. Still, she kept going, willing herself to speak slowly. Clearly. "And millions of people see it as a holy place. Christians. Muslims. Jews."

"Well, yes, it's where Jesus lived and all that," Virginia said. "But as for the rest of it—"

"Jews have a historic connection to Palestine—I mean Israel." Anne had dared to interrupt Virginia. "And since I'm Jewish, I wanted to see for myself what that was all about."

Once more, the girls fell silent. Tabbie and Polly stared. Midge's mouth had actually dropped open, though she closed it in a hurry. Carol looked down at her knees. But it was too late for Anne to change her mind, and anyway, she didn't want to.

"You're one of them?" Virginia seemed incredulous.

"Yes. One of *them*."

"But you never said so. You let us think . . ." Virginia looked confused, as if her power might be in question. She looked around, as if seeking confirmation from the others.

"I had no idea—" Polly said.

"Neither did I. None of us did." Carol talked right over Polly.

"I never actually said what I was. Or wasn't. You were the ones who made the assumption."

"Because you *wanted* us to make it. What kind of person does that?"

"The kind of person who wants to fit in and not be excluded. Or gossiped about. Insulted. Like the way you excluded, gossiped about, and insulted Delia Goldhush."

"Delia! She was an awful girl. Everyone knew it. Besides, you went along with it. All of it," said Virginia. "I remember the things you said about her. And you signed that letter I wrote to the dean."

"I know. And I'm ashamed that I didn't have the backbone to speak up." Was she really doing this? Taking on Virginia, and in public no less? She felt like she'd jumped off a cliff. But instead of crashing, she was floating, and from way up here, she could see more clearly. Virginia wasn't used to anyone talking back. It made her nervous. Very nervous, in fact, which was all the more reason for Anne to keep going.

"She deserved what she got." Virginia's voice lowered. "She was a . . . slut."

"Was she? Because she fell in love and did what people in love have always done?" Anne looked around at the rest of them. "Can you really say that none of you have been tempted? Or even gone all the way?" Midge's face was turning a bright pink, and Carol was looking rather desperately around the room. Anne knew she'd hit a nerve. "And maybe you were even jealous—jealous that he picked Delia." She paused to let the comment sink in. "And anyway, it was never about that. You didn't like her because she was Jewish, and seemed like a foreigner with all her French ways. Because of that, you did a terrible thing. We all did. I've apologized to her for my part in it, by the way. Not that an apology makes things right. She was still expelled."

For a few seconds, Virginia didn't reply. Then she said, "I should have known there was something not right about you. Something off. You never really talked about your family, where you were from. You didn't want us to know. And now it comes out. No wonder you're defending Delia Goldhush—you're two of a kind."

"I'll take that as a compliment." Anne stood up, accidentally knocking the cup from its saucer; tea splashed all over Virginia's lap.

"Look at what you did!" Virginia dabbed her skirt with a napkin.

Anne felt the smile forming. She didn't even try to hide it as she walked out of the Rose Parlor, without looking back.

After that, she braced herself for the fallout. Of course Virginia would start a campaign against her, and all the others would get on board. She imagined the snubbing, the whispering, and the looks. Rumors too, like what they—and she—had circulated about Delia. And there was a bit of backlash—those girls kept away from her at first, looking away if they saw her, or passing her by without stopping to talk. But then Polly showed up at Anne's door one night after dinner. Anne was so surprised that she just stood there and blinked.

"Could I come in?" Polly finally asked.

"Oh, of course."

Polly sat down, and the words poured out in a rush. She said they had all felt bullied by Virginia, and though they'd grown tired of it, they were all too cowed to confront her.

"Until you did," said Polly. "None of us could believe it at first. I mean, I—we—didn't think of you as someone—"

"Who could stand up for herself? Well, I wasn't. At least not then."

"So what changed?"

"It wasn't just one thing—it was everything coming together. Paris. Running into Delia. Palestine." She wanted to add, *Falling in love*. But she wasn't ready to talk about that. She couldn't imagine when she would be.

"Delia Goldhush? You saw her in Paris?" Polly leaned forward. "What was *that* like? It must have been . . . awkward."

Anne told Polly about that chance meeting in Paris, and their trip to Palestine. When she was finished, she saw that Polly seemed uncomfortable. Was it hearing about Delia?

"Can I ask you something?" Polly said. "Something kind of personal?"

"Maybe. It depends." Anne's guard went up.

"I wanted to ask you about being a Jew. I mean, being Jewish."

This wasn't at all what Anne expected. "I don't understand. What would you like to know?"

"I'm not even sure. I've never really known anyone Jewish. I mean, I knew Delia from a distance, but I don't think I ever had an actual conversation with her. Or any other Jewish people. Jews just weren't in my circle."

"You knew me."

"Well, yes, but I didn't know you were Jewish."

"Isn't that the point?" When Polly looked blank, she added, "Jews are pretty much like anyone else."

After that, Anne found that those girls from freshman year in Main considered her something of a leader—they asked her opinion and sought her advice. They invited her, included her, and were influenced by what she wore and said and did. This was a totally unexpected turn of events. She liked this new version of herself. And seeing herself in a new way opened new possibilities about what she might want to do after graduation. She was majoring in art history with a minor in French, which made her lean toward a job in a museum or gallery. Hadn't Delia said her father had a gallery in Greenwich Village? But why was she worrying about this now? She had more pressing concerns, like working on the long final paper that was due in the spring, along with the final comprehensive exam that was part of the requirement for graduation. She'd selected her topic: the stained glass windows at Chartres Cathedral. She knew that there had been many books and articles on the topic, and worried that she might not have anything new to say. But she'd been there, experienced for herself the power of that space, and felt the exaltation it created. She'd seen the saturation of those colors, their glow. She hoped all that would lead to something that truly was her own. She'd already started listing the sources she wanted to consult; many of them were in French, but by now she felt like she could read them comfortably, if not with total ease.

But after that, she came to a mental roadblock. Or more like an electrified fence. Every time she sat down to work on her paper, something pushed her away, and she let herself get easily diverted by anything else instead. After a couple of weeks, she realized what should have been obvious: she just didn't want to write about Chartres. That's why she was avoiding it. She needed to change her topic and her adviser. The chairman of the art history department might not allow this; she'd have to come up with both a compelling topic and an equally compelling reason for the switch to be approved at this late date. But as she walked briskly across the quad toward Taylor Hall, she felt sure she could figure it out. The answer was somewhere inside her, buzzing, humming, and just waiting to be let out.

"Hey, wait up!"

Anne turned to see Diana Beckham waving at her, and she stopped so Diana could fall into step with her.

"Are you headed to Miss Grayson's class? You're early," Diana said. "I guess I am too."

"She's so good, you don't want to miss a minute."

Diana, like Anne, was on her way to Miss Grayson's 300-level seminar, Rodin: Modern Master. There were just ten students in the class, and three of them—Diana Beckham, Margaret Bailey, and Evangeline Roberts—were seniors and art history majors Anne knew from other classes. The others were juniors she knew only by sight. But all of them were united in their awe of the professor, Pamela Grayson, who possessed the kind of glamour not typically found either among academics or in Poughkeepsie. Miss Grayson had started teaching at Vassar last year, when Anne was in France, but when she was signing up for the course, Anne discovered that there was already a kind of fan club surrounding the professor. Anne could see why. Her lectures were nothing short of scintillating, delivered with the kind of passion and verve that belong on the stage more than in the classroom. She couldn't keep still when she talked and tended to pace around the room. As she roamed, her words poured out in a rush, as if mere speech couldn't keep up with the speed of her thinking. Anne tried her best to follow, but sometimes she'd be writing so quickly that she couldn't decipher her notes later on.

And then there were Miss Grayson's clothes. She'd show up to class wearing a velvet cape or a hat with several large feathers sprouting from the brim. Her lips and nails were always painted a deep scarlet, and she tended toward fanciful jewelry—ropes of pearls that may or may not have been real, a brooch in the shape of a giraffe, a turtle, or a mushroom on her jacket lapel, earrings of colored stones that winked and sparkled near her face. One week she might wear long leather gloves in a burnt-orange color, with a billowing silk scarf whose design was a series of interlocking orange and brown squares; the next, she'd pair a green mohair suit with a blouse of green, teal blue, and yellow. She was unlike any professor Anne had ever known, and Anne considered herself lucky to have gotten into the class. They all did.

"I heard twenty-six people tried to sign up," Diana was saying this morning. "But she wouldn't allow any more than ten because she said she wanted us to learn from each other, not just from her."

Anne considered this. The discussions they had in class were interesting and even exciting. But as interesting or exciting as Miss Grayson? It wasn't possible. When they got to Taylor Hall, they went upstairs and took their seats around the seminar table. At the front of the room, Miss Grayson—today she wore a chocolate-brown velvet suit with a cameo pinned at the neck of her peach-colored silk blouse—sat with a sheaf of papers in front of her. After greeting all the students, Miss Grayson asked one of the girls to dim the lights, and she began to show the slides. Anne was struck by the enormous range of Rodin's work—marble, bronze, and plaster. He worked on monumental pieces that were meant for public spaces and small-scale table-size ones that could easily find a place in someone's home.

Professor Grayson spoke for a bit about Rodin in general—how he was a rule breaker, an iconoclast—and then clicked on a slide of a small bronze figure. "Here's Rodin's interpretation of Danaë. Can someone tell us who she was?"

Anne had read about her for another class. "She was a Greek princess. Her father was told he'd be killed by his own grandson, so he locked her up. But Zeus wanted her, and he turned himself into a shower of gold dust that poured down into the tower where she was a prisoner."

"That's right," Professor Grayson said. "But even though she's a mythological figure, she's presented as a real, flesh-and-blood young woman."

Anne looked at the small body, tucked in upon itself. "It's like she's trying to protect herself," she said. "Even to hide."

"Exactly!" said the professor. "And look at how realistically she's rendered—the evidence of her bone structure, the texture of her skin."

The class continued: more slides, more questions, more conversation. But something about that small bronze form stayed with Anne, and when the lights went back on, and everyone was filing out of the room, she stayed behind. That little figure might be the answer to the question that had been on her mind since last night.

"Miss Grayson, I'd like to change the topic of my final paper. I want to work on Rodin's sculpture, but specifically the small pieces, like the *Danaë* you showed us today. Would you consider being my adviser?"

"I thought you were doing something on Chartres," said the professor.

"I was. But this is calling to me. There's something special about the small works—they're intimate. Personal."

"I see what you mean," said the professor. "And I think it's an interesting perspective." She put her lecture notes in a leather folder and snapped it closed. "If you can get permission to change topics, come and see me during my office hours. We can discuss it then."

"I would really like that. Thank you." Anne was excited at the idea of working with her—much more than she had been with tedious Professor Abbott.

"And didn't you spend your junior year in Paris?" Miss Grayson asked. "You must have seen a lot of sculpture, including Rodin's, there.

You could place those small pieces within the context of other work on that scale."

"I did," said Anne. "At the Louvre and other places too. But one of my favorite pieces was in a gallery, and made by someone not very well known."

"Who was that?"

"Sophie Rossner. She's American, but she lived and worked in Paris for many years."

"Sophie Rossner. That name is ringing a bell." The professor began walking down the stairs.

"You're familiar with her work?" Anne fell into step beside her.

"I remember now. I was out on Long Island recently, visiting an alum who's considering a donation to the art gallery."

"She's donating a piece of Sophie Rossner's?"

"She was planning to donate two paintings, both from the nineteenth century. But she and her husband bought a very large lot of sculpture from a warehouse in Paris that had gone out of business, and I think some of them—quite a number actually—were made by Rossner."

"Sophie Rossner's daughter Delia was a student at Vassar, and—"

"She is?"

"Well, no. She was." Anne did not want to go into that story, especially not now. "She grew up in Paris, but she and her father escaped when the war started. Sophie stayed behind, and so did the sculpture. Delia's been trying to find it for months."

"Where was she looking?"

"Paris. She went back last year to find her mother's work."

"If these are the works she's looking for, they're in a pool house in Old Westbury. Only a few had been unwrapped. I remember now, because I thought they were very strong. Adele—that is, Mrs. Bancroft—wasn't sure what to do with them, and I suggested that some of them might be part of the donation."

"Do you think she would let us see them?"

"I've already seen them."

"No, I mean Delia Goldhush, Sophie's daughter. And me. Delia's been looking and looking and thought that she'd never find them. She'll be so happy to know that they're safe—and not only safe, but here in the United States. Do you think Mrs. Bancroft would agree?"

"I don't see why not," the professor said. "I'll give you the address, and you can use my name when you write to her."

"Oh, that would be wonderful!"

"And this girl . . . Delia. Where is she now?"

"I don't know. I've lost track of her." The last time Anne had seen Delia, she had been in the hospital in Be'er Sheva. She might still be there. Or she could be in Paris, New York, or anywhere else in the world. Anne hadn't tried to contact her since she'd returned to school. But the discovery of the sculptures changed everything. Miss Grayson wanted to know where Delia was? So did Anne, and Anne was going to try her best to find her.

TWENTY-SIX

ANNE

1948–1949

When Anne arrived at the Old Westbury train station, she took a cab to the address Mrs. Bancroft had given her; they'd been corresponding for a couple of weeks. The driver whistled softly when he came to the stone wall where he let Anne out. "Some spread," he said—more to himself than to her, but she had to agree. The red-brick house beyond that wall was three stories high; on one side there were extensive gardens, on the other a swimming pool, now empty, and beyond that a pool house and tennis court. Anne paid the man before turning back to the house and walking up the flagstone path leading to the front door. That door was a glossy black, which matched the shutters, and in the center was the face of a large brass lion that functioned as a knocker. She lifted it—it was so heavy—and the sound brought someone almost immediately. A maid in a black uniform topped by a white apron said, "Miss Bishop? Mrs. Bancroft is expecting you. May I take your coat?"

Anne handed the coat—not the fur she'd bought in Paris, she couldn't bring herself to wear that anymore, but a black-and-brown tweed that she'd bought in New York and thought was very chic—to the maid and waited while it was hung in the closet. Then she followed her across the marble-floored entryway into a vast carpeted room whose large windows were covered by sheer, ivory panels that let in the light—which was abundant—but obscured the view into the house.

"Anne!" Mrs. Bancroft got up from the champagne-colored silk sofa and crossed the room. "It's good to meet you. I'm so intrigued that you know something about those pieces of sculpture. My husband and I called them the mystery statues—we hadn't a clue about what they were or how they got packed and shipped to us, because we hadn't seen them in Paris—there must have been some mix-up."

"And I'm so happy the sculpture has been found. I can't wait to tell Delia."

"The artist's daughter? You haven't told her yet?"

"I don't know where she is."

"What about the artist herself?" asked Mrs. Bancroft. "Surely she'd want to know where they are now."

"I will let her know. She's overseas."

"Paris?" asked Mrs. Bancroft.

"No. Israel, actually."

Mrs. Bancroft looked exceedingly surprised but said nothing. Anne followed her through a dining room with an elaborately carved marble mantelpiece and an oval table that looked like it would seat twenty people, then through an enormous kitchen with two sinks, two refrigerators, and a stove that had six burners.

Mrs. Bancroft opened a door at the kitchen's far end, and they went through a little covered passageway that led to the pool house. It was dark at first, but when the light was switched on, Anne was so entranced, overwhelmed even, by the twenty or so sculptures placed around the space that she hardly knew where to look first. At the life-size figures of a man and a woman embracing, her hair streaming down her back? The young woman coiled upon herself, arms wrapped around her knees? Or the group of animals, none of them more than fifteen inches high, that formed an impromptu menagerie? Some were more conventional in their naturalism, while others were streamlined and spare, verging on abstraction.

Most of the surfaces were shiny and sleek, almost glazed, like the female figure Anne had bought in Paris. But a few were rougher, pebbly or almost gritty—were they unfinished, or had Sophie been trying to achieve a different effect? And the colors! Burnt orange, wine, green, greenish gray, rich brown flecked with black or white.

"They're quite something, aren't they?" Mrs. Bancroft said. "Walter and I had no idea."

"What will you do with them?" Anne asked.

"That's a good question, especially now that you've told me the artist's daughter has been looking for them. I was thinking of giving a couple to the Vassar College Art Gallery. But now it seems that the artist—or her daughter—might want them back? Am I right in thinking that you know the daughter? She's a friend of yours?"

"I do know her." Anne couldn't really claim friendship. "She was in my year at Vassar."

"Oh! Will she graduate with you this spring?"

"She took a leave of absence," Anne lied. "But she'll be so thrilled to know that they're safe and that they're here." She kept looking at the sculptures: their arresting forms, their range of color, of texture, of subject. For the last several years they'd been wrapped up and hidden away; now they deserved to be seen and appreciated again. And maybe she could find a way to make that happen.

Back at Vassar, Anne sought out Miss Grayson, who had only seen a couple of the sculptures, while Anne had seen them all. She described the different kinds of stone, the finishes, as well as the range and scope of the subject matter. "There was one—a small crouching woman—that reminded me of Rodin's *Danaë*. Maybe Rossner had seen it and was inspired by it? But instead of bronze, she used porphyry," Anne said. "It's such a gorgeous color, and it gave the figure a wholly different look. Compared to the metal, the stone seemed warm, almost animate."

"You sound very excited by seeing these statues," Miss Grayson said. "They made a real impression on you."

"They did."

"Did Mrs. Bancroft say what she intended to do with them?"

"She talked about possibly returning them to Sophie Rossner. Or to Delia."

"I'm guessing you haven't been in touch with either of them yet?"

"I don't know where they are."

"I'm sure the college has an address on file. I can write to her and let her know the sculpture has been found."

Anne didn't say anything.

"You want to be the one to tell her, don't you?" Professor Grayson asked.

"Yes, I do."

Professor Grayson considered this. "I think that would be all right. You can send her a letter, and then the school will follow up in an official way."

Anne didn't think Delia would be so pleased to hear from anyone at Vassar. But she wasn't going to say that now. She took the address back to her dorm room and wrote Delia a brief note, which she mailed that afternoon. She couldn't predict how or even if Delia would respond, but she didn't have time to dwell on that. There were the preparations for her final exam, and her paper, which had once again stalled. What was the matter with her? She had switched topics from Chartres to Rodin because she'd felt stuck, and now it was happening again.

She had a meeting with Miss Grayson the following day, and she was dreading it. She trudged to Taylor and went up the stairs. The door to the professor's office was open, and the professor was seated at her desk. She wore a powder-blue brocade suit with a mouton collar; two pale-blue enamel cuffs adorned each wrist.

"Come in, Miss Bishop."

Anne sat down. She didn't have a single thing to say.

The professor waited, and when Anne still didn't speak, she said, "Is something wrong?"

"I just haven't been able to move ahead with the paper," Anne confessed. "I don't know why. I was enthusiastic about working on Rodin at first. But now it's as if the light went out. And I've already changed my topic once. I can't do it again."

Well, now she'd said it, and there was some relief in that. She expected Miss Grayson to say that the paper had to be completed in order for Anne to graduate, and that she would simply have to buckle down and get to work, light or no light. The professor said something quite different, though.

"Miss Bishop, do you remember that conversation we had about Sophie Rossner's work?" Anne nodded. "Well, I do too, and I think that may solve the problem."

"How?"

"Mrs. Bancroft would like to move those sculptures out of her pool house, and since she's donating two paintings to the art gallery, she wondered if she couldn't send the paintings and the sculpture together."

"Sophie Rossner's sculpture would be sent here, to Vassar?"

"Well, yes. You've written to Delia Goldhush?" When Anne nodded, she continued, "It seems impractical to think about shipping them overseas. And until arrangements can be made to ship them to New York, they'll be safe here. Since they're going to be here, what if you put together a small show in the art gallery, and wrote a catalogue to accompany it? Students are allowed to do an independent study. That could be yours. And the final paper could dovetail with the show—you could write about Rodin and his influence on successive generations of sculptors, Rossner included. You even said one of her pieces reminded you of Rodin."

"That sounds like a terrific idea."

"Put together a proposal, and I'll share it with the chair. I think I can get him to agree. But you'll have to buckle down and work very hard, because you're behind schedule. Do you think you can do that?"

"I know I can."

"Good." Professor Grayson smiled. Then she said, "There is one more thing. I took it upon myself to do a bit of research, and found out that Delia Goldhush was expelled." She paused. "But of course you know that."

Anne looked down at her shoes, the rug, the bottom of the metal file cabinet against the wall—anywhere but at Miss Grayson. "I did know," she said finally. "I just didn't think it was my story to tell."

"You were involved in it, though. I saw the file, and the letter that was sent to the dean. Your signature is on it."

"It is." Anne forced herself to look up. "And I've been sorry about it ever since."

For the next several weeks, Anne devoted herself almost exclusively to her schoolwork. No more walks over to the diner or Alumnae House, no dances at West Point, and especially not at Yale. She was going to graduate with the best grades she could, and that meant she had to put aside almost everything else. There was the paper, and there was the preparation for the exam. And then there was the task of curating the show for the art gallery. Mrs. Bancroft had twenty-two pieces of Rossner's sculpture in her possession, and she sent them all to Vassar.

When they arrived, Anne was able to go through them more carefully and from those twenty-two, select twelve for the exhibition. Most were small pieces, meant to sit on a table or shelf, but she decided to open the show with a life-size piece, and then selected another life-size piece to end it. Her aim was not only to describe the trajectory of Rossner's work and analyze her subject matter, but also to speculate on the visual references in her work and put it into an art historical context.

As she considered the sculptures, arranged them—first as a series of index cards, laid out and moved around on her desk, and then, with help from the gallery assistants, in the actual space allocated to them—Anne had so many questions. Was Sophie's choice of stone determined by the subject, or did the subject arise out of her response to a particular piece of stone? Since she worked in both large and small scale, how did she decide on the size of each piece? And what about thematic connections? Women, figures drawn from myth or literature, animals—was there a connection, and if so, what was it? She wrote to Sophie in Be'er Sheva, hoping she would provide answers, and in her letter, asked if Delia was still there. It took a while but when Anne received an envelope with a postmark from Israel, she tore it open eagerly.

> *. . . I worked with stone, not words, so whatever I have to say will be more of a distraction than an illumination. And your questions are so perceptive that I'd rather let you speculate and draw your own conclusions than burden you with any prosaic, humdrum information I might share. Let your imagination take you where it will and pay no mind to me. I'll be interested to see where you land. As for Delia, she left in the spring and said she was going to New York. You can write to her there.*

Reading these lines, Anne felt a mixture of annoyance, frustration, and admiration. Delia had stressed, more than once, how unconventional her mother was and here was the proof. She refolded the letter and put it back in its envelope. Even this nonanswer might be an answer of sorts; maybe she would find a way to use it. And at least Sophie had told her where to find Delia. She wrote and when she didn't hear back, she called, twice, but both times the phone just rang and rang. She knew she could get on a train to New York and knock on the door of Delia's house but really, how much punishment was she supposed to take? Delia clearly wanted nothing to do with her and it was time to accept that.

Anne continued to work on the project. She found it challenging, at times frustrating, but also thrilling in a way she had not anticipated. She burrowed into the research, prepared wall texts, and produced a catalogue essay that went through seven separate drafts before she was finally satisfied. She began to think that she could make a life doing this. The breakup with Drew, while no longer as consuming or painful, had left her feeling soured on the idea of romance. Maybe she would never get married, but instead forge a path as a thoroughly modern career woman, devoted to her work, not a husband or children. What if this show was only the first of many she would go on to curate?

Throughout the process, Anne continued to feel Delia's presence and, simultaneously, her absence. Even now, she harbored the hope that if Delia saw firsthand the effort Anne had made on her behalf, she would finally forgive Anne's execrable behavior in their sophomore year. Yet when the show opened, Delia was not there to see it. Still, it was a festive gathering. Students and faculty came into the gallery. They nibbled the nuts from silver bowls, took cheese-topped crackers or pastel mints from trays that were circulating, and drank cups of fizzy red punch. The small group of girls Anne knew from freshman year—Peggy, Carol, Midge, and Tabitha—were all there. All except Virginia. Peggy and Tabitha congratulated Anne, and then, lowering her voice, Peggy said, "Delia Goldhush's mother is the artist?"

"She is," Anne said.

"I had no idea," said Peggy.

"We didn't really know anything about her, did we?" Tabitha said.

Anne was surprised by the comment, and even more surprised when Peggy said, "Well, now we do," and touched her cup of punch to Anne's. "To Delia—and her mother."

Anne thanked them both for coming and went to greet Miss Grayson, who for this occasion wore an ivory silk blouse and a long satin evening skirt that shimmered when she moved. The hem of the skirt was deeply scalloped, and when she turned, Anne saw that there was a large bow at the back. Her earrings were faceted, sparkling drops, and rings adorned all her fingers but her thumbs. She was more dressed up than anyone here, and Anne loved that. Delia would have loved it too.

"Miss Bishop!" her professor said. "Congratulations. You did a fine job with this. You should be proud."

Anne was quiet. She had been hoping for something more effusive.

"I'm sorry Miss Goldhush isn't here," Miss Grayson said.

"She never answered my letter."

"Nor mine, which is a pity. This exhibition would make her happy," said Miss Grayson. Then she added, "Do you see that man? He's from the *Poughkeepsie Journal*. They're going to run a piece about the show in their Arts and Culture section. And that girl, the one over there?" Anne followed her gaze. "She's taking pictures for the *Miscellany News*. You can get copies of both, keep a record. It may be useful one day."

"Yes, I will," Anne said. But she was still disappointed: no article or photographs could ever be the same as being here, face-to-face with these works of art.

The event was winding down when Miss Grayson came to find her again. "Miss Bishop, may I have a word with you?"

"Of course," said Anne.

"Let's go into my office. We won't be disturbed there."

Anne followed her out of the gallery and up the stairs. When they were alone, the professor said, "I told you that I reviewed Delia Goldhush's file."

Anne wished this conversation were not happening. Reviewing the file meant dredging up Anne's role in what happened; did they really need to discuss this a second time?

"Going over it again made me wonder about Mr. McQuaid. So I made some inquiries. It seems that Miss Goldhush was not . . . the only one."

"I don't understand." Anne could guess, but she needed it spelled out.

"Just that his name has been associated with other students here at the college. Three of them." She paused, presumably to let that sink in. "In the light of that information, the dean's response to Miss Goldhush's situation may have been an overreaction. Perhaps some of the blame should have been extended to Mr. McQuaid as well."

"I didn't know any of that," Anne said. "None of us did."

"Of course not. It was kept quiet. But this has been Mr. McQuaid's last year at Vassar. He's been offered a tenure-track position elsewhere. In California, I think. He'll be starting there in the fall. And Dean Schoales retired last year, which means that the two people who were most involved in Miss Goldhush's expulsion will no longer be associated with the college. That changes things."

"Do you mean . . ."

"Perhaps Miss Goldhush can come back. That is, if she wants to. I'm going to bring the whole matter to the attention of President Blanding. I have a strong feeling she'll agree with me."

Anne felt herself breaking into a wide smile. Yes, she had been instrumental in getting Delia expelled from Vassar. But now it seemed she might be instrumental in her being invited back. And wouldn't *that* be something?

TWENTY-SEVEN

DELIA

1948

Delia got back to New York in the middle of a week-long heat wave. The days were steamy and oppressive, and unlike the desert, which never failed to cool down after dark, the nights were essentially the same. She spent most of her time on West Eleventh Street, with fans set up all over the house; it was just too hot to go anywhere. Helga was happy to see her and declared fattening her up as a personal mission. “You so skinny!” she clucked repeatedly. “You must eat more!” To that end, she baked pies, layer cakes, and muffins in shocking numbers; the kitchen was so hot that Delia wouldn’t even enter it and sought refuge outside, in the yard. Sometimes she spied her neighbor George Frost out behind his house. His garden was lush, filled with flowers and vegetables too; where there wasn’t greenery, there was a patch of slate on which stood four wrought-iron chairs, and a table topped by an umbrella. She never saw him sitting there, though, and she never made any attempt to engage with him.

If Helga seemed unchanged, the same was not true for her father. He was very glad to see Delia, and when she first came home, held her in a long embrace. She studied his face, where new lines had appeared, and his hair, which badly needed a trim and was now almost entirely gray. And talk about skinny—Simon's clothes hung from his frame, shirts billowing and pants pooling. What had happened? The answer came quickly: Harriet had moved out and left a gaping hole in his life.

While Delia was away, she and her father had exchanged letters intermittently—she told him about Paris, the search for the sculpture, and reconnecting with Gaby. At first Simon's letters had been newsy and upbeat; he wrote about his trip out west, meeting O'Keeffe—"a living legend," he called her—his plans for the gallery, and other trips he wanted to take, on which he urged her to join him. But then the letters essentially stopped; now she knew why.

"What happened with Harriet, Papa?" she asked one night over dinner. They were sitting in the dining room, where three table fans had been set out, the gentle whir of the blades a soothing sound. Helga had made a cold beet soup, which was perfect for the sultry weather. "I thought you two were happy together."

"I thought so too." Simon swirled his spoon around in the soup but didn't eat any of it.

"So then . . . ?"

"She met someone else."

Delia looked at her father's haggard face and felt a rush of pity. But that didn't mean she wasn't going to initiate the difficult conversation she knew they had to have. There were things she needed to ask and had to say, whether or not he wanted to answer.

Helga took the uneaten soup away and brought in a salad. Simon seemed more interested and speared a lettuce leaf, then a chunk of tomato.

"Did you ever find the sculpture?" he asked.

"No." So he was taking the lead on this; good.

"I didn't think you would. Were you in Paris the whole time? Is that where you were looking?"

"I was in Paris for a month or so. Everywhere I looked led to a dead end. Then I saw one of Sophie's sculptures in a gallery right near our old apartment on the rue Vavin."

"You saw one of her pieces? Which one?"

"Nothing you or I had ever seen before. It was done in 1946."

"But that's impossible. Your mother was killed before that."

"Marie-Pierre was wrong. Papa, Sophie is alive, and living in Palestine—well, Israel now. I went there to find her."

"Sophie is alive! What are you talking about?" He looked more alert than he had since she'd arrived.

"She wasn't killed. Though she nearly was—she had a narrow escape." Delia then told him the entire story Sophie had told her, including her having given birth to Asher.

"I can't believe any of this. She made it up, every bit of it."

"No, Papa! It's true. I've seen her. I spent weeks with her and . . . my brother."

"He's not your brother."

"Oh, but he is, Papa."

"Well, maybe he's your half brother, but this business about a Nazi soldier—it's a lie. And it does sound like your mother. She loved telling stories, the more outlandish the better. This is just another example."

"I believe her," Delia said. "And if you'd seen her and met Asher, you'd believe her too." She'd been thinking about Asher, and to her own surprise, she missed him. And Sophie—did she miss her too?

The next day, Delia took a walk to the gallery. Simon told her it had been closed for a while. She tried to get him to go with her, but he refused, so she went herself. The shades were pulled down, and when she stepped inside, she saw that the place was a wreck. Also dusty—she sneezed several times. Her first impulse was to turn around, lock the door, and not look back. But something kept her rooted to the spot; she wasn't going to abandon it.

A large canvas was facing the wall; she turned it around. It was a lovely Fauvist seascape—brightly colored boats bobbing on a choppy blue sea, pink puffy clouds above. Then she looked at some of the other canvases, and opened a drawer of the flat files, where she found several watercolors depicting different kinds of marine life, as well as a very finely rendered ink drawing of a ship with three masts and full sails. What if she opened the gallery again? She could mount a little show of work related to water. Not the most original idea, but better than leaving things as they were now. She spent a couple of hours at the gallery, and though there was far more to do, she felt that she had made a good start.

At dinner that night, she told her father about what she'd done that day. Though he nodded and made a few comments, he didn't seem truly engaged, and as soon as he finished eating, he went upstairs to his study. Delia was alone. Restless, she wandered through the rooms downstairs, stopping by the front doors. Maybe she would take a walk; it wasn't late, and it might be a bit cooler outside. She reached for the key ring hanging on the brass rack of hooks, but it dropped and slid under the small chest of drawers where Helga always stacked the mail. Getting down on her knees, Delia reached under the chest, feeling around for what she could not see. There were the keys, but wait, there was something else. It turned out to be a letter—no, two, both a bit dusty and both addressed to her. The postmarks showed that they had been mailed from Poughkeepsie some weeks ago. She opened the first one.

Dear Delia,

I wanted to tell you that the missing sculpture you were looking all over Paris for has been found—it was in the United States, on Long Island, of all places. I've been to see the work, and think your mother is a very gifted artist; I understand why you were so intent on getting it back. And it just seems like great good luck that after all those months, it ended up so close to home.

The sculptures have been shipped to Poughkeepsie, but they can be shipped to your house or your father's gallery. Please let me know what you prefer. This year I'm in Cushing, so you can find me there. Please write back. There's a lot for us to talk about.

Always,

Anne

Delia put the letter down on the chest of drawers. Her mother's sculpture was now in Poughkeepsie, of all places. How astonishing! But before she could even feel the full impact of this information, she was now even more curious about the other letter. This one was on Vassar stationery and sent by someone named Professor Pamela Grayson. Delia didn't know her. She too was writing about the sculpture, some of which was apparently going to be exhibited at the Vassar Art Gallery, in a small show curated by Anne. Anne curating a show of Sophie's work? Professor Grayson was inviting her to the opening, which, Delia could see, had already taken place; she'd missed it. But Grayson said the show would be up until November; that meant she could take the train up to see it. Did she want to do that? She kept reading. Miss Grayson brought up the subject of Delia's expulsion and said that the president of the college had revisited the decision and decided to reverse it. Delia could have a place in the class of 1952 or 1953, depending on how many courses she was willing to take in a semester. This was the most astonishing of all.

The next morning Delia went to the gallery. There was still plenty of work to do but it did look better and that was encouragement enough to keep going. Once she got started, she became immersed and didn't even stop to eat lunch. But she had an apple with her and had just taken a bite when she saw that there was someone at the door. She was prepared to say that they were not open for business yet until she saw it was her neighbor George Frost. Delia let him in.

"Well, hello," he said. Today he wore a pale-blue shirt under a light-tan jacket, its left arm pinned, as usual, to his shoulder.

"Hello, George," she said uncertainly. Had he come to see her, or was he just passing by?

"I brought you these," he said. "Since you have such a good eye for color, I thought you'd like them." He handed her a bunch of peonies in a deep, rich magenta.

"They're beautiful." She was glad to be occupied by finding a vase and going to the sink in the back to fill it. Then she set the flowers out on the desk and picked up her apple.

"Lunch," she said apologetically. "And it's all I brought, so I can't even offer you one."

"That's all right," he said. "I've already eaten."

Delia concentrated on the apple, trying not to make excessive noise while chewing it. She still didn't know quite why he'd come by.

"I've passed the gallery a bunch of times," he said. "It's been closed for a while, hasn't it? But then yesterday I saw it looked different inside and I guessed you'd been here."

"Now that I'm back in New York, it's going to be open more regularly."

"You were away for a long time." It was not a question. "Where were you?"

"Paris," she said. "And Israel."

His eyebrows—unexpectedly dark for his light hair—shot up. "There's a big difference between those two places. Must have been interesting, right? Compare and contrast?"

"It was very . . . interesting." Really, what *was* he doing here?

As if he'd read her mind, he said, "Well, I'll be going now. I just wanted to give you the flowers." He moved toward the door. "Oh—and I also wanted to invite you and your father to dinner sometime. I've got so many vegetables out back that I've taken up cooking."

So not only did he garden with one hand, but he cooked too?

". . . since I'm by myself now, I can't eat them all fast enough," he was saying.

"By yourself?" Delia remembered the woman she'd seen him with, the ease in each other's company they seemed to have.

"My mother passed away during the winter."

"Oh, I'm so sorry." She had no idea. Then she blurted out, "Her coffee cake. It was delicious."

He looked confused, so Delia said, "When we moved in, she sent over a cake she'd made. You brought it, remember?"

"Oh, that's right. She loved to bake," he said. "Me? Not so much. But I've been experimenting. With mixed results." He smiled, a kind of shy, touching smile.

"We'd love to come to dinner," Delia said. "Did you have a night in mind?"

"How about tomorrow at seven?" he said. "Is tomorrow good?"

Tomorrow. Why the rush? Delia was going to say something about tomorrow night not being convenient, but then she saw it on his face: hope, like a bright, syrupy glaze, and she couldn't disappoint him.

"Tomorrow would be just fine," she said. "I'll tell my father. Is there something we can bring?"

"Just bring yourselves." That smile again.

After he'd left, Delia looked at the flowers. He was a nice man. Dinner might even be fun. When she got into bed that night, she remembered that she hadn't answered Anne or Professor Grayson and had no intention of responding to either of them until she'd thought things through. And that, she realized, was going to take a little while.

TWENTY-EIGHT

ANNE

1949

After the opening of Sophie Rossner's exhibition, the days seemed to gallop along until June 13 finally arrived—graduation day for the class of 1949. Anne woke early and walked over to the window. The campus seemed to sparkle in the morning light; everything outside was a brilliant, electric green, and there were already people on the paths and the lawn. While the actual commencement ceremony was today, there had been a whole weekend of events leading up to it—the senior class banquet, the glee club concert, the president's reception, and the commencement supper were just some of them. And it was also reunion weekend, so alumnae—from the classes of 1899 through the teens and more recent—were here too.

The chapel doors were open, and though she could not see inside, Anne knew that the space was decorated with the daisy chain, a tradition in which the sophomores—their sister class—used the flowers to honor the older girls. Years ago, the sophomores had actually picked the daisies from a field where the quad dorms now stood and woven them into a chain to mark off the section of the chapel reserved for the seniors. Now a local florist handled the whole thing, though there were still sophomores in white dresses—chosen by the seniors; it was an honor to be asked—who carried the chain. Anne had not been chosen when she was a sophomore, though Virginia Worthington had. She remembered feeling envious back then, but Virginia Worthington no longer inspired her envy.

Anne turned away from the window and toward the mirror. Yesterday she'd gone to the Glamour Girl beauty parlor in town, where she'd sat under a stiff pink cloth and had a trim, after which her hair was parted on the side and coaxed into soft, natural-looking waves that framed her face. Of course the waves weren't natural at all, and she'd had to sleep with a fat, padded cap—also pink—to keep her new coif from getting mussed. It had been uncomfortable, but it was worth it, because today her hair was perfect.

She went down the hall to take a shower and found the communal bathroom filled with steam, high voices, and giggling. Four other seniors were already there, brushing their teeth, combing their hair, putting on cologne, lipstick, rouge, mascara. It reminded Anne of the nights before a dance, though today's excitement wasn't about boys or romance. Just as well; since she broke up with Drew, there hadn't been anyone else. Or at least anyone else she liked nearly as much. He hadn't written or called. Of course she hadn't written either, though she had badly wanted to. But reaching out invited the possibility of rejection, and Anne didn't think she could endure that.

Why was she brooding about this? Today was her graduation day, a time to celebrate. Barney Weiss and his wife Ida would be here, as would her aunt Betty, her uncle Sol, and her three cousins. They would watch her walk across the stage in her cap and gown, mingle at the reception, and then take her to lunch at the Beekman Arms in Rhinebeck. She got ready and made her way over to the chapel. The program would begin at ten o'clock.

First there was an organ recital, through which Anne fidgeted. She'd never liked organ music—she found it too somber and pretentious—

and she liked it even less today. It was warm in the chapel, so she used her program to fan herself as she waited for the organ to finally be still. Then the calling of the names began. Good. It wouldn't be long; the degrees were presented alphabetically. When she heard her name, she stood up and walked across the stage. The furled-up roll of paper, tied with a ribbon, was not the actual diploma; that would come a little later on. She'd made sure it would say Miriam Anne Bishop. She'd been Anne since she got here, but Miriam for the prior eighteen years; she wanted the diploma to encompass both.

She sat back down on the other side of the stage, faux diploma in her lap. Now she could relax a little, and she let her gaze stray out over the audience assembled in the wooden pews. There was Aunt Betty, dabbing her eyes with a hankie. Uncle Sol's eyes were closed; was he actually asleep? Her cousin Arthur was whispering something to his brother Ben, and Ruthie, the youngest of the three, was leaning over, straining to hear what Arthur was saying. Uncle Sol's eyes opened, and he shushed the three of them. Barney and Ida were sitting on the other side, and he gave her the smallest wave, a mere flutter of the fingers. Barney had been good to her, and she was very fond of him. Yet though Barney and Aunt Betty had each invited Anne to spend the summer at their respective houses, she'd turned down both invitations. Instead, she was going to spend a few weeks in Maine, with Elizabeth and the rest of the Hunnewells, of all people.

Over the winter break, Anne had been in New York and stopped in at Lord & Taylor, mostly to get out of the cold. While browsing the ground floor—did she want that adorable red tam with the pompom at the top?—she decided to go upstairs to the Bird Cage, where she ordered a coffee and the prune whip with custard sauce, one of her favorites. As she spooned the creamy concoction down, she saw that Mrs. Hunnewell was sitting two tables away, and before Anne could even decide whether she wanted to talk to her, Mrs. Hunnewell had seen her and walked right over.

"Miriam!" She used the name Anne had answered to back then.

"Hello, Mrs. Hunnewell."

"Please, it's Priscilla. But you know that—we were like family. Though we haven't seen you in a long time."

"I know," Anne said. "A very long time."

"Can I join you?" Mrs. Hunnewell—Priscilla—said. "Unless you're meeting someone."

"I'm not meeting anyone," Anne said.

Priscilla sat down, and though she didn't explicitly mention the Colony Club or the ill-fated lunch, she seemed to want to reminisce, and brought up times they'd spent together that Anne had either forgotten or hadn't thought of in years. It was, Anne understood, her way of apologizing. "And I did want to say that I was so sorry to hear about your father. I know how close you were to him."

Anne just nodded; she didn't trust herself to speak, because her eyes had filled with tears. Priscilla reached over and took Anne's hands in hers. "I do hope you'll be in touch with Elizabeth—I know she'd love to hear from you—and that we'll see more of you in the future."

Anne had called Elizabeth that very evening, and on a gray day in early January, they met at Rumpelmayer's, a café and ice cream parlor in the Hotel St. Moritz, overlooking Central Park. Most of Elizabeth's birthday parties—skating at the Rockefeller Center, a Broadway matinee, a visit to the zoo—would conclude there, the girls digging into the thick, almost-have-to-eat-it-with-a-spoon hot chocolate, or sharing the outsize ice cream sundaes. Looking around, Anne saw that the walls were still pink and still adorned with Egyptian-style mosaics. There were still shelves filled with stuffed animals; you could take down a teddy bear and hold him while you ate. Being back there with Elizabeth felt a little bit like coming home.

"You were right," Elizabeth said. "I shouldn't have gone to the Colony for that lunch. None of us should have. I somehow thought that once it was over, everything would go back to the way it had been, that we'd never have to think about it again."

"And it seemed like it was *all* I could think about. I brooded over it for a long time. Too long," said Anne. "And even when I stopped thinking about it so much, it kind of burrowed into my mind. It warped things for me."

"Warped? How?"

"When I got to Vassar, I let everyone think I wasn't Jewish."

"I don't understand."

"I just never let on that I was a Jew, and no one assumed I was. My last name threw people off track, and I used my middle name, so I became Anne Bishop. I never came out and said I was Christian, but I never said I wasn't either, so I sort of slid by."

"So that night at Yale, at the dance . . . you *were* there."

"I was. But I couldn't admit to knowing you, or even take the chance of seeing you. I was afraid you'd say something that would give me away. I couldn't have that."

"And that's why you never answered my letter."

"That's why," Anne said. "I behaved badly."

"We both did." Elizabeth looked straight at her. "But that was the past. We can do better. We *will* do better."

"Do you think so?" Anne asked. And returning Elizabeth's frank gaze, she thought, Yes. Yes, we will.

When they got to the G's, Anne thought of Delia, whose name was not called out. She should have been here, not only today, but last month too, at the opening of the show. But Delia hadn't responded to either Anne's letter or the one sent by Miss Grayson. Now they were at the M's, and as Dominique Martin crossed the stage, followed by Sarabeth Miller and Constance Moody, Anne looked upward, at the towering interior space with its brilliantly blue Tiffany rose window. This was quite different from any window she'd seen at Chartres, but mysterious and beautiful in its own way. Chartres. It was coming back from the cathedral that she'd first met Drew. And in an instant, she was back on that Parisian street, watching as he hugged Nancy, her heart doing an unexpected flip when he turned her way.

Now they'd gotten to the *T*'s—there were quite a number of those: Taylor, Tellin, Thomas, Travis . . . Anne shut her eyes, and the blue of the window disappeared. When she opened them again, she looked for her family. Now Uncle Sol really was asleep, his head tilted back. Ruth was leaning against Aunt Betty, who was stroking her hair. Anne was getting impatient too. The chapel was stuffy; she wanted the ceremony to be over. Longingly, she looked at the closed doors and imagined them wide open to the soft spring air, the sunshine. She wanted to walk out into this glowing day, college and graduation behind her, and walk straight toward her future. Only what would that be? She had plans for the summer, but that was all.

Her gaze continued to roam the sea of faces and then quite suddenly stopped. Who was that man off to the side? He looked so much like Drew Gilchrist, it was unsettling. Thinking about Chartres and Drew must have created a kind of mirage here in the chapel. But the man was now looking at *her*. Then he looked down and put a hand on something gray or silvery in his lap. It *was* Drew; that was his Leica. When had he gotten to campus? And why?

Anne wanted to jump up and rush down from the stage. But she had to wait for the *W*'s, and watch Virginia Worthington cross the stage. Anne looked down; she had never made peace with Virginia and never would. There was an *X*, and two *Y*'s, and the lone *Z*. Even then she had to sit through the interminable remarks made by some visiting college president. Finally, the ceremony was over, and she could make her way down the stairs, along with the other graduates. She jostled past people offering congratulations, hugging and kissing. Where was Drew? She'd lost sight of him.

But Betty, Sol, and her cousins had found her; they were joined by Barney and Ida. Now she was the object of the congratulations and the hugs. And then, out of nowhere, there was Drew, standing right in front of her. He wore a dark suit, white shirt, and a tie. She'd never seen him in such clothes, and he looked unfamiliar, even strange. But then he smiled, and there was that dimple she'd loved from the start. "Congratulations, Anne. You did it." He leaned in a for hug. She was overwhelmed by the familiar scent of him; it was all she could do not to bury her face in his neck. She would do no such thing, of course, and simply introduced him to Barney and her family as "a friend from my time in Paris."

Aunt Betty invited him to join them for lunch, an invitation that he accepted, and for twenty-three minutes she had to sit squeezed in next to him in the back of Uncle Sol's blue-and-brown station wagon. She was very aware of his thigh pressing against hers. Drew didn't seem affected by it, though, and chatted amiably with her aunt and uncle. Anne could feel Aunt Betty's questions hovering in the air as if they were thought bubbles rising from her head. *Is this a boyfriend? How old is he? Is he Jewish?* Anne knew the answers to the last two questions, but as for the first, she was as in the dark as Aunt Betty.

The restaurant was able to fit in another place setting, and fortunately—or was it unfortunately?—Drew was seated at the other end of the long table. She could only sneak glances at him in between conversations at her end of the table and spoonfuls of corn chowder. Finally—finally!—the dessert cart glided over to the table, choices were made, and servings of apple pie and chocolate layer cake devoured before the sticky plates were cleared. Barney and Ida were headed back to New York, while Uncle Sol and Aunt Betty drove Anne—and now Drew—back to Vassar. She waved goodbye to them and promised to write from Maine. And then, at last, she and Drew were alone.

"What are you doing here?" she burst out. "Nothing, not a word, in over a year, and then you show up at my graduation? And how did you even know about it?"

"Nancy graduated from Northeastern last week, and you two were the same year, so I knew you'd be graduating too. It's a big milestone, and I wanted to surprise you."

"Well, you did." She was aware she sounded a little angry; well, she *was* angry. Anger was a buffer, protecting her from the cutting silence of those months, from the hurt.

"Anne . . ." He moved closer, but she stepped back. He couldn't just show up and expect her to forget all that had happened between them. "I'm sorry if I upset you. I didn't mean to. It's just that I . . . I missed you." That disarmed her. And she had missed him too. So much. But she wasn't ready to say it yet. Instead she said, "Let's take a walk." She didn't have a specific place in mind, but most anywhere they went would be better than standing here by Main Gate, where there were still so many people milling around. She set off toward the New England Building, where the science classes were held.

"This is where we're going?" He pointed to a building with a semicircular extension at the back.

"No. Here." She led him behind it, to the entrance of a well-tended garden with brick paths, neatly trimmed shrubs, and tidy beds of flowers. The brass plaque said it was planted with all the flowers and shrubs mentioned in Shakespeare's canon.

Pansy season was over, but there were several roses in bloom—pink, red, and white.

Anne read the names—Musk, Damask, Eglantine—as Drew stopped to photograph. The soft clicks of the shutter were familiar; she remembered that day together in Paris—the last time she'd seen him—and how his picture taking had infuriated her. Today, she didn't mind; the activity was a distraction from the new awkwardness between them. All those months of thinking about him, longing for him—and yet now that he was here, there was a barrier. Who was he, anyway? She no longer felt like she knew. They came to a stone bench, and when she sat down, he sat down beside her.

"Now that we're alone, I can ask: Why are you here?"

"I missed you. And I wanted to say I'm sorry for how I behaved back in Paris. I should have understood why you wouldn't want to meet with a priest or go to church. I should have just respected your religion and left it alone."

Anne paused before replying; it was important that she get this right. "It's not exactly religion. Religious observance wasn't even a big part of my upbringing. It's about my background, my family. My essence. My father once told me that being Jewish was part of who he was. He couldn't change or excise it, even if he wanted to. Well, the same is true for me."

"I understand," he said. "I do." They sat in silence for a moment, and then he asked, "Have you been dating anyone since you got back?"

"No." So he cared about that. But wait—maybe there was another reason he was asking. "Have you?" When he hesitated, she knew the answer was yes.

"There was someone," he said. "She worked at the paper."

Anne had to stop herself from pelting him with questions. "Oh?" was all she said.

"A reporter. Mary Rafferty."

Irish, Anne thought. And more to the point: *Catholic.*

"So, are you and Mary still an item?"

"No. If we were, I wouldn't be here." He paused. "She's a nice girl. Very nice. Smart. Pretty. Lots of get-up-and-go. My mother really liked her."

Of course.

"What went wrong?"

"She wasn't you." He reached for her hand.

The words mollified her. Also the gesture. But it wasn't enough. "If we *did* start seeing each other again, what would you do about your mother? She's not going to like me any better the second time around."

"No, she won't."

This was the response she wanted; it was honest, and if they were going to start up again, she couldn't accept anything less. "And that won't bother you?"

"I'd be lying if I said no. But not being with you would bother me more. A lot more. I think it's worth another try. Do you?" Before she could answer, he released her hand and reached into his pocket for a small white box. "For you," he said.

"Is it—"

"The ring," he said. "Aren't you going to open it?"

She undid the white ribbon and saw the simple, elegantly wrought band, the striations and subtle green weave of the stone. "You kept it." She didn't add that she was glad he hadn't given it to Mary Rafferty. "Why?"

"Maybe I hoped you would wear it again." He paused. "Will you?"

She looked into his eyes and saw just how much he wanted her to say yes. And part of her wanted that too. But somehow she couldn't. "I don't know," she said honestly.

"When?" he said. "When will you know?"

She looked at him and shrugged.

TWENTY-NINE

DELIA

1949

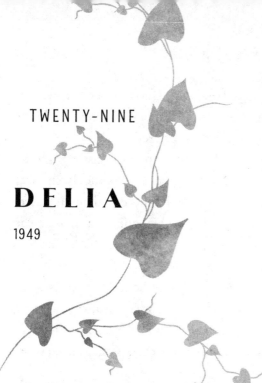

George Frost's house was identical, at least in floor plan, to the one in which Delia and her father lived. The two had been built by the same developer sometime around 1850. But while Delia's house was filled with artwork and an eclectic mix of furniture and rugs, George's house was chiefly filled with books. Oh, there was a sofa, a couple of chairs, and a few other pieces, but they seemed overwhelmed, almost engulfed, by all those books—some small and thin, others thick as doorstops, some with dust jackets and others whose faded cloth covers were unadorned. Some were neatly arranged on shelves, others stacked in equally neat piles. On the coffee table, lavish art books were open to double-page spreads. Books, books, and more books.

"I'm glad you could come," George said as he ushered Delia and her father in. Today he wore a short-sleeved shirt that he hadn't bothered to pin. The empty sleeve rustled when he moved, which to Delia suggested a phantom arm, invisible but somehow still present.

"Thank you for inviting us." Delia handed him the bottle of wine Simon had selected, and then froze. She should have thought more about the gift—he couldn't very well open it with only a single hand.

But he didn't seem at all bothered and went into the kitchen, returning with a corkscrew, which he handed to Simon. "Would you do the honors?" The cork was popped, the wine poured.

Delia continued to look around. She saw poetry, history, and an entire shelf devoted to the works of Shakespeare. Suddenly she was back in Ian's class reading Juliet's lines, and in his car, then his office, and finally staring through the window as his wife took in what she was seeing. The memories singed. Shakespeare was ruined for her; she looked away in a hurry.

". . . I've always been a reader, but I like books as objects too," George was saying. "The feel of them, the weight. I'm always looking for the rare ones, the special ones, you know? The thrill of the hunt is exciting, especially now—what with my mother gone. I need some distraction."

Delia admired his candor. There was a lot to like about George Frost.

"You've read this?" Simon reached for a book on top of a stack and read its title aloud: "*Insect Adventures*, by J. H. Fabre."

"You know Fabre?" George asked.

"Know Fabre?" said Simon. "I revere Fabre!" When George looked surprised, he added, "We lived in France for many years. Fabre is well known there. And look—you have *The Life and Love of Insects*, and *The Life of the Fly* too." He picked up one book and then another.

"He's a naturalist who writes like a novelist," George said to Delia. "A born storyteller."

The Life of the Fly? Delia shuddered. So in addition to worms, George was interested in flies and other insects, an interest Delia most decidedly did not share. She stopped listening and, leaving books and bug talk behind, stepped out into the garden through the kitchen door. The light was just beginning to fade, but she could still see the rows of orderly beds, vegetables on one side, flowers on the other. And herbs—Delia smelled basil. Separating the two sides was a narrow slate walkway and, close to the house, the table and chairs she'd seen from her own yard. It was lovely out here, an oasis.

From inside, she heard her father's voice, sounding more animated than it had in a while. Delia hoped he wasn't drunk, especially so early in the evening. Then George appeared in the doorway. "Dinner's ready," he said. "Come in and join us." Delia followed him inside. A small bunch of roses in a white ironstone pitcher sat at the center of a table that was set with unmatched plates, all with floral designs; heavy white napkins, each with a different border, sat atop the plates. Somehow, despite the variety of patterns, colors, and textures, it all seemed intentional, even harmonious. The napkins were pressed and starched; had George done that? Delia was inordinately curious about how he managed with a single arm. Was there something unseemly about her interest?

"You have quite a collection," Simon said as they ate. "Impressive really. Have you ever thought about selling any of it? You could open a bookshop."

"Funny you should say that, because I've been thinking the same thing," said George. "I've even been inquiring about places to rent along Fourth Avenue. But there are a lot of shops there already. I'd need to set myself apart in some way."

"Yes! Exactly!" Simon drained what was left in his wineglass, and when George refilled it, he brought it right to his lips. Delia shook her head when George tried to refill her glass; someone had to stay sober. "You could focus on books about nature—flora and fauna, if you will. And you could sell plant and animal prints too."

George got up and started clearing the plates; without asking, Delia helped. On the kitchen counter was a round cake stand; the cake sitting on it was white and sprinkled with coconut. "Did you make this too?" she asked.

"No. I bought it. As I told you, I've been teaching myself to bake, but I'm not ready to share the results with company."

"You've taught yourself a lot of things."

"I've got a lot of time on my hands. Or hand." He smiled again.

Delia couldn't imagine how he could poke fun at himself. Unable to look at him just then, she went over to the sink, where she started washing dishes.

"Oh, you don't need to do that," he said. "Let's have dessert and keep talking."

She rinsed a final plate before following him back to the table and watching him while he cut the cake and served each of them a little glass of sherry. Simon drank his in a single gulp and took the bottle to pour himself another. But he missed the glass and spilled sherry all over the table.

"Papa! Look what you did!" Delia cried.

"Don't worry about it," George said.

"I'm sorry." Simon started dabbing at the little puddle with his napkin; now the sherry was dripping onto the floor.

"You're just making it worse." Delia took the napkin from his hand and set it beside his glass.

"Here, let me." George went to the kitchen and returned with a sponge.

"He's had too much to drink," said Delia. "I need to get him home."

"I'll go with you." George helped Simon to his feet, then together they ushered him out of George's house and into the house next door. Delia settled her father on the sofa, eased off his shoes, and turned on one of the fans. "Better," he mumbled. "Much better." His eyelids fluttered, and then closed. Delia waited a moment and then said to George, "He'll probably be all right, but I'd rather not leave him. Can we stay here?"

"Of course. I'll just go get the cake." He went next door and returned with the two slices and two sherry glasses all on a tray he supported with his single, spread hand. There was another piece of cake wrapped in wax paper. "For your father. He can eat it tomorrow. But we can have ours now. Do you want to go out back?"

"Our yard is pretty overgrown—a mess, really. Let's sit on the stoop out front instead."

"Perfect," he said.

Outside, the street was quiet with few passersby: a couple holding hands, a young man with what appeared to be an old dog and an old one with a puppy; the puppy wouldn't walk in a straight line but pranced and frolicked on the sidewalk. The moon, full and golden, rose slowly over the low brick and brownstone buildings.

"Is that a harvest moon?" Delia asked. "Or a strawberry moon?" The cake was delicious, moist and sweet. She hadn't even known she liked coconut cake.

"I don't know my moons," said George. "But I know about the stars, constellations and all. Though of course you can't see them here."

"Stars," Delia mused. "Where did you learn about them?"

"All over. We went camping a lot."

"Your family?"

"My cousins. We were close as kids. We still are."

"So you're an only child—like me."

"I had two brothers—twins, actually. They were killed, along with my father, in a car accident. That was a long time ago. For years, it was just my mother and me."

Scratch at the surface of any life, Delia thought, any life at all, and you'll find the loss that lies beneath it. Sometimes it was right there; sometimes it was buried deep. Nothing surprising about that. What was surprising, though, was George's response to that loss: sad, but not broken. Accepting, but not beaten down. Delia licked the tines of her fork and set her empty plate down beside her. She thought of the losses she'd endured; could she say she'd handled them as well?

"What about you?" he asked. "Your mother—I never saw her here at all."

"She stayed in France. We thought she'd been killed during the war, but that turned out not to be true. She's living in Israel."

"You said you went to Israel—to see her?"

"Yes." That was all Delia was going to say about it, at least right now.

George seemed to understand that because he took a forkful of cake and said, "I'm going to learn to make this. Expand my repertoire." He smiled at her. "Maybe that sounds silly, but I like to give myself goals, even small ones."

"That's not silly at all. What other goals have you set for yourself?"

"Well, after tonight, I think opening a bookstore might be one of them. Also, I want to learn French."

"French? Why?"

"Why not? You speak French, don't you? My mother said you and your parents lived in Paris."

"We did."

"I've never been there, but I'd love to go, and if I do, I want to be able to talk to people. And I like the sound of it—subtle, murmuring even. Like someone's telling you a secret. Not harsh, like German."

"You were in Germany." She didn't need to ask.

"I was. For a few months. It's not a happy memory."

She waited, looking up at the sky. A cloud was passing the moon, obscuring its light. When he still didn't say anything more, she asked, "Do you want to tell me about it? Because if you do, I'd like to hear."

His gaze searched her face as if he was trying to decide whether or not to say more. "It was near the end of the war. April, late in the month," he said. "We'd already won, we knew it, we were sure of it. It was just a matter of time. We were out in the country, not in the cities that were being bombed. The country seemed peaceful, even safe by comparison. We saw a small band of German soldiers coming toward us, and they didn't even stay to fight—they just scattered and ran away. Ran away!"

So he must have still had his arm then, Delia thought. He couldn't have been there, in the thick of things, without it.

"We laughed about it, laughed at them. Spring was coming, and there we were, marching down a road on a sunny morning, laughing. And singing too. Singing as loud as we could . . ."

Delia waited before she spoke. "And then?"

"Then the shooting started. Bullets were coming from every direction."

"German troops?"

"The soldiers we'd seen earlier, the ones who ran away? The ones we mocked? It turns out that they hadn't run away at all, they were just hiding, waiting to ambush us. The guy marching next to me—Fred, he was my buddy—was hit in the chest. I reacted out of instinct, trying to shield him even though I knew that he was already dead. That's when I was hit—my shoulder, my arm, sprayed with bullets. They just kept coming. The next thing I remember was waking up in the hospital. The doctor told me they tried to save it"—he touched the empty sleeve—"but they couldn't."

Whatever she might say would be inadequate; Delia kept quiet.

"They kept me pretty doped up for a while, so the full impact didn't hit me right away. And as soon as I was able to travel, they sent me home. They even gave me a citation for bravery."

"So you came back here? To your mother?"

"I did. She'd already lost a husband and two kids. Instead of mourning my missing arm, she woke up every day grateful that I was still here, still alive. She got me through the worst of it. And somehow the fact that she was able to tolerate the loss helped me to do the same."

"It sounds like she deserved a citation too."

He nodded, and they sat in silence for a while. A group of young people—a handful of girls and boys—came down the street, giggling and talking to each other in high, excited voices. The boys wore light jackets over button-down shirts and belted pants; three of the girls were in skirts with sleeveless blouses while the fourth was in a flouncy dress with a sash that tied in a bow at the back.

"College kids," George said when they had passed. "You went to college, right? Vassar?"

"How did you know?"

"Your father told my mother. She said he was very proud of you."

"Well, there's not so much to be proud of now. I was asked to leave. Expelled."

"Oh," George said. "I guess I shouldn't have brought it up."

"That's all right," Delia said. "You didn't know. Aren't you going to ask why?"

"No. You'll tell me if you want to."

Delia hadn't planned to reveal this, at least not so soon. But it had come up; here she was. "I had an affair with one of my professors. A married professor. The dean found out. I was gone by the end of the week." She scanned his face and in it saw no shock, no disapproval or distaste. He didn't judge, he just listened to the story and then said, "What happened to him? Was he asked to leave too?"

"No. And I heard he was offered a tenured position somewhere else."

"So his situation got better. Yours got worse. That hardly seems fair."

"I suppose not."

"I didn't finish college either," he said.

"Because you were drafted?"

"I enlisted. I'd just started at City College, but when I saw so many guys signing up, it felt wrong to stay behind."

"You could go back now," she said.

"I could," he agreed. "But I'm not sure I could stand the looks, the pity." He gestured toward his missing arm.

"You don't need anyone's pity," she said. She hoped he knew that she was being utterly sincere.

"Thank you." He turned to look at her, and between the moonlight and the streetlamp, she could read the expression on his face and saw that yes, he did.

"There's something else . . ." she said. "Something I haven't told anyone."

"What's that?"

"I got a letter from a professor at Vassar. They're offering to take me back."

"That's good, isn't?" he said. "Problem solved."

"No," she said. "It's not."

"I don't understand."

"How can I go back there? Everyone would know, they would talk about me."

"Forget all that," he said. "You said I could go back to college? Well, *you* can too. That's the only thing that matters—whether you want to or not. What other people think or say isn't as important as that. And don't let yourself get waylaid by too much thinking. This is a decision you make with your heart, not your head."

George made it sound so simple, so self-evident. She thought of a quote by Blaise Pascal that had been in one of her textbooks, long ago. "Le cœur a ses raisons que la raison ne connaît point." *The heart has its reasons, which reason knows nothing of.* And she knew what her heart was telling her. "Do you think I really could?"

"Yes. You could, and what's more, you should." He sounded so sure. She felt herself drawn, like a moth in one of those books by Fabre, to his certainty, to his ease with himself. And he was sitting very close to her now; when had that happened? But before she could figure it out, he'd leaned over and was kissing her. And to her surprise—and slowly unfurling delight—she was kissing him back.

THIRTY

ANNE & DELIA

1949

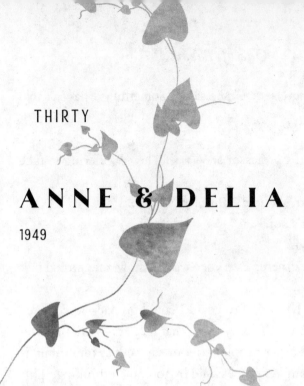

Anne got out of the taxi in front of Main Gate and walked through it onto campus. It was late September, and some of the trees had just started to turn; star-shaped golden leaves glittered the lawn. What a lovely place this was; in a way she could appreciate it even more now that her official time here had ended. She checked her watch; it was just one o' clock, the time she and Delia had agreed to meet. After Professor Grayson had written to tell Anne that Delia was returning to Vassar, Anne had immediately written to her. In her letter, Anne said she wanted to visit and go walk through Sophie's show with her. She also wanted to see Delia back at Vassar; it was brave of her to return, and Anne wanted to witness her triumph.

But Delia's response, though cordial, had not been overly enthusiastic, and Anne was hurt. She'd wanted something more effusive, more encouraging. Yet Delia had agreed to this meeting, which was something. Now Anne had to hope she would keep her word.

Looking around, she saw girls—singly, in pairs, or sometimes in groups—walking along the paths, most likely coming from their classes, on their way to lunch. She remembered that first lunch she'd had with Delia at the diner in town and wondered if she should suggest they go there after seeing the show. But no; Delia wasn't as apt to be nostalgic about that day as Anne was.

She looked at her watch again. Now it was a quarter past the hour. It was possible, of course, that Delia wouldn't come, and then Anne would have made the trip for nothing. She'd been back in the city after several weeks in Maine with Elizabeth, and what a wonderful, restorative time that had been. She hadn't realized how much she'd missed not just Elizabeth, but her whole family. She and Elizabeth had been able to pick up where they left off, and the Hunnewells took her seamlessly back into the fold. By the end of those weeks, she and Elizabeth had decided to rent an apartment together; they had just moved into a two-bedroom on East Seventy-Fourth Street between Park and Lexington Avenues. The bedrooms were small, and both faced the back, but the living room faced the tree-lined street and had a working fireplace besides. Elizabeth had just started a job as a secretary at *McCall's* magazine, and Anne would be starting as an assistant in decorative arts at the Parke-Bernet auction house.

"Look at us," Elizabeth had said, sitting in their nearly empty apartment as they unpacked the boxes all around them. "Two working girls."

"No," Anne said. "Two career women." Because that's how she felt—a young woman, making her way, mapping out a path for herself. She had snagged this job—how proud her father would have been—and now this apartment; she'd gone to the warehouse and picked out pieces that had been in storage for the last four years to bring to her new home; they would be delivered next week. It wouldn't replicate the apartment where she'd grown up, but that was all right. No, more than all right. She was building a new life, not trying to climb back into the old one. And part of that new life did include Drew Gilchrist again. They were seeing each other now, navigating the physical distance between them—he was still based in Boston, and traveled frequently for work—as well as the less tangible but more significant emotional distance. Mrs. Gilchrist still didn't approve of her; that made Anne resentful, and that in turn made Drew feel torn—he loved his mother, he loved Anne. They'd fought about it more than once. There had been harsh words, and plenty of them. Anne remembered how naive she'd been boarding that train to Poughkeepsie, how she'd actually thought that simply disavowing her Jewishness would solve everything. She had no such illusions now. Through all this, the silver ring remained in her top bureau drawer, nestled in its box. She wasn't ready to wear it, but she wasn't ready to give it back either.

Now it was 1:25—Delia was almost thirty minutes late, and Anne was annoyed. Why agree to meet if she was only going to stand Anne up? But still, Anne didn't want to leave yet. Maybe she could go upstairs and see if Professor Grayson was in her office. She could tell her about the new job; Miss Grayson would be pleased about that. And she could see the show she had curated one final time and Sophie Rossner's sculptures would be sent back to New York. So much for Delia. Anne turned and went into Taylor Hall.

Delia walked briskly across the quad toward Taylor Hall. She was living in Lathrop, on the quad, having decided against Main; too many memories. Even though she'd agreed to this meeting with Anne, when the day actually came, she found herself ambivalent. But then, being back at Vassar was filled with ambivalence. Had she thought she'd just resume her old life here? After all, that life had hardly been smooth. She'd always been a bit of a loner—set apart, not fully woven into the social fabric. And this time around, the added distinction—or notoriety—of her past was part of the experience. She recognized girls who'd been underclassmen back then giving her covert but still discernible looks. She was aware of their judgment, and the concomitant chill.

But on the brighter side—and there was a bright side, most days—

she'd made friends with two freshmen in her dorm, Rachel Rosen and Theodora Day. Rachel was Jewish and a fellow New Yorker; she, like Delia, had been snubbed, sometimes subtly, sometimes openly. But because she and Delia were able to commiserate—and even laugh—about it, those snubs felt less wounding. Theodora was Rachel's roommate, and she'd been horribly homesick—and horribly embarrassed by it—when she first got to school. Rachel had listened and consoled and as a result, they had become close. Both of them looked up to Delia—now a junior—admiring her style, her French je ne sais quoi. Neither of them knew about Ian McQuaid; he wasn't on campus any longer. The three of them formed a little group of their own, sitting together at meals, going to the library, casual visits to one another's dorm rooms late at night.

Then there were her classes: a survey of ancient history, and another on epic poetry. She was also taking a seminar on the pre-Raphaelites, as well as a seminar with Miss Grayson on the Italian neoclassical sculptor Antonio Canova. And a first-level class in Spanish. She was fluent in French and thought it wouldn't be too difficult to achieve some proficiency in another Romance language. All in all, it was a rich smorgasbord of intellectual pursuits, demanding but rewarding. And it meant she could graduate in two years.

Miss Grayson's class was her favorite; Delia loved both the smooth, polished surfaces of Canova's marble statues and the professor's way of talking about them and placing them in both artistic and historical context. Had Sophie been at all inspired by Canova's work? His *Cupid and Psyche*—a miracle of intertwined limbs and tender gestures—was in the Louvre, and so would have been easy for her to have seen. She had been writing to Sophie, and she would ask in her next letter.

Yet despite her feelings about the class, and her gratitude for Miss Grayson's role in her return to Vassar and in getting Sophie's sculpture there, she had still not been to see the exhibition. She knew the statues were there, waiting for her. Maybe she was waiting too—waiting for Anne. After all, it was Anne who had found them.

But when she got to Taylor Hall, Anne wasn't there. How strange. She had been the one to campaign for this meeting, and now she failed to show up? Delia felt something it took her a moment to identify: disappointment. She remained waiting in the cool, almost fall air as five, and then ten minutes went by. Her watch had said it was 12:45 when she arrived. When she checked again, the two hands were still in the same place—it must have stopped. She opened the door and stepped into the vestibule outside the gallery. Maybe Anne was waiting inside? But no, the vestibule was empty. Well, she wouldn't wait any longer, she'd see the show by herself.

Then she heard footsteps and turned. Someone had just come through the corridor that linked Taylor Hall to the art gallery. That someone was Anne. Delia almost didn't recognize her. She was not the timid, uncertain girl Delia had first seen in the hallway of Main. Now everything about her—hair, neatly tailored brown-and-cream tweed jacket, cream-colored leather gloves—was stylish and projected confidence. The transformation Delia had seen starting in Paris was complete.

"Delia!" Anne said. "There you are. I was afraid you weren't going to show up." She looked so happy, so *relieved*, that something stubborn in Delia thawed.

"Sorry I kept you waiting. My watch stopped." Delia held up her wrist.

"That's all right. We found each other, didn't we?"

Together, they went into the exhibition of her mother's work. Delia paused, wanting to let the immediate impression settle over her before she started moving around. Here were the works she remembered from childhood, along with at least two or three she'd never seen. These pieces reflected not only the trajectory of Sophie's career but also Delia's own history. There was the mermaid from that day when she'd gone to Sophie's studio; here was another pregnant woman in gleaming black marble that she'd never seen before. Delia wove in and out between them, stepping in for a close-up view and then back to see how the pieces read from a distance. Anne stayed nearby the entire time, saying nothing. Delia realized that Anne wasn't going to say anything until Delia spoke first.

"You've done a wonderful job," she said at last. "Such an interesting, intelligent arrangement. I honestly didn't know what to expect. But this"—she gestured around the gallery—"this is even better than what I could have imagined."

"Thank you." Anne felt satisfaction and pride sifting down lightly, sweet as a dusting of powdered sugar. "Does that mean there's a chance we might be friends again?"

Delia said nothing. Anne had done a terrible thing. But so many people did terrible things and walked away, too ashamed to own up to what they had done. Anne was different. She'd done her best to make amends. And she made it possible for Delia to come back to Vassar. Delia hadn't understood how much she'd wanted this until she was here again. "I think we already are." As Delia linked her arm through Anne's she realized that yes, it was true.

Anne smiled—no, beamed—and she was still beaming as, arm in arm, she and Delia took a final turn around the gallery. By the time they left the building, the day had turned cloudy, yet against the gray of the sky, the just-starting-to-turn leaves were stunningly, shockingly bright. The two girls walked toward Main. Anne looked at the imposing brick edifice and said, "They're about to start serving tea. Should we go upstairs?"

"Tea in the Rose Parlor . . ." Delia said. "You know, I've never actually gone."

"Well, then," Anne said. "Maybe it's time for you to give it a try."

ACKNOWLEDGMENTS

Every novel that comes into the world needs a team behind it, and I am extremely grateful for mine. I would like to thank Emily Griffin, who first saw the promise in this book, and Sara Nelson for the intelligence, thought, and care she put into its editing. Susanna Einstein, your advice and guidance have been and continue to be invaluable. To the crew at HarperCollins—Edie Astley, Heather Drucker, Lisa Erikson, Olga Grlic, and Katie O'Callaghan—thank you for all the work you do and for always having my back. Susan Weidman Schneider at *Lilith* magazine has been the most loyal and enthusiastic of supporters as well as having been my role model for years. My friends in the writing and book-loving community also deserve a shout-out: Bonnie Bender, Jennie Fields, Suzanne Leopold, Janet Schneider, Ken Silver, Renee Weingarten, and Linda Zagon. Ron Patkus, Dean Rogers, and Tom Hill, all at Vassar, have added greatly to my knowledge of the college's history and culture. My sincere and heartfelt thanks to all.

ABOUT THE AUTHOR

The author of *Not Our Kind* and *The Dressmakers of Prospect Heights*, Kitty Zeldis is the pseudonym for a novelist and nonfiction writer of books for adults and children. She lives with her family in Brooklyn, New York.